語用為綱國際漢語教學系列教材

Book 3

CANTONESE
in Communication:
Listening and Speaking

邊學邊用
粵語聽說教材（三）

總主編　吳偉平

編　審　李兆麟　沈嘉儀

商務印書館

Cantonese in Communication: Listening and Speaking [Book 3]

Series editor: Weiping Wu
Editor：Siu-lun LEE　Ka-yee SHUM
Reviewer: The Yale-China Chinese Language Center of the Chinese University of Hong Kong
Executive Editor: Elma Zou
Cover Designer: KI

Published by
The Commercial Press (H.K.) Ltd.
8/F, Eastern Central Plaza, 3 Yiu Hing Road, Shau Kei Wan, Hong Kong
http://www.commercialpress.com.hk

Distributed by
SUP Publishing Logistics (H.K.) Ltd.
3/F, C & C Building, 36 Ting Lai Road, Tai Po, N.T., Hong Kong

Printed by
Elegance Printing & Book Binding Co., Ltd.
Block A, 4/F, Hoi Bun Industrial Building, 6 Wing Yip Street, Kwun Tong, Kowloon, Hong Kong

First Edition and first printed in January 2019
©2018 by The Commercial Press (H.K.) Ltd.
ISBN 978 962 07 0535 9
Printed in Hong Kong

All rights reserved. No part of this publication may be reproduced, stored in a retrieval system, or transmitted in any form or by any means, electronic, mechanical, photocopying, recording and/or otherwise without the prior written permission of the publisher

邊學邊用：粵語聽説教材（三）

總　主　編：吳偉平

編　　審：李兆麟　沈嘉儀

審　　訂：香港中文大學雅禮中國語文研習所

責任編輯：鄒淑樺

封面設計：黎奇文

出　　版：商務印書館 (香港) 有限公司
　　　　　香港筲箕灣耀興道 3 號東滙廣場 8 樓
　　　　　http://www.commercialpress.com.hk

發　　行：香港聯合書刊物流有限公司
　　　　　香港新界大埔汀麗路 36 號中華商務印刷大廈 3 字樓

印　　刷：美雅印刷製本有限公司
　　　　　九龍觀塘榮業街 6 號海濱工業大廈 4 樓 A

版　　次：2019 年 1 月第 1 版第 1 次印刷
　　　　　©2019 商務印書館 (香港) 有限公司
　　　　　ISBN 978 962 07 0535 9
　　　　　Printed in Hong Kong

版權所有，不准以任何方式，在世界任何地區，以中文或其他文字翻印、
仿製或轉載本書圖版和文字之一部分或全部。

Table of Content

LESSON 1   Pearl of the Orient　東方之珠

LESSON 4   Smoking ban   無煙香港

LESSON 6

Proposing casinos　開設賭場

LESSON 7

Hong Kong for Sports Events　申辦賽事

LESSON 8   Holidays and cultures   節日文化

LESSON 9

Law and society 法律與社會

LESSON 10

Environmental Protection 環境保護

PREFACE

The Yale-China Chinese Language Center (CLC), founded in 1963, became part of the Chinese University of Hong Kong (CUHK) and has been responsible for teaching Chinese as a Second Language (CSL) to university students in the past decades. In 2004, we launched the Teaching Materials Project (TMP) to meet the needs of students in different programs. Over the years, the hallmark of all TMP products is the use of the Pragmatic Framework, which reflects findings from research in sociolinguistics and their applications in CSL.

Compared with the two published series designed for learners with background in Chinese languages and cultures (*Putonghua for Cantonese Speakers* and *Cantonese for Putonghua Speakers*), the current series, designed for non-Chinese learners [*Chinese (Putonghua) in Communication* and *Cantonese in Communication*], has moved further in making pragmatic factors an integrated part of CSL teaching materials. Some of the salient features common to the series are highlighted below, while characteristics in each volume and guide to use the textbook are explained in the INTRODUCTION following this PREFACE.

Guiding principle: Language learning is a process that includes four key stages based on the counter-clockwise approach in CSL learning (assessment, curriculum design, teaching materials, teaching and teacher training), all of which ideally should follow the same guiding principle. Using a textbook designed with theories in structuralism for a curriculum with a communicative approach, for example, will lead to confusion and frustrations for both teachers and learners. The compilation of this series follows the same principle that guides the other three key stages in CSL teaching and learning as practiced at CLC, which treats contextual factors as part of the learning process.

Aims: By using this textbook with the matching learning and teaching strategies, it is expected that communication in Chinese by learners will be not only correct linguistically, but appropriate culturally. It is also expected that, with the focus on using while learning, the speaking proficiency of the learner will improve in both quality and quantity (from sentence to paragraph to discourse).

Authenticity (from oral to oral): Teaching materials for speaking Chinese, to the best extent possible, should come from spoken Chinese. Instead of "writing the texts according to the lists of vocabulary and grammatical points", a common practice in almost all teaching materials preparation, we have pioneered the approach that starts from spoken data and, based on authentic spoken data, works out a list of vocabulary for active use, grammatical points and pragmatic points. This challenging approach, dubbed "from oral to oral", is believed to bring learners closer to the authenticity of spoken Chinese in oral communication.

Pragmatic factors: Attempts have been made to turn pragmatic knowledge in communication from oblivious to obvious, as indicated by the summary table at the beginning of each lesson, which includes information related to participants, setting and timing (or purpose) of the communication event. A limited number of "pragmatic points" are also listed together with "grammatical points" to draw the awareness of learners, and to serve as an indication of the importance to learning such points.

Style and register of spoken Chinese (*Yuti*): Since culturally appropriateness is regarded as a major goal of learning, it becomes an unavoidable task to show the differences in style and register of the language used. Efforts have been made to illustrate the characteristics of style and register in communication for different purposes in different settings, including the choice of vocabulary, grammatical and discourse structure, as well as formulaic patterns. More information in this area can be found in the INTRODUCTION for volume three of this series.

In today's world, it is paradoxical that there are actually far too many textbooks in the CSL field and, at the same time, far too few that can be used as it is when it comes to specific programs and teaching methodology. The following notes are therefore provided to put the current series in perspective:

1. They are designed to meet the changing needs of CSL learners, most of whom are now motivated by the desire to use the language they learn in real life communication.

2. Each of the three volumes in the series can be used for one semester (6 hours

per week for 12-14 weeks). For programs with a longer duration, supplementary materials will be needed.

3. The focus of this series is on the learner's ability in speaking and listening, which will establish a solid foundation for further study that may focus on all the four skills including reading and writing.

As the Director of CLC, it's my privilege to launch this project more than a decade ago with support from the University, to serve as the TMP leader and series editor and to see it become one of the four major academic projects of the Center. I am pleased to see yet one more product from this Project, which will not only meet the immediate needs of our own students, but also serve the CSL community for the sustainable development of the field.

Weiping M. Wu, Ph.D.
TMP Leader and CSL Series Editor
Director of the Chinese Language Center
The Chinese University of Hong Kong
Shatin, Hong Kong SAR

INTRODUCTION

This is the third book of the book series, "Cantonese in Communication". The book series is designed for learners learning Cantonese as a second language. The third book of this series is targeted to upper intermediate or advanced learners of Cantonese as a second language and is suitable to use in programmes designed for university students and working professionals who want to learn practical Cantonese and to use Cantonese in their daily life as well as in their professional life. All examples and sample conversations demonstrated in this series are drawn from AUTHENTIC speaking materials collected from native Hong Kong speakers and focus on spoken Cantonese used in Hong Kong. This whole series emphasizes on appropriate use of Cantonese and prioritizes the use of language to finish different communication tasks in real world situations. This book series wishes to help learners to increase their Cantonese proficiency with accurate pronunciation and use of linguistic forms in authentic linguistic situations. This book puts "pragmatic factors" and "style and register of spoken Chinese (*Yuti*)" together in the lesson texts, as well as in most examples and exercises to train learners to use the linguistic forms appropriately in actual communications. We know that when a language is used in different settings (formal verses informal), to different people (single audience verses group audience), to people of different status, and in different occasions; the choice of wordings/phrases and even sentence patterns could be very different. As a result, "style and register" are very important factors for upper-intermediate and advanced learners. This book not only aims at arousing learners' awareness of these factors, but also provides authentic inputs to train learners when using the different "styles and registers" in different real world situations.

The third book of the series focus on semi-formal to formal language scenarios. Useful vocabulary, lively language inputs and exercises to train intermediate/advanced learners to be able to use Cantonese appropriately in work situations and handle semi-formal to formal situations. This book uses Yale-romanization system to transcribe Cantonese and has the following characteristics:

The third book is,

1. Providing authentic input (from oral to oral) to learners

2. Emphasizing pragmatic factors and language functions in using the language

3. Demonstrating different styles and registers of spoken Chinese with reference to different linguistic situations

4. Focusing on practical use of Cantonese

5. Setting clear stage goals to improve oral proficiency and providing exercises for practicing speaking and listening skills

There is very few upper-intermediate to advanced Cantonese learning materials in the market and as one of the editors of this book, I would sincerely wish this book provides guidance and valuable assistance to Cantonese second language learners. Wish all Cantonese learners would enjoy their learning journey.

How to use the book

This book is an upper-intermediate to advanced book targeted learners who need to use the language in semi-formal and formal language scenarios. Useful vocabulary, authentic language input and exercises with specific demonstration of "style and register" factors are provided in this book to train upper-intermediate to advanced learners to use Cantonese in a practical way. This book consists of 10 lessons and 2 general review lessons. The 10 lessons include language scenarios happened in work life (including semi-formal and formal situations) and cover various language functions, such as persuading, exploring, expressing opinion, introducing (in formal situations), defensing, discussing, criticizing, drawing conclusion and expressing gratitude (in formal situations). Each lesson consists of the following 8 parts:

1. **Pragmatic factors, *Yuti* features and linguistic functions**　語用因素、語體特 與語言功能

   Each lesson of this book states clearly the core linguistic functions presented in the lesson texts and in "Notes on pragmatic knowledge". One outstanding feature of this book is that the "style and register" factors are demonstrated in the lesson texts and explained, when necessary, in "Notes on pragmatic knowledge". This sets a goal of what learners can do by using Cantonese appropriately after finishing each lesson. The whole book contains different language contexts ranging from semi-formal to formal situations.

2. **Texts**　課文

   All the lesson texts in this book are based on real life topics and situations. All texts used in this book are adopted from AUTHENTIC speaking materials taken from native Cantonese speakers in Hong Kong. Speaking data of 4 native speakers were collected and specific pragmatic and stylistic features were adopted in preparing the lesson texts.

   Cantonese characters and Yale-romanization are presented in the lesson for learners to follow. All the texts are also written in Standard Written Chinese and attached in the appendix for reference.

3. **Vocabulary in use**　活用詞彙

   Each lesson presents vocabulary items which are frequently used when in each language contexts and pragmatic functions. All vocabulary items are presented with Yale-Romanization, Cantonese characters, part of speech and English translation for learners and teachers to use. All vocabulary items are listed in the appendix for easy reference.

4. **Notes on language and discourse structure**　語言及篇章結構知識

   This book provides a step-by-step guide on language structure. Each lesson presents syntactic structures and patterns that relate to the language contexts and pragmatic functions of the lesson. Since this book is catering for upper-intermediate to advanced learners, discourse structures are demonstrated and explained in order to help learners to achieve construction of connected discourse and paragraphs.

5.   **Notes on pragmatic knowledge**   語用因素與相關知識

Pragmatic use is the major concern of this book. Each lesson provides pragmatic notes relating to the language contexts and linguistic functions, as well as syntactic structures in relation to different styles and registers. Cultural factors are also explained in this section. Discussions and examples are given in each lesson to illustrate pragmatic knowledge.

6.   **Contextualized speaking practice**   情境說話練習

There are contextualized speaking practices in each lesson to provide pre-class preparation guidelines and a post-class assessment on each stage. Learners can work on the exercises to reinforce what they have learnt and at the same time check what aspects need further assistance.

7.   **Listening and speaking**   聽說練習

Listening skills are as important as speaking skills. This section provides exercise and training on listening and speaking skills on various topics discussed in semi-formal or formal situations.

8.   **Additional texts**   附加課文

Reinforcement is important in language learning. In view of this, each lesson provides extended texts or speaking samples for learners to reinforce and consolidate their language skills. At the end of each lesson, pre-edited authentic oral data are given to learners for their reference.

Apart from the 10 core lessons, there are 2 review lessons to provide training and consolidation of learners' language skills. The first review lesson is placed after Lesson 5 and it reviews knowledge and skills presented in the first 5 lessons. The second review lesson is located after Lesson 10 and it is a general revision of all knowledge and skills presented in this book.

Acknowledgement

I would like to express my gratitude to the many people who saw me through this book; to all those who provided support, talked things over, read, wrote, offered comments, and assisted in the editing, proofreading and design.

I would like to thank my co-worker, Ms. Ka-yee Shum, for working together on this book. I would like to express my very great appreciation to the Director of Yale-China Chinese Language Centre, Dr. Weiping Wu, enabling us to publish this book and this book series. Dr. Wu provided valuable theoretical inspirations throughout the whole process of this publication. I would also like to thank Dr. Ho-put Wong and Ms. Yun Li for their professional supports and continuous encouragement in the making of this book.

I would like to offer my special thanks to Mr. Tianxiao Wang and the Administration Team of Yale-China Chinese Language Centre who have been helping us for clerical supports. I would also thank Commercial Press (Hong Kong)'s supports and assistance on the printing and publishing stage. I am particularly grateful for the assistance given by Mr. Yongbo Mao of Commercial Press (Hong Kong) for his long-lasting supports and encouragement.

Last and not least, I beg forgiveness of all those who have been with me over the course of the years and whose names I have failed to mention.

Siu-lun, LEE (Dr.)
Head of the Cantonese Programme Division, CLC, CUHK.
Editor of *Cantonese in Communication, Book 3*

ABBREVIATIONS AND SYMBOLS

Adj.	Adjective
Adv.	Adverb
Att.	Attributive
AV	Auxiliary Verb
BF	Bound Form
CV	Co-Verb
DW	Directional Word
IE	Idiomatic Expressions
lit.	literally
M	Measure
MA	Movable Adverb
N	Noun
Nu	Number
P	Particle
Patt	Sentence Pattern
PH	Phrase
PN	Pronoun
PW	Place Word
Q/A	Question & Answer
QW	Question Word
RV	Resultative Verb
RVE	Resultative Verb Ending
S	Subject
SP	Specifier
T Sp	Time Spent
TW	Time Word
V	Verb
VO	Verb-Object Compound
/	or
( )	word(s) that can be left out

Lesson 1 Pearl of the Orient
東方之珠

1. Pragmatic factors, Yuti features and linguistic functions
語用因素、語體特徵與語言功能
Yúhyuhng yānsou, yúhtái dahkjīng yúh yúhyìhn gūngnàhng

Pragmatic factors/ Yuti features 語用因素 / 語體特徵	Linguistic function 語言功能
Pragmatic factors: Pragmatic factors: Although this is a typical scenario for a formal situation, which tends to call for some formal features of language, the content is about tourists and daily life. Thus the tone and the use of words may sometimes be less solemn. 語用因素： 場合正式，但內容相對輕鬆，所以語體較為包容。 **Yuti features:** Formality index: 1-2 語體特徵：1-2 級之間	**Linguistic function:** Persuading Bringing your audience to your perspective to effectively introduce a subject and make recommendations by using a suitable method to bridge the distance between audience and writer/speaker. 語言功能：勸說 把聽眾當成「自己人」來進行推介，用適當的方式拉近與聽眾的距離。

Notes on pragmatic knowledge 語用知識	Notes on structure 語言及篇章結構知識

I. Politeness and other relevant features
禮貌與其他相關因素
 	
  1. Honorable guests and friends
    「各位來賓，各位朋友」
  2. Let me introduce myself
    「等我介紹一下自己」
 	
II. Related knowledge
相關知識
 	
  1. Born and grow up here「土生土長」
  2. Bureau of Tourism and Development
    「旅發局」
  3. Multi-culture「多元文化」
  4. People "addicted" to a hobby「發燒友」
  5. Race course「馬場」
	I. Grammar and sentence patterns
	語法和句型
	
	  1. Sentence particle, "lā", "a", used for listing items or examples
	  2. "yauh…yauh…"
	  3. "jihnghaih… ja / jē"
	  4. "hóuchíh……yātyeuhng" just like…
	  5. "gónghéi séuhng làih" speaking of…
	  6. "m̀jí…juhng / dōu", not only…, but also…
	  7. "jauhhaih…" in other words; that is to say…
	  8. "yuhtlàihyuht……", "yuht…yuht…" getting more and more…
	
	II. Paragraph and discourse
	語段和篇章
	
	  1. "sáusīn……yìhnhauh……juhngyáuh ……" first…then…besides/in addition…

2. Text 🔊

課文 Fomàhn

局長先生、各位業界嘅朋友、各位來賓,大家好。	Guhkjéung sīnsāang, gokwái yihpgaaige pàhngyáuh, gokwái lòihbān, daaihgā hóu.
我係來自旅遊業界嘅劉家寶。等我嚟介紹一下自己,我係土生土長嘅香港人,我好榮幸能夠喺呢度介紹香港。首先我要借呢個機會喺呢度代表業界向香港旅遊發展局表示感謝,感謝旅發局舉辦呢次大型展銷活動,俾各行各業一個展示香港嘅平台。	Ngóh haih lòihjih léuihyàuh yihpgaai ge Làuh Gābóu, dáng ngóh làih gaaisiuh yātháh jihgéi, ngóh haih tóusāng tóujéungge Hēunggóng yàhn, ngóh hóu wìhnghahng nàhnggau hái nīdouh gaaisiuh Hēunggóng. Sáusīn ngóh yiu je nīgo gēiwuih hái nīdouh doihbíu yihpgaai heung Hēunggóng Léuihyàuh Faatjín Guhk bíusih gámjeh, gámjeh Léuihfaatguhk géuibaahn nīchi daaihyìhng jínsīu wuhtduhng, béi gok hòhng gok yihp yātgo jínsih Hēunggóngge pìhngtòih.

香港有一個好靚嘅名叫做「東方之珠」，咁細嘅香港每年可以吸引咁多遊客，旅遊業係香港最重要嘅經濟支柱之一。其中嘅原因，首先，我哋有著名嘅城市景觀——譬如尖沙咀呀、中環呀、山頂呀。然後喺購物方面，如果你想喺香港買嘢，有好多唔同嘅選擇。去執平貨你可以去旺角，幾十蚊一件嘅衫，又平又襟著嘅鞋，又有一啲女士們十分鍾意嘅首飾，淨係喺旺角你都可以搵到。如果你唔係咁鍾意執平貨，你可以去中環一啲高級嘅商場買名牌貨。世界各國嘅牌子你都可以搵到。我哋又有大型主題樂園，仲有好多其他城市好難搵到嘅自然風景。離市區唔遠嘅地方，就有郊野公園或者離島，遊客即刻就可以投身大自然，放鬆身心。香港嘅東平洲就係國家級嘅地質公園，嗰度嘅石十分之特別，好似仙景一樣。你喺香港中文大學附近嘅碼頭搭船去，大概一個鐘多啲。好多人都會喺嗰度玩一日。圍住個島行一個圈，就可以喺碼頭附近嘅士多食一啲特色食物。咁樣嚟到過一日真係好寫意㗎。

Hēunggóng yáuh yātgo hóuleng ge méng giujouh "Dūngfōng jījyū", gam saige Hēunggóng múihnìhn hóyíh kāpyáhn gam dō yàuhhaak, léuihyàuhyihp haih Hēunggóng jeui juhngyiuge gīngjai jīchyúh jīyāt. Kèihjūngge yùhnyān, sáusīn, ngóhdeih yáuh jyumìhngge sìhngsíh gínggūn—peiyùh Jīmsājéui a, Jūngwàahn a, Sāandéng a. Yìhnhauh hái kaumaht fōngmihn, yùhgwó néih séung hái Hēunggóng máaihyéh, yáuh hóudō m̀tùhngge syúnjaahk. Heui jāp pèhngfo néih hóyíh heui Wohnggok, géisahp mān yātgihnge sāam, yauh pèhng yauh kāmjeukge hàaih, yauh yáuh yātdī néuihsihmùhn sahpfān jūngyige sáusīk, jihnghaih hái Wohnggok néih dōu hóyíh wándóu. Yùhgwó néih m̀haih gam jūngyi jāp pèhng fo, néih hóyíh heui Jūngwàahn yātdī gōukāp ge sēungchèuhng máaih mìhngpàaih fo. Saigaai gokgok ge pàaihjí néih dōu hóyíh wándóu. Ngóhdeih yauh yáuh daaihyìhng jyútàih lohkyùhn, juhngyáuh hóudō kèihtā sìhngsíh hóunàahn wándóuge jihyìhn fūnggíng. Lèih síhkēui m̀yúhnge deihfōng, jauhyáuh gāauyéh gūngyún waahkjé Lèihdóu, yàuhhaak jīkhāk jauh hóyíh tàuhsān daaihjihyìhn, fongsūng sānsām. Hēunggóngge Dūngpìhngjāu jauhhaih gwokgākāpge deihjāt gūngyún, gódouhge sehk sahpfānjī dahkbiht, hóuchíh sīngíng yātyeuhng. Néih hái Hēunggóng Jūngmàhn Daaihhohk fuhgahnge máhtàuh daapsyùhn heui, daaihkoi yātgo jūng dōdī. Hóudō yàhn dōu wúih hái gódouh wáan yātyaht. Wàihjyuh godóu hàahng yātgo hyūn, jauh hóyíh hái máhtàuh fuhgahnge sihdō sihk yātdī dahksīk sihkmaht. Gámyéung làihdou gwo yātyaht jānhaih hóu séyi ga.

講起上嚟，遊客嚟到香港，就會發現喺香港唔只可以觀光同娛樂，仲可以了解呢度嘅風土人情同歷史文化，品嚐呢度嘅美食。鍾意刺激嘅運動發燒友呢，可以試試滑翔傘呀、滑浪風帆呀呢啲活動，又或者入馬場睇賽馬。除此之外，香港氣候溫和，交通方便，香港人友善好客，好多遊客嚟咗仲想再嚟。

Gónghéi séuhnglàih, yàuhhaak làihdou Hēunggóng, jauh wúih faatyihn hái Hēunggóng m̀jí hóyíh gūngwōng tùhng yùhlohk, juhng hóyíh líuhgáai nīdouhge fūngtóu yàhnchìhng tùhng lihksí màhnfa, bánsèuhng nīdouhge méihsihk. Jūngyi chitgīkge wahnduhng faatsīuyáu nē, hóyíh sisi waahtchèuhngsaan a, waahtlohng fūngfàahn a nīdī wuhtduhng, yauh waahkjé yahp máhchèuhng tái choimáh. Chèuihchí jīngoih, Hēunggóng heihauh wānwòh, gāautūng fōngbihn, Hēunggóng yàhn yáuhsihn houhaak, hóudō yàuhhaak làihjó juhng séung joi làih.

喺呢度我要特別感謝旅遊業嘅同行，因為你哋多年嘅努力，香港成為國際旅遊城市。我希望政府以後繼續支持旅遊業，令我哋業界可以開發新嘅景點同旅遊項目，改善服務質素，令旅遊業持續發展，越做越好，俾更多人認識香港。

Hái nīdouh ngóh yiu dahkbiht gámjeh léuihyàuhyihpge tùhnghòhng, yānwaih néihdeih dōnìhn ge nóuhlihk, Hēunggóng sìhngwàih gwokjai léuihyàuh sìhngsíh. Ngóh hēimohng jingfú yíhhauh gaijuhk jīchìh léuihyàuhyihp, lihng ngóhdeih yihpgaai hóyíh hōifaat sānge gíngdím tùhng léuihyàuh hohngmuhk, góisihn fuhkmouh jātsou, lihng léuihyàuhyihp chìhjuhk faatjín, yuht jouh yuht hóu, béi gangdō yàhn yihngsīk Hēunggóng.

多謝。

Dōjeh.

3. Vocabulary in use 🔊

活用詞彙 Wuhtyuhng chìhwuih

3.1 Common vocabulary

Number	Word	Yale Romanization	POS	English
1	各位	gokwái	PH	every; everybody
2	來自	lòihjih	V	to come from
3	土生土長	tóu sāng tóu jéung	PH	locally born and bred
4	榮幸	wìhnghahng	Adj	to be honored
5	感謝	gámjeh	N/V	thanks; to thank; to be grateful
6	大型	daaihyìhng	Adj	large-scale
7	展銷活動	jínsīu wuhtduhng	N	trade fair
8	展示	jínsih	V	to show
9	平台	pìhngtòih	N	platform
10	吸引	kāpyáhn	Adj/V	attractive; to attract
11	著名	jyumìhng	Adj	famous, well-known
12	城市景觀	sìhngsíh gínggūn	N	urban landscape
13	購物	kaumaht	N/V	shopping; to do shopping
14	首飾	sáusīk	N	jewelry
15	執平貨	jāp pèhngfo	VO	to buy cheap products
16	牌子	pàaihjí	N	brand
17	主題樂園	jyútàih lohkyùhn	PW	theme park
18	自然風景	jihyìhn fūnggíng	N	natural scenery
19	仙境	sīngíng	N	fairyland
20	圍住	wàihjyuh	V	to surround
21	寫意	séyi	Adj	enjoyable, relaxed

22	觀光	gūngwōng	V	to go sightseeing
23	風土人情	fūngtóu yàhnchìhng	N	local conditions and customs
24	歷史文化	lihksí màhnfa	N	history and culture
25	品嚐	bánsèuhng	V	to taste (food and drinks)
26	刺激	chigīk	Adj	exciting
27	除此之外	chèuih chí jī ngoih	PH	besides, in addition
28	氣候溫和	heihauh wānwòh	PH	the climate is moderate
29	友善好客	yáuhsihn houhaak	PH	friendly and hospitable
30	景點	gíngdím	N	tourist spot, tourist attraction
31	服務質素	fuhkmouh jātsou	N	quality of service

3.2 Proper nouns, people and place words

1	局長	guhkjéung	N	Director of Bureau
2	業界嘅朋友	yihpgaai ge pàhngyáuh	PH	friends from the industry
3	來賓	lòihbān	N	guest
4	同行	tùhnghòhng	N	people of the same industry
5	劉家寶	Làuh Gā-bóu	PN	Lau Ka-po
6	香港旅遊發展局	Hēunggóng Léuihyàuh Faatjín Guhk	PN	Hong Kong Tourism Board
7	東方之珠	Dūngfōng Jī Jyū	PN	Pearl of the Orient
8	市區	síhkēui	PW	urban area
9	離島	Lèihdóu	PW	Outlying island(s)
10	東平洲	Dūngpìhngjāu	PW	Tung Ping Chau
11	郊野公園	gāauyéh gūngyún	PW	country park
12	地質公園	deihjāt gūngyún	PW	geopark

3.3 About tourism and economy

1	旅遊業界	léuihyàuh yihpgaai	N	tourism industry
2	各行各業	gok hòhng gok yihp	PH	all walks of life
3	經濟支柱	gīngjai jīchyúh	N	economic pillar
4	投身大自然	tàuhsān daaihjihyìhn	PH	to throw oneself into the nature
5	放鬆身心	fongsūng sānsām	PH	to relax the body and mind
6	國家級	gwokgā kāp	PH	national level
7	旅遊項目	léuihyàuh hohngmuhk	N	tourism project
8	持續發展	chìhjuhk faatjín	PH	to sustain the development

3.4 About hobbies

1	發燒友	faatsīuyáu	N	enthusiast
2	滑翔傘	waahtchèuhngsaan	N	paragliding
3	滑浪風帆	waahtlohng fūngfàahn	N	windsurfing
4	睇跑馬	tái páaumáh	VO	to watch horse racing

4. Notes on language and discourse structure
語言及篇章結構知識 Yúhyìhn kahp pīnjēung gitkau jīsīk

4.1. Grammar and sentence patterns 語法和句型

4.1.1. Sentence particles, "lā", "a", used for listing items or examples

1. M̀tùhng gwokgā ge mìhngpàaihfo dōu hóyíh hái Hēunggóng wándóu, peiyùh, Faatgwok lā, Yidaaihleih lā, Yahtbún lā, Hòhngwok lā.

2. Nīgo deihfōng fēisèuhng hóuwáan, sēungchèuhng a, jyútàih gūngyún a, chāantēng a, dōu yáuh.

3. Heui léuihhàhng jīchìhn yiu gímchàhháh, wuhjiu a, chīmjing a, gēipiu a, nīdī yéh.

4. Nīdouh tói a, dihnnóuh a, mātyéh dōu yáuh, ngóhdeih jauh hái nīdouh wānsyū lā.

4.1.2. Compound predicate, "S yauh…yauh…"

This pattern means "(both)...and...", e.g.: Kéuih yauh gōu yauh daaih. (He is tall and big.)

1. Gógāan poutáu maaih ge yéh yauh pèhng yauh leng.

2. Hēunggóng ge hahtīn yauh yiht yauh sāp, lihng yàhn gokdāk hóu sānfú.

3. Ngoihbihn yauh daaihfūng yauh daaihyúh, néih m̀hóu chēutheui lo.

4. Néih yauh hohk Gwóngdūngwá yauh hohk sé Jūngmàhn jih, jānhaih sānfú lo.

5. Kéuih góng Jūngmàhn góngdāk yauh faai yauh jeng.

6. Kéuih sáisāam sáidāk yauh faai yauh gōnjehng.

7. Ngóhdeih chéng ge jīkyùhn yauh yiu sīk dihnnóuh yauh yiu sīk Yahtmán.

8. Gódouh yauh séuijam yauh sāannàihkīngse, jānhaih ngàihhím lo.

4.1.3. Compound predicate, "jihnghaih……ja/jē"

The pattern means '……only/merely'.

1. Ngóh jihnghaih jyújó néihge faahn ja, móuh jyú kéuihge faahn.

2. Jihnghaih ngóh tùhng néih (heui)ja, kéuihdeih dōu m̀heui.

3. Ngóh jihnghaih hohk Gwóngdūngwá jē, móuh hohk Jūngmàhn jih.

4. Jihnghaih nī léuhng bún syū ja, jauh yiu yih chīn mān la.

4.1.4. Compound predicate, "hóuchíh… (yātyeuhng)" just like...

1. Nīdouh hóuchíh ngóh ūkkéi yātyeuhng, yauh fōngbihn yauh syūfuhk.

2. Kéuihge Gwóngdūngwá góngdāk hóuchíh Hēunggóng yàhn yātyeuhng.

3. Néih yìhgā haih daaihhohksāang la, m̀hóu hóuchíh síu pàhngyáuh yātyeuhng.

4.1.5. "gónghéi séuhnglàih…" speaking of...

1. Gónghéi séuhnglàih, Hēunggóng haih yātgo gwokjai sìhngsíh, dōu haih yātgo méihsihk tīntòhng (tīntòhng = heaven).

2. Ngóh haih gauhnín būnlàih Hēunggóngge. Gónghéi séuhnglàih, gójahnsìh jānhaih yáuhdī m̀jaahpgwaan.

3. A : Gāmnìhn baatyuht, ngóhge jái wúih heui Yīnggwok chāamgā yātgo yàuhhohk tyùhn.

   B : Gónghéi séuhnglàih, ngóh dōu hóu noih móuh heuigwo Yīnggwok, ngóh dōu séung heui hàahngháh.

4.1.6. Compound predicate, "S m̀jí......juhng/dōu......(tīm)"

This pattern means "not only...but also...", e.g.: Kéuih m̀jí sīk Jūngmàhn, juhng sīk Yahtmán tīm. (He not only knows Chinese, but also knows Japanese.)

1. Ngóh ge gūngyàhn m̀jí yiu jouh gāmouh, juhng yiu chau bìhbī tīm.
2. Hēunggóng ge hahtīn, m̀jí hóu yiht, juhng hóu sāp tīm.
3. Yānwaih lohkjó géi yaht daaih yúh, sóyíh gāai seuhngbihn m̀jí séuijam, juhng yáuh sāannàihkīngse tīm.
4. Tīnhei bougou wah gāmyaht m̀jí yáuh daaih yúh, juhng yáuh lèuihbouh tīm.
5. Kéuih m̀jí sáisāam sáidāk hóu gōnjehng, jyúsung juhng jyúdāk hóu hóusihk tīm.
6. Kéuih m̀jí gaausyū gaaudāk hóugwo ngóh, dá móhngkàuh dōu dádāk lēkgwo ngóh tīm.
7. Kéuih haih m̀haih jihnghaih jūngyi hàahngsāan a? M̀haih, kéuih m̀jí jūngyi hàahngsāan, juhng jūngyi waahtsyut tīm.
8. M̀jí néih m̀heui, Chàhn síujé dōu m̀heui.
9. Kéuih m̀jí sihkfaahn sihkdāk dōgwo ngóh, jouhyéh dōu jouhdāk hóugwo ngóh tīm.
10. Kéuih m̀jí tàahnkàhm tàahndāk hóu lēk, yàuhséui dōu yàuhdāk hóu faai tīm.

4.1.7. "jauhhaih..." in other words; that is to say...

1. Sīngkèihyaht hóudō yàhn jūngyi heui jáulàuh sihk dímsām, jauhhaih Gwóngdūngyàhn góngge yámchàh la.
2. Làihdou Hēunggóng gánghaih yiu siháh "chàh chāantēng", "chàh chāantēng" jauhhaih Hēunggóng dahksīk chāantēng.

4.1.8. Compound predicate, " S yuht làih yuht..." and "S yuht ...yuht..."

"S yuht làih yuht..." means something "becomes more and more...", e.g.: Kéuih yuht làih yuht leng. (She is getting more and more beautiful.)

"S yuht ...yuht..." means "the more..., the more...", e.g.: Kéuihge néui yuht daaih yuht leng. (Her daughter becomes prettier the more she grows up.)

1. Yìhgā dī gūngyàhn yuht làih yuht nàahnchéng.
2. Kéuih yuht làih yuht sānfú.
3. Yàhngūng yuht làih yuht dāi.
4. Kéuih góng Gwóngdōngwá góngdāk yuht làih yuht hóu.
5. Kéuih sáisāam sáidāk yuht làih yuht m̀gōnjehng.
6. Néih cheunggō cheungdāk yuht làih yuht hóutēng.

7. Gahnlói ge tīnhei yuht làih yuht yiht.

8. Poutáu ge sāangyi dím a? Yuht làih yuht nàahnjouh.

9. Sānséui yuht jouh yuht dō.

10. Yàhn yuht lóuh tàuhfaat yuht síu.

11. Kéuihge Jūngmàhn jih yuht sé yuht leng.

12. Gwóngdūngwá hóu nàahnhohk, ngóh yuht hohk yuht sānfú.

13. Kéuih jyúsung jyúdāk yuht làih yuht hóusihk, ngóh yuht sihk yuht jūngyi sihk.

14. Gógāan poutáu ge sāangyi yuht jouh yuht hóu.

15. Kéuih ge Gwóngdūngwá dím a? Yuht hohk yuht hóu.

16. (Néih) yuht jouhdāk noih yàhngūng yuht dō.

17. Ngoihbihn yuht làih yuht daaihfūng, dī yúh yuht lohk yuht daaih.

18. Néih yuht góng ngóh yuht m̀mìhngbaahk.

4.2. Paragraph and discourse 語段和篇章

4.2.1. "sáusīn … yìhnhauh … juhngyáuh…" first…then… besides / in addition…

1. Heui chàhlàuh yámchàh, sáusīn yiu lówái, yìhnhauh fógei wúih mahn néih yám mātyéh chàh. Fógei wúih bōng néih hōichàh. Juhngyáuh hóu hóusihkge dímsām. Néih hóyíh yātbihn yámchàh, yātbihn kīnggái.

2. Yùhgwó néih yiu heui ngoihgwok làuhhohk, sáusīn yiu háausíh, yìhnhauh yiu wán yàhn bōng néih sé tēuijinseun (recommendation letter). Juhngyáuh néih yiu gáan séung duhkge fōmuhk.

3. Jōu'ūk ge sìhhauh, sáusīn yiu táiháh jāuwàihge wàahngíng, yìhnhauh táiháh go dāanwái, juhngyáuh yiu tùhng yihpjyú kīngháh gachìhn.

5. Notes on pragmatic knowledge

語用因素與相關知識 Yúhyuhng yānsou yúh sēunggwāan jīsīk

5.1. 禮貌與其他相關因素 Politeness and other relevant features

5.1.1. "各位來賓，各位朋友 Gokwái lòihbān, gokwái pàhngyáuh" honorable guests and friends.

The order of greeting at the beginning is important and follows accepted social and cultural norms according to the contexts. Here "guests" comes before "friends". Among other factors that affect the order of such greetings are official ranking (from high to low) and age (from old to young). "Ladies and gentlemen" is becoming globally common nowadays.

- Dōjeh jyúchìh yàhn! Gokwái lòihbān, gokwái pàhngyáuh, daaihgā hóu!
- Jyūngingge haauhjéung, gokwái lòihbān, gokwái lóuhsī, gokwái tùhnghohk, ngóh gāmyaht hóu wìhnghahng doihbíu bātyihpsāng séuhngtòih faatyìhn.

5.1.2. "等我介紹一下自己 Dáng ngóh gaaisiuh yātháh jihgéi" Let me introduce myself.

There are certain phrases that a good speaker would use to draw the audience close, especially the use of "you"and "me"to make it sound like a conversation. In most formal contexts, the speaker is already introduced before he or she speaks and the need to have a self introduction is really not necessary. So such a phrase as used here is for rapport and pragmatic purposes and is an indication of pragmatic ability.

- Dáng ngóh gaaisiuh yātháh jihgéi…

5.2. Related knowledge 相關知識

5.2.1. "土生土長 tóusāng tóujéung" born and grow up here

The use of "tóu" (土), literally "soil", in phrases like the one here often refers to "local" or "native" and is often in contrast to "yèuhng (洋)" or "fāan (番)", which is "foreign" or "abroad". The speaker in the text used this to claim "sameness" with the audience to whom the speaker speaks, presenting the identity that says "I'm one of you", which sometimes is believed to contribute to credibility.

- Ngóh haih yātgo tóusāng tóujéungge Hēunggóng yàhn…

5.2.2. " 旅發局 Léuihfaat Guhk" Bureau of Tourism and Development

There are rules about abbreviation in Chinese that are socially and culturally recognized and the most common of which is to take the first syllable of a word in a long phrase to create an abbreviated form. Thus " 旅遊發展局 Léuihyàuh Faatjín Guhk" becomes " 旅發局 Léuihfaat Guhk", " 中文大學 Jūngmàhn daaihhohk" becomes " 中大 Jūngdaaih". Most Chinese have no problem in understanding the meaning of an abbreviation when they hear it or, if they don't, they try to get the full form by making educated guesses.

- Ngóh bātyihp jīhauh jauh yātjihk hái Léuihfaat Guhk gūngjok.
- Néih góngge "Jūng Daaih" haih Jūngmàhn daaihhohk dihnghaih Jūngsāan daaihhohk a?

5.2.3. " 多元文化 dōyùhn màhnfa" multi-culture

This phrase can be used in a variety of ways, referring to the situation in which different cultures, including concepts and value systems, among others, are tolerated, practiced or encouraged.

- Ngóh gokdāk Hēunggóng haih yātgo dōyùhn màhnfa ge deihfōng.

5.2.4. " 發燒友 faatsīuyáu" people with the same hobby

" 發燒 faatsīu" literally means "having a fever", but " 發燒友 faatsīuyáu" is used as metaphor to refer to a group of people who share the same hobby.

- Ngóh dōu haih dihnnóuh faatsīuyáu, yáuh gēiwuih yātchàih yìhngau háh lā.

5.2.5. " 馬場 máhchèuhng" race course

Living in Hong Kong where the race course is the hallmark of the city, a CSL learner here should at least understand the meaning of " 馬場 máh chèuhng", which consists of the character for horse " 馬 máh" and the one for court " 場 chèuhng". It is owned by " 馬會 máh wúi", which is the Chinese word for the Jockey Club.

- Hēunggóng yáuh léuhnggo máhchèuhng, yātgo hái Sātìhn, yātgo hái Góngdóu.

6. Contextualized speaking practice

情境説話練習 Chìhnggíng syutwah lihnjaahp

【課前預習】 **Class preparation**

6.1. Please answer the following True/False questions according to the lesson text.

1. Làuh Gābóu haih tóusāng tóujéungge Hēunggóng yàhn. (T/F)

2. Léuihfaat Guhk géuibaahnjó nīgo daaihyìhng gwokjai wuihyíh. (T/F)

3. Hēunggóng yáuh yātgo méng giujouh "Dūngfōng jījyū", léuihyàuh yihp haih Hēunggóng jeui juhngyiuge gīngjai jīchyúh jīyāt. (T/F)

4. Hái Wohnggok hóu nàahn wándóu géisahp mān yātgihnge sāam tùhng yauh pèhng yauh kāmjeuk ge hàaih. (T/F)

5. Hái Jūngwàahn yātdī gōukāp sēungchèuhng, ngóhdeih hóyíh máaihdóu lòihjih Hēunggóngge mìhngpàaih fomaht. (T/F)

6. Lèih síhkēui m̀yúhnge deihfōng, jauhhaih gāauyéh gūngyún waahkjé Lèihdóu. (T/F)

7. Dūngpìhngjāu haih gwokgā kāp ge deihjāt gūngyún, gódouhge sehktàuh fēisèuhng dahkbiht. (T/F)

8. Hēunggóng m̀sīkhahp jūngyi chigīk wahnduhng ge faatsīu yáu. (T/F)

9. Hēunggóng heihauh hòhnláahng, gāautūng fōngbihn, Hēunggóng yàhn yáuhsìhn houhaak. (T/F)

10. Làuh Gābóu hēimohng meihlòih hóyíh hōifaat sānge gíngdím tùhng léuihyàuh hohngmuhk, góisìhn fuhkmouh jātsou. (T/F)

6.2 Please explain the following phrases in Cantonese

1 土生土長 tóusāng tóujéung
2 東方之珠 dūngfōng jījyū
3 發燒友 faatsīu yáu
4 執平貨 jāp pèhngfo

【課後練習】 **Post-class exercises**

6.3 Fill in the blanks with the given vocabularies. Each vocabulary can be chosen once only.

lòihjih	jínsih	kāpyáhn	jyumìhng
sīngíng	séyi	gūngwōng	bánsèuhng
wìhnghahng	chigīk	kaumaht	jāp pèhngfo

1. Kéuih múihyaht ge sāngwuht hóu hīngsūng _____, yātdī ngaatlihk dōu móuh.
2. Wa! Nīdouh ge jihyìhn fūnggíng jānhaih hóu leng wo, lengdou hóuchíh heuijó _____ yātyeuhng.
3. Gahnnìhn, yuht làih yuht dō yàhn jūngyi hái móhngseuhng _____, yānwaih fomaht júngleuih hóu dō, yìhché juhng hóyíh ōnpàaih séuhngmún sungfo (home delivery) tīm.
4. Nīgo jyútàih lohkyùhn yauh _____ yauh hóuwáan, bātyùh wán yaht yātchàih heui gódouh wáan lo!
5. Gokwái lòihbān, gokwái pàhngyáuh, daaihgā hóu! Ngóh hóu _____ nàhnggau hái nīdouh gaaisiuh ngóh ge gwokgā.
6. Hái nīgo jínsīu wuhtduhng léuihmihn, hóudō gūngsī dōu _____ jó kéuihdeih m̀tùhng júngleuih ge cháanbán, yáuhdī juhng maaihdāk hóu pèhng tīm, sóyíh _____ jó hóu dō yàhn làih _____.
7. Múihnìhn yáuh hóu dō _____ m̀tùhng gwokgā ge léuihhaak làih Hēunggóng léuihyàuh, kéuihdeih wúih heui hóu dō m̀tùhng ge _____ gíngdím _____, dōu wúih _____ Hēunggóng ge deihdouh síusihk.

6.4 Complete the following sentences using the given patterns.

1. ...... a, ... a, ... a
   Hēunggóng ge baakfo gūngsī yáuh hóu dō m̀tùhng ge yéh maaih, hóuchíh _____ dángdáng.
2. yauh ...... yauh ......
   Waahtchèuhngsaan haih yātjúng _____ ge wahnduhng.
3. jihnghaih ......
   Nīgāan chāantēng ge sihkmaht syúnjaahk hóu síu, _____.
4. hóuchíh ...... yāt yeuhng
   Gahnlòih tīnhei hóu yiht, yihtdou _____.
5. góng héi séuhng làih, ...
   _____. Bātyùh wángo sìhgaan yātchàih sihkfaahn lo!

6. m̀jí ...... juhng ......

   Ngóh heui léuihhàhng gójahnsìh, _____.

7. jauhhaih

   "Dūngfōng jī jyū" jauhhaih _____.

8. yuht làih yuht ......

   Ngóh ge pàhngyáuh _____, yānwaih kéuih sèhngyaht dōu jouh wahnduhng.

9. yuht ...... yuht ......

   Jínsīu wuhtduhng ge cháanbán _____.

7. Listening and speaking 🔊

聽說練習 Tingsyut lihnjaahp

7.1 Listening comprehension exercises

Please listen to the recording and answer the following T/F questions:

1. Yíngóngge yàhn bātyihp jīhauh yātjihk hái Hēunggóng Léuihyàuh Faatjín Guhk gūngjok. (T/F)

2. Yíngóngge yàhn m̀haih búndeih yàhn. (T/F)

3. Hēunggóng jí yáuh yihndoih mōtīn daaihlàuh. (T/F)

4. Hēunggóng haih yātgo jūngsāi hahpbīk, yihndoih yúh gúdín bihngchyùhnge sìhngsíh. (T/F)

5. Yíngóngge yàhn wah Hēunggóng gāautūng hóu fōngbihn. (T/F)

6. Hēunggóng yáuh gwokjai gēichèuhng tùhng fóchē jaahm. (T/F)

7. Hēunggóng haih yātgo kaumaht tīntòhng (shopping paradise), yānwaih yáuh hóudō búndeih bánpàaih. (T/F)

8. Hēunggóng sēuiyihn yáuh hóudō gūngyún, daahnhaih móuh Lèihdóu. (T/F)

9. Yíngóngge yàhn yihngwàih Hēunggóng m̀haih yātgo sīkhahp louhyìhng tùhng sipyíngge deihfōng. (T/F)

10. Hóiyèuhng Gūngyún haih Hēunggóng yātgo sīkhahp gokgo nìhnlìhngchàhngge yùhlohk chèuhngsó. (T/F)

7.2 Speech topics

1. Deui yàuhhaak làih góng, néih yihngwàih Hēunggóng (waahkjé néih ge gwokgā) yáuh mātyéh kāpyáhn ge deihfōng?

2. Néih haih Hēunggóng Léuihyàuh Faatjín Guhk ge doihbíu, chéng néih gaaisiuhháh Hēunggóng m̀tùhng deihkēui ge léuihyàuh hohngmuhk.

3. Néih yihngwàih Hēunggóng (waahkjé néih ge gwokgā) yáuh mātyéh baahnfaat hóyíh kāpyáhn dōdī lòihjih m̀tùhng deihkēui ge yàuhhaak làih léuihyàuh nē?

7.3 Speaking exercise: Please use at least 10 of the following vocabularies/patterns to say on the following topic in one to two minutes.

"Léuihhàhng gójahnsìh, néih jūngyi jouh mātyéh a? Dímgáai jūngyi jouh nīdī yéh nē?"

kāpyáhn	syúnjaahk	pàaihjí	séyi
gūngwōng	chigīk	gíngdím	jāp pèhngfo
chèuih chí jīngoih	fuhkmouh jātsou	jihnghaih	
yauh ...... yauh	hóuchíh ...... yātyeuhng		
m̀jí ...... juhng	yuht làih yuht	yuht ...... yuht	

8. Additional texts
附加課文 Fuhgā fomàhn

8.1 Additional text 附加課文

中國人嘅收入提高咗，選擇去國外旅遊嘅人越嚟越多。而且，好多國家開放咗對中國嘅簽證政策，令到中國出境遊客人數增加得好快。美國、加拿大 (Gānàhdaaih, Canada)、新加坡 (Sāngabō, Singapore)、韓國、日本同澳洲 (Oujāu, Australia) 等好多國家同地方都開始俾多次入境 (Multiple Entry) 簽證中國遊客。

Jūnggwok yàhnge sāuyahp tàihgōujó, syúnjaahk heui gwokngoih léuihyàuhge yàhn yuht làih yuht dō. Yìhché, hóudō gwokgā hōifongjó deui Jūnggwokge chīmjing jingchaak, lihngdou Jūnggwok chēutgíng yàuhhaak yàhnsou jānggā dāk hóu faai. Méihgwok, Gānàhdaaih, Sāngabō, Hòhngwok, Yahtbún tùhng Oujāu dáng hóudō gwokgā tùhng deihfōng dōu hōichí béi dōchi yahpgíng chīmjing Jūnggwok yàuhhaak.

根據最新嘅「中國遊客境外旅遊」嘅調查報告，中國嘅境外旅遊出現咗一啲新情況。譬如話，而家嘅中國遊客更加重視旅遊體驗，唔再鍾意跟住導遊旅行，自由行越嚟越受歡迎。值得一提嘅係，唔同年齡層嘅中國遊客，都出現咗呢個變化。

Gāngeui jeui sānge "Jūnggwok yàuhhaak gíngngoih léuihyàuh" ge diuhchàh bougou, Jūnggwokge gíngngoih léuihyàuh chēutyihnjó yātdī sān chìhngfong. Peiyùhwah, yìhgāge Jūnggwok yàuhhaak ganggā juhngsih léuihyàuh táiyihm, m̀joi jūngyi gānjyuh douhyàuh léuihhàhng, jihyàuh hàhng yuht làih yuht sauh fūnyìhng. Jihkdāk yāttàihge haih, m̀tùhng nìhnlìhngchàhng ge Jūnggwok yàuhhaak, dōu chēutyihnjó nīgo binfa.

60後遊客非常希望走出國門，去更遠嘅地方，感受更多唔一樣嘅文化。80後同90後嘅年輕遊客更加係咁樣，為咗有更加多嘅機會同時間出去睇下、去了解下呢個多元嘅世界，一啲年輕人甚至推遲結婚、生小朋友呢啲傳統嘅人生階段。喺選擇旅遊方式嘅時候，如果父母同仔女一齊旅行，佢哋會互相影響。作為子女，選擇旅遊目的地同活動嘅時候，要考慮父母嘅興趣同身體情況。而年輕人更加鍾意刺激，可能都比父母更加熟悉外語同高科技，都會令父母放心選擇更加獨立嘅國際旅行方式。

Luhksahp hauh yàuhhaak fēisèuhng hēimohng jáuchēut gwokmùhn, heui gang yúhnge deihfōng, gámsauh gangdō m̀yātyeuhngge màhnfa. Baatsahp hauh tùhng Gáusahp hauhge nìhnhīng yàuhhaak ganggā haih gámyéung, waihjó yáuh ganggā dō ge gēiwuih tùhng sìhgaan chēuteui táiháh, heui líuhgáiháh nīgo dōyùhnge saigaai, yātdī nìhnhīngyàhn sahmji tēuichìh gitfān, sāang síupàhngyáuh nīdī chyùhntúngge yàhnsāng gāaidyuhn. Hái sýunjaahk léuihyàuh fōngsīk ge sìhhauh, yùhgwó fuhmóuh tùhng jáinéui yātchàih léuihhàhng, kéuihdeih wúih wuhsēung yínghéung. Jokwàih jínéuih, sýunjaahk léuihyàuh muhkdīkdeih tùhng wuhtduhng ge sìhhauh, yiu háauleuih fuhmóuhge hingcheui tùhng sāntái chìhngfong. Yìh nìhnhīngyàhn ganggā jūngyi chigīk, hónàhng dōu béi fuhmóuh ganggā suhksīk ngoihyúh tùhng gōu fōgeih, dōu wúih lihng fuhmóuh fongsām sýunjaahk ganggā duhklahpge gwokjai léuihhàhng fōngsīk.

另外，購物對中國遊客嘅吸引力都唔似以前咁大喇，旅行最重要嘅原因係放鬆同休息。中國污染問題好嚴重，因此好多遊客都會選擇自然環境乾淨、同環境優美嘅地方去旅行。呢個調查報告仲講，最近幾年選擇去海島嘅中國遊客數量都越嚟越多。

Lihngngoih, kaumaht deui Jūnggwok yàuhhaakge kāpyáhnlihk dōu m̀chíh yíhchìhn gam daaih la, léuihhàhng jeui juhngyiuge yùhnyān haih fongsūng tùhng yāusīk. Jūnggwok wūyíhm mahntàih hóu yìhmjuhng, yānchí hóudō yàuhhaak dōu wúih sýunjaahk jihyìhn wàahngíng gōnjehng tùhng wàahngíng yāuméih ge deihfōng heui léuihhàhng. Nīgo diuhchàh bougou juhng góng, jeuigahn géinìhn sýunjaahk heui hóidóuge Jūnggwok yàuhhaak souleuhng dōu yuht làih yuht dō.

8.2 Additional vocabulary 附加詞彙

Number	Word	Yale Romanization	POS	English
1	開放	hōifong	V	to release; to open up
2	增加	jānggā	V	to increase
3	跟	gān	V	to follow
4	導遊	douhyàuh	N	guide; tour guide
5	~後	~hauh	Part	post-, the ~ generation
6	推遲	tēuichìh	V	to put off; to delay; to postpone; to defer
7	階段	gāaidyuhn	N	stage; phase; period
8	方式	fōngsīk	N	way; mode; manner; pattern
9	高科技	gōu fōgeih	N	high technology
10	數量	souleuhng	N	number; quantity; amount

8.3 Please answer the following T/F questions after reading the additional text:

1 Yānwaih Jūnggwok yàhnge sāuyahp yuht làih yuht gōu, sóyíh heui gwokngoih léuihhàhngge yàhn yuht làih yuht dō. (T/F)

2 Yìhgā, Jūnggwok yàuhhaak baahn chīmjing tùhng yíhchìhn yātyeuhng, dōu haih fēisèuhng nàahn. (T/F)

3 Jūnggwok yàuhhaak jeui jūngyige léuihhàhng fōngsīk haih chāamgā léuihhàhng tyùhn. (T/F)

4 Nìhngéi daaihge yàhn béi nìhnchīngyàhn ganggā jūngyi jihyàuh hàhng. (T/F)

5 Waihjó léuihhàhng, yātdī nìhnchīngyàhn séung jóudī gitfān. (T/F)

6 Yùhgwó yātchàih léuihhàhng, fuhmóuh wúih yínghéung nìhnchīngyàhnge syúnjaahk. (T/F)

7 Yānwaih fuhmóuh yáuhchín, sóyíh hóyíh syúnjaahk ganggā duhklahpge gwokjai léuihhàhng fōngsīk. (T/F)

8 Máaihyéh haih Jūnggwok yàuhhaak chēutgwok léuihhàhng jeui juhngyiuge muhkdīk. (T/F)

9 Jūnggwok yàhn jūngyi heui gōnjehng, wàahngíng yāuméihge deihfōng. (T/F)

10 Jeuigahn géi nìhn, Jūnggwok yàuhhaak hōichí heui hóidóu léuihhàhng. (T/F)

8.4 Topics for discussions

1 Dímgáai Jūnggwok yàuhhaak yuht làih yuht dō? Dímgáai yuht làih yuht dō Jūnggwok yàhn jūngyi chēutgwok léuihhàhng nē?

2 Néih jūng m̀jūngyi léuihhàhng a ? Néih jūngyi yuhng dímyéungge fōngsīk léuihhàhng a ? Chéng néih góngháh yùhnyān.

8.5 Authentic oral data 1 🔊
真實語料 1

8.6 Authentic oral data 2 🔊
真實語料 2

Lesson 2　Eating in Hong Kong
香港美食

1. Pragmatic factors, Yuti features and linguistic functions
語用因素、語體特徵與語言功能
Yúhyuhng yānsou, yúhtái dahkjīng yúh yúhyìhn gūngnàhng

Pragmatic factors/ Yuti features 語用因素/語體特徵	Linguistic function 語言功能
Pragmatic factors: Between casual and semi-formal, with no particular requirement for polite forms but slang and frozen expressions should be avoided.	**Linguistic function:** Detailed Description Besides sharing basic information, better employing rhetoric and emotion or adding a literary flavor in one's description.
語用因素： 半正式，因為沒有特定的物件，說話者一般不會用表示禮貌的語言，描述的時候會避免特別俚俗和太正式的用語。	語言功能：詳細描述 在傳遞資訊的基礎上，通過添加文學色彩、個人感情及修辭手段來進行詳細描述。
Yuti features: Formality index: 1-2	
語體特徵：1-2 級之間	

Notes on pragmatic knowledge 語用知識	Notes on structure 語言及篇章結構知識
I. Spoken features and euphemism 口語特徵與委婉語 　1. The use of sentence final particles 句末語氣詞：「呢」，「啦」，「啊」等 II. Related knowledge 相關知識 　1. Heaven of delicious food 「美食天堂」 　2. Hong Kong style "tea restaurant" 「茶餐廳」 　3. Foreign helpers 「外籍傭工（菲傭）」 　4. Cantonese style herbal tea 「廣式涼茶」 　5. Indigenous inhabitants 「原居民」 　6. Indigenous food: Pot-dish 「盆菜」 　7. Eating is the most important thing in life 「民以食為天」	I. Grammar and sentence patterns 語法和句型 　1. "yìh ……" as to; with regards to … 　2. "jokwàih……" as … 　3. "jauhsyun……dōu……" even if... 　4. "gei……yauh……" both...and... 　5. "jihkdāk" to be worth 　6. "……yíhlàih" ever since … 　7. Resultative verbs 　8. Sentence particles : Double finals II. Paragraph and discourse 語段和篇章 　1. "m̀léih ……dōu……jiyū……jauh ganggā m̀sái góng la" no matter...as to...let alone...

22

2. Text 🔊

課文 Fomàhn

我代表香港海鮮協會向各位推廣香港旅遊嘅魅力。廣東菜係中國最有代表性嘅菜系之一，而廣東菜最特別嘅就係蒸海鮮。香港以前作為一個漁村，二百年前，香港好多人住喺船上面，需要時時出海。今日雖然水上人越嚟越少，但係香港嘅漁村風味仲可以喺離島同避風塘搵到。香港嘅海鮮嚟自唔同嘅地方，有啲離香港比較近，例如廣東啦、海南島啦，有啲離香港遠啲，例如菲律賓啦、印尼啦、甚至澳洲附近嚟嘅都有，所以海鮮嘅種類好豐富。食海鮮，唔一定要去酒樓，香港每個街市每日都有海鮮賣，就算打風落大雨，都一樣買到最新鮮嘅海鮮。

Ngóh doihbíu Hēunggóng Hóisīn Hipwúi heung gokwái tēuigwóng Hēunggóng léuihyàuhge meihlihk, Gwóngdūngchoi haih Jūnggwok jeui yáuh doihbíusing ge choihaih jīyāt, yìh Gwóngdūngchoi jeui dahkbihtge jauhhaih jīng hóisīn. Hēunggóng yíhchìhn jokwàih yātgo yùhchyūn, yihbaak nìhn chìhn, Hēunggóng hóudō yàhn jyuhhái syùhn seuhngmihn, sēuiyiu sìhsìh chēuthói. Gāmyaht sēuiyìhn séuiseuhngyàhn yuht làih yuht síu, daahnhaih Hēunggóngge yùhchyūn fūngmeih juhng hóyíh hái Lèihdóu tùhng beihfūngtòhng wándóu. Hēunggóng ge hóisīn làihjih m̀tùhngge deihfōng, yáuhdī lèih Hēunggóng béigaau káhn, laihyùh Gwóngdūng lā, Hóinàahm Dóu lā, yáuhdī lèih Hēunggóng yúhndī, laihyùh Fēileuhtbān lā, Yannèih lā, sahmji Oujāu fuhgahn làihge dōu yáuh. Sóyíh hóisīnge júngleuih hóu fūngfu. Sihk hóisīn, m̀yātdihng yiu heui jáulàuh, Hēunggóng múihgo gāaisíh múih yaht dōu yáuh hóisīn maaih, jauhsyun dáfūng lohk daaihyúh, dōu yātyeuhng máaihdóu jeui sānsīnge hóisīn.

近年海水污染，每年又有「休漁期」，為咗保持海鮮嘅供應，養海鮮變成另外一個選擇。香港嘅元朗、西貢同南丫島嘅碼頭，我哋仲見到好多人養魚、養蝦、養龍蝦。香港自己養嘅海鮮，客人可以放心食，既新鮮又衛生，因為我哋有嚴格嘅衛生標準。食海鮮，係所有嚟香港旅行嘅人一定要做嘅嘢。除咗西貢同離島，香港仔、元朗、屯門、鯉魚門都係食海鮮嘅好地方。如果想試吓新嘅體驗，銅鑼灣避風塘都值得去嘅，客人可以喺船上面一面食海鮮，一面欣賞維多利亞港嘅夜景。唔理你鍾唔鍾意食海鮮，我都推介遊客去行下睇下，認識下香港嘅文化。至於鍾意食海鮮嘅朋友就更加唔使講喇。

香港係海邊嘅城市，幾百年以嚟，都離唔開魚。除咗海鮮，香港人仲鍾意將啲魚曬乾，變成蝦米呀、蝦醬呀、魚粉呀、魚露呀、鹹魚呀等等。好多遊客都知道，大澳仲保留住以前漁村嘅風味，所以特登去大澳買蝦醬。如果唔想去咁遠，香港島嘅上環同西營盤有好多賣海味嘅鋪頭，香港人叫嗰度做「鹹魚欄」或者「海味街」，嗰度一百年前已經係好熱鬧嘅貿易中心，附近嘅碼頭人來人往。我提議嚟香港旅行嘅人一定要去上環行吓，噉樣唔止可以買啲海味做手信，仲可以睇吓附近嘅舊建築，好似西港城啦、醫學博物館啦、孫中山紀念館啦，知道多啲香港嘅歷史。我代表香港海鮮協會，歡迎世界各地嘅遊客嚟呢度體驗香港嘅另一面。

Gahnnìhn hóiséui wūyíhm, múihnìhn yauh yáuh"Yāuyùh kèih", waihjó bóuchìh hóisīn ge gūngying, yéuhng hóisīn binsìhng lihngngoih yātgo syúnjaahk. Hēunggóng ge Yùhnlóhng, Sāigung tùhng Nàahmngādóu ge máhtàuh, ngóhdeih juhng gindóu hóudō yàhn yéuhng yú, yéuhng hā, yéuhng lùhnghā. Hēunggóng jihgéi yéuhngge hóisīn, haakyàhn hóyíh fongsām sihk, gei sānsīn yauh waihsāng, yānwaih ngóhdeih yáuh yìhmgaak ge waihsāng bīujéun. Sihk hóisīn, haih sóyáuh làih Hēunggóng léuihhàhngge yàhn yātdihng yiu jouhge yéh. Chèuihjó Sāigung tùhng Lèihdóu, Hēunggóngjái, Yùhnlóhng, Tyùhnmùhn, Léihyùhmùhn dōu haih sihk hóisīnge hóu deihfōng. Yùhgwó séung siháh sānge táiyihm, Tùhnglòhwāan beihfūngtòhng dōu jihkdāk heui ge, haakyàhn hóyíh hái syùhn seuhngmihn yātmihn sihk hóisīn, yātmihn yānséung Wàihdōleihnga Góng ge yehgíng. M̀léih néih jūng m̀jūngyi sihk hóisīn, ngóh dōu tēuigaai yàuhhaak heui hàahngháh táiháh, yihngsīkháh Hēunggóngge màhnfa. Jiyū jūngyi sihk hóisīn ge pàhngyáuh jauh ganggā m̀sái góng la.

Hēunggóng haih hóibīn ge sìhngsíh, géi baak nìhn yíhlàih, dōu lèihm̀hōi yú. Chèuihjó hóisīn, Hēunggóngyàhn juhng jūngyi jēung dī yú saaigōn, binsìhng hāmáih a, hājeung a, yùhfán a, yùhlouh a, hàahmyú a dángdáng. Hóudō yàuhhaak dōu jīdou, Daaih'ou juhng bóulàuhjyuh yíhchìhn yùhchyūn ge fūngmeih, sóyíh dahkdāng heui Daaih'ou máaih hājeung. Yùhgwó m̀séung heui gam yúhn, Hēunggóng Dóu ge Seuhngwàahn tùhng Sāiyìhngpùhn yáuh hóudō maaih hóiméi ge poutàu, Hēunggóngyàhn giu gódouh jouh "Hàahmyùh Lāan" waahkjé "Hóiméi Gāai", gódouh yāt baak nìhn chìhn yíhgīng haih hóu yihtnaauhge mauhyihk jūngsām, fuhgahnge máhtàuh yàhn lòih yàhn wóhng. Ngóh tàihyíh làih Hēunggóng léuihhàhng ge yàhn yātdihng yiu heui Seuhngwàahn hàahngháh, gámyéung m̀jí hóyíh máaih dī hóiméi jouh sáuseun, juhng hóyíh táiháh fuhgahnge gauh ginjūk, hóuchíh Sāi Góng Sìhng lā, Yīhohk Bokmahtgún lā, Syūn Jūng-sāan Geinihm Gún lā, jīdou dōdī Hēunggóngge lihksí. Ngóh doihbíu Hēunggóng Hóisīn Hipwúi, fūnyìhng saigaai gokdeih ge yàuhhaak làih nīdouh táiyihm Hēunggóngge lihng yātmihn.

3. Vocabulary in use 🔊

活用詞彙 Wuhtyuhng chìhwuih

3.1 Common vocabulary

Number	Word	Yale Romanization	POS	English
1	有代表性	yáuh doihbíu sing	Adj	typical
2	菜系	choihaih	N	cuisine
3	蒸	jīng	V	to steam
4	漁村	yùhchyūn	N	fishing village
5	街市	gāaisíh	N	wet market
6	海水污染	hóiséui wūyíhm	PH	marine pollution
7	保持	bóuchìh	V	to keep, to maintain
8	供應	gūngying	N/V	supply; to supply
9	碼頭	máhtàuh	N	pier
10	養	yéuhng	V	to keep (animals)
11	衞生	waihsāng	Adj/N	hygienic; hygiene
12	嚴格	yìhmgaak	Adj	strict
13	標準	bīujéun	Adj/N	standard
14	體驗	táiyihm	N/V	experience; to learn through practice, to learn through one's personal experience
15	欣賞	yānséung	V	to admire, to appreciate
16	推介	tēuigaai	N/V	recommendation; to recommend
17	遊客	yàuhhaak	N	tourist
18	曬乾	saaigōn	RV	to dry in the sun
19	變成	binsìhng	RV	to become, to change into

20	保留	bóulàuh	V	to reserve, to retain
21	貿易中心	mauhyihk jūngsām	N	trade centre
22	人來人往	yàhn lòih yàhn wóhng	PH	many people hurrying back and forth
23	提議	tàihyíh	N/V	suggestion; to suggest, to propose
24	手信	sáuseun	N	souvenir
25	舊建築	gauh ginjūk	N	old building and structure
26	另一面	lihngyātmihn	PH	the other side

3.2 Proper nouns and place words

1	香港海鮮協會	Hēunggóng Hóisīn Hipwúi	PN	Hong Kong Seafood Association
2	海南島	Hóinàahm Dóu	PW	Hainan Island
3	澳洲	Oujāu	PW	Australia
4	元朗	Yùhnlóhng	PW	Yuen Long
5	西貢	Sāigung	PW	Sai Kung
6	南丫島	Nàahmngādóu	PW	Lamma Island
7	屯門	Tyùhnmùhn	PW	Tuen Mun
8	鯉魚門	Léihyùhmùhn	PW	Lei Yue Mun
9	維多利亞港	Wàihdōleihnga Góng	PW	Victoria Harbour
10	大澳	Daaih'ou	PW	Tai O
11	上環	Seuhngwàahn	PW	Sheung Wan
12	西營盤	Sāiyìhngpùhn	PW	Sai Ying Pun
13	鹹魚欄	Hàahmyùh Lāan	PW	Salted Fish Market
14	海味街	Hóiméi Gāai	PW	Dried Seafood Street
15	西港城	Sāi Góng Sìhng	PW	Western Market

| 16 | 醫學博物館 | Yīhohk Bokmahtgún | PW | Museum of Medical Sciences |
| 17 | 孫中山紀念館 | Syūn Jūng-sāan Geinihm Gún | PW | Dr Sun Yat-sen Museum |

3.3 Food

1	龍蝦	lùhnghā	N	lobster
2	蝦米	hāmáih	N	dried shrimp
3	蝦醬	hājeung	N	shrimp paste
4	魚粉	yùhfán	N	fish meal
5	魚露	yùhlouh	N	fish sauce
6	鹹魚	hàahmyú	N	salted fish
7	海味	hóiméi	N	dried seafood

3.4 About the life at sea

1	漁村風味	yùhchyūn fūngmeih	N	taste of fishing village
2	避風塘	beihfūngtòhng	N	typhoon shelter
3	休漁期	yāuyùh kèih	PH	fishing moratorium

4. Notes on language and discourse structure

語言及篇章結構知識 Yúhyìhn kahp pīnjēung gitkau jīsīk

4.1 Grammar and sentence patterns 語法和句型

4.1.1. "yìh......" as to; with regards to

1. Gwóngdūngchoi haih Jūnggwok jeui yáuh doihbíusing ge choihaih jīyāt, yìh Gwóngdūngchoi jeui dahkbihtge jauhhaih jīng hóisīn.

2. Kéuih wah tīngyaht fāanlàih, yìh doudái géidím, ngóh jauh m̀jīdou la.

3. Nīdouh ge síuhohk, jūnghohk dōu haih míhnfai ge, yìh daaihhohk hohkfai yiu géidō chín nē, ngóh jauh m̀jīdou la.

4.1.2. "jokwàih ......" as ...

1. Jokwàih Hēunggóng Léuihfaat Guhk ge doihbíu, ngóh gāmyaht hóu hōisām hóyíh hái nīdouh gaaisiuh Hēunggóng.

2. Jokwàih yātgo leuhtsī, ngóh fēisèuhng gwāansām Hēunggóngge faatleuht mahntàih.

3. Jokwàih yātgo lihksí faatsīu yáu, ngóh jūngyi heui lihksí bokmahtgún, dōu jūngyi tái tùhng lihksí yáuhgwāange syū.

4.1.3. "jauhsyun......dōu......" even if...

1. Ngóh gokdāk Hēunggóng Lihksí Bokmahtgún fēisèuhng jihkdāk hēui, jauhsyun heuigwo dōu hóyíh joi heui.

2. Gógāan daaihhohkge yīukàuh dahkbiht gōu, jauhsyun háausíh sìhngjīk hóu, dōu m̀yātdihng hóyíh yahp.

3. Jauhsyun bàhbā màhmā m̀tùhngyi, ngóh dōu yiu tùhng kéuih gitfān!

4.1.4. "gei......yauh......" both...and...

1. Nīgo sìhngsíh gei yáuh daaih sēungchèuhng, yauh yáuh lihksí ginjūk.

2. Sātìhnge daaihpàaihdong gei hóusihk gachìhn yauh hahpléih, néih séung m̀séung tùhng ngóhdeih yātchàih heui a?

3. Nīgo yàhn gei móuh gūngjok gīngyihm, yauh m̀sīk ngoihyúh, yīnggōi hóu nàahn wándóu gūngjok.

4.1.5. "jihkdāk" to be worth

1. Hah sīngkèih yáuh sāam yaht gakèih, néih wah bīndouh jihkdāk heui nē?

2. Gógāan ūk hóu gwai, néih wah jihk m̀jihkdāk máaih nē?

3. Sihkyīn hóuchíh hóu yáuhyìhng, daahnhaih wúih jouhsìhng hóudō gihnhōng mahntàih, néih wah jihk m̀jihkdāk nē?

4.1.6. "……yíhlàih" ever since …

1. Gāmyaht haih ngóh yahp daaihhohk yíhlàih jeui hōisāmge yātyaht.

2. Ngóh hóu jūngyi heui léuihhàhng, nī géinìhn yíhàih ge gīngyihm wah béi ngóh jī, Hēunggóng jānhaih saigaai seuhng jeui ōnchyùhnge deihfōng jīyāt.

3. Ngóh làihjó Hēunggóng sahpgéi nìhn, nī sahpgéi nìhn yíhlàih, Hēunggóng binjó hóudō.

4. Daaihhohk bātyihp yíhlàih, ngóh yātjihk hái Léuihfaat Guhk gūngjok.

4.1.7　Resultative verbs (RV)

Resultative verbs are compound verbs in which the first, or main verb describes the principle action, and the second indicates the extent to, or manner in which the action has been carried through or achieved.

1. -dóu

"dóu" is a resultative verb ending (RVE). It indicates that an objective has been successfully achieved.

1. Gāmmáahn lohkdaaihyúh, sóyíh tái m̀dóu yuhtgwōng.

2. Néih tēng m̀tēngdóu kéuih giu néih a?

3. Ngóhdeih hàahnglàih, yānwaih wán m̀dóu dīksí.

4. Néih nám m̀námdóu máaih mātyéh láihmaht béi kéuih a?

5. Ngóh yānwaih daap m̀dóu góbāan syùhn, sóyíh chìhdou.

6. Gójoh sāan gam gōu, kéuih séuhng m̀dóu.

7. Chàhn síujé máaih m̀dóu góbún syū.

8. M̀jī dímgáai kéuih ló m̀dóu Méihgwokge chīmjing.

9. A: Néih sāudóu ngóhge fēksí meih a?

　　B: Juhng meih sāudóu.

10. Gógāan chīukāpsíhchèuhng jauh hái chìhnbihn, néih gin m̀dóu mē?!

11. Ngàhnhòhng yíhgīng sāanjó mùhn la, kéuihdeih ló m̀dóu chín.

12. A: Néih tái m̀táidākdóu kéuih gihn lāu mātyéh sīk a?

　　B: Táidākdóu, hùhngsīk.

2. -dou

"dou" (RVE) indicates that (1) a goal has been reached, arrival at a place (2) something has been done to the extent of one's ability.

1. Wòhng sīnsāang heuidou Mahksāigō la.

2. Kàhmmáahn kéuihdeih hàahng fāsíh hàahngdou hóu yeh.

3. Mìhngjái jouh gūngfo jouhdou yehmáahn yātdím.

4. Léuhnggo jūngtàuh hóyíh séuhngdou gógo sāandéng ma?

5. Gógo màhnyùhn dájih dádou luhkdím juhng meih fonggūng.

6. Kéuih fāandou ngūkkéi gójahnsí, chéng néih giu kéuih dá dihnwá béi ngóh.

7. Gógihn T-sēut yíhgīng jeukdou gauhsaai.

8. Gāmyaht lóuhsī gaaudou daihgéi fo a?

9. Gāmmáahn kéuih heui m̀heuidāk dou Seuihsih a?

10. Hahgo láihbaai ngóhdeih duhk m̀duhkdākdou daih yahsāamfo a?

11. A: Néih baatdím fāan m̀fāandākdou ngūkkéi a?

    B: M̀fāandākdou, gáudím lā.

12. Ngóhdī chín yuhngdou tīngyaht jauh yuhngyùhn la.

3. –hóu

"hóu" (RVE) indicates satisfactory completion of a task.

1. Jēung táai jyúhóu faahn la.

2. Dī saimānjái jeukhóu hàaih meih a?

3. Néih yiu sóhóu douh mùhn sīnji chēutgāai.

4. Néihge tùhnghohk jouhhóu dī gūngfo meih a?

5. Ngoihbihn lohkyúh, néih yiu sāanhóu dī chēung.

6. Dī sāam géisìh sīnji tongdākhóu a?

7. Gihn sēutsāam jouhjó yātgo láihbaai juhng meih jouhdākhóu.

4. -fāan

"fāan" (RVE) indicates return to an original state or position; repayment, replacement or recovery.

1. Chéng néih béifāan go tòuhsyūjing ngóh.

2. Néih lófāan go hohksāangjing meih a?

3. Néih sihkjó ngóhge pìhnggwó, néih yiu máaihfāan go béi ngóh.

4. Kéuih wah kéuih jeukfāan gihn sāam jauh làih wóh.

5. Mìhngjái yiu geifāan fūng seun heui hohkhaauh.

6. A: A-Mēi hóufāan meih a?

    B: Hóufāan hóudō la, yáuhsām!

7. Néih hái gógāan ngàhnhòhngge chín ló m̀lódākfāan a?

8. Góbún syū ngóh juhng meih táiyùhn, sóyíh m̀béidākfāan néih.

9. Kéuih ge behng m̀hóudākfāan.

5. –màaih

"màaih"(RVE) indicates that something has been closed, locked or finished off.

1. Kéuih yámmàaih būi gafē jauh làih.

2. Màhmā giu kéuih sihkmàaih dī faahn.

3. Ngóh sāanmàaih dī chēung la, daahnhaih douh mùhn só m̀màaih.

4. Ngóh jouhmàaih nīdī yéh jauh tùhng néih yātchàih heui táihei.

5. Yāusīksāt douh mùhn só m̀sódākmàaih a?

6. Dímgáai yīyún dī chēung m̀sāandākmàaih a?

6. "- chān" indicates the effectiveness of the action of the verb and implies a degree of unpleasant sense.

1. láahngchān (catch cold)

2. haakchān (scare/be scared)

3. jíngchān jek sáu (get hurt in the hand)

Sometimes 'V chān' means 'everytime ……'.

1. Ngóh yāt góngchān nīgihn sih kéuih dōu hóu nāu.

2. Kéuih sihkchān nīdī yéh dōu m̀syūfuhk.

3. Ngóh heuichān kéuih ngūkkéi kéuih dōu m̀háidouh.

4. Ngóh giuchān kéuih kéuih dōu m̀làih.

4.1.8. Sentence particles: Double Finals

1. ......la gwa

(surely; probably; I think so; I guess so, don't you agree?)

1. Kéuih dáhóu fahn màhngín la gwa?!

2. Chàhn sīnsāang lódóu chīmjing la gwa?!

3. A-Yān heuijó Méihgwok la gwa?!

2. ......la wóh

(it is said......, I was told......)

1. Kéuih wah kéuih ge chīmjing yìhndóukèih la wóh!

2. A-Mēi yíhgīng heuidou Gānàhdaaih la wóh!

3. Jēung sīnsāang wah kéuih ge behng hóufāansaai la wóh!

3. ......la bo

(as far as I can see; in my opinion/mild suggestion, usually to children or students)

1. Néih yiu jouh gūngfo la bo!

2. M̀hóu tái gam dō dihnsih la bo!

3. Yìhgā dī choi móuh seuhnggo láihbaai gam gwai la bo!

4. ......la mē?

(implies surprise at someone's change of mind or opinion, sometimes used sarcastically)

1. Máaih la mē? Kàhmyaht néih wah m̀máaih ge bo.

2. Kéuih būnjó heui Sāngaai la mē?

3. Jīdou ngóh sāileih la mē?

5. ......lāma

(seeks clarification or further assurance about someone's action or intention)

1. Néih m̀duhksyū lāma? Hóu, yātjahngāan néih móuh dāk heui yámchàh.

2. Néih jānhaih heui lāma? Gám ngóh bōng néih béichín la!

3. Néih m̀fāanhohk lāma? Gám néih hái ūkkéi jouhháh gāmouh lā!

6. ......je mē?

(only, implies surprise or disbelief)

1. Gam síu je mē?

2. Néih sāudóu yātfahn láihmaht je mē?

3. Sēunmahnchyu jíyáuh yātgo jipdoihyùhn je mē?

4.2. Paragraph and discourse 語段和篇章

4.2.1. "m̀léih......dōu......jiyū......jauh ganggā m̀sái góng la" no matter...as to...let alone...

1. M̀léih néih haih daaihyàhn, dihnghaih síu pàhngyáuh, néih dōu wúih jūngyi nīgo deihfōng. Jiyū lóuhyàhngā, jauh ganggā m̀sái góng la.

2. Deui ngoihgwok yàhn, m̀léih haih Gwóngdūngwá, dihnghaih Póutūngwá, dōu m̀léih haih sīngdiuh dihng haih yúhfaat, dōu géi nàahn. Jiyū Jūngmàhn jih, jauh ganggā m̀sáigóng la.

3. Jokwàih yātgo jūngyi sihkyéhge yàhn, ngóh jūngyi heui m̀tùhng deihfong sihkyéh, m̀léih bīngo gwokgā ge choi, ngóh dōu séung siháh, jiyū deihdouhge méihsihk, jauh ganggā m̀sái góng la.

5. Notes on pragmatic knowledge

語用因素與相關知識 Yúhyuhng yānsou yúh sēunggwāan jīsīk

5.1. Spoken features and euphemism 口語特徵與委婉語

5.1.1. The use of sentence final particles 句末語氣詞：" 呢 nē"，" 啦 lā"，" 啊 a" 等

The use of sentence final particles, " 呢 nē"，" 啦 lā"，" 啊 a", can soften the tone of abrupt suggestions and orders.

- Ngóhdeih yātchàih jouh, hóu m̀hóu nē?
  (compare with "Ngóhdeih yātchàih jouh, hóu m̀hóu?")
- Néih faaidī lā, ngóhdeih móuh sìhgaan la.
  (compare with "Néih faaidī, ngóhdeih móuh sìhgaan la".)
- A: Néih sihkm̀aaih nīdī yéh hóu m̀hóu a? B: Hóu a.
  (compare with "A: Néih sihkm̀aaih nīdī yéh hóu m̀hóu a? B: Hóu.")

5.2. Related knowledge 相關知識

5.2.1. " 美食天堂 méihsihk tīntòhng" heaven of delicious food

It is used for describing a place where you can find all kinds of delicious food. You can find other similar expressions in Chinese such as " 人間天堂 yàhngāan tīntòhng", meaning "heaven on earth". It is common in the Chinese culture to use this word as an exaggerating way of expressing something superb.

- Hēunggóng haih yātgo léuihyàuh tīntòhng, dōu haih yātgo méihsihk tīntòhng.

5.2.2. " 茶餐廳 chàh chāantēng" Hong Kong style "tea restaurant"

It is commonly referring to a special kind of small and local restaurants in Hong Kong with low price, fast service and limited variety on the menu.

- Gāmyaht, ngóhdeih jauh heui chàh chāantēng sihkngaan, hóu m̀hóu a?

5.2.3. " 外籍傭工（菲傭） ngoihjihk yùhnggūng (Fēiyùhng)" foreign helpers (Philipino helpers)

It is a general term referring to domestic helpers with foreign passports, sometimes referred by local people as "Fēiyùhng" (Philipino helpers) because they were introduced to Hong Kong first and has been the largest group in this category.

Hái Hēunggóng, hóudō gātìhng dou yáuh ngoihjihk yùhnggūng bōngmòhng.

5.2.4. " 廣式涼茶 Gwóngsīk lèuhngchàh" Cantonese style herbal tea

Literally, it means "cool tea", referring to a variety of drinks made from herbs or Chinese medicine. This is a very popular drink for the Chinese and it can either go with meals or by itself.

- Gwóngdūng yàhn chèuihjó jūngyi yám tōng, dōu jūngyi yám lèuhngchàh.

5.2.5. " 原居民 yùhngēuimàhn" Indigenous inhabitants

It is referring to the people who lived in the New Territories of Hong Kong since eight hundred years ago and still enjoy some special rights after Hong Kong was returned to China in 1997. They also have some unique culture legacy, such as the "pùhnchoi" described here.

- Tēngginwah jeui hóusihkge pùhnchoi haih Sāngaai yùhngēuimàhnge pùhnchoi.

5.2.6. " 盆菜 pùhnchoi" pot-dish

It is a special kind of pot-dish that put together different kinds of meat, poultry, seafood and vegetables, cooked as one dish and this single dish is usually large enough to serve the whole table. It is popular during special cultural occasions such as the Chinese New Year.

- Pùhnchoi haih mātyéh choi nē? Yáuhdī mātyéh sihk ge nē?

5.2.7. " 民以食為天 màhn yíh sihk wàih tīn" eating is the most important thing in life

Literally, the phrase means"eating is the 'sky' for people". The word "tīn" here is used figuratively in the Chinese culture to refer to something very important.

- Hēunggóng yáuh hóudō sihkyéhge deihfōng, jānhaih "màhn yíh sihk wàih tīn" la.

6. Contextualized speaking practice

情境説話練習 Chìhnggíng syutwah lihnjaahp

【課前預習】 Class preparation

6.1. Please answer the following True/False questions according to the lesson text.

1. Góngjé (speaker) doihbíu Hēunggóng Hóisīn Hipwúi faatyìhn.(T/F)
2. Sāamsahp nìhn chìhn, Hēunggóng yáuh hóudō yàhn jyuhhái syùhn seuhngmihn, sēuiyiu

sìhsìh chēuthói. (T/F)

3. Hēunggóng ge hóisīn lòihjih m̀tùhngge deihfōng, yáuhdī lèih Hēunggóng béigaau káhn, yáuhdī lèih Hēungóng béigaau yúhn, júngleuih fūngfu.(T/F)

4. Waihjó bóuchìh hóisīnge gūngying, sóyíh yáuh yéuhngge hóisīn. (T/F)

5. Hēunggóngge Yùhnlóhng, Sāigung tùhng Nàahmngādóu ge máhtàuh, ngóhdeih yíhgīng hóu nàahn táidóu yáuh yàhn yéuhng hóisīn. (T/F)

6. Jíyáuh hóusíu làih Hēunggóngge yàhn wúih sihk hóisīn. (T/F)

7. Hái Tùhnglòhwāan beihfūngtòhng, haakyàhn hóyíh hái syùhn seuhngmihn yātbīn sihk hóisīn, yātbīn yānséung bíuyín. (T/F)

8. Hēunggóng yàhn jūngyi jēung yātdī yú saaigōn, binsìhng jōngsīk bán. (T/F)

9. Hēunggóng Dóu ge Seuhngwàahn tùhng Sāiyìhngpùhn yáuh hóudō maaih hóiméi ge poutáu, Hēunggóng yàhn giu gódouh jouh "Hàahmyùh Lāan" waahkjé "Hóiméi Gāai". (T/F)

10. Hái Seuhngwàahn, ngóhdeih hóyíh máaih yātdī hóiméi jouh sáuseun, tùhng táiháh fuhgahnge gauh ginjūk. (T/F)

6.2 Please explain the following phrases in Cantonese

1 避風塘 beihfūng tòhng
2 休魚期 yāuyùh kèih
3 漁村風味 yùhchyūn fūngmeih
4 海味 hóiméi

【課後練習】 Post-class exercises

6.3 Fill in the blanks with the given vocabularies. Each vocabulary can be chosen once only.

yéuhng	jīng	bóuchìh	gūngying
waihsāng	yìhmgaak	yānséung	yáuh doihbíusing
bóulàuh	tàihyíh	tēuigaai	yàhn lòih yàhn wóhng

1. Jímsājéui Jūnglàuh haih Hēunggóng kèihjūng yātgo hóu _____ ge gauh ginjūk, hóudō yàhn dōu jūngyi làih nīdouh gūngwōng.

2. Lóuhsai deui ngóhdeih ge yīukàuh hóu _____, kéuih hēimohng ngóhdeih mātyéh dōu jouhdou jeui hóu.

3. Ngóh ūkkéi _____ jó yātjek gáu tùhng yātjek māau.

4. Nīgāan jáulàuh m̀jí yáuh hóudō nìhn lihksí, yìhché juhng yìhngyìhn (still) _____ chyùhntúng ge dímsām chē tīm.

5. Nīgāan chīukāp síhchèuhng múihyaht dōu yáuh sānsīn sōchoi _____.

6. Ngóh jeui _____ kéuih ge deihfōng haih kéuih jouh yéh yauh yihngjān yauh saisām.

7. Nīgo gāaisíh yātdī dōu m̀ _____, seijāuwàih dōu haih laahpsaap.

8. Yāt doujó yehmáahn waahkjé jāumuht, Tùhnglòhwāan jauh _____ gám, hóu dō yàhn dōu jūngyi heui gódouh hàahnggāai máaih yéh.

9. Ngóh tàuhsīn hái gāaisíh máaihjó tìuh hóu sānsīn ge yú a, bātyùh gāmmáahn _____ làih sihk lòh?

10. Nīgāan chāantēng ge sihkmaht tùhng fuhkmouh jātsou dōu hóu hóu, jihkdāk _____.

11. Máaihsung jyúfaahn, jeui gányiu haih sihkmaht yiu _____ sānsīn gōnjehng.

12. A: Jauhlàih fāan Hēunggóng la wo, máaih mātyéh sáuseun fāan heui hóu a?

   B: Ngóh _____ máaih dī síusihk fāanheui lā!

6.4 Fill in the blanks with the given double final particles or resultative verb endings. Each double final particle or resultative verb ending can be chosen once only.

la bo   la mē   lāma   je mē

dóu   dou   hóu   fāan   màaih

1. Seuhnggo yuht kéuih mahn ngóh jejó ge sāamchīnmān, kéuih yíhgīng wàahn _____ béi ngóh la.

2. Nīgāan gūngsī dāk yātgo màhnyùhn _____?!

3. Hái Léihyùhmùhn sihk hóisīn, jeui nàhnggau táiyihm _____ yùhchyūn fūngmeih.

4. A: Wai, yìhgā sahpyātdím géi _____, yiu faaidī daap chē fāan ūkkéi la!

   B: Māt yìhgā sahpyātdím géi _____?! Ngóh juhng yíhwàih haih gáudím géi tīm!

5. Kéuihdeih gāmyaht wáanjó sèhngyaht, wáan _____ hóu guih sīnji fāan ūkkéi.

6. Kéuih juhng meih jyú _____ chāan faahn, yiu dáng dō yātjahn sīnji yáuh dāk sihk.

7. Néih jānhaih m̀sihk _____?! Gám ngóh bōng néih sihk _____ ga la!

6.5 Complete the following sentences or answer the following questions using the given patterns.

1. yìh
    A: Néih gokdāk Hēunggóng tùhng néih ge gwokgā yáuh mātyéh m̀tùhng a?
    B: _____.

2. jokwàih ......
    _____, ngóh séung heui dōdī deihfōng táiyihmháh m̀tùhng ge màhnfa.

3. jauhsyun ...... dōu ......
    Hēunggóng ge láu yuht làih yuht gwai, _____.

4. gei ...... yauh ......
    Hēunggóng _____, sóyíh hóudō yàuhhaak dōu jūngyi làih nīdouh léuihyàuh.

5. jihkdāk ......
    Hēunggóng yáuh hóudō m̀tùhng júngleuih ge méihsihk, _____.

6. ...... yíhlàih
    _____, ngóh dōu móuh heuigwo gódouh wáan.

7. Listening and speaking 🔊

聽説練習 Tingsyut lihnjaahp

7.1 Listening comprehension exercise

Please use the words below to fill in the blanks in the following questions:

dímsām	méihsihk	yámchàh
chīngdaahm	jūngyeuhk	daaihpàaihdong
lóuhfó tōng	chāutīn	hóisīn	pùhnchoi

1. Hēunggóng haih yātgo _____ tīntòhng.
2. Sīngkèih Yaht gójahnsìh, Hēunggóng yàhn jūngyi heui chàhlàuh_____.
3. Hái chàhlàuh léuihmihnge_____haih Hēunggóng kèihjūng yātgo dahksīk.

4. Chèuihjó gōukāp jáudim, ngóhdeih juhng hóyíh syúnjaahk hái chàh chāantēng waahkjé_____sihkfaahn.

5. Ngóhdeih hóu yùhngyih hái daaihpàaihdong wándóu háumeih béigaau_____ge Gwóngdūng choi.

6. Hēunggóng yàhn hóu gónggau_____, yáuhdī yiu bōu hóu noih.

7. Gwóngdūng lèuhngchàh yuhngge _____yáuh gonngaat tùhng heuifó jokyuhng.

8. Hēunggóng yùhnjyuhmàhnge dahksīk sihkmaht haih_____.

9. Hēunggóng yàhn jūngyi sihk_____, galìhm mahtméih (cheap but good).

10. _____gójahnsìh, Hēunggóng yàhn wúih tùhng gāyàhn yātchàih sihk daaihjaahp háaih.

7.2 Speech topics

1. Deui néih làih góng, néih gokdāk mātyéh sihkmaht jeui nàhnggau doihbíu Hēunggóng (waahkjé néih ge gwokgā)? Dímgáai nē?

2. Chéng néih heung tùhnghohk gaaisiuhháh néih ge gwokgā jeui yáuh doihbíusing ge méihsihk, gauh ginjūk, lihksí gíngdím, léuihyàuh gíngdím waahkjé màhnfa wuhtduhng.

3. Néih haih Hēunggóng Léuihyàuh Faatjín Guhk ge doihbíu, chéng néih heung yàuhhaak tēuigaai Hēunggóng m̀tùhng deihkēui jeui yáuh doihbíusing ge méihsihk tùhngmàaih yātdī gwāanyū méihsihk ge deihfōng.

7.3 Speaking exercise: Please use at least 10 of the following vocabularies/patterns to say on the following topic in one to two minutes.

"Ngoihgwok yàuhhaak làihdou Hēunggóng léuihyàuh, jeui hóu heui bīndouh máaih sáuseun a? Máaih mātyéh sáuseun hóu nē?"

yáuh doihbíusing	yàhn lòih yàhn wóhng		
yānséung	binsìhng	tēuigaai	tàihyíh
waihsāng	yàuhhaak	sáuseun	bīujéun
lihng yāt mihn	jokwàih	......, yìh	
gei ...... yauh	jihkdāk	jauhsyun ...... dōu	

8. Additional texts

附加課文 Fuhgā fomàhn

8.1. Additional text 附加課文

民以食為天

中國人鍾意食，當然對食嘅嘢都相當講究。噉大家平時係點樣揀餐廳嘅呢？喺外面食飯嘅時候鍾意食乜嘢呢？

最近有網站分析咗啲人喺一個美食APP上嘅食評，話俾我哋知中國人嘅口味到底係點樣嘅。

（一）揀乜嘢餐廳

結果係「服務」最重要，然後係「環境」、「口味」、「價錢」等等。有意思嘅係，第九個關鍵詞係「老闆」。有個生得好睇、態度又好嘅老闆，會令唔少顧客想下次再嚟。服務唔好就一定唔受歡迎，但係如果特別好食，環境簡陋一啲、地方遠啲、服務差啲，對於好多鍾意食嘅人嚟講都唔係問題。

（二）食乜嘢

揀好咗餐廳，就應該決定食乜嘢喇。最受歡迎嘅食物係牛肉。無論係重口味嘅水煮牛肉（séuijyú ngàuhyuhk, sliced beef in chili oil），定係最近流行嘅牛肉火鍋，牛肉都越嚟越受歡迎。排喺第二嘅係蝦（hā, shrimp,prawn）。喺前十名之中，大部分都係肉類。年輕人鍾意嘅芝士（jīsí, cheese）排第六，唯一嘅素菜豆腐排喺第十位。

Màhn yíh sihk wàih tīn

Jūnggwok yàhn jūngyi sihk, dōngyìhn deui sihkge yéh dōu sēungdōng gónggau. Gám daaihgā pìhngsìh haih dímyéung gáan chāantēng ge nē? Hái ngoihmihn sihkfaahn ge sìhhauh jūngyi sihk mātyéh nē?

Jeuigahn yáuh móhngjaahm fānsīkjó dī yàhn hái yātgo méihsihk APP seuhngge sihkpìhng, wah béi ngóhdeih jī Jūnggwok yàhnge háumeih doudái haih dímyéung ge.

(1) Gáan mātyéh chāantēng

Gitgwó haih "fuhkmouh" jeui juhngyiu, yìhnhauh haih "wàahngíng", "háumeih", "gachìhn" dángdáng. Yáuh yisī ge haih, daih gáugo gwāangihnchìh haih "lóuhbáan". Yáuh go sāangdāk hóutái, taaidouh yauh hóuge lóuhbáan, wúih lihng m̀síu guhaak séung hahchi joi làih. Fuhkmouh m̀hóu jauh yātdihng m̀sauh fūnyìhng, daahnhaih yùhgwó dahkbiht hóusihk, wàahngíng gáanlauh yātdī, deihfōng yúhndī, fuhkmouh chādī, deuiyū hóudō jūngyi sihk ge yàhn làihgóng dōu m̀haih mahntàih.

(2) Sihk mātyéh

Gáanhóujó chāantēng, jauh yīnggōi kyutdihng sihk mātyéh la. Jeui sauh fūnyìhngge sihkmaht haih ngàuhyuhk. Mòuhleuhn haih chúhng háumeihge séuijyú ngàuhyuhk, dihnghaih jeuigahn làuhhàhngge ngàuhyuhk fówō, ngàuhyuhk dōu yuht làih yuht sauh fūnyìhng. Pàaih hái daihyihge haih hā. Hái chìhn sahp mìhng jījūng, daaih bouhfahn dōu haih yuhkleuih. Nìhnhīngyàhn jūngyige jīsí pàaih daihluhk, wàihyāt ge souchoi dauhfuh pàaihhái daihsahp waih.

（三）口味

「辣」係好多中國人好鍾意嘅口味，「甜」同「香」排喺第二、第三位。四川菜、湖南菜都好辣，江蘇（Gōngsōu, Jiangsu Province）、浙江（Jitgōng, Zhejiang Province）、廣東菜「甜甜地」，北方人好鍾意「香」。安徽（ōnfāi, Anhui Province）有名嘅「臭鱖魚」（Chau gwaiyú, soy braised mandarin fish）係臭崩崩嘅，都受到唔少人嘅歡迎。

(3) Háumeih

"Laaht" haih hóudō Jūnggwok yàhn hóu jūngyige háumeih, "tìhm" tùhng "hēung" pàaihhái daihyih, daihsāam waih. Seichyūnchoi, Wùhnàahmchoi dōu hóu laaht, Gōngsōu, Jitgōng, Gwóngdūngchoi "tìhmtím déi", bākfōngyàhn hóu jūngyi "hēung". Ōnfāi yáuhméngge "Chau gwai yú" haih chau bāngbāngge, dōu sauhdou m̀síu yàhnge fūnyìhng.

（四）點做

中國菜嘅做法非常豐富。喺呢個 APP 上面，第一名係「烤」，然後係「炸」、「煮」、「燒」同「炒」。排名第八嘅「拉」，指嘅係「拉麵」（lāaimihn, hand-pulled noodle soup）。講咗咁多，你最鍾意食乜嘢呢？

(4) Dímjouh

Jūnggwok choi ge jouhfaat fēisèuhng fūngfu. Hái nīgo APP seuhngmihn, daihyāt mìhng haih "hāau", yìhnhauh haih "ja", "jyú", "sīu" tùhng "cháau". Pàaihmìhng daihbaat ge "lāai", jí ge haih "lāaimihn". Góngjó gamdō, néih jeui jūngyi sihk mātyéh nē?

8.2 Additional vocabulary 附加詞彙

Number	Word	Yale Romanization	POS	English
1	分析	fānsīk	N/V	analysis; to analyze
2	食評	sihkpìhng	N	food review
3	受歡迎	sauh fūnyìhng	PH	popular; be well liked
4	流行	làuhhàhng	Adj	popular
5	排	pàaih	V	to rank
6	唯一	wàihyāt	Adj	the only
7	香	hēung	Adj	fragrant; aromatic
8	臭	chau	Adj	smelly
9	煮	jyú	V	to boil
10	拉	lāai	V	to pull

8.3 Please answer the following T/F questions after reading the additional text：

1　Nīpīn màhnjēung haih gāngeui yātgo méihsihk APP sé ge. (T/F)

2　Jūnggwok yàhn gáan chāantēng ge sìhhauh, gokdāk háumeih jeui gányiu. (T/F)

3　Yáuhdī chāantēngge yéh fēisèuhng hóusihk, jauhsyun fuhkmouh m̀haih géi hóu, dōu yáuh yàhn heui sihk. (T/F)

4　Jeui sauh fūnyìhngge sahpjúng sihkmaht léuihmihn, yáuh chīugwo yātbun haih jāai. (T/F)

5　Hái Jūnggwok jeui làuhhàhng ge sihkmaht haih jyūyuhk. (T/F)

6　Jūngyi jīsí ge yàhn jíjūng, dōsou haih nìhnchīng yàhn. (T/F)

7　Gōngsōu, Jitgōng choi béigaau laaht. (T/F)

8　Yáuh dī Jūnggwok choi chauchàudéi, daahnnhaih yáuh yàhn jūngyi. (T/F)

9　Jūnggwok choi yáuh hóudō júng jouhfaat. (T/F)

10　Ja tùhng jīn haih jeui sauh fūnyìhngge Jūnggwok choi jouhfaat. (T/F)

8.4 Topics for discussions

1　Néih suhk m̀suhksīk Jūnggwokge méihsihk a？Néih hó m̀hóyíh gaaisiuh yātgo néih jeui jūngyige choi a？

2　Deui néih làihgóng, gáan chāantēng, mātyéh jeui juhngyiu a? Dímgáai a？

3　Hái néihge gwokgā, jeui sauh fūnyìhngge ńgh júng sihkmaht haih mātyéh a？

4　Yáuhdī sihkmaht sēuiyìhn chauchàudéi waahkjé fúfúdéi, daahnnhaih dōu sauh fūnyìhng, néih yáuh móuh sihkgwo gámge sihkmaht a？Chéng néih gaaisiuh háh.

5　Néih sīk m̀sīk jyúfaahn a？Néih hó m̀hóyíh gaau ngóh jyú yātgo sung a？

8.5 Authentic oral data 1　🔊
真實語料 1

8.6 Authentic oral data 2　🔊
真實語料 2

Lesson 3　The Joy of Reading

樂在閱讀

1. Pragmatic factors, Yuti features and linguistic functions
語用因素、語體特徵與語言功能
Yúhyuhng yānsou, yúhtái dahkjīng yúh yúhyìhn gūngnàhng

Pragmatic factors/ Yuti features 語用因素 / 語體特徵	Linguistic functions 語言功能
Pragmatic factors: The situation is not formal but, because of the content (or the subject being talked about), many formal words and phrases are used. 語用因素： 場合並非正式，所以有很明顯的口語特徵。因為內容的關係，說話者還是用了不少正式詞彙。 **Yuti features:** Formality index: 1-2 語體特徵：1-2 級之間	**Linguistic function:** Exploring In an informal context, one uses a relatively relaxed tone to discuss formal subjects. 語言功能：深入探討 在非正式場合用相對輕鬆的語氣討論比較正式的話題。

Notes on pragmatic knowledge 語用知識	Notes on structure 語言及篇章結構知識

I. Features of spoken style and self-demeaning 口語特徵與自貶
  1.1 Pardon my shallowness 「可能係我個人比較膚淺」
 	
II. Related knowledge 相關知識
  1. Things like fighting and killing 「打打殺殺嘅嘢」
  2. The four famous literary works 「四大名著」
  3. Very interested in.... 「⋯迷」
	I. Grammar and sentence patterns 語法和句型
	  1. "tùhng…yáuh gwāan(haih); tùhng… móuh gwāan(haih)" be (not) related to...
	  2. "m̀haih…jauhhaih…" "yāthaih… yāthaih…"
	  3. "Chèuihjó… jīngoih"
	  4. "waihjó；…haih waihjó…"
	  5. "yātmihn…,yātmihn…"
	  6. "mòuhleuhn yùhhòh" no matter what
	  7. "hóuchíh…gám"; "hóuchíh…gam…"
	  8. "dou…ge chìhngdouh" to the extent of ; to the point of...
	  9. "chādī" almost; nearly
	  10. Advanced degree complement "Adj. dou bāt dāk líuh"
	
	II. Paragraph and discourse 語段和篇章
	  1. "…haih…,dōuhaih…, juhnghaih…"

2. Text 🔊

課文 Fomàhn

你問我平時睇啲咩嘢書嚤？我自細就好鍾意睇書，小學嘅時候係，大學嘅時候都係，而家出嚟做嘢都係好鍾意睇書。我鍾意好多類型嘅書。我鍾意睇歷史書、人物傳記、翻譯文學同埋旅遊書。首先講吓歷史書先啦。我平時去開書店，一定會留意吓有冇一啲同中國、日本同埋東南亞有關嘅新書。我對古代歷史特別有興趣，我最近唔係睇中國歷史就係睇日本歷史。

Néih mahn ngóh pìhngsìh tái dī mēyéh syū àh? Ngóh jihsai jauh hóu jūngyi táisyū, síuhohk ge sìhhauh haih, daaihhohk ge sìhhauh dōu haih, yìhgā chēutlàih jouhyéh dōuhaih hóu jūngyi táisyū. Ngóh jūngyi hóudō leuihyìhng ge syū. Ngóh jūngyi tái lihksí syū, yàhnmaht jyuhngei, fāanyihk màhnhohk tùhngmàaih léuihyàuh syū. Sáusīn góngháh lihksí syū sīn lā. Ngóh pìhngsìh heui hōi syūdim, yātdihng wúih làuhyiháh yáuh móuh yātdī tùhng Jūnggwok, Yahtbún tùhngmàaih Dūngnàahmnga yáuh gwāange sān syū. Ngóh deui gúdoih lihksí dahkbiht yáuh hingcheui, ngóh jeuigahn m̀haih tái Jūnggwok lihksí jauhhaih tái Yahtbún lihksí.

古代嘅中國同日本有好多來往，有啲中國人去咗日本做生意，而日本無論係宗教、建築、藝術、音樂都受到中國好多方面嘅影響。最近買咗一本書，係講一千三百年前一般中國人嘅日常生活，例如佢哋平時着啲咩嘢衫呀、買餸去邊度買呀、病咗去邊度睇醫生呀、去旅行要準備啲咩呀等等。我發現佢哋嘅生活同電影裏面或者電視劇入面嘅形象有好大嘅分別。譬如話街上面其實好污糟，夜晚唔可以隨便出街，仲有普通人好難搵到乾淨嘅水煮飯同沖涼，生活都幾辛苦、幾慘㗎。

Gúdoihge Jūnggwok tùhng Yahtbún yáuh hóudō lòihwóhng, yáuhdī Jūnggwok yàhn heuijó Yahtbún jouh sāangyi, yìh Yahtbún mòuhleuhn haih jūnggaau, ginjūk, ngaihseuht, yāmngohk dōu sauhdou Jūnggwok hóudō fōngmihnge yínghéung. Jeuigahn máaihjó yātbún syū, haih góng yāt chīn sāam baak nìhn chìhn yātbún Jūnggwok yàhnge yahtsèuhng sāngwuht, laihyùh kéuihdeih pìhngsìh jeuk dī mēyéh sāam a, máaihsung heui bīndouh máaih a, behngjó heui bīndouh tái yīsāng a, heui léuihhàhng yiu jéunbeih dī mē a dángdáng. Ngóh faatyihn kéuihdeihge sāngwuht tùhng dihnyíng léuihmihn waahkjé dihnsih kehk yahpmihnge yìhngjeuhng yáuh hóudaaih ge fānbiht. Peiyùhwah gāai seuhngmihn kèihsaht hóu wūjōu, yehmáahn m̀hóyíh chèuihbín chēutgāai, juhngyáuh póutūng yàhn hóu nàahn wándóu gōnjehngge séui jyúfaahn tùhng chūnglèuhng, sāngwuht dōu géi sānfú, géi cháam ga.

除咗歷史書之外，我都鍾意睇一啲人物傳記。呢一類嘅書比較容易讀。因為佢嘅故事嘅發展十分之吸引。搭車嘅時候睇都得。人物傳記通常都分為兩種啦，一種就係改編成小説嘅，一種就係比較寫實嘅記錄。改編成小説嘅人物傳記，為咗令故事比較吸引，通常都會加入一啲原本冇喺嗰個人身上發生嘅情節。一啲寫實性嘅人物傳記通常就會將一啲細節或者嗰個人嘅成長，好忠實嘅樣記錄低。所以兩種嘅人物傳記都有佢哋各自吸引人嘅地方。兩種我都鍾意睇。

Chèuihjó lihksí syū jīngoih, ngóh dōu jūngyi tái yātdī yàhnmaht jyuhngei. Nī yāt leuihge syū béigaau yùhngyih duhk. Yānwaih kéuihge gusihge faatjín sahpfānjī kāpyáhn. Daapchē ge sìhhauh tái dōu dāk. Yàhnmaht jyuhngei tūngsèuhng dōu fānwàih léuhngjúng lā, yātjúng jauhhaih góipīn sìhng síusyut ge, yātjúng jauhhaih béigaau sésahtge geiluhk. Góipīn sìhng síusyutge yàhnmaht jyuhngei, waihjó lihng gusih béigaau kāpyáhn, tūngsèuhng dōu wúih gāyahp yātdī yùhnbún móuh hái gógo yàhn sānseuhng faatsāngge chìhngjit. Yātdī sésahtsing ge yàhnmaht jyuhngei tūngsèuhng jauh wúih jēung yātdī saijit waahkjé gógo yàhnge sìhngjéung, hóu jūngsaht gámyéung geiluhkdāi. Sóyíh léuhng júng ge yàhnmaht jyuhngei dōu yáuh kéuihdeih gokjih kāpyáhn yàhn ge deihfōng. Léuhng júng ngóh dōu jūngyi tái.

我係一個小説迷。各國嘅小説我都經常睇。台灣出嘅翻譯小説不嬲都好多，但係呢幾年我都買多咗好多大陸出版嘅翻譯小説，因為佢哋翻譯嘅速度好快，而且書嘅設計越嚟越好，種類越嚟越多。你平時咁鍾意睇書，你一定知道好多外國嘅文學同小説唔止翻譯成中文，仲保留返本來嘅文字，你可以一面睇中文，一面睇英文；或者一面睇中文，一面睇日文。無論如何，我覺得睇小説可以放鬆心情，我唔鍾意嗰啲打打殺殺嘅戰爭故事，我比較膚淺，都唔鍾意嗰啲經典名著，我一係睇愛情小説，一係睇偵探小説，當你進入小説嘅世界，就會唔記得好多生活中嘅麻煩事，有時我會諗，如果好似小説裏面嘅人噉，我會點做。我中學時代非常鍾意睇愛情小説，鍾意到差啲連飯都唔食嘅程度。有啲小説仲會改編成為電影，我會去睇小説改編嘅電影，都係一種有趣嘅消遣。電影《達文西密碼》你睇過啦嘛，真係好睇到不得了，原版小説你睇過未呀？呢本書我可以送俾你，我已經睇完喇。

Ngóh haih yātgo síusyut màih, gokgwokge síusyut ngóh dōu gīngsèuhng tái. Tòihwāan chēut ge fāanyihk síusyut bātnāu dōu hóudō, daahnhaih nīgéi nìhn ngóh dōu máaih dōjó hóudō Daaihluhk chēutbáange fāanyihk síusyut, yānwaih kéuihdeih fāanyihkge chūkdouh hóu faai, yìhché syūge chitgai yuht làih yuht hóu, júngleuih yuht làih yuht dō. Néih pìhngsìh gam jūngyi táisyū, néih yātdihng jīdou hóudō ngoihgwok ge màhnhohk tùhng síusyut m̀ji fāanyihk sìhng Jūngmán, juhng bóulàuhfāan búnlòihge màhnjih, néih hóyíh yātmihn tái Jūngmàhn, yātmihn tái Yīngmán; waahkjé yātmihn tái Jūngmán, yātmihn tái Yahtmán. Mòuhleuhn yùhhòh, ngóh gokdāk tái síusyut hóyíh fongsūng sāmchìhng, ngóh m̀jūngyi gódī dá dá saat saat ge jinjāng gusih, ngóh béigaau fūchín, dōu m̀jūngyi gódī gīngdín mìhngjyu, ngóh yāthaih tái ngoichìhng síusyut, yāthaih tái jīngtaam síusyut, dōng néih jeunyahp síusyutge saigaai, jauh wúih m̀geidāk hóudō sāngwuht jūng ge màhfàahn sih, yáuhsìh ngóh wúih nám, yùhgwó hóuchíh síusyut léuihmihnge yàhn gám, ngóh wúih dím jouh. Ngóh jūnghohk sìhdoih fēisèuhng jūngyi tái ngoichìhng síusyut, jūngyi dou chādī lìhn faahn dōu m̀sihk ge chìhngdouh. Yáuhdī síusyut juhng wúih góipīn sìhngwàih dihnyíng, ngóh wúih heui tái síusyut góipīnge dihnyíng, dōu haih yātjúng yáuhcheuige sīuhín. Dihnyíng "Daahtmàhnsāi Mahtmáh" néih táigwo lāmáh, jānhaih hóutái dou bāt dāk líuh, yùhnbáan síusyut néih táigwo meih a ? Nībún syū ngóh hóyíh sungbéi néih, ngóh yíhgīng táiyùhn la.

3. Vocabulary in use 🔊

活用詞彙 Wuhtyuhng chìhwuih

3.1 Common vocabulary

Number	Word	Yale Romanization	POS	English
1	類型	leuihyìhng	N	type
2	古代	gúdoih	N	ancient times
3	來往	lòihwóhng	N/V	contact, dealings; to come and go
4	宗教	jūnggaau	N	religion
5	電視劇	dihnsihkehk	N	TV drama
6	形象	yìhngjeuhng	N	image
7	污糟	wūjōu	Adj	dirty
8	發展	faatjín	N/V	development; to develop
9	改編	góipīn	V	to adapt, to rearrange, to reorganize
10	小說	síusyut	N	novel
11	寫實	sésaht	Adj	appearing to be existing or happening in fact
12	記錄	geiluhk	N/V	record; to record
13	原本	yùhnbún	Adj/Adv	original; originally
14	情節	chìhngjit	N	plot
15	細節	saijit	N	details
16	速度	chūkdouh	N	speed
17	設計	chitgai	N/V	design; to design
18	打打殺殺	dá dá saat saat	PH	blood and guts, fighting and killing
19	膚淺	fūchín	Adj	shallow, superficial, skin-deep

20	程度	chìhngdouh	N	degree, level
21	消遣	sīuhín	N	pastime

3.2 Proper noun and place name

1	東南亞	Dūngnàahmnga	PW	Southeast Asia
2	達文西密碼	Daahtmàhnsāi Mahtmáh	PN	Da Vinci Code (movie & novel)

3.3 Types of books

1	人物傳記	yàhnmaht jyuhngei	N	biography
2	翻譯文學	fāanyihk màhnhohk	N	translated literature
3	旅遊書	léuihyàuh syū	N	travel guide
4	戰爭故事	jinjāng gusih	N	war story
5	經典名著	gīngdín mìhngjyu	N	the classics
6	偵探小說	jīngtaam síusyut	N	detective novel
7	愛情小說	ngoichìhng síusyut	N	romantic novel

4. Notes on language and discourse structure

語言及篇章結構知識 Yúhyìhn kahp pīnjēung gitkau jīsīk

4.1. Grammar and sentence patterns 語法和句型

4.1.1. "tùhng …yáuh gwāan (haih)；tùhng…móuh gwāan(haih)" be (not) related to...

1. Nīdī syū dōu tùhng lihksí yáuh gwāan.
2. Daaih bouhfahn ngóh jūngyi táige syū dōu tùhng màhnfa yáuh gwāan.
3. Nīgihn sih tùhng néih móuh gwāanhaih, néih m̀hóu joi mahn la.

4.1.2. Alternative phrases: "m̀haih...jauhhaih..."; "yāthaih…, yāthaih…"

The pattern "m̀haih...jauhhaih..." means "either...or...". The literal meaning for this pattern is "if not..., then must be/then it is..."

1. Kéuih m̀haih heui dábō jauhhaih heui yàuhséui.
2. Wòhng sāang jūngyi ge sīuhín m̀haih tái dihnsih jauhhaih dá màhjéuk.
3. M̀haih Héui táai heuijó waahtséui jauh haih Máhlaih heuijó waahtséui la!
4. A-Mān m̀haih hái ngūkkéi waahkwá jauhhaih hái ūkkéi tàahnkàhm.
5. Kéuih yìhgā m̀haih dágán cheukkàuh jauhhaih dágán gōuyíhfūkàuh.
6. Mìhngjái m̀haih heuijó choichē jauhhaih heuijó choimáh.
7. Kéuih m̀haih heui Yahtbún làuhbīng jauhhaih heui Yahtbún waahtsyut.

The English meaning of "yāthaih…, yāthaih…" is almost the same as "m̀haih...jauhhaih...". It means "either...or..."

1. Néihdeih hóyíh dá yātjúng bō jē, yāthaih bīkkàuh, yāthaih làahmkàuh.
2. Sāanbún táai yāthaih heui kālāōukēi jáulòhng cheunggō, yāthaih heui tēng yāmngohk.
3. Yāthaih Chàhn sāang heui tek jūkkàuh, yāthaih Wòhng sāang heui tek jūkkàuh, ngóh m̀geidāk haih bīngo.
4. Yāthaih ngóh heui dá gōuyíhfūkàuh, yāthaih néih heui dá gōuyíhfūkàuh, ngóhdeih m̀hóyíh léuhnggo dōu heui.
5. Chīnggit tùhng dásou ngūkkéi ge yéh, yāthaih gūngyàhn jouh, yāthaih jihgéi jouh.
6. Yāthaih go màhnyùhn sīkjó jáan dāng, yāthaih gīngléih sīkjó jáan dāng, ngóh m̀jī haih bīngo.
7. Yāthaih néih fongga, yāthaih ngóh fongga, ngóhdeih léuhnggo m̀hóyíh yātchàih fong.

4.1.3. "Chèuihjó......jīngoih, juhng/dōu......tīm" and "Chèuihjó......jīngoih, jauh......"

The meaning of "chèuihjó......jīngoih" is either "besides" or "except". There are several variations of this pattern:

-   Chèuihjó ..… jīngoih, (S) juhng/dōu V/Adj. tīm.
-   S chèuihjó V/Adj. jīngoih, juhng/dōu V/Adj. tīm.
-   Chèuihjó N V/Adj. jīngoih, jauh m̀/móuh/meih ......

If "chèuihjó......jīngoih" is followed by a clause with "juhng" or "dōu", the whole pattern means "besides…, …". If "chèuihjó......jīngoih" is followed by a clause with "jauh" and negative words, the whole pattern means "… no/not/not yet…, except…".

1. Gāmyaht néih yáuh dī mātyéh sīuhín a? Chèuihjó heui kālāōukēi jáulòhng jīngoih, ngóh juhng séung táihei tīm.
2. Heui sātāan chèuihjó hóyíh saai taaiyèuhng jīngoih, dōu hóyíh yàuhséui tīm.
3. Chèuihjó néih jīngoih, juhng yáuh bīngo wúih góng Yīngmàhn a?
4. Chèuihjó Wòhng sāang jīngoih, ngóh jauh yātgo dōu m̀sīk la!
5. Chèuihjó néih gaaugwo ngóh jīngoih, jauh móuh yàhn gaaugwo ngóh.

4.1.4. Stating the purpose "...haih waihjó..."; "waihjó..."

1. Duhksyū haih waihjó kāpsāu (absorb) jisīk, dōu haih waihjó gáamhēng ngaatlihk (ease pressure).
2. M̀síu yàuhhaak làih Hēunggóngge muhkdīk haih waihjó kaumaht.
3. Hóudō Hēunggóng yàhn chéng ngoihjihk yùhnggūng haih waihjó jihgéi yáuh sìhgaan chēutheui gūngjok.
4. Hóudō yàhn heui léuihhàhng, haih waihjó táiháh dōngdeih ge lihksí tùhng màhnfa.
5. Waihjó bánsèuhngháh deihdouh ge Hēunggóng méihsihk, kéuihdeih gāmyaht heui chàh chāantēng sihkfaahn.

4.1.5. Paired clause to form coordinate compound sentence: "yātmihn...yātmihn.../yātbihn... yātbihn..."

There are two basic meanings to this pattern :

(1) "At the same time", indicates two actions carried at the same time.
e.g. Bàhbā jūngyi yātmihn sihk jóuchāan yātmihn tái boují.
(Father likes to have breakfast and read newspaper at the same time.)

(2) "On the one hand...on the other hand"; "while...meanwhile", have the two actions carried out at the same time and contradict each other.
e.g. A-Mēi yātbihn wah jihgéi taai fèih, yātbihn sèhngyaht sihk jyūgūlīk.
(On the one hand, May said she is too fat, on the other hand she eats chocolate all day long.)

1. Ngóh m̀mìhngbaahk dímgáai dī hohksāang hóyíh yātmihn cheunggō yātmihn duhksyū.
2. Hóudō ngoihgwok hohksāang hái Méihgwok duhksyū gójahnsìh dōu haih yātmihn duhksyū, yātmihn jouhgūng, jānhaih sānfú.
3. Yātmihn jāchē yātmihn dádihnwá ge yàhn jānhaih hóu ngàihhím.
4. A-Wáih yātmihn wah hóu báau yātmihn yauh sihkdō yātgo chāsīubāau.

5. Néih yáuh móuh gingwo yàhn yātbihn haam(cry) yātbihn siu ge nē?

6. Hóudō hohksāang chóh fóchē gójahnsìh, yātbihn táisyū, yātbihn tēng yāmngohk, hóu m̀dākhàahn.

4.1.6 "mòuhleuhn yùhhòh" no matter what

1. Yùhgwó néih mahn ngóh yáuh mātyéh syū jihkdāk tái, ngóh nám "Jūnggwok sei daaih mìhngjyu" mòuhleuhn yùhhòh dōu yātdihng yiu tái.

2. Ngóh jíyáuh néih yātgo pàhngyáuh, mòuhleuhn yùhhòh, néih dōu yiu bōng ngóh.

3. Ngóh jīdou yìhgā hóu nàahn máaih gēipiu, daahnhaih mòuhleuhn yùhhòh ngóh dōu yiu heui Bākgīng. M̀gōi néih bōng bōngsáu lā.

4.1.7. "Hóuchíh…gám…" and "hóuchíh…gam…"

The pattern "hóuchíh......gám,....." means: (1) N₁ is similar to N₂; and (2) It seems that PN/N is Adj.

1. Gāmyaht ge tīnhei hóuchíh dūngtīn gám, yauh dung yauh daaih fūng.

2. Sāanbún táai hóuchíh kéuih sīnsāang gám, dōu haih gam jūngyi sihk Yidaaihleih choi ge.

3. Ngóh hóuchíh Wòhng sāang gám, nìhnnìhn fongga dōu heui Daaihyùhsāan ge douhga'ūk jyuhháh.

4. Sāanbún síujé hóuchíh Tìhnjūng sīnsāang gám, chìhmséui chìhmdāk hóu hóu.

5. Kéuih hóuchíh hóu m̀dākhàahn gám.

6. Kéuih hóuchíh hóu dung gám. Béi gihn sāam kéuih jeuk lā!

"Hóu chíh N gam......" means "just like...so..."

1. Ngóh m̀haih hóuchíh néih gam jūngyi máaihyéh, ngóh béigaau jūngyi heui dábō.

2. Hóuchíh néih gam jūngyi wahnduhng ge yàhn yātdihng hóu gihnhōng ge la.

3. Móuh yàhn hóuchíh kéuih gam jūngyi waahtsyut ge.

4. Ngóh hēimohng ngóh hóyíh hóuchíh kéuih gam gihnhōng.

5. Ngóh yiu sāamgo hóuchíh nīgo gam leng ge bīu.

6. Kéuih m̀haih hóuchíh ngóh gam jūngyi fāangūng.

7. Ngóh ge tùhnghohk hóuchíh ngóh gam jūngyi tēng yāmngohk tùhng cheunggō.

4.1.8. "dou…ge chìhngdouh" to the extent of...; to the point of...

1. Ngóh jūngyi táisyū jūngyi dou faahn dōu m̀sihk ge chìhngdouh.

2. Hēunggóngge làuhga (property price) yíhgīng gōu dou móuhyàhn máaih dākhéi ge chìhngdouh.

3. Kéuih hóu jūngyi yámjáu, jūngyi dou m̀yám jauh fan m̀jeuhk (cannot fall asleep) ge chìhngdouh.

4.1.9. "chādī" almost; nearly

1. Duhk daaihhohk ge sìhhauh, chādī gānjó néih duhk Jūnggwok lihksí, sāumēi ngóh faatyihn souhohk (Mathematics) sīnji ngāam ngóh.

2. Āiya, ngóh chādī m̀geidāk yiu dádihnwá béi néuih pàhngyáuh, chādī m̀geidāk gāmyaht haih kéuih sāangyaht.

3. Kàhmyaht fandāk m̀hóu, gāmyaht héi m̀dóu sān, chādī chìhdou.

4.1.10. Advanced degree complement "Adj.dou bāt dāk líuh"

1. Ngóh jeui jūngyi tái ngoichìhng síusyut, jānhaih hóutái dou bāt dāk líuh.

2. Kéuih tùhng lóuhbáange gwāanhaih hóu dou bāt dāk líuh, néih yiu síusām dī a!

3. Kéuihge néui yahpjó hóu hóuge daaihhohk, kéuih jānhaih hōisām dou bāt dāk líuh.

4.2. Paragraph and discourse 語段和篇章

4.2.1. "…haih…, dōuhaih…, juhnghaih…"

1. Ngóh haih yātgo síusyut màih, dōuhaih yātgo lihksí màih, juhnghaih yātgo màhnhohk màih, sóyíh néih mìhngbaahk dímgáai ngóh gam jūngyi tái nīdī yàhnmaht jyuhngei.

2. Wūyíhm (pollution) haih yātgo wàahngíng mahntàih, dōuhaih yātgo gīngjai (economic) mahntàih, juhnghaih yātgo séhwúi (social) mahntàih, sóyíh ngóhdeih yiu séung baahnfaat gáaikyut (solve) wūyíhm mahntàih.

3. Hēunggóng haih yātgo léuihyàuh tīntòhng, dōuhaih yātgo méihsihk tīntòhng, juhnghaih yātgo gwokjai gāmyùhng jūngsām, sóyíh múihnìhn dōu yáuh hóudō yàuhhaak làih Hēunggóng.

5. Notes on pragmatic knowledge

語用因素與相關知識 Yúhyuhng yānsou yúh sēunggwāan jīsīk

5.1. Features of spoken style and self-demeaning 口語特徵與自貶

5.1.1. " 可能係我個人比較膚淺 hónàhng haih ngóh go yàhn béigaau fūchín", pardon my shallowness

This is another example of being modest in Chinese culture. The word "膚淺 fūchín" (shallow) is derogatory and should be avoided when referring to others. The use of " 比較 béigaau" (relatively) softens the tone a little bit and, together with "可能 hónàhng" （perhaps）, the whole phrase can be treated as a "set phrase" that you can use in various situations when you are invited to speak in formal situations to express humbleness.

5.2. Related knowledge 相關知識

5.2.1. " 打打殺殺嘅嘢 dá dá saat saat ge yéh" things like fighting and killing

Most native speakers would use a "general word" to express themselves when not clear or not sure about the exact wording, such as the word " 嘢 yéh" here, which literally means "thing" or "something". Similar example would be the use of "fruit" to replace the exact name of any fruit that you cannot name. The phrase " 打打殺殺嘅嘢 dádá saatsaatge yéh" can also be treated in the same category.

5.2.2. " 四大名著 Seidaaih mìhngjyu" the four famous literary works

Referring to the four well-known literary works in modern Chinese literature: Dream of the Red Mansions, Journey to the West, Romance of the Three Kingdoms and Heroes of the Marshes. This is common knowledge for most educated native speakers and, although there are many famous literary works in Chinese, the unmarked meaning of this phrase is always the four listed above.

5.2.3. "… 迷 …màih" very interested in

The best translation for "…… 迷 ……màih"in this context is perhaps "to be crazy about……". As you can see from the text, it can be used after almost anything to indicate your enthusiasm to the point of being addicted.

6. Contextualized speaking practice

情境説話練習 Chìhnggíng syutwah lihnjaahp

【課前預習】Class preparation

6.1. Please answer the following True/False questions according to the lesson text.

1. Góngyéh ge yàhn jūngyi tái lihksí syū, yàhnmaht jyuhngei, fāanyihk màhnhohk tùhng léuihyàuh syū. (T/F)

2. Góngyéh ge yàhn deui gúdoih lihksí dahkbiht yáuh hingcheui, jeuigahn tái ge syū dōu haih gwāanyū Jūnggwok tùhng Méihgwokge lihksí. (T/F)

3. Góngyéh ge yàhn jeuigahn máaihjó yātbún syū, haih gwāanyū yātchīn sāam baak nìhn chìhn yātbūn Yahtbún yàhnge sāngwuht. (T/F)

4. Góngyéh ge yàhn dōu jūngyi tái yàhnmaht jyuhngei yānwaih gusih faatjín dahkbiht kāpyáhn. (T/F)

5. Yātdī sésaht ge yàhnmaht jyuhngei tūngsèuhng jauh wúih jēung yātdī saijit waahkjé gógo yàhnge sìhngjéung, hóu jūngsaht gám geiluhk lohklàih. (T/F)

6. Góngyéh ge yàhn nī géi nìhn máaihjó hóudō Daaihluhk chēutbáange fāanyihk síusyut. (T/F)

7. Daaihluhk chēutbáange fāanyihk síusyut fāanyihk ge chūkdouh hóu faai, yìhché syūge chitgai hóu, júngleuih dō. (T/F)

8. Góngyéh ge yàhn yihngwàih tái síusyut hóyíh fongsūng sāmchìhng. (T/F)

9. Góngyéh ge yàhn m̀jūngyi tái ngoichìhng síusyut, dōu m̀jūngyi tái jīngtaam síusyut. (T/F)

10. Góngyéh ge yàhn yáuh táigwo dihnyíng "Daahtmàhnsāi Mahtmáh", daahnhaih móuh táigwo síusyut. (T/F)

6.2 Please explain the following phrases in Cantonese

1 東南亞 Dūngnàahm Nga
2 人物傳記 Yàhnmaht jyuhngei
3 名著 mìhngjyu
4 旅遊書 léuihyàuh syū

【課後練習】Post-class exercises

6.3 Fill in the blanks with the given vocabularies. Each vocabulary can be chosen once only.

leuihyìhng   lòihwóhng   yìhngjeuhng   wūjōu
faatjín   góipīn   sésaht   geiluhk
chìhngjit   saijit   fūchín   chitgai

1. Nītou dihnyíng haih yàuh jān yàhn jān sih _____ ge, jihkdāk heui táiháh.

2. Nīgāan syūdim maaih hóu dō m̀tùhng _____ ge syū, hóuchíh síusyut a, léuihyàuh syū a, sáanmàhn (prose) a dáng dáng.

3. Sēuiyìhn ngóh hái Hēunggóng jyuhjó sahpnìhn, daahnhaih ngóh deui Hēunggóng màhnfa ge yihngsīk juhng haih hóu _____ .

4. Nībún lihksí syū _____ jó Hēunggóng dímyéung yàuh baak géi nìhn chìhn ge yātgo síu yùhchyūn _____ sìhng gāmyaht ge gwokjai daaih sìhngsíh.

5. Kéuih bōng gūngsī _____ jó yātgo chyùhn sān ge móhngjaahm, hēimohng hóyíh bōng gūngsī góibin _____ .

6. Nīchēut dihnsihkehk ge _____ hóu _____ , hóu dō yàhn tái yùhn dōu wah gokdāk hóuchíh gónggán jihgéi pìhngsìh ge sāngwuht gám.

7. Néih hó m̀hóyíh tùhng ngóh góngháh nīgo wuhtduhng ge sóyáuh _____ a?

8. Néih jī m̀jī Hēunggóng yáuh mātyéh gāautūng gūnggeuih _____ síhkēui tùhng gēichèuhng a?

9. Nīgo deihfōng hóu noih dōu móuh yàhn làih chīnggit, sóyíh _____ dou bāt dāk líuh.

6.4 Complete the following sentences or answer the following questions using the given patterns.

1. tùhng ...... yáuh gwāan
   Nībún syū ge noihyùhng haih _____ ge.

2. m̀haih ...... jauhhaih ......
   Kéuih yāt fongga jauh chēutgāai wáan, _____ .

3. ......, haih waihjó ......
   A: Dímgáai néih làih Hēunggóng duhksyū a?
   B: _____ .

4. yātmihn ...... yātmihn ......
   Ngóh jeui jūngyi _____ .

5. mòuhleuhn yùhhòh, ...

Yáuh yàhn wah nītou dihnyíng taai dō dá dá saat saat ge yéh, daahnhaih dōu yáuh yàhn wah nītou dihnyíng ge kehkchìhng hóu gánjēung chigīk. Ngóh gokdāk,

_____.

6. hóuchíh ...... gám

Kéuih jeuigahn _____, chichi ngóh séung yeuk kéuih kéuih dōu wah m̀dākhàahn.

7. dou ...... ge chìhngdouh

Kéuih hohk Gwóngdūngwá, hohk _____.

8. chādī

Ngóh gāmjīu chìhjó héisān, _____.

9. Adj dou bātdāklíuh

Wa, nīgaan jáudim _____.

10. Chèuihjó ......, juhng ......

A: Néih sīk góng Gwóngdūngwá, juhng sīk góng mātyéh yúhyìhn a?

B: _____.

7. Listening and speaking 🔊

聽説練習 Tingsyut lihnjaahp

7.1 Listening comprehension exercise

Please listen to the recording and answer the following T/F questions：

1. Yíngóngge yàhn jūngyi tái tùhng gwānsih lihksí yáuhgwāange syū. (T/F)
2. Yíngóngge yàhn táiyùhn sei daaih mìhngjyu. (T/F)
3. Sāiyàuhgei ge noihyùhng haih tùhng yātbaak lìhng baat go hóuhon yáuhgwāan ge. (T/F)
4. Yíngóng ge yàhn jūngyi tái lihksí syū yānwaih kéuih jūngyi jinjāng bokmahtgún. (T/F)
5. Yíngóng ge yàhn yihngwàih gwānsih tùhng lihksí móuh gwāanhaih. (T/F)
6. Yíngóngge yàhn deui sāngmaht (biology) hóu yáuh hingcheui, dahkbiht haih jihkmaht (plants). (T/F)
7. Yíngóngge yàhn daaihhohk ge sìhhauh duhk sāngmaht hohk. (T/F)
8. Yíngóngge yàhn yìhgā hóusíu táisyū. (T/F)

9. Yíngóngge yàhn m̀jūngyi tái gwāanyū ngoichìhng ge syū. (T/F)

10. Yíngóngge yàhn gokdāk sāam daaih mìhngjyu m̀jihkdāk tái. (T/F)

7.2 Speech topics

1. Néih jeui jūngyi tái mātyéh leuihyìhng ge syū a? Dímgáai nē?

2. Yíhchìhn ge yàhn jí wúih tái jíjāt (paper) ge syū, daahnhaih gahnnìhn yuht làih yuht dō yàhn yuhng dihnnóuh tái syū. Nīléuhngjé deui syūsēung (book sellers) tùhng duhkjé (readers) làih góng yáuh mē fānbiht nē? Tùhngmàaih yáuh mē hóuchyu tùhng waaihchyu nē?

3. Néih jūngyi tái jíjāt ge syū dihnghaih yuhng dihnnóuh táisyū dōdī a? Dímgáai nē?

7.3 Speaking exercise: Please use at least 10 of the following vocabularies/patterns to say on the following topic in one to two minutes.

"Néih jeui jūngyi tái mātyéh syū? Jeui m̀jūngyi tái mātyéh syū a? Dímgáai nē?"

leuihyìhng	jūnggaau	geiluhk	góipīn
síusyut	sésaht	chìhngjit	fūchín
dá dá saat saat	chādī	mòuhleuhn yùhhòh	
dou ...... ge chìhngdouh		Adj dou bātdāklíuh	
tùhng ...... yáuh gwāan		chèuihjó ......, juhng	
m̀haih ...... jauhhaih			

8. Additional texts

附加課文 Fuhgā fomàhn

8.1. Additional text 附加課文

唔同嘅人對睇書呢件事有唔同嘅想法，有啲人因為工作或者考試去讀書，有啲人係為咗打發時間，有啲人想喺節奏快、壓力大嘅社會中搵到一個安靜嘅角落。但係無論係因為乜嘢原因，讀書呢件事都進入咗我哋每個人嘅生活，就好似食飯、瞓覺一樣，係生活中唔可以缺少嘅一部分。

Mtùhngge yàhn deui táisyū nīgihn sih yáuh m̀tùhngge séungfaat, yáuhdī yàhn yānwaih gūngjok waahkjé háausíh heui duhksyū, yáuhdī yàhn haih waihjó dáfaat sìhgaan, yáuhdī yàhn séung hái jitjau faai, ngaatlihk daaihge séhwúi jūng wándóu yātgo ōnjihngge goklohk. Daahnhaih mòuhleuhn haih yānwaih mātyéh yùhnyān, duhksyū nīgihn sih dōu jeunyahpjó ngóhdeih múihgo yàhnge sāngwuht, jauh hóuchíh sihkfaahn, fangaau yātyeuhng, haih sāngwuhtjūng m̀hóyíh kyutsíuge yāt bouhfahn.

前幾年聽到唔少書店閂門嘅消息，但係我覺得書店唔會消失，因為嗰度嘅氣氛同體驗都係獨特嘅。你去一間書店睇書買書，周圍都有人睇書，你知道嗰啲人同你有相同嘅愛好、相同嘅想法。你可以同店員傾偈，都可以坐低飲杯咖啡，呢種體驗係網上書店冇辦法俾到你嘅。

Chìhn géi nìhn tēngdóu m̀síu syūdim sāanmùhnge sīusīk, daahnhaih ngóh gokdāk syūdim m̀wúih sīusāt, yānwaih gódouhge heifān tùhng táiyihm dōu haih duhkdahkge. Néih heui yātgāan syūdim táisyū máaihsyū, jāuwàih dōu yáuh yàhn táisyū, néih jīdou gódī yàhn tùhng néih yáuh sēungtùhng ge oi'hou, sēungtùhng ge séungfaat. Néih hóyíh tùhng dimyùhn kīnggái, dōu hóyíh chóhdāi yám būi gafē, nījúng táiyihm haih móhngseuhng syūdim móuh baahnfaat béidóu néih ge.

我覺得紙質書都唔會消失。雖然電子書越嚟越普遍，但係我哋各有各嘅興趣，有人鍾意電子書方便同平，都有人鍾意紙質書擇喺手裏面嘅獨特感覺。

Ngóh gokdāk jíjāt syū dōu m̀wúih sīusāt. sēuiyìhn dihnjí syū yuht làih yuht póupin, daahnhaih ngóhdeih gok yáuh gok ge hingcheui, yáuh yàhn jūngyi dihnjí syū fōngbihn tùhng pèhng, dōu yáuh yàhn jūngyi jíjāt syū lóhái sáu léuihmihnge duhkdahk gámgok.

而且，無論睇嘅係電子書，或者係紙質書，都係睇書。紙質書少咗，並唔係話我哋唔鍾意讀書。不過而家嘅人去書店，可能唔只係買書同睇書，而係更加似係一種休閒活動。我相信，就算有電子書，唔少讀者都願意花時間去書店行下、睇下、坐下。

Yìhché, mòuhleuhn táige haih dihnjí syū, waahkjé haih jíjāt syū, dōu haih táisyū. Jíjāt syū síujó, bihng m̀haih wah ngóhdeih m̀jūngyi duhksyū. Bātgwo yìhgā ge yàhn heui syūdim, hónàhng m̀jíhaih máaihsyū tùhng táisyū, yìhhaih ganggā chíh haih yātjúng yāuhàahn wuhtduhng. Ngóh sēungseun, jauhsyun yáuh dihnjí syū, m̀síu duhkjé dōu yuhnyi fā sìhgaan heui syūdim hàahnghńáh, táiháh, chóhháh.

對我哋大部分人嚟講，睇書係一種享受。雖然電腦網絡發展得好快，我哋嘅生活方式改變咗好多，但係睇書喺我哋嘅生活中，仲係唔可以缺少嘅一部分。	Deui ngóhdeih daaih bouhfahn yàhn làihgóng, táisyū haih yātjúng héungsauh. Sēuiyìhn dihnnóuh móhnglohk faatjín dāk hóufaai, ngóhdeihge sāngwuht fōngsīk góibinjó hóudō, daahnhaih táisyū hái ngóhdeihge sāngwuht jūng, juhnghaih m̀hóyíh kyutsíuge yāt bouhfahn.

8.2 Additional vocabulary 附加詞彙

Number	Word	Yale Romanization	POS	English
1	閱讀	yuhtduhk	V	to read
2	打發	dáfaat	V	to kill (the time), to pass (the time)
3	角落	goklohk	N	corner
4	缺少	kyutsíu	V	to lack; to be short of
5	消失	sīusāt	V	to disappear; to vanish; to fade away
6	體驗	táiyihm	N/V	experience; to experience
7	相同	sēungtùhng	Adj	the same; identical; equal; alike
8	店員	dimyùhn	N	shop assistant; clerk; salesclerk
9	同樣	tùhngyeuhng	Adj	same; similar; equal
10	熱愛	yihtngoi	V	to ardently love

8.3 Please answer the following T/F questions after reading the additional text

1 M̀tùhngge yàhn yáuh m̀tùhngge yùhnyān táisyū. (T/F)
2 Ngóhdeihge sāngwuht lèih m̀hōi táisyū. (T/F)
3 "Ngóh" dāamsām syūdim wúih sīusāt. (T/F)
4 Heui syūdim máaihsyūge yàhn dōu haih hóuyàhn. (T/F)
5 Hái syūdim máaihsyū, juhng hóyíh yám būi gafē, gámyéungge táiyihm hóu dahkbiht. (T/F)
6 "Ngóh" gokdāk jíjāt syū m̀wúih sīusāt, yānwaih béigaau pèhng tùhng fōngbihn. (T/F)
7 Yìhgā jíjātsyū yuht làih yuht síu, yānwaih jūngyi táisyūge yàhn síujó. (T/F)
8 Yìhgā ngóhdeih heui syūdim táisyū, hónàhng haih waihjó fōngbihn. (T/F)

9 Jeuigahn, deui yātdī yàhn làihgóng, heui syūdim haih yātjúng yāuhàahn wuhtduhng. (T/F)

10 "Ngóh" yihngwàih dihnnóuh móhnglohk móuh góibin ngóhdeih táisyūge jaahpgwaan tùhng taaidouh. (T/F)

8.4 Topics for discussions

1 Néih jūng m̀jūngyi táisyū a ? Dímgáai a ?

2 Chéng néih gónggóng néih deui dihnjí syū ge táifaat.

3 Hái néihge gwokgā, dō m̀dō yàhn jūngyi táisyū a ? Néih gokdāk haih mātyéh yùhnyān nē ?

8.5 Authentic oral data 1 🔊
真實語料 1

8.6 Authentic oral data 2 🔊
真實語料 2

8.7 Authentic oral data 3 🔊
真實語料 3

Lesson 4 Smoking ban
無煙香港

1. Pragmatic factors, Yuti features and linguistic functions
語用因素、語體特徵與語言功能

Yúhyuhng yānsou, yúhtái dahkjīng yúh yúhyìhn gūngnàhng

Pragmatic factors/ Yuti features 語用因素 / 語體特徵	Linguistic function 語言功能
Pragmatic factors: A live interview on TV is typically a formal situation in which the speaker should pay attention to their use of words while expressing their opinion. 語用因素： 正式場合，說話者會用到表示禮貌的語言，也會用到一些客氣話和場面話。 **Yuti features:** Formality index: 2 語體特徵：2 級之間	**Linguistic function:** Expressing Opinion Explicitly stating one's viewpoint and providing sufficient proof, while simultaneously considering your counterpart's reasonable claims. 語言功能：發表意見 明確提出自己的觀點並進行充分論證，同時也考慮到對方的合理訴求。

Notes on pragmatic knowledge 語用知識	Notes on structure 語言及篇章結構知識
I. Politeness and expressing thanks 禮貌與感謝 1. Thanks for the opportunity 「多謝……機會」 2. Knowing that you have a time limit 「知道你哋嘅採訪有時間限制」 II. Related knowledge 相關知識 1. Three meals a day「一日三餐」 2. Second-hand smoking「二手煙」 3. Journals with authority「權威雜誌」 4. How can you (lit. "depending on what")「憑乜嘢」 5. A matter of life and death 「人命關天嘅事」 6. Addictive to smoking「煙癮起」	I. Grammar and sentence patterns 語法和句型 1. "Baak fahn jī baak" one hundred percent; absolutely 2. "Jeun yāt bouh" further; go a step further 3. "Lihng yàhn (gámdou)…" to make one (feels)... 4. Rhetorical questions with "m̀tūng… mē?" 5. "pàhng……" rely on; base on 6. "Sēuiyìhn…, daahnhaih…" 7. " Búnlòih…sāumēi/hauhlòih/yìhgā…" 8. "Mòuhleuhn dím dōu…" II. Paragraph and discourse 語段和篇章 1. "Sáusīn…jeun yāt bouh…lihng yāt fōngmihn…jeuihauh…" ; first..., furthermore..., on the other hand..., in the end...

2. Text 🔊

課文 Fomàhn

室內場所應唔應該全面禁煙，我自己都明白係一個非常之具爭議性嘅題目，因為本身我自己屋企都係有人係食煙嘅。噉所以當我哋出街食飯嘅時候都面對唔少嘅矛盾。一方面我哋都想遷就屋企人啦，另一方面我哋都明白其實，食煙的確係對自己同身邊嘅人嘅健康都係有一個十分之大嘅影響。所以喺呢個議題上面，我自己嘅，我自己嘅立場係非常之清晰。我自己係百分之百贊成酒樓餐廳同室內公共場所應該全面禁煙嘅。

Sātnoih chèuhngsó yīng m̀yīnggōi chyùhnmihn gamyīn, ngóh jihgéi dōu mìhngbaahk haih yātgo fēisèuhngjī geuih jāngyíhsing ge tàihmuhk, yānwaih búnsān ngóh jihgéi ngūkkéi dōu haih yáuh yàhn haih sihkyīn ge. Gám sóyíh dōng ngóhdeih chēutgāai sihkfaahn ge sìhhauh dōu mihndeui m̀síuge màauhtéuhn. Yāt fōngmihn ngóhdeih dōu séung chīnjauh ngūkkéi yàhn lā, lihng yāt fōngmihn ngóhdeih dōu mìhngbaahk kèihsaht, sihkyīn dīkkok haih deui jihgéi tùhng sānbīnge yàhn ge gihnhōng dōuhaih yáuh yātgo sahpfānjī daaihge yínghéung. Sóyíh hái nīgo yíhtàih seuhngmihn, ngóh jihgéige, ngóh jihgéige lahpchèuhng haih fēisèuhngjī chīngsīk. Ngóh jihgéi haih baak fahnjī baak jaansìhng jáulàuh chāantēng tùhng sātnoih gūngguhng chèuhngsó yīnggōi chyùhnmihn gamyīnge.

首先我哋要留意一個好重要嘅基礎，就係吸煙危害健康，係人命關天嘅大事。相信喺呢一個觀點上面係絕對冇討論嘅空間嘅。權威雜誌上有數字顯示其實食煙嘅人，佢哋患癌嘅機會係非常之高啦。無論係咽喉癌，口腔癌，肺癌都係十分之常見。進一步嚟睇我哋都知道其實食煙亦都會影響下一代呀。如果懷孕嘅人佢係有吸煙嘅習慣，胎兒嘅發展係會嚴重受到影響。另一方面當我哋見到，其實市面上有好多戒煙用品、戒煙中心啦、輔助熱線啦、心理輔導啦等等，其實亦都證明咗啲人係知道食煙對健康係冇益，但係係十分之難去戒甩。

Sáusīn ngóhdeih yiu làuhyi yātgo hóu juhngyiuge gēichó, jauhhaih kāpyīn ngàihhoih gihnhōng, haih yàhn mehng gwāantīn ge daaih sih. Sēungseun hái nī yātgo gūndím seuhngmihn haih jyuhtdeui móuh tóuleuhn ge hūnggāan ge. Kyùhnwāi jaahpji seuhng yáuh soujih hínsih kèihsaht sihkyīnge yàhn, kéuihdeih waahn ngàahm ge gēiwuih haih fēisèuhngjī gōu lā. Mòuhleuhn haih yīnhàuh ngàahm, háuhōng ngàahm, fai ngàahm dōu haih sahpfānjī sèuhnggin. Jeun yātbouh làih tái ngóhdeih dōu jīdou kèihsaht sihkyīn yihkdōu wúih yínghéung hah yātdoih a. Yùhgwó wàaihyahnge yàhn kéuih haih yáuh kāpyīnge jaahpgwaan, tōiyìhge faatjín haih wúih yìhmjuhng sauhdou yínghéung. Lihng yāt fōngmihn dōng ngóhdeih gindóu, kèihsaht síhmihn seuhng yáuh hóudō gaaiyīn yuhngbán, gaaiyīn jūngsām lā, fuhjoh yihtsin lā, sāmléih fuhdouh lā dángdáng, kèihsaht yihkdōu jingmìhngjó dī yàhn haih jīdou sihkyīn deui gihnhōng haih móuhyīk, daahnnaih haih sahpfānjī nàahn heui gaailāt.

冇錯，有人話食煙係個人嘅選擇同自由，你鍾意食煙，唔關我事。不過個人嘅選擇同自由係必須建立喺唔影響其他人嘅基礎上面嘅。意思係如果你喺巴士上便食煙，其他乘客聞到啲煙味覺得唔舒服，唔通要佢哋落車咩？噉你就即係影響咗佢哋㗎。呢個情形就好似幾個人喺圖書館裏面大聲講嘢一樣。傾偈係佢哋嘅自由，但係喺圖書館裏面大聲講嘢，就一定會影響其他想靜靜哋讀書嘅人，令其他人唔開心。

Móuhcho, yáuh yàhn wah sihkyīn haih goyàhnge syúnjaahk tùhng jihyàuh, néih jūngyi sihkyīn, m̀gwāan ngóh sih. Bātgwo goyàhnge syúnjaahk tùhng jihyàuh haih bītsēui ginlahp hái m̀yínghéung kèihtā yàhnge gēichó seuhngmihn ge. Yisī haih yùhgwó néih hái bāsí seuhngbihn sihkyīn, kèihtā sìhnghaak màhndóu dī yīnmeih gokdāk m̀syūfuhk, m̀tūng yiu kéuihdeih lohkchē mē? Gám néih jauh jīkhaih yínghéungjó kéuihdeih la. Nīgo chìhngyìhng jauh hóuchíh géigo yàhn hái tòuhsyūgún léuihmihn daaihsēng góngyéh yātyeuhng. Kīnggái haih kéuihdeihge jihyàuh, daahnhaih hái tòuhsyūgún léuihmihn daaihsēng góngyéh, jauh yātdihng wúih yínghéung kèihtā séung jihngjíngdéi duhksyū ge yàhn, lihng kèihtā yàhn m̀hōisām.

或者有人會話，唔係喎，食煙同飲酒一樣，都係一個人嘅嗜好啫。我鍾意食煙，你鍾意飲啤酒，我唔反對你喺室內公共場所飲啤酒喎，你憑乜嘢反對我食煙。雖然我覺得啤酒嘅味道好臭，好奇怪，但係我唔會理你。你哋覺得呢個講法啱唔啱呢？我想講，其實食煙同飲酒係唔一樣嘅。人人都知道食煙對身體有害無益，而且食二手煙嘅害處多過食煙本身。就算我自己唔食煙，但係喺室內空氣唔流通嘅場所，吸咗人哋嘅煙，我都一樣會病。聽講有啲人因為噉樣就患肺癌死咗。佢哋唔食煙都有肺癌，點解？就係因為食二手煙嘅關係。何況喺酒樓同餐廳呢啲地方有好多小朋友、老人家、孕婦、仲有香港有好多人鼻敏感。如果其他人食煙，對佢哋無論點都有影響。所以為咗社會大多數人嘅利益，其實室內禁煙係好嘅，因為呢一個方法可以幫人去盡量減少吸煙。長遠嚟講，室內禁煙係對我哋社會可持續發展係有一個十分之大嘅益處，譬如話醫療費用啦，整體社會嘅醫療費用我相信係會下降，對於家庭嘅美滿，屋企人呀，能夠更加多嘅時間去相聚。咁所以喺各方面嘅理據底下，其實我哋明白室內禁煙係對個人同社會整體都有好處嘅。

Waahkjé yáuh yàhn wúih wah, m̀haih wo, sihkyīn tùhng yámjáu yātyeuhng, dōuhaih yātgo yàhnge sihou jē. Ngóh jūngyi sihkyīn, néih jūngyi yám bējáu, ngóh m̀fáandeui néih hái sātnoih gūngguhng chèuhngsó yám bējáu wo, néih pàhng mātyéh fáandeui ngóh sihkyīn. Sēuiyìhn ngóh gokdāk bējáuge meihdouh hóu chau, hóu kèihgwaai, daahnhaih ngóh m̀wúih léih néih. Néihdeih gokdāk nīgo góngfaat ngāam m̀ngāam nē? Ngóh séung góng, kèihsaht sihkyīn tùhng yámjáu haih m̀yātyeuhngge. Yàhn yàhn dōu jīdou sihkyīn deui sāntái yáuh hoih mòuh yīk, yìhché sihk yihsáu yīnge hoihchyu dōgwo sihkyīn búnsān. Jauhsyun ngóh jihgéi m̀sihkyīn, daahnhaih hái sātnoih hūnghei m̀làuhtùngge chèuhngsó, kāpjó yàhndeihge yīn, ngóh dōu yātyeuhng wúih behng. Tēnggóng yáuhdī yàhn yānwaih gámyéung jauh waahn faingàahm séijó. Kéuihdeih m̀sihkyīn dōu yáuh faingàahm, dímgáai? Jauhhaih yānwaih sihk yihsáu yīn ge gwāanhaih. Hòhfong hái jáulàuh tùhng chāantēng nīdī deihfōng yáuh hóudō síu pàhngyáuh, lóuhyàhngā, yahnfúh, juhngyáuh Hēunggóng yáuh hóudō yàhn beih máhngám. Yùhgwó kèihtā yàhn sihkyīn, deui kéuihdeih mòuhleuhn dím dōu yáuh yínghéung. Sóyíh waihjó séhwúi daaih dōsou yàhn ge leihyīk, kèihsaht sātnoih gamyīn haih hóu ge, yānwaih nī yātgo fōngfaat hóyíh bōng yàhn heui jeuhnleuhng gáamsíu kāpyīn. Chèuhngyúhn làih góng, sātnoih gamyīn haih deui ngóhdeih séhwúi hó chìhjuhk faatjín haih yáuh yātgo sahpfānjī daaih ge yīkchyu, peiyùhwah yīlìuh faiyuhng lā, jíngtái séhwúi ge yīlìuh faiyuhng ngóh sēungseun haih wúih hahgong, deuiyū gātìhng ge méihmúhn, ngūkkéi yàhn a, nàhnggau ganggā dō ge sìhgaan heui sēungjeuih. Gám sóyíh hái gok fōngmihnge léihgeui dáihah, kèihsaht ngóhdeih mìhngbaahk sātnoih gamyīn haih deui goyàhn tùhng séhwúi jíngtái dōu yáuh hóuchyu ge.

我好明白，對於煙民嚟講，食煙唔止係嗜好，仲係生活習慣。佢哋煙癮起嗰陣時，要佢哋特登行到好遠，真係幾麻煩幾唔方便嘅。不過，我覺得唔可以因為噉樣，就唔理其他人。室內公共場所需要照顧其他人嘅需要，唔可以咁自私嘅。如果因為你嘅自由，影響到其他人，噉樣社會就會更加唔公平嘑。其實有啲城市連室外都唔俾食煙，呢度淨係室內唔俾食，都算幾自由㗎嘑。我知道你哋嘅採訪時間有限制，所以我想總結，我贊成室內公共場所全面禁煙嘅同時，政府應該指定一啲吸煙區，唔應該剝奪煙民食煙嘅自由。	Ngóh hóu mìhngbaahk, deuiyū yīnmàhn làihgóng, sihkyīn m̀jí haih sihou, juhnghaih sāngwuht jaahpgwaan. Kéuihdeih yīnyáhn héi gójahnsìh, yiu kéuihdeih dahkdāng hàahng dou hóu yúhn, jānhaih géi màhfàahn géi m̀fōngbihn ge. Bātgwo, ngóh gokdāk m̀hóyíh yānwaih gámyéung, jauh m̀léih kèihtā yàhn. Sātnoih gūngguhng chèuhngsó sēuiyiu jiugu kèihtā yàhnge sēuiyiu, m̀hóyíh gam jihsī ge. Yùhgwó yānwaih néihge jihyàuh, yínghéung dou kèihtā yàhn, gámyéung séhwúi jauh wúih ganggā m̀gūngpìhng la. Kèihsaht yáuhdī sìhngsíh lìhn sātngoih dōu m̀béi sihkyīn, nīdouh jihnghaih sātnoih m̀béi sihk, dōu syun géi jihyàuh ga la. Ngóh jīdou néihdeihge chóifóng sìhgaan yáuh haahnjai, sóyíh ngóh séung júnggit, ngóh jaansìhng sātnoih gūngguhng chèuhngsó chyùhnmihn gamyīnge tùhngsìh, jingfú yīnggōi jídihng yātdī kāpyīn kēui, m̀yīnggōi mōkdyuht yīnmàhn sihkyīnge jihyàuh.

3. Vocabulary in use

活用詞彙 Wuhtyuhng chìhwuih

3.1 Common vocabulary

Number	Word	Yale Romanization	POS	English
1	非常之	fēisèuhngjī	Adv	very, extremely
2	具爭議性	geuih jāngyíhsing	Adj	controversial
3	題目	tàihmuhk	N	topic
4	矛盾	màauhtéuhn	Adj/N	contradictory; contradiction
5	的確	dīkkok	Adv	indeed
6	議題	yíhtàih	N	issue

7	立場	lahpchèuhng	N	standpoint
8	清晰	chīngsīk	Adj	clear
9	百分之百	baak fahn jī baak	PH	a hundred percent; absolutely
10	贊成	jaansihng	V	to approve of, to be in favour of
11	基礎	gēichó	N	foundation
12	危害	ngàihhoih	V	to endanger, to harm
13	討論	tóuleuhn	N/V	discussion; to discuss
14	空間	hūnggāan	N	space
15	十分之	sahpfānjī	Adv	very, fully
16	常見	sèuhng gin	Adj	common
17	下一代	hah yāt doih	N	the next generation
18	戒煙	gaaiyīn	VO	to quit smoking
19	冇益	móuhyīk	Adj	unhelpful, not beneficial
20	戒甩	gaailāt	RV	to successfully quit (a habit)
21	自由	jihyàuh	Adj/N	free; freedom
22	嗜好	sihou	N	hobby
23	反對	fáandeui	V	to oppose
24	本身	búnsān	N	self, itself
25	利益	leihyīk	N	benefit
26	社會	séhwúi	N	society
27	下降	hahgong	V	to decrease
28	家庭	gātìhng	N	family
29	美滿	méihmúhn	Adj	happy, good and perfect (for marriage or family)
30	相聚	sēungjeuih	V	to gather together
31	理據	léihgeui	N	justification
32	自私	jihsī	Adj	selfish
33	公平	gūngpìhng	Adj	fair

34	限制	haahnjai	N/V	restriction; to restrict
35	總結	júnggit	N/V	conclusion; to conclude
36	剝奪	mōkdyuht	V	to deprive

3.2 About smoking and smoking ban

1	全面禁煙	chyùhnmihn gamyīn	PH	total ban on smoking
2	減少吸煙	gáamsíu kāpyīn	PH	to reduce smoking
3	煙味	yīn meih	N	smoke smell
4	煙癮起	yīnyáhn héi	PH	to have an urge to smoke
5	煙民	yīnmàhn	N	smoker
6	吸煙區	kāpyīn kēui	N	smoking area

3.3 About medical issues and physical condition

1	患癌	waahn ngàahm	VO	to suffer from cancer
2	咽喉癌	yīnhàuh ngàahm	N	cancer of the pharynx and larynx
3	口腔癌	háuhōng ngàahm	N	oral cavity cancer
4	肺癌	fai ngàahm	N	lung cancer
5	懷孕	wàaihyahn	V	to be pregnant
6	胎兒	tōiyìh	N	fetus
7	孕婦	yahnfúh	N	pregnant woman
8	鼻敏感	beih máhngám	N	nasal allergy
9	醫療費用	yīlìuh faiyuhng	N	medical expenses

3.4 Other vocabularies

1	室內場所	sātnoih chèuhngsó	N	indoor place
2	權威雜誌	kyùhnwāi jaahpji	N	reputed journal
3	用品	yuhngbán	N	articles for use
4	輔助熱線	fuhjoh yihtsin	N	assistance hotline
5	心理輔導	sāmléih fuhdouh	N	psychological counselling
6	採訪	chóifóng	N/V	news gathering; to interview and gather news
7	指定	jídihng	V	to appoint, to assign

3.5 Useful expressions

1	憑乜嘢反對	pàhng mātyéh fáandeui	PH	what to base on to oppose
2	有害無益	yáuh hoih mòuh yīk	PH	harmful and unhelpful
3	空氣唔流通	hūnghei m̀làuhtūng	PH	poorly rentilated
4	可持續發展	hó chìhjuhk faatjín	PH	sustainable development

4. Notes on language and discourse structure

語言及篇章結構知識 Yúhyìhn kahp pīnjēung gitkau jīsīk

4.1. Grammar and sentence patterns 語法和句型

4.1.1 "Baak fahn jī baak" one hundred percent; absolutely

1. Ngóh m̀sihkyīn, sóyíh ngóh baak fahn jī baak jīchìh hái sātnoih gūngguhng chèuhngsó chyùhnmihn gamyīn.
2. Kéuih haih ngóh jeui hóuge pàhngyáuh, ngóh baak fahn jī baak sēungseun kéuih.
3. Kéuih haih baak fahn jī baakge Hēunggóng yàhn, kéuih hái Hēunggóng chēutsai, hái Hēunggóng duhksyū, yìhgā juhnghái Hēunggóng jouh yéh.

4.1.2 "Jeun yātbouh" further; go a step further

1. Chèuihjó kāpyīn ngàihhoih gihnhōng jīngoih, ngóh juhng hóyíh jeun yātbouh gónggóng sihkyīnge kèihtā hoichyu.

2. Yihsáuyīnge hoihchyu yáuh géi daaih, ngóhdeih juhng yiu jeun yātbouh yìhngau.

3. Yùhgwó néih séung hái Hēunggóng gūngjok, néih jeui hóu jeun yātbouh líuhgáaiháh Hēunggóngge màhnfa.

4.1.3 "Lihng yàhn (gámdou)…" to make one (feels)…

1. Lihng yàhn gámdou hōisām ge haih, jeuigahn sihkyīnge yàhn síujó.

2. Kéuih cheunggō hóu hóutēng, kéuihge yíncheungwúi (concert) lihng yàhn gīkduhng (excited).

3. Sātnoih chèuhngsó yáuh hóudō yàhn sihkyīn, lihng yàhn gámdou m̀syūfuhk.

4.1.4 Rhetorical questions with "m̀tūng…mē?"

1. Ngóh jūngyi sihkyīn, m̀tūng ngóh móuh sihkyīnge jihyàuh (freedom) mē?

2. Néih làihjó Hēunggóng sāamnìhn, m̀tūng néih m̀jī Hēunggóng yáuh hóudō hóusihk ge dímsām mē?

3. Sihkyīn deui sāntái yáuh mātyéh yínghéung (effect), m̀tūng néih m̀jī mē?

4.1.5 "Pàhng ……" rely on; base on

1. Néih pàhng mātyéh yiu kéuih bōng néih a?

2. Hái nīdouh, lóuhyàhn hóyíh pàhng sānfánjing míhnfai chóh bāsí.

3. Néih m̀haih ngóh lóuhbáan, pàhng mātyéh yiu tēng néihge syutwah a?

4.1.6 "Sēuiyìhn…daahnhaih…"meaning"though…yet…"

1. Sēuiyìhn Gwóngdūngwá hóu nàahnhohk daahnhaih Máhlaih hóu jūngyi hohk.

2. Sēuiyìhn gógāan jáulàuh hóu gwai, daahnhaih yānwaih gódouh dī yéh hóusihk, sóyíh sìhsìh dōu yáuh hóudō yàhn.

3. Sēuiyìhn séjihlàuh yáuh hóudō yéh jouh, daahnhaih gógo beisyū juhng sèhngyaht dá dihnwá tùhng pàhngyáuh kīnggái.

4. Sēuiyìhn kéuih múihyaht jíhaih yámséui, daahnhaih juhnghaih hóu fèih.

5. Sēuiyìhn tīnhei hóu dung, daahnhaih kéuih juhng yahtyaht yàuhséui.

6. Sēuiyìhn kéuih làihjó Hēunggóng chāam̀dō yātnìhn, daahnhaih juhng meih yáuh gēiwuih heui Hēunggóng yàhn ngūkkéi sihkfaahn.

   Please note that in Cantonese, when "sēuiyìhn…" is used, it is mostly followed by "daahnhaih…". These two clauses usually contradict each other in meaning.

4.1.7 "Búnlòih...sāumēi/hauhlòih/yìhgā..." meaning "Originally...later/now…"

1. Búnlòih kéuih m̀jūngyi Hēunggóng, sāumēi hohksīk Gwóngdōngwá, yìhgā fēisèuhngjī jūngyi jyuhhái nīdouh la.

2. Búnlòih lóuhbáan séung giu kéuih heui Yahtbún gūnggon, bātgwo sāumēi lóuhbáan jihgéi heuijó.

3. Búnlòih kéuih hóu pa tēng Jūnggwok yāmngohk, daahnhaih yìhgā yuhtlàih yuht jūngyi tēng.

4. Búnlòih Máhlaih séung sung laahpjūk béi Wòhng sāang, sāumēi kéuih sung yāthahp béng béi Wòhng sāang.

5. Búnlòih sáutàih dihnwá hóu gwai, hauhlòih yuht làih yuht pèhng.

6. Búnlòih kéuih jāchē jādāk géi maahn, yìhgā kéuih máaihjó yātga sānchē, jādāk faai jó hóudō.

4.1.8 "Mòuhleuhn dím dōu… " means "no matter how…, …"

1. Dī séui taai yiht, mòuhleuhn dím yám dōu yám m̀lohk.

2. Dī jih taai sai, mòuhleuhn dím tái dōu táim̀dóu.

3. Kéuih góng dāk taai faai, mòuhleuhn dím ngóh dōu tēngm̀mìhng.

4. Sēuiyìhn dī gūngfo taaidō, daahnhaih dī hohksāang mòuhleuhn dím dōu wúih jouh yùhn.

5. Wòhng táai jyú gamdō choi, ngóhdeih mòuhleuhn dím dōu yiu sihksaai.

6. Gógo saimānjái m̀haih hóu gwāai, mòuhleuhn dím dōu m̀tēng néih góng.

7. Góbún gaau Yīngmàhn ge syū mòuhleuhn dím dōu máaih m̀dóu.

8. Fóchējaahm taai dō yàhn, ngóh mòuhleuhn dím séuhng dōu séuhngm̀dóu fóchē.

9. Néih joi daaihsēngdī góng lā, néih gam saisēng, ngóhdeih mòuhleuhn dím tēng dōu tēng m̀dóu .

10. Kéuih mòuhleuhn dím dōu jīchìh (support) kéuih sīnsaang.

11. Chèuihfēi (Unless) néih háng duhksyū tùhng góng dōdī, yùhgwó m̀haih (otherwise), Gwóngdūngwá dím hohk dōu hohk m̀sīk ge la.

4.2 Paragraph and discourse 語段和篇章

4.2.1. "Sāusīn…jeun yātbouh …lihng yāt fōngmihn …jeuihauh …" first..., furthermore..., on the other hand..., in the end.

1. Sáusīn, sihkyīn wúih wūyíhm sātnoihge hūnghei…, ngóh juhng hóyíh jeun yātbouh góngháh sihkyīn deui gihnhōngge yínghéung…, lihng yāt fōngmihn, ngóh dōu jīdou yáuh yàhn wúih wah, sihkyīn haih jihgéige jihyàuh…, jeuihauh ngóh séung góng

ngóh haih fáandeui (oppose) gūngguhng chèuhngsó sihkyīn ge.

2. Sáusīn, ngóh yiu góngge haih Jūnggwok yàhn hóu jūngyi sihk, gānjyuh wúih jeun yātbouh góng dímgáai Jūnggwok yàhn deui sihkmaht gam gónggau,... lihng yāt fōngmihn, ngóh séung góng, sihkyéh m̀jíhaih sāngwuht, juhnghaih yātjúng màhnfa,... jeuihauh ngóh wúih tùhng daaihgā yātchàih tái yāttou yáuhgwāan sihkge dihnyíng.

3. Néih séung sānchíng duhk yìhngausāng (postgraduate study), yiu sé yātfūng seun. Sáusīn gaaisiuhháh néih jihgéi, gónghán néih dímgáai séung duhk yìhngausāng, yìhnhauh jeun yātbouh gónghán néih dímgáai jūngyi nīyāt fō. Lihng yāt fōngmihn, néih dōu yiu béi lóuhsī jīdou néih haih yātgo hóu kàhnlihkge hohksāang, jeuihauh néih hóyíh gónghán néih jēunglòih yáuh mātyéh gaiwaahk.

5. Notes on pragmatic knowledge
語用因素與相關知識 Yúhyuhng yānsou yúh sēunggwāan jīsīk

5.1. Politeness and expressing thanks 禮貌與感謝

5.1.1 "多謝 dōjeh...... 機會 gēiwuih" Thanks for the opportunity.

It is natural, and pragmatically desirable, to express thanks before speaking in a formal situation. You can express thanks to the host, the organizer or the MC for the event, someone who introduces you before your talk or someone who recommends you for the occasion, etc.

-   Dōjeh dihnsihtòih béi ngóh nīgo gēiwuih, ngóh séung gónghán...

5.1.2 "知道你哋嘅採訪有時間限制 jīdou néihdeihge chóifóng yáuh sìhgaan haahnjai" knowing that you have a time limit

Like the phrase "due to the limitation of time", this is a common "excuse" used by many Chinese speakers to end their talk. Even though it may or may not be true in reality, the use of phrases like this seems to lead to a more natural conclusion when compared with a somewhat abrupt ending.

-   Jīdou néihdeihge chóifóng yáuh sìhgaan haahnjai, ngóh jauh góngdou nīdouh, dōjeh daaihgā.

-   Jīdou daaihgā dōu hóu mòhng, ngóh hahchi joi góng.

5.2. Related knowledge 相關知識

5.2.1 "一日三餐 yātyaht sāamchāan" three meals a day

Stating the obvious, such as 3 meals a day, 365 days a year, etc. is often used to indicate "every" or "all the time". These phrases are treated as idiomatic expressions and cannot be created anytime you want. Thus you may hear in Chinese "4 seasons a year"as part of an utterance because many native speakers would use it, but will perhaps never hear "60 minutes an hour" in similar contexts.

- Hóudō yàhn yātyaht sāamchāan dōu chēutgāai sihkfaahn.
- Yātnìhn seigwai, néih dōu hóyíh dá bīnlòuh (hot pot).

5.2.2 "二手煙 yihsáu yīn" second-hand smoking

Although "second-hand" means "used" here and is now a common phrase with indication of being cheap, it is often used with only a limited set of nouns such as "car", "house" or other durable goods. The ability to form appropriate phrases with "second-hand" is related to one's pragmatic knowledge.

- Yahtyaht sihk yihsáu yīn, ngóh dāamsām ngóhge sāntái wúih yáuh sih.
- Ngóh m̀gauchín, jihnghaih hóyíh máaih yihsáu chē.

5.2.3 "權威雜誌 kyùhnwāi jaahpji" journals with authority

The use of "權威 kyùhnwāi (authority)" together with "journal" or "magazine" reflects some subtle aspect of the Chinese culture. People tend to hear "a reputable journal" or "a journal with dependable sources" in English because trustworthy publications in the media may not come from the "authority".

- Kyùhnwāi jaahpji wah sihkyīn deui sāntái yáuh hoih.
- Kéuih haih nī fōngmihnge kyùhnwāi yàhnsih.

5.2.4 "憑乜嘢 pàhng mātyéh" literally meaning "depending on what"

The phrase "憑乜嘢 pàhng mātyéh", in terms of style and register, is often seen in spoken argumentation when used as a rhetorical question. Pragmatically many people would consider it "rude" or at least "impolite" if you use it when talking to them in Chinese.

- Néih pàhng mātyéh yiu ngóh jechín béi néih a?
- Néih pàhng mātyéh wah ngóhdeih m̀yahpdāk heui a ?

5.2.5 "人命關天嘅事 yàhn mehng gwāan tīn ge sih" a matter of life and death.

Similar to the use of "天 tīn" in "民以食為天 màhn yíh sihk wàih tīn" (eating is the most important thing for all people), the phrase "人命關天 yàhn mehng gwāan tīn" is here used figuratively to refer to something of extreme importance, like a matter of life and death. It can be used literally to refer to a situation in which life is indeed at stake, or figuratively to refer to something with serious consequences.

- Nīgihn haih yàhn mehng gwāan tīn ge sih!

5.2.6 "煙癮起 yīnyáhn héi" addictive to smoking

The use of "癮 yáhn", often found together with cigarette smoking or drugs, is often derogatory in Chinese. It can also be used in a relatively neutral way to show a very strong desire to do something, but is seldom, if ever, used to refer to things of a positive nature.

- Kéuihge yīnyáhn hóu sāileih, yīnyáhn héi kéuih jauh gokdāk hóu m̀syūfuhk.
- Yáuh duhkyáhn (addictive to drugs) ge yàhn giu jouh yáhn gwānjí (drug addicts).

6. Contextualized speaking practice

情境説話練習 Chìhnggíng syutwah lihnjaahp

【課前預習】 Class preparation

6.1. Please answer the following True/False questions according to the lesson text.

1. Góngsyutwahge yàhn ge gāyàhn yáuh yàhn sihkyīn. (T/F)
2. Góngsyutwahge yàhn fáandeui jáulàuh chāantēng tùhng sātnoih gūngjung chèuhngsó chyùhnmihn gamyīn. (T/F)
3. Góngsyutwahge yàhn yihngwàih kāpyīn ngàihhoih gihnhōng. (T/F)
4. Yáuh soujih hínsih kèihsaht sihkyīnge yàhn waahn ngàahm ge gēiwuih tùhng póutūng yàhn yātyeuhng. (T/F)
5. Yahnfúh yùhgwó yáuh sihkyīnge jaahpgwaan, tōiyìhge faatjín haih wúih yìhmjuhng sauhdou yínghéung ge. (T/F)
6. Sātnoih gamyīn haih tùhng ngóhdeih séhwúi hóchìhjuhk faatjín móuh gwāanhaih ge. (T/F)

7. Góngsyutwahge yàhn yihngtùhng sihkyīn tùhng yámjáu yātyeuhng. (T/F)

8. Góngsyutwahge yàhn yihngwàih hái sātnoih gūngjung chèuhngsó jauh sēuiyiu jiugu kèihtā yàhn ge sēuiyiu. (T/F)

9. Góngsyutwahge yàhn yihngwàih yùhgwó yānwaih goyàhn jihyàuh, yínghéungjó kèihtā yàhn, séhwúi jauh wúih ganggā m̀gūngpìhng. (T/F)

10. Góngsyutwahge yàhn tàihchēut jingfú yīnggōi jídihng yātdī fēi kāpyīn kēui. (T/F)

6.2 Please explain the following phrases in Cantonese

1 二手煙 yihsáu yīn

2 人命關天 yàhnmehng gwāan tīn

3 煙癮 yīnyáhn

4 可持續發展 hóchìhjuhk faatjín

【課後練習】 Post-class exercises

6.3 Fill in the blanks with the given vocabularies. Each vocabulary can be chosen once only.

tóuleuhn	ngàihhoih	jaansìhng	fáandeui
màauhtéuhn	chīngsīk	haahnjai	gūngpìhng
jihsī	jihyàuh	móuhyīk	gaailāt

1. Lóuhsai yeukjó ngóhdeih tīngyaht _____ gūngsī meihlòih ge gaiwaahk tùhng faatjín fōngheung.

2. Yáuh dī fuhmóuh yìhmgaak _____ jáinéui múihyaht séuhngmóhng tùhngmàaih chēutgāai ge sìhgaan.

3. Kéuih fahn yàhn hóu _____, mātyéh dōu jihnghaih nám jihgéi ge leihyīk tùhng gámsauh, m̀nám kèihtā yàhn.

4. Chīnkèih m̀hóu hōichí sihkyīn, yānwaih jíyiu sihkgwo yātchi jauh wúih séuhngyáhn (to be addicted), yíhhauh hóu nàahn _____ ga la.

5. Ngóh baak fahn jī baak _____ yámsihkgaai chyùhnmihn gamyīn gamjáu, yānwaih sihkyīn yámjáu deui sāntái yātdī dōu _____.

6. Hóudō yīnmàhn dōu _____ gūngjung chèuhngsó chyùhnmihn gamyīn, kéuihdeih yihngwàih gámyéung jí wúih mōkdyuht kéuihdeih sihkyīn ge _____, deui kéuihdeih hóu m̀ _____.

7. Ngóh yihngwàih jingfú deui chyùhnmihn gamyīn ge lahpchèuhng hóu m̀ _____ .
   Jingfú yātmihn hái gwónggou léuihmihn wah béi yàhn tēng "kāpyīn _____ gihnhōng",
   yātmihn yauh gaijuhk béi chīukāp síhchèuhng tùhng bihnleihdim maaih yīn, ngóh gokdāk
   gámyéung sahpfānjī _____ .

6.4 Complete the following sentences or answer the following questions using the given patterns.

1. baak fahn jī baak ......
   A: Deuiyū jingfú "chyùhnmihn gamyīn" ge kyutdihng, néih yáuh mātyéh yigin a?
   B: Ngóh _____ .

2. jeun yāt bouh ......
   Hēunggóng ge hūnghei yíhgīng m̀hóu, yìh sihkyīn juhng wúih _____ .

3. lihng yàhn gámdou ......
   A: Néih deui hohkhaauh háausi yáuh mātyéh táifaat a?
   B: Ngóh yihngwàih hohkhaauh háausi _____ .

4. m̀tūng ......mē
   Gogo yeuk chān kéuih, kéuih dōu chìhdou, _____ ?!

5. pàhng ......
   Kéuihdeih _____ dākdóu nīgo jéung (prize).

6. sēuiyìhn ...... daahnhaih ......
   _____ , yānwaih gámyéung gihnhōngdī.

7. búnlòih ...... sāumēi ......
   _____ , yānwaih kéuih hái nīdouh sīkjó hóu dō pàhngyáuh.

8. mòuhleuhn dím dōu ......
   Sēuiyìhn ngóh jeuigahn jānhaih mòhng dou bātdāklíuh, daahnhaih

   _____ .

7. Listening and speaking 🔊

聽説練習 Tingsyut lihnjaahp

7.1 Listening comprehension exercise

Please listen to the recording and fill in the blanks with the following words.

wūyíhm   fahohk mahtjāt   jīchìh   chāantēng   fójōi
síu pàhngyáuh   hūnghei làuhtūng   bātnàhng   kāpyīn kēui   geihseuht

1. Yíngóngge yàhnge lahpchèuhng (standpoint) haih _____ gamyīn.
2. Yíngóng ge yàhn góngge noihyùhng jyúyiu gwāanyū _____tùhng sātnoih
   gūngguhng chèuhngsó chyùhnmihn gamyīn.
3. Yíngóngge yàhn yihngwàih sihkyīn wúih_____sātnoih hūnghei.
4. Yíngóngge yàhn góng yìhngau bougou jíchēut, yīnmouh léuihmihn yáuh sāam chīn géi júng
   _____.
5. Hái sātnoih waahkjé _____béigaau chā ge wàahngíng léuihmihn, kāp yihsáu yīn
   tùhng jihgéi sihkyīn haih yātyeuhng.
6. _____ tùhng yahnfúh deui yīnmouh jūng ge yáuhhoih mahtjāt ge dáikonglihk
   béigaau chā.
7. Yíngóngge yàhn yihngwàih bóujeung kāpyīnjé ge jihyàuhge sìhhauh, _____
   mōkdyuht (deprive) m̀sihkyīn ge yàhn ge jihyàuh.
8. Yíngóng ge yàhn jíchēut chèuihjó gihnhōng mahntàih, sātnoih kāpyīn juhngwúih yáhnji
   _____.
9. Yíngóngge yàhn tàihchēut hái gēichèuhng tùhng chāantēng chitlahp _____ ge
   ginyíh.
10. Hái béigaau daaihge chāantēng léuihmihn, yīnggōi _____seuhng kokbóu
    m̀sihkyīnge guhaak m̀sauh yínghéung.

7.2 Speech topics

1. Néih jaan m̀jaansìhng sātnoih chèuhngsó chyùhnmihn gamyīn a? Dímgáai nē?
2. Yáuh dī yīnmàhn fáandeui chyùhnmihn gamyīn, yáuh mātyéh yùhnyān a? Deuiyū kéuihdeih
   ge léihgeui, néih yáuh mē táifaat a?

3. Yùhgwó jingfú tēuihàhng chyùhnmihn gamyīn tùhng chyùhnmihn gamjáu (total ban on alcoholic drinks), deui goyàhn, gātìhng, séhwúi tùhng gīngjai wúih yáuh mātyéh yínghéung nē?

7.3 Speaking exercise: Please use at least 10 of the following vocabularies/patterns to say on the following topic in one to two minutes.

"Sihk yīn tùhng yám jáu deui goyàhn, gātìhng tùhng séhwúi dángdáng yáuh mē m̀hóu ge deihfōng?"

ngàihhoih	sèuhnggin	hah yāt doih	gātìhng
méihmúhn	móuhyīk	jihsī	gūngpìhng
jihyàuh	sihou	búnsān	gaailāt
lihng yàhn gámdou		sēuiyìhn ...... daahnhaih	
búnlòih ...... sāumēi		mòuhleuhn dím dōu	

8. Additional texts
附加課文 Fuhgā fomàhn

8.1 Additional text 附加課文

世界衛生組織（WHO）同聯合國（UN）最近有一份報告講，每年大概有 600 萬左右嘅人因為食煙死亡。而且，食煙唔只係對個人健康有害，對經濟發展都有好處。	Saigaai Waihsāng Jóujīk tùhng Lyùhnhahp Gwok jeuigahn yáuh yātfahn bougou góng, múihnìhn daaihkoi yáuh luhk baak maahn jóyáuge yàhn yānwaih sihkyīn séimòhng. Yihché, sihkyīn m̀jí haih deui goyàhn gihnhōng yáuhhoih, deui gīngjai faatjín dōu móuh hóuchyu.
食煙造成各種疾病。喺中國，因為同吸煙有關嘅疾病死亡嘅人佔每年死亡總人數嘅 80% 以上。	Sihkyīn jouhsìhng gokjúng jahtbehng. Hái Jūnggwok, yānwaih tùhng kāpyīn yáuhgwāange jahtbehng séimòhngge yàhn jim múihnìhn séimòhng júngyàhnsou ge baakfahnjī baatsahp yíhseuhng.

中國係全球最大嘅煙草生產國同消費國。中國大概 28% 嘅成年人都食煙。所以，如果有嚴格嘅規定，因為食煙死亡嘅人仲會越嚟越多。嗰樣會為中國經濟帶嚟好大嘅損失。首先買煙要用錢，如果因為食煙病咗，唔能夠工作，甚至死亡，家庭就會變得貧窮，同時，公司、企業同社會醫療保險嘅壓力都會更加大。另外，國家要喺醫療方面花更多嘅錢。

Jūnggwok haih chyùhnkàuh jeuidaaihge yīnchóu sāngcháan gwok tùhng sīufai gwok. Jūnggwok daaihkoi baakfahnjī yihsahpbaat ge sìhngnìhn yàhn dōu sihkyīn. Sóyíh, yùhgwó móuh yìhmgaak ge kwāidihng, yānwaih sihkyīn séimòhngge yàhn juhngwúih yuht làih yuhtdō. Gámyéung wúih waih Jūnggwok gīngjai daailàih hóu daaih ge syúnsāt. Sáusīn máaihyīn yiu yuhng chín, yùhgwó yānwaih sihkyīn behngjó, m̀nàhnggau gūngjok, sahmji séimòhng, gātìhng jauhwúih bindāk pàhnkùhng, tùhngsìh, gūngsī, kéihyihp tùhng séhwúi yīlìuh bóuhímge ngaatlihk dōu wúih ganggā daaih. Lihngngoih, gwokgā yiu hái yīlìuh fōngmihn fā gangdō ge chín.

都有人認為，煙草行業為國家經濟作出咗好大嘅貢獻，交咗好多稅。但係值得注意嘅係，食煙帶嚟嘅健康損失同其他方面嘅損失（例如社會、經濟、環境等等），大大超過貢獻！

Dōu yáuh yàhn yihngwàih, yīnchóu hòhngyihp waih gwokgā gīngjai jokchēutjó hóu daaih ge gunghin, gāaujó hóudō seui. Daahnhaih jihkdāk jyuyi ge haih, sihkyīn daailàihge gihnhōng syúnsāt tùhng kèihtā fōngmihn ge syúnsāt (laihyùh séhwúi, gīngjai, wàahngíng dángdáng), daaihdaaih chīugwo gunghin!

喺中國大部分城市，甚至係北京、上海呢啲大城市，幾年前仲未有嚴格嘅禁煙規定，隨便入去一間餐廳、咖啡室，可能會發現周圍都係煙霧。不過最近幾年禁煙嘅規定越嚟越嚴格，呢種情況有好大嘅改善。

Hái Jūnggwok daaih bouhfahn sìhngsíh, sahmji haih Bākgīng, Seuhnghói nīdī daaih sìhngsíh, géi nìhn chìhn juhng meih yáuh yìhmgaak ge gamyīn kwāidihng, chèuihbín yahpheui yātgāan chāantēng, gafē sāt, hónàhng wúih faatyihn jāuwàih dōu haih yīnmouh. Bātgwo jeuigahn géi nìhn gamyīnge kwāidihng yuht làih yuht yìhmgaak, nījúng chìhngfong yáuh hóu daaihge góisihn.

譬如話北京政府規定，十種公共場所全面禁煙，包括醫院、學校、戲院、博物館、圖書館、銀行、巴士站、體育館等等。而家，呢啲地方嘅空氣越嚟越乾淨，環境越嚟越舒服，食煙嘅人慢慢習慣咗唔喺公共場所食煙，所有市民都支持呢個改變。

Peiyùhwah Bākgīng jingfú kwāidihng, sahp júng gūngguhng chèuhngsó chyùhnmihn gamyīn, bāaukut yīyún, hohkhaauh, heiyún, bokmahtgún, tòuhsyūgún, ngàhnhòhng, bāsí jaahm, táiyuhk gún dángdáng. Yìhgā, nīdī deihfōngge hūnghei yuht làih yuht gōnjehng, wàahngíng yuht làih yuht syūfuhk, sihkyīnge yàhn maahnmáan jaahpgwaanjó m̀hái gūngguhng chèuhngsó sihkyīn, sóyáuh síhmàhn dōu jīchìh nīgo góibin.

8.2 Additional vocabulary 附加詞彙

Number	Word	Yale Romanization	POS	English
1	死亡	séimòhng	N/V	death; to die
2	疾病	jahtbehng	N	disease, sickness
3	佔	jim	V	to occupy; to make up, to account for
4	煙草	yīnchóu	N	tobacco, bacco, baccy
5	生產	sāngcháan	V/N	to produce; manufacture
6	消費	sīufai	V/N	to consume, to expend, to use; comsumption, expense
7	成年人	sìhngnìhn yàhn	N	adult, grown-up
8	損失	syúnsāt	V/N	to lose, to suffer loss; loss, damage
9	醫療	yīlìuh	N	medical treatment
10	貧窮	pàhnkùhng	Adj	poor, needy, impoverished
11	貢獻	gunghin	V/N	to contribute, to dedicate, to devote; contribution
12	稅	seui	N	tax, duty
13	超過	chīugwo	V	to exceed, to surpass, to overtake

8.3 Please answer the following T/F questions after reading the additional text:

1 Jeuigahn yātfahn bougou wah sihkyīn deui yàhnge gihnhōng tùhng gīngjai faatjín dōu yáuhhoih. (T/F)

2 Sihkyīnge yàhn 80% dōu yáuh behng. (T/F)

3 Jūnggwok haih saigaaiseuhng sāngcháan tùhng sīufai yīnchóu jeuidōge gwokgā. (T/F)

4 Hái Jūnggwok, sihkyīn ge sìhngnìhn yàhn síugwo baakfahn jī sāamsahp. (T/F)

5 Yùhgwó yáuh yàhn yānwaih sihkyīn behngjó, chèuihjó gātìhng hónàhng bindāk pàhnkùhng, gūngsī tùhng jínggo séhwúi dōu wúih sauh yínghéung. (T/F)

6 Yīnchóu hòhngyihp móuh waih gwokgā jokchēut gunghin. (T/F)

7 Yīnchóu yihp jouhsìhngge syúnsāt béi gunghin daaih hóudō. (T/F)

8　Hái Jūnggwok daaih bouhfahn sìhngsíh, jeuigahn sīnji hōichí gamyīn. (T/F)

9　Hái Jūnggwok, tòuhsyū gún m̀hóyíh sihkyīn, daahnnhaih daaihhohk hóyíh. (T/F)

10　Fēi kāpyīnjé jūngyi gamyīn, daahnnhaih sihkyīnge yàhn juhng m̀jaahpgwaan. (T/F)

8.4　Topics for discussions

1　Néih gokdāk sihkyīn deui goyàhn, gātìhng tùhng séhwúi yáuh mātyéh yínghéung nē?

2　Yīnchóu yihp deui gwokgāge gīngjai yáuh gunghin, daahnnhaih dōu jouhsìhng hóudaaihge syúnsāt, chéng néih góngháh néih deui yīnchóuyihp ge táifaat.

3　Néih gokdāk bīndī gūngguhng chèuhngsó yīnggōi gamyīn? Bīndī deihfōng m̀sái gamyīn? Dímgáai nē?

8.5　Authentic oral data 1　🔊
真實語料 1

8.6　Authentic oral data 2　🔊
真實語料 2

Lesson 5 Education in Hong Kong
香港教育

1. Pragmatic factors, Yuti features and linguistic functions
語用因素、語體特徵與語言功能

Yúhyuhng yānsou, yúhtái dahkjīng yúh yúhyìhn gūngnàhng

語用因素 / 語體特徵 Pragmatic factors/ Yuti features	語言功能 Linguistic function
Pragmatic factors: A typical scenario for a formal situation in which the speaker should pay attention to their use of words according to the status of the audience. 語用因素： 正式場合，説話者會用到表示禮貌的語言，也會用到一些客氣話和場面話。 Yuti features: Formality index: 1-2 語體特徵：1-2 級之間	**Linguistic function:** Introduction When introducing something, strike the balance between a general description and a detailed exploration of important characteristics such that you give the reader a comprehensive general impression of the subject while also explaining its prominent features in sufficient depth. 語言功能：介紹 介紹某一事物時，在概括和重點之間掌握平衡，既全面介紹又突出重點。

Notes on pragmatic knowledge 語用知識	Notes on structure 語言及篇章結構知識
I. Yuti and opening 語體與開場 　1. Honorable leaders and guests 　　「各位領導，各位嘉賓」 II. Related knowledge 相關知識 　1. I'm honoured「(我) 好榮幸」 　2. Due to the limitation of time 　　「由於時間關係」 　3. My introduction will stop here 　　「我嘅介紹到此結束」 　4. Thank you all「多謝大家」 　5. Two written languages and three spoken 　　forms「兩文三語」	I. Grammar and sentence patterns 語法和句型 　1. "…. yauh hóu, … yauh hóu" 　2. "waihjó……" in order to; for; for the sake of 　3. Using "só+V+ge" to form one kind of 　　nominal construction 　4. Emphasizing a negation with "bihng" 　5. "m̀hóu … jyuh" and "m̀ … jyuh " 　6. "yàuhyū……ge gwāanhaih" because of; due 　　to 　7. Making "-ize" and "-ify" verbs with "-fa" 　8. More about manner of action 　9. "Adj.jó dī" 　10. "yáuh gam … dāk gam…" II. Paragraph and discourse 語段和篇章 　1. "…yáuh…, kèihjūng…,kèihtā……" there 　　is…, among (which)…, and the other… 　2. "chùhng…héi/hōichí, …, (yìhnhauh)…, 　　gānjyuh…, (jeuihauh)…" to begin 　　with…(then)…, next…, in the end…

2. Text 🔊

課文 Fomàhn

局長先生、各位業界嘅朋友、各位來賓，大家好。	Guhkjéung sīnsāang, gokwái yihpgaai ge pàhngyáuh, gokwái lòihbān, daaihgā hóu.

我係來自教育界嘅陸小慧。我好榮幸有呢個機會喺呢度介紹一下香港嘅教育。香港嘅教育主要由教育局嚟到管理。可以分為幾個部分。第一個部分係學前教育。通常就係三歲至到六歲期間。學前教育有幼兒園同幼稚園，其中有私人機構，其他亦都有一啲非牟利機構嚟到去開辦。係私人機構開辦嘅又好，非牟利機構開辦嘅又好，每一個家庭都可以按照自己嘅需要嚟到去選擇幼稚園。跟住落嚟就係十二年免費教育。小學一年級至到六年級，跟住就係初中，中一至到中三，跟住就係中四至到中六高中嘅課程。喺高中階段 DSE 呢個英文字就象徵住高中學生嘅生活。呢個時期就係為咗呢個考試每日嘅樣努力，希望可以入到自己所喜愛嘅大學。如果 DSE 嘅成績理想，就可以進入專上課程嘅階段。專上課程當然有香港八大所提供嘅學士學位課程啦。但係如果成績並唔係太好，就要選擇一啲其他嘅課程喇。譬如係副學士或者係高級文憑課程等等。讀完專上學位，如果唔想工作住，想繼續深造，香港嘅大學都提供優質嘅研究生課程俾想繼續進修嘅學生選讀。從學前教育開始，然後到小學教育，跟住中學教育，最後到專上教育，政府都提供唔少嘅資助。香港嘅教育其實喺世界嚟講，水平都係十分之穩定。包括香港大學畢業生嘅英語水平，同埋小學生嘅識字量同閱讀能力，其實都係排喺世界嘅首位。相信香港嘅教育發展落去係有一個光明嘅前途。

Ngóh haih lòihjih gaauyuhk gaai ge Luhk Síu Waih. Ngóh hóu wìhnghahng yáuh nīgo gēiwuih hái nīdouh gaaisiuh yātháh Hēunggóngge gaauyuhk. Hēunggóngge gaauyuhk jyúyiu yàuh gaauyuhkguhk làihdou gúnléih. Hóyíh fānwàih géigo bouhfahn. Daih yātgo bouhfahn haih hohkchìhn gaauyuhk. Tūngsèuhng jauhhaih sāam seui jidou luhk seui kèihgāan. Hohkchìhn gaauyuhk yáuh yauyìhyún tùhng yaujihyún, kèihjūng yáuh sīyàhn gēikau, kèihtā yihkdōu yáuh yātdī fēi màuhleih gēikau làihdou heui hōibaahn. Haih sīyàhn gēikau hōibaahn ge yauh hóu, fēi màuhleih gēikau hōibaahnge yauh hóu, múih yātgo gātìhng dōu hóyíh onjiu jihgéige sēuiyiu làihdou heui syúnjaahk yaujihyún. Gānjyuh lohklàih jauhhaih sahpyih nìhn míhnfai gaauyuhk. Síuhohk yāt nìhnkāp jidou luhk nìhnkāp, gānjyuh jauhhaih chōjūng, jūngyāt jidou jūngsāam, gānjyuh jauhhaih jūngsei jidou jūngluhk gōujūngge fochìhng. Hái gōujūng gāaidyuhn DSE nīgo Yīngmàhn jih jauh jeuhngjīngjyuh gōujūng hohksāangge sāngwuht. Nīgo sìhkèih jauhhaih waihjó nīgo háusíh múihyaht gámyéung nóuhlihk, hēimohng hóyíh yahpdóu jihgéi só héingoi ge daaihhohk. Yùhgwó DSE ge sìhngjīk léihséung, jauh hóyíh jeunyahp jyūnseuhng fochìhngge gāaidyuhn. Jyūnseuhng fochìhng dōngyìhn yáuh Hēunggóng baat daaih só tàihgūng ge hohksih hohkwái fochìhng lā. Daahnhaih yùhgwó sìhngjīk bihng m̀haih taai hóu, jauh yiu syúnjaahk yātdī kèihtā ge fochìhng la. Peiyùh haih fu hohksih waahkjé haih gōukāp màhnpàhng fochìhng dángdáng. Duhkyùhn jyūnseuhng hohkwái, yùhgwó m̀séung gūngjok jyuh, séung gaijuhk sāmchou, Hēunggóngge daaihhohk dōu tàihgūng yāujāt ge yìhngau sāng fochìhng béi séung gaijuhk jeunsāuge hohksāang syúnduhk. Chùhng hohkchìhn gaauyuhk hōichí, yìhnhauh dou síuhohk gaauyuhk, gānjyuh jūnghohk gaauyuhk, jeuihauh dou jyūnseuhng gaauyuhk, jingfú dōu tàihgūng m̀síu ge jījoh. Hēunggóngge gaauyuhk kèihsaht hái saigaai làihgóng, séuipìhng dōu haih sahpfānjī wándihng, bāaukut Hēunggóng daaihhohk bātyihpsāng ge Yīngyúh séuipìhng, tùhngmàaih síuhohksāang ge sīkjihleuhng tùhng yuhtduhk nàhnglihk, kèihsaht dōu haih pàaih hái saigaai ge sáuwaih. Sēungseun Hēunggóngge gaauyuhk faatjín lohkheui haih yáuh yātgo gwōngmìhngge chìhntòuh.

每日我哋喺街上面行，除咗睇到匆匆忙忙嘅香港人之外，仲有來自唔同國家嘅遊客，但係我哋可能唔係每日都睇到喺香港讀書嘅留學生。其實每年嚟香港留學嘅學生有超過三萬，香港嘅學校喺世界上有非常好嘅聲譽。我哋有先進嘅設備，由於香港好多大學都希望培養學生有國際化嘅視野嘅關係，加上政府好重視對教育嘅投資，我哋可以從世界唔同地方請到優秀嘅老師。另外，香港係世界上最安全嘅城市之一，呢度嘅生活質素比較高，大學裏面環境優美，城市公共交通方便。有啲留學生因為喺呢度讀書而愛上香港，畢業之後仲留喺香港，成為香港社會嘅一份子。

Múihyaht ngóhdeih hái gāai seuhngmihn hàahng, chèuihjó táidóu chūngchūngmòhngmòhngge Hēunggóng yàhn jīngoih, juhngyáuh lòihjih m̀tùhng gwokgāge yàuhhaak, daahnhaih ngóhdeih hónàhng m̀haih múihyaht dōu táidóu hái Hēunggóng duhksyūge làuhhohksāang. Kèihsaht múihnìhn làih Hēunggóng làuhhohkge hohksāang yáuh chīugwo sāam maahn, Hēunggóngge hohkhaauh hái saigaai seuhng yáuh fēisèuhng hóuge sīngyuh. Ngóhdeih yáuh sīnjeunge chitbeih, yàuhhyū Hēunggóng hóudō daaihhohk dōu hēimohng pùihyéuhng hohksāang yáuh gwokjaifa ge sihyéh ge gwāanhaih, gāséuhng jingfú hóu juhngsih deui gaauyuhkge tàuhjī, ngóhdeih hóyíh chùhng saigaai m̀tùhng deihfōng chéngdóu yāusauge lóuhsī. Lihngngoih, Hēunggóng haih saigaai seuhng jeui ōnchyùhnge sìhngsíh jīyāt, nīdouhge sāngwuht jātsou béigaau gōu, daaihhohk léuihmihn wàahngíng yāuméih, sìhngsíh gūngguhng gāautūng fōngbihn. Yáuhdī làuhhohksāang yānwaih hái nīdouh duhksyū yìh ngoiséuhng Hēunggóng, bātyihp jīhauh juhng làuhhái Hēunggóng, sìhngwàih Hēunggóng séhwúi ge yāt fahnjí.

由於時間關係，我好快咁介紹咗香港嘅教育。我嘅介紹到此結束。我相信香港作為一個擁有多元文化嘅國際城市，香港嘅教育環境可以培養出兩文三語嘅國際級人才。我哋歡迎所有人士嚟香港享受高質素嘅教育。

Yàuhhyū sihgaan gwāanhaih, ngóh hóu faai gám gaaisiuhjó Hēunggóngge gaauyuhk. Ngóhge gaaisiuh douchí gitchūk. Ngóh sēungseun Hēunggóng jokwàih yātgo yúngyáuh dōyùhn màhnfage gwokjai sìhngsíh, Hēunggóngge gaauyuhk wàahngíng hóyíh pùihyéuhng chēut léuhngmàhn sāamyúh ge gwokjaikāp yàhnchòih. Ngóhdeih fūnyìhng sóyáuh yàhnsih làih Hēunggóng héungsauh gōujātsouge gaauyuhk.

多謝各位。

Dōjeh gokwái.

3. Vocabulary in use 🔊

活用詞彙 Wuhtyuhng chìhwuih

3.1 Common vocabulary

Number	Word	Yale Romanization	POS	English
1	管理	gúnléih	N/V	management; to manage
2	部分	bouhfahn	N	part
3	通常	tūngsèuhng	Adv	usually, ordinarily
4	開辦	hōibaahn	V	to set up
5	課程	fochìhng	N	course, curriculum
6	階段	gāaidyuhn	N	stage
7	象徵	jeuhngjīng	N/V	symbol; to symbolize
8	努力	nóuhlihk	V	to strive, to make an effort
9	喜愛	héingoi	V	to be fond of
10	理想	léihséung	Adj/N	ideal
11	提供	tàihgūng	V	to provide
12	成績	sìhngjīk	N	achievement, academic result
13	深造	sāmchou	V	to pursue advanced studies
14	優質	yāujāt	Att	high-quality; of high quality
15	進修	jeunsāu	V	to pursue further studies
16	資助	jījoh	N/V	subsidy; to subsidize
17	水平	séuipìhng	N	level, standard
18	穩定	wándihng	Adj	stable
19	畢業生	bātyihpsāng	N	graduate
20	光明	gwōngmìhng	Adj	bright
21	前途	chìhntòuh	N	prospects
22	匆匆忙忙	chūngchūngmòhngmòhng	PH	in a hurry

23	留學生	làuhhohksāang	N	overseas student; student studying abroad
24	超過	chīugwo	V	to exceed, to surpass
25	聲譽	sīngyuh	N	reputation
26	先進	sīnjeun	Adj	advanced (for equipment, technology, etc.)
27	培養	pùihyéuhng	V	to cultivate
28	國際化	gwokjaifa	PH	internationalization; internationalized
29	視野	sihyéh	N	field of vision
30	關係	gwāanhaih	N	relations; relationship
31	重視	juhngsih	V	to attach importance to
32	優秀	yāusau	Adj	outstanding, excellent
33	一份子	yātfahnjí	PH	a member of, a part of
34	由於	yàuhyū	Adv	due to
35	享受	héungsauh	N/V	enjoyment; to enjoy
36	高質素	gōu jātsou	PH	high-quality, of high quality

3.2 Proper nouns

| 1 | 陸小慧 | Luhk Síu-waih | PN | Luk Siu-wai |
| 2 | 教育局 | Gaauyuhk Guhk | PN | Education Bureau |

3.3 About education (gaauyuhk 教育)

1	教育界	gaauyuhk gaai	N	education sector
2	學前教育	hohk chìhn gaauyuhk	N	pre-primary education
3	免費教育	míhnfai gaauyuhk	N	free education
4	私人機構	sīyàhn gēikau	N	private organization

5	非牟利機構	fēi màuhleih gēikau	N	non-profit-making organisation
6	幼兒園	yauyìhyún	N	nursery
7	幼稚園	yaujihyún	N	kindergarten
8	高中	gōujūng	Att/N	senior secondary
9	專上課程	jyūnseuhng fochìhng	N	post-secondary programme
10	八大	baat daaih	PH	the eight major universities in Hong Kong
11	學士學位	hohksih hohkwái	PN	Bachelor's Degree
12	副學士	fu hohksih	PN	Associate Degree
13	高級文憑	gōukāp màhnpàhng	PN	Higher Diploma
14	研究生課程	yìhngausāng fochìhng	N	postgraduate programme
15	選讀	syúnduhk	V	to choose to study (e.g. courses, curriculum)
16	識字量	sīkjihleuhng	N	repertoire of words (number of words that one knows)
17	閱讀能力	yuhtduhk nàhnglihk	N	reading literacy
18	兩文三語	léuhngmàhn sāamyúh	PH	biliteracy and trilingualism

3.4 Other vocabularies

1	投資	tàuhjī	N/V	investment; to invest
2	環境優美	wàahngíng yāuméih	PH	the environment is beautiful
3	公共交通	gūngguhng gāautūng	N	public transport
4	方便	fōngbihn	Adj/V	convenient; to make things easy

3.5 Useful expressions

| 1 | 首位 | sáuwaih | PH | to be in the first place |
| 2 | 發展落去 | faatjín lohkheui | PH | keep on developing |

3	由於時間關係	yàuhyū sìhgaan gwāanhaih	PH	due to time constraints
4	到此結束	dou chí gitchūk	PH	that's the end (of …)
5	多元文化	dōyùhn màhnfa	PH	multi-culturalism
6	國際級人才	gwokjai kāp yàhnchòih	N	talented people at international level

4. Notes on language and discourse structure

語言及篇章結構知識 Yúhyìhn kahp pīnjēung gitkau jīsīk

4.1. Grammar and sentence patterns 語法和句型

4.1.1. …yauh hóu, …yauh hóu

This pattern means 'either……or…..'. "Mòuhleuhn" can be used here.

1. Néih heui Bākgīng yauh hóu, heui Seuhnghói yauh hóu, dōu hóyíh hohkdóu Póutūngwá ge.
2. (Mòuhleuhn) hàahnglouh yauh hóu, jouh gāmouh yauh hóu, dōu haih hóu ge wahnduhng.
3. (Mòuhleuhn) yàuhséui yauh hóu, tiumóuh yauh hóu, dōu hóyíh gáam fèih.
4. Waahkwá yauh hóu, tàahn gittā yauh hóu, dōu haih hóu hóu ge yùhlohk sīuhín.
5. Chēutgāai sihkfaahn yauh hóu, jihgéi hái ngūkkéi jyúfaahn sihk yauh hóu, ngóh dōu móuh māt sówaih.
6. Kéuih tēngdóu yauh hóu, tēng m̀dóu yauh hóu, ngóhdeih dōu m̀hóu joi giu kéuih.

4.1.2. "waihjó…" in order to; for; for the sake of

1. Waihjó pùihyéuhng (nurture) hohksāang ge yuhtduhk tùhng sīháau nàhnglihk, ngóhdeih sēuiyiu dímyéungge daaihhohk nē?
2. Wàihjó sihk hóusihkge yéh, ngóhdeih dángjó chām̀dō yātgo jūngtàuh.
3. Waihjó hái gwokjaifage wàahngíng duhksyū, m̀síu hohksāang làih Hēunggóng duhk daaihhohk.

4.1.3. Using "só+V+ge" to form one kind of nominal construction

1. Hēunggóng jēung yaujihyún tùhng yāuyìh jūngsām só tàihgūng ge fuhkmouh giujouh "hohkchìhn fuhkmouh".

2. Ngóh jēung hái Hēunggóng só táiyihm dóu ge dōu fong hái Facebook seuhngmihn. Néih dākhàahn hóyíh táiháh.

3. Múihgo hohkhaauh só jēuikàuh ge dōu haih hohkseuht jihyàuh (academic freedom) tùhng yāujāt (excellent) gaauyuhk.

4.1.4. Emphasizing a negation with "bihng"

"bihng" is often used when expressing disagreement, or pointing out a flaw in someone's argument.

1. Jānjing yínghéung ngóhdeihge, yáuhsìh bihng m̀haih máuhdī (certain) hàhngwàih (behavior) tùhng sihgín (incident), yìhhaih hàhngwàih tùhng sihgín só doihbíuge yiyih (meaning).

2. Gógo síupàhngyáuh hohkjó sahpnìhn gongkàhm, kèihsaht kéuih bihng m̀jūngyi gongkàhm, dōu haih Bàhbā Màhmā yiu kéuih hohkge.

3. Ngóh hái daaihhohk duhk gīngjai, daahnhaih jouh gīngjai fōngmihnge gūngjok bihng m̀haih ngóhge léihséung.

4.1.5. Action temporarily suspended

- m̀hóu… jyuh

The pattern means 'don't do it now', e.g.:
Ngóhdeih m̀hóu góng jyuh, heui gūnghéi sānnéung sīn.

1. Ngóhdeih m̀hóu sihk jyuh, dáng sóyáuh ge haakyàhn làihsaai sīn.
2. Néih m̀hóu jáu jyuh, néih juhng meih jouhyùhn dī yéh.
3. Néih m̀hóu yahplàih jyuh, kéuih juhng meih wuhnhóu sāam.
4. Néih m̀hóu nāu jyuh, ngóh chèuihbín mahnháh jē.

- m̀…jyuh

The pattern means 'not now', e.g.:
Nīdī yéh m̀hóyíh sihk jyuh, yānwaih juhng meih suhk.
(We can't eat it now, because it's not yet done/cooked.)

1. Kéuih m̀séung gitfān jyuh, kéuih yiu wán dōdī chín sīn.

2. Nīdī yéh ngóh m̀yuhng jyuh, néih lóheui yuhng lā.

3. Ngóh daai m̀gau chín, sóyíh yìhgā m̀máaih jyuh, tīngyaht sīnji máaih.

4. Ngóh gāmyaht taai mòhng, sóyíh m̀làih jyuh.

4.1.6. " yàuhyū…(ge) gwāanhaih" because of; due to

1. Yàuhyū sìhgaan gwāanhaih, ngóh jí hóyíh gaaisiuh juhngdím.

2. Yàuhyū sìhgaan gwāanhaih, ngóhdeih gāmyaht jíhaih tóuleuhn chìhnmihn sāamgo mahntàih.

3. Yàuhyū hohkfaige gwāanhaih, ngóhdeih kyutdihng m̀sung síupàhngyáuh heui gwokjai hohkhaauh.

4.1.7. Making "-ize" and "-ify" verbs with "-fa"

You can take some Chinese nouns and adjectives and add a "-fa" to the end of them to make "-ize" or "-ify" them

1. Dímyéung sahtyihn (realize) hohkseuht jihyàuh tùhng dōyùhnfa nē?

2. Hēunggóng haih yātgo sēungdōng gwokjaifage sìhngsíh, chùhng màhnfa tùhng yàhnmàhn sāngwuht seuhng dōu hóyíh táidóu.

3. Hēunggóng yàhn yáuhdī fōngmihn hóu sāifa, yáuhdī fōngmihn hóu jūnggwokfa.

4.1.8. More about manner of action

- Adv.(gám) V

1. Kéuih yáuh hóudō sìhgaan, sóyíh kéuih maahnmáan (gám) sihk.
    (He's got much time, so he eats leisurely/slowly.)

2. Kéuih seiwàih(gám) táiháh.

3. Ngóh chèuihbín(gám) mahnháh jē, néih m̀hóu nāu.

4. Ngóh síusām(gám) hàahng, yùhgwó m̀haih (otherwise), yáuh ngàihhím.

- 'Gám' can also be omitted in a request or command, e.g.:

1. M̀gōi néih daaihsēng góng.
    (Please speak up/loudly.)

2. M̀hóu chèuihbín ló yàhn ge yéh.

3. Sunghaak ge sìhhauh, ngóhdeih wúih deui pàhngyáuh góng, "síusām, maahnmáan hàahng."

4. Néih yiu síusām táiháh yáuh móuh m̀ngāam.

- hóu Adj. gám V

This pattern is translated into an adverb, i.e. Adj.-ly, in English.

1. Kéuih hóu hōisām gám wahbéi ngóhdeih tēng, "ngóh gitfān la!"
2. Kéuih hóu nāu gám jáujó chēutheui.
3. Ngóh hóu faai gám jouhyùhn gūngfo jauh heui fangaau.
4. Ngóh hóu daaihsēng gám giu kéuih, kéuih dōu tēng m̀dóu.

- V-Adj.-dī-(O)-lā !

Request involving manner of action.
The comparison degree of an adjective is used here.

1. Sihk dōdī lā.
2. Hàahng faaidī lā.
3. Néih góngdāk taai faai, ngóh tēng m̀dóu, góng maahndī lā.
4. Néih séung gáamfèih, jauh yiu sihk síudī yéh, jouh dōdī wahnduhng.
5. Néih hàahng káhndī jauh wúih táidóu la.

- V dō/síu Nu-M-(N)

For 'dō' or 'síu', a NU-M-N can take the place of 'dī' to denote an exact amount of the thing mentioned, e.g.:

1. Daaihgā yám dō (yāt) būi.
2. Sihk dō (yāt) gihn béng lā.
3. Duhk yātchi m̀sīk, duhk dō géi chi jauh sīk ge la.
4. Néih yātyaht sihk sei chāan gam dō, gánghaih fèih lā, sihk síu léuhng chāan jauh wúih sau ge la.
5. Nīgo yuht fāan síu sāam yaht gūng, sóyíh yàhngūng síudī.

4.1.9. "Adj. jó dī" to mean 'a little too'
1. Dī sung hàahmjó dī.
2. Kéuih go yéung géi leng, daahnhaih fèihjó dī.
3. Nītou sāijōng ge ngàahnsīk sāmjó dī.
4. Yātgo fosāt hóyíh chóh sahpgo yàhn, chóh sahpyihgo yàhn jauh bīkjó dī.

4.1.10. yáuh gam Adj. dāk gam Adj.

This pattern means 'as Adj. as possible', e.g.:

Ngóh yāt fongjó gūng jauh yáuh gam faai dāk gam faai fāan ngūkkéi wuhnsāam heui jáulàuh.

1. Màhmā wah, "Néihdī gūngfo yiu jouhdāk yáuh gam hóu dāk gam hóu sīnji hóyíh chēutheui wáan."

2. Kéuih lèih ngóh hóu yúhn, sóyíh ngóh yáuh gam daaihsēng dāk gam daaihsēng giu kéuih.

3. Nīdī sung taai hóusihk, ngóh yiu sihk dōdī, yáuh gam dō dāk gam dō.

4. Nīdī yéh móuh māt yàhn máaih, ngóhdeih yiu maaihdāk yáuh gam pèhng dāk gam pèhng sīnji dāk.

5. Kéuih yāt fongga jauh heui léuihhàhng, heui dāk yáuh gam yúhn dāk gam yúhn.

6. Nīgo hohksāang hóu gwāai, dī jih sédāk yáuh gam leng dāk gam leng.

7. Dī hóisīn yiu jyúdāk yáuh gam suhk dāk gam suhk sīnji hóu sihk.

4.2. Paragraph and discourse 語段和篇章

4.2.1. "…yáuh…, kèihjūng…, kèihtā …" there is…, among (which)…, and the other…

1. Hēunggóng yáuh sahpgéi gāan daaihjyūn yúnhaauh (tertiary institutions), kèihjūng baatgāan haih jingfú jījohge, kèihtā haih sīlahpge.

2. Ngóhdeih bāan yáuh sahpluhk go hohksāang, kèihjūng chātgo haih Yahtbún yàhn, kèihtā tùhnghohk haih hái Hòhngwok, Yandouh, Méihgwok làihge.

3. Jūngmàhn daaihhohk yáuh gáugo syūyún, kèihjūng seigo lihksí béigaau chèuhng, kèihtā dōu haih hōijó móuh géi noih.

4.2.2 "chùhng…héi /hōichí…, (yìhnhauh)…, gānjyuh…, (jeuihauh)…" to begin with…(then)…, next…, in the end…

1. Gaaisiuh Hēunggóngge gaauyuhk, ngóh wúih chùhng hohkchìhn gaauyuhk gónghéi, gānjyuh jauhhaih síuhohk tùhng jūnghohk…

2. Ngóh múihyaht duhksyū dōu haih chùhng fomàhn duhkhéi, jīhauh wānjaahp sāangjih, gānjyuh haih yúhfaat, jeuihauh haih jouh gusih.

3. Tùhng Jūnggwokyàhn kīnggái, hóyíh chùhng hēunghá (hometown) gónghéi, góngháh yáuh mātyéh hóusihk, yáuh mātyéh hóuwáan, gānjyuh hóyíh góngháh gāyàhn lā, gūngjok lā, jeuihauh maahnmáan jauh wúih yuht kīng yuht dō.

5. Notes on pragmatic knowledge

語用因素與相關知識 Yúhyuhng yānsou yúh sēunggwāan jīsīk

5.1. Yuti and opening 語體與開場

5.1.1. "各位領導 gokwái líhngdouh，各位嘉賓 gokwái gābān" honorable leaders and guests

In a formal situation where participants include officials and invited guests, it is polite, and very important in terms of pragmatic ability, to start your speech with greetings to the leaders and guests. What we have here is a general term for the officials (領導 líhngdouh), but in really formal situations, the leaders and guests are often acknowledged with their official titles, starting from the one with the highest rank or status.

Gokwái líhngdouh, gokwái gābān…

Gokwái lóuhsī, gokwái tùhnghohk, ngóh doihbíu…

5.2. Related knowledge 相關知識

5.2.1. " (我) 好榮幸 (Ngóh) hóu wìhnghahng" I'm honoured

Similar to politeness strategies found in formal situations, the speaker would use words of this kind to indicate the humbleness as a speaker, thus giving honor to the audience, the sponsor, the situation, or to all.

Ngóh gāmyaht hóu wìhnghahng doihbíu Hēunggóng gaauyuhkgaai waih daaihgā gaaisiuh Hēunggóngge gaauyuhk.

Ngóh hóyíh hái nīdouh doihbíu bātyihpsāng faatyìhn, haih ngóhge wìhnghahng.

5.2.2. " 由於時間關係 yàuhyū sìhgaan gwāanhaih" due to the limitation of time

This is perhaps true but you often hear it even if it is not. In addition to the lack of time, the speaker can also refer to the lack of his/her own knowledge, expertise, etc.

Yàuhyū sìhgaan gwāanhaih, ngóh gaaisiuhge juhngdím haih…

5.2.3. " 我嘅介紹到此結束 ngóhge gaaisiuh douchí gitchūk" My introduction will stop here

A good speaker will always lead the audience to make sure they are not lost. Saying the obvious (telling them you have finished when you finish) is one way of doing things in a formal situaiton like this.

Ngóhge gaaisiuh douchí yùhnbāt (end).

Ngóh gāmyahtge faatyìhn jauh dou nīdouh,…

5.2.4. "多謝大家 dōjeh daaihgā" Thank you all

Expressing thanks at the end is polite and often expected for someone who is invited to speak.

Dōjeh daaihgā !

Dōjeh gokwáige gwāanjyu !

5.2.5. "兩文三語 léuhngmàhn sāamyúh" two written languages and three spoken forms

Both English and Chinese have official status according to the language policy of Hong Kong after 1997. While each language has the written and spoken form, Chinese in Hong Kong officially has two spoken codes, Cantonese and Putonghua.

"Léuhngmàhn sāamyúh" haih Hēunggóngge yúhyìhn jingchaak.

Ngóhdeih hēimohng hóyíh pùihyéuhng hohksāang léuhngmàhn sāamyúhge nàhnglihk.

6. Contextualized speaking practice

情境説話練習 Chìhnggíng syutwah lihnjaahp

【課前預習】Class preparation

6.1. Please answer the following True/False questions according to the lesson text.

1. Hēunggóngge gaauyuhk jyúyiu yàuh Gaauyuhk Guhk làih gúnléih. (T/F)
2. Hohkchìhn gaauyuhk jíhaih bāaukut yauyìhyún. (T/F)
3. Yauyìhyún tùhng yaujihyún jíhaih yàuh fēi màuhleih gēikau làih hōibaahn. (T/F)
4. Hēunggóng yáuh gáu nìhn míhnfai gaauyuhk, jí ge haih síuhohk yātnìhn kāp ji luhk nìhnkāp tùhng chō jūng fochìhng. (T/F)
5. Hēunggóng yáuh baat gāan daaihhohk tàihgūng hohksih hohkwái fochìhng. (T/F)
6. Hēunggóngge gaauyuhk kèihsaht hái saigaai làihgóng, séuipìhng haih sahpfān wándihngge. (T/F)

7. Hēunggóng síuhohksāangge sīkjihleuhng tùhng yuhtduhk nàhnglihk, pàaih hái saigaai daihsāam waih. (T/F)

8. Múih nìhn làih Hēunggóng làuhhohkge hohksāang chīugwo ńgh maahn. (T/F)

9. Hēunggóngge hohkhaauh hái saigaaiseuhng yáuh fēisèuhng hóuge sīngyuh, yānwaih ngóhdeih yáuh sīnjeunge chitbeih, daaihhohk tùhng jingfú hóu juhngsih deui gaauyuhkge tàuhjī.(T/F)

10. Daaih bouhfahn làuhhohksāang yānwaih hái nīdouh duhksyū yìh ngoiséuhng Hēunggóng, bātyihp jīhauh juhng làuh hái Hēunggóng. (T/F)

6.2 Please explain the following phrases in Cantonese

1 非牟利機構 fēimàuhleih gēikau
2 兩文三語 léuhngmàhn sāamyúh
3 私立學校 sīlahp hohkhaauh
4 多元文化 dōyùhn màhnfa

【課後練習】 Post-class exercises

6.3 Fill in the blanks with the given vocabularies. Each vocabulary can be chosen once only.

fochìhng	sìhngjīk	sīngyuh	jeunsāu
wándihng	chìhntòuh	séuipìhng	pùihyéuhng
héungsauh	tàihgūng	jījoh	nóuhlihk

1. Yìhgā hóudō yàhn yiu yātmihn gūngjok, yātmihn _____.

2. Fuh móuh yiu bōng jáinéui _____ hóu ge jaahpgwaan, laihyùh jéunsìh jouhhóu gūngfo, jóu seuih jóu héi dáng dáng.

3. Hái Hēunggóng, hóudō daaihjyūn yúnhaauh dōu hōibaahn m̀tùhng leuihyìhng ge _____ béi joihjīk yàhnsih (working people) bouduhk.

4. Kéuih jeuigahn jyunjó gūng, sān gūng ge sāuyahp tùhng gūngjok sìhgaan dōu hóu _____.

5. Sóyáuh gūngsī dōu yīnggōi waih yùhngūng (staff) _____ léihséung ge gūngjok wàahngíng.

6. Ngóh hóu _____ yìhgā ge sāngwuht, gei jihyàuh yauh séyi.

7. Hái Hēunggóng, hóudō gātìhng ge sāuyahp _____ m̀gōu, ngóh yihngwàih jingfú yīnggōi _____ kéuihdeih.

8. Sēuiyìhn kéuih pìhngsìh hóu _____ duhksyū, daahnhaih hái gāmchi háausi dōu háau m̀dóu hóu ge _____.

9. Nīgāan hohkhaauh ge lihksí yàuhgáu (long history), _____ lèuhnghóu (good), waihjó jáinéui ge _____, hóu dō fuhmóuh dōu jāangjyuh bōng jáinéui bouméng yahpduhk.

6.4 Fill in the blanks with the given words with "-fa". Each word can be chosen once only.

gwokjaifa   dihnnóuhfa   yihndoihfa

luhkfa   yúhnfa   méihfa   okfa/ngokfa

1. Waihjó _____ wàahngíng, jingfú dásyun hái m̀tùhng ge deihfōng jung (to plant) dōdī jihkmaht (plants).

2. Yìhgā hóu dō gūngsī jouh mātyéh dōu _____, yùhgwó néih m̀sīk yuhng dihnnóuh jauh wúih hóu màhfàahn.

3. Búnlòih kéuih haih baak fahn jī baak fáandeui ngóhdeih gámyéung jouh ge, sāumēi kéuih ge lahpchèuhng _____ jó.

4. Nījoh daaihhah ge chitgai sēungdōng _____, ngoihyìhng (appearance) hóu dahkbiht, tùhng yātbūn ge ginjūkmaht hóu m̀yātyeuhng.

5. Kéuih waahn ngàahmjing yíhlàih, sāntái yuht làih yuht chā, jeuigahn behngchìhng juhng jeun yāt bouh _____.

6. Waihjó pùihyéuhng jáinéui yáuh _____ ge sihyéh, hóudō fuhmóuh dōu wúih sung jáinéui heui ngoihgwok duhksyū.

7. Ngóh gokdāk nīchēut dihnsihkehk _____ jó kéuih ge yìhngjeuhng la, kéuih hái lihksí seuhng búnlòih dōu m̀haih hóu yàhn.

6.5 Complete the following sentences or answer the following questions using the given patterns.

1. ...... yauh hóu, ... yauh hóu

   _____, dōu haih hohk Gwóngdūngwá ge hóu baahnfaat.

2. waihjó ......

   A: Kéuih yíhgīng daaihhohk bātyihp la, dímgáai juhng yiu gaijuhk duhksyū a?

   B: Sēuiyìhn kéuih yíhgīng daaihhohk bātyihp la, daahnhaih _____.

3. N só V ge

   Ngóh m̀haih géi mìhngbaahk_____, néih hó m̀hóyíh joi góng yātchi a?

4. yíhwàih ……, kèihsaht bihng……

   Hóudō yàhn_____.

5. m̀hóu …… jyuh

   Néih _____, dáng bàhbā màhmā fāanjó làih sīn.

6. yàuhyū …… ge gwāanhaih

   _____, gāmchi ngóhdeih ge wuhtduhng yiu chéuisīu.

7. hóu Adj gám

   Kéuih _____ wah béi ngóhdeih jī kéuih hahgo yuht gitfān la!

8. yáuh gam …… dāk gam ……

   Ngóh yāt fonggūng jauh _____.

7. Listening and speaking 🔊

聽説練習 Tingsyut lihnjaahp

7.1. Listening comprehension exercise

Please listen to the recording and answer the following T/F questions:

1. Yíngóngge yàhn hái daaihhohk gūngjok, kéuih doihbíu gaauyuhkgaai faatyìhn. (T/F)
2. Hēunggóngge hohkchìhn gaauyuhk m̀bāaukut yauyìhyún. (T/F)
3. Hēunggóngge síuhohk tùhng jūnghohk hóyíh fānsìhng: gūnglahp, jījoh tùhng sīlahp sāam júng. (T/F)
4. Hēunggóng jingfúge gaauyuhk léihnihm haih tàihgūng dōyùhnfa hohkhaauh gaauyuhk. (T/F)
5. Hēunggóng hohksāang jíhaih hohk Gwóngdūngwá tùhng Póutūngwá. (T/F)
6. Hēunggóng yáuh baatgāan daaihhohk, dōu yàuh jingfú jījoh. (T/F)
7. Gaauyuhk Guhk fuhjaak gúnléih Hēunggóngge gaauyuhk. (T/F)
8. Hēunggóng gōudáng gaauyuhk ge màhnfa jeuhkjuhng hohkseuht jihyàuh tùhng dōyùhnfa. (T/F)
9. Hēunggóngge síuhohkge dahkdím haih gwokjaifa. (T/F)
10. Hēunggóng Jūngmàhn Daaihhohk ngoihjihk lóuhsī béilaih chīugwo 40%. (T/F)

7.2 Speech topics

1. Hēunggóng tùhng néih ge gwokgā ge gaauyuhk jaidouh (system) yáuh mātyéh yātyeuhng waahkjé m̀tùhng ge deihfōng a? Nī léuhnggo deihfōng ge gaauyuhk jaidouh yáuh mātyéh hóu, yáuh mātyéh m̀hóu nē?

2. Gātìhng gaauyuhk tùhng hohkhaauh gaauyuhk deui síupàhngyáuh ge sìhngjéung (growth) yáuh géi juhngyiu a? Néih yihngwàih deui síupàhngyáuh làih góng, gātìhng gaauyuhk dihnghaih hohkhaauh gaauyuhk juhngyiudī nē? Dímgáai a?

3. Néih haih yātgo fēimàuhleih gēikau ge doihbíu, chéng néih hái yātgo gājéung'wúi seuhng heung gājéung gaaisiuh néihdeih gēikau hōibaahn ge hohkhaauh tùhng fochìhng.

7.3 Speaking exercise: Please use at least 10 of the following vocabularies/patterns to say on the following topic in one to two minutes.

"Chéng néih béigaauháh Hēunggóng tùhng néih ge gwokgā ge hohkhaauh, fochìhng, hohksāang dángdáng."

tūngsèuhng	hōibaahn	gāaidyuhn	sìhngjīk
chìhntòuh	chīugwo	héungsauh	gwokjaifa
pùihyéuhng	yāusau	bātyihpsāng	waihjó ……
chūngchūngmòhngmòhng	yáuh gam …… dāk gam ……		
yàuhyū …… ge gwāanhaih	bihng ……		

8. Additional texts
附加課文 Fuhgā fomàhn

8.1 附加課文 Additional text

舊年有人調查咗全世界唔同國家八千幾個家庭，了解家長對教育嘅睇法。	Gauhnín yáuh yàhn diuhchàhjó chyùhn saigaai m̀tùhng gwokgā baat chīn géi go gātìhng, líuhgáai gājéung deui gaauyuhk ge táifaat.

結果發現：唔理係邊度嘅中國父母，佢哋對教育嘅睇法都有唔少相同嘅地方。香港家庭嘅平均教育費用係 132161 美元，係全世界排第一。臺灣（Tòihwāan, Taiwan）56424 美元，排第四，中國內地 42892 美元，係第五名。即係話，中國家長用喺小朋友教育上嘅錢差唔多係世界上最多嘅。

Gitgwó faatyihn: m̀léih haih bīndouhge Jūnggwok fuhmóuh, kéuihdeih deui gaauyuhkge táifaat dōu yáuh m̀síu sēungtùhngge deihfōng. Hēunggóng gātìhngge pìhnggwān gaauyuhk faiyuhng haih sahpsāam maahn yih chīn yāt baak luhksahp yāt méihyùhn, haih chyùhn saigaai pàaih daihyāt. Tòihwāan ńgh maahn luhk chīn sei baak yihsahp sei méihyùhn, pàaih daihsei, Jūnggwok noihdeih sei maahn yih chīn baat baak gáusahp yih méihyùhn, haih daihńgh mìhng. Jīkhaih wah, Jūnggwok gājéung yuhng hái síupàhngyáuh gaauyuhk seuhng ge chín chā m̀dō haih saigaai seuhng jeui dō ge.

因為中國家長對教育非常重視，所以名校嘅競爭非常激烈。特別係香港嘅國際學校，由於有國際化同多元文化嘅特色，受到國內外家長嘅信賴，因此成為好多家長追求嘅目標。

Yānwaih Jūnggwok gājéung deui gaauyuhk fēisèuhng juhngsih, sóyíh mìhnghaauhge gingjāng fēisèuhng gīkliht. Dahkbiht haih Hēunggóngge gwokjai hohkhaauh, yàuhyū yáuh gwokjaifa tùhng dōyùhn màhnfage dahksīk, sauhdou gwoknoihngoih gājéungge seunlaaih, yānchí sìhngwàih hóudō gājéung jēuikàuhge muhkbīu.

香港有超過 50 間國際學校，教學以英文為主，國際學校都有中文堂。每個國際學校都有好長嘅候選名單。好多名人、富商都將小朋友送入國際學校。除咗香港人同住喺香港嘅外國人之外，最近幾年，越嚟越多內地小朋友都入咗香港嘅國際學校讀書。

Hēunggóng yáuh chīugwo ńghsahp gāan gwokjai hohkhaauh, gaauhohk yíh Yīngmàhn wàihjyú, gwokjai hohkhaauh dōu yáuh Jūngmàhn tòhng. Múihgo gwokjai hohkhaauh dōu yáuh hóuchèuhngge hauhsyún mìhngdāan. Hóudō mìhngyàhn, fusēung dōu jēung síupàhngyáuh sungyahp gwokjai hohkhaauh. Chèuihjó Hēunggóng yàhn tùhng jyuhhái Hēunggóngge ngoihgwok yàhn jīngoih, jeuigahn géinìhn, yuht làih yuht dō noihdeih síupàhngyáuh dōu yahpjó Hēunggóngge gwokjai hohkhaauh duhksyū.

為咗令小朋友有更加好嘅將來，亞洲嘅有錢人用幾多錢喺仔女身上呢？

Waihjó lihng síupàhngyáuh yáuh ganggā hóuge jēunglòih, Ngajāuge yáuhchín yàhn yuhng géidō chín hái jáinéui sānseuhng nē?

喺香港，一間國際學校，每年學費大概係 17 萬港元，小學、中學 13 年讀完需要超過 200 萬港元。其他有名嘅國際學校情況都差唔多。	Hái Hēunggóng, yātgāan gwokjai hohkhaauh, múih nìhn hohkfai daaihkoi haih sahp chāt maahn góngyùhn, síuhohk, jūnghohk sahp sāam nìhn duhkyùhn sēuiyiu chīugwo yihbaak maahn góngyùhn. Kèihtā yáuhméng ge gwokjai hohkhaauh chìhngfong dōu chā m̀dō.
到咗讀大學嘅時候，要用幾多錢就要睇所選嘅專業同學校喇。除咗學費，仲有生活費、活動費、遊學費等等。	Doujó duhk daaihhohk ge sìhhauh, yiu yuhng géidō chín jauh yiu tái sósyúnge jyūnyihp tùhng hohkhaauh la. Chèuihjó hohkfai, juhngyáuh sāngwuht fai, wuhtduhng fai, yàuhhohk fai dángdáng.
為咗提高學生嘅學習成績，好多香港父母仲要小朋友上補習班。呢啲補習班有幾受歡迎呢？睇睇香港嘅街上面、巴士上面嘅補習班廣告，你就會明白。除咗學會知識、打好基礎，中國父母都會考慮其他方面嘅教育，譬如話音樂、舞蹈、運動等等，都好早就安排好喇。	Waihjó tàihgōu hohksāangge hohkjaahp sìhngjīk, hóudō Hēunggóng fuhmóuh juhngyiu síupàhngyáuh séuhng bóujaahp bāan. Nīdī bóujaahp bāan yáuh géi sauh fūnyìhng nē? Táitái Hēunggóng ge gāai seuhngmihn, bāsí seuhngmihnge bóujaahp bāan gwónggou, néih jauh wúih mìhngbaahk. Chèuihjó hohkwúih jisīk, dáhóu gēichó, Jūnggwok fuhmóuh dōu wúih háauleuih kèihtā fōngmihnge gaauyuhk, peiyùhwah yāmngohk, móuhdouh, wahnduhng dángdáng, dōu hóu jóu jauh ōnpàaih hóu la.

8.2 Additional vocabulary 附加詞彙

Number	Word	Yale Romanization	POS	English
1	調查	diuhchàh	V/N	to investigate, to survey; investigation, survey
2	平均	pìhnggwān	Att./Adj	average; equally, on the average
3	費用	faiyuhng	N	cost, expenditure, expense, charges
4	信賴	seunlaaih	V/ N	to trust, to count on, to have faith in
5	候選名單	hauhsyún mìhngdāan	N	shortlist
6	富商	fusēung	N	wealthy merchant

| 7 | 補習班 | bóujaahp bāan | N | tutoring classes |
| 8 | 舞蹈 | móuhdouh | N | dance |

8.3 Please answer the following T/F questions after reading the additional text:

1 Gauhnín yáuhyàhn diuhchàhjó baat chīn géigo Jūnggwok gātìhng ge gaauyuhk hōijī. (T/F)
2 Hēunggóng, Tòihwāan tùhng Jūnggwokge gājéung dōu hóu juhngsih gaauyuhk. (T/F)
3 Jūnggwok yáuhméng ge hohkhaauh gingjāng hóu sāileih. (T/F)
4 Gwokjai hohkhaauhge dahkdím haih gwokjaifa tùhng dōyùhn màhnfa. (T/F)
5 Hēunggóng ge gwokjai hohkhaauh síugwo nghsahp gāan. (T/F)
6 Hēunggóngge gwokjai hohkhaauh yáuh Hēunggóng hohksāang, ngoihgwok hohksāang, juhngyáuh noihdeih hohksāang. (T/F)
7 Hēunggóng yáuhméngge gwokjai hohkhaauh yātnìhn hohkfai chāṁdō yiu yih baak maahn. (T/F)
8 Duhk daaihhohk yiu yuhng géidō chín, tùhng jyūnyihp tùhng hohkhaauh yáuh gwāanhaih. (T/F)
9 Daaihhohk wúih hái bāsí jouh gwónggou. (T/F)
10 Chèuihjó hohk jīsīk, yáuhdī síupàhngyáuh dōu yiu hohk tiumóuh, yāmngohk dángdáng. (T/F)

8.4 Topics for discussions

1 Néih deui Hēunggóngge gaauyuhk yáuh mātyéh líuhgáai tùhng táifaat?
2 Néih gokdāk Jūnggwokge gājéung dímgáai gam juhngsih gaauyuhk nē?
3 Néihge gwokgā deui gaauyuhk yáuh mātyéh táifaat nē?
4 Yáuhdī fuhmóuh yiu síupàhngyáuh chāamgā hóudō wuhtduhng tùhng hingcheui bāan, néih yáuh mātyéh táifaat nē? Fuhmóuh deui síupàhngyáuh ge gaauyuhk yáuh mātyéh yínghéung nē?

8.5 Authentic oral data 1 🔊
真實語料 1

8.6 Authentic oral data 2 🔊
真實語料 2

Mid-term Review L1-L5

1. Speaking topics

1. Yùhgwó néih heui ngoihgwok léuihhàhng, néih béigaau jūngyi kaumaht, gūngwōng, bánsèuhng méihsihk, dihnghaih wáan chigīk ge wahnduhng a? Dímgáai nē?

2. Yùhgwó néih ge gāyàhn pàhngyáuh làih Hēunggóng léuihhàhng, néih wúih dímyéung bōng kéuihdeih ōnpàaih hàhngchìhng a? (Peiyùhwah, néih wúih tēuigaai kéuihdeih heui dī mātyéh gíngdím gūngwōng, kaumaht tùhng bánsèuhng mātyéh deihdouh méihsihk a?)

3. Néih làihjó Hēunggóng gam noih, gokdāk Hēunggóng gokjúng (every kind of) gāautūng gūnggeuih ge fuhkmouh jātsou dímyéung a? Dímgáai néih gám góng nē?

4. Néih gokdāk Hēunggóng ge gāaisíh tùhng sáisáugāan ge waihsāng chìhngfong dímyéung a? Kèihtā gwokgā/sìhngsíh nē? Dímgáai néih gám góng a?

5. Néih pìhngyaht dākhàahn waahkjé fongga gójahnsìh, yáuh dī mātyéh sīuhín a? Néih gokdāk Hēunggóng yáuh dī mātyéh sīuhín ge hóu deihfōng a?

6. Yáuh dī yàhn gokdāk tái lihksí syū hóu yáuhcheui, daahnhaih dōu yáuh yàhn gokdāk tái lihksí syū hóu muhn. Néih jihgéi nē? Néih jūng m̀jūngyi tái lihksí syū a? Dímgáai a?

7. Deuiyū chāantēng tùhng sātnoih chèuhngsó chyùhnmihn gamyīn, m̀tùhng ge yàhn fānbiht (respectively) pàhng mātyéh léihgeui jaansìhng waahkjé fáandeui nē?

8. Néih gokdāk yātgo méihmúhn ge gātìhng sāngwuht yáuh dī mātyéh yiusou (essential factor) nē? (Peiyùhwah, chín, gāyàhn ge gūngjok tùhng sihóu, pìhngyaht sēungjeuih sìhgaan, dángdáng.)

9. Néih yihngwàih fuhmóuh yiu bōng jáinéui chùhng síu (since childhood) pùihyéuhng dī mātyéh jaahpgwaan tùhng sihou a? Dímgáai nē?

10. Néih jaan m̀jaansìhng jingfú jījoh ngāamngāam chēutlàih séhwúi gūngjok ge bātyihpsāng jeunsāu a? Dímgáai nē?

2. Make a sentence with each of the following vocabulary.

1. séyi

2. sésaht

3. jījoh

4. chīngsīk

5. bóuchìh

6. bóulàuh

7. jyumìhng

8. lòihwóhng

9. léihséung

10. yìhmgaak

11. mōkdyuht

12. yìhngjeuhng

13. héungsauh

14. gaailāt

15. tóu sāng tóu jéung

3. Make a sentence with each of the following pattern.

1. ...... jihkdāk ......

2. ...... lihng yàhn gámdou ......

3. m̀jí ...... juhng ......

4. ...... dou ...... ge chìhngdouh

5. ...... yauh hóu, ... yauh hóu, ...

4. Oral Skills Practice

4.1. Complete the following sentences or answer the following questions using the given patterns.

1. Yānwaih gwokjai hohkhaauh ge sīngyuh hóu hóu, sóyíh _____.
    (jauhsyun ...... dōu ......)

2. Néihdeih _____, yīnggōi hóuhóu nóuhlihk duhksyū.
    (jokwàih ......)

3. Kéuih yahtyaht dōu sihkyīn, _____.
    (m̀tūng ......?)

4. Kéuihdeih _____, yānwaih kéuihdeih yìhgā juhng meih gau chín.
    (m̀ ...... jyuh)

5. Kéuih hóu gwajyuh kéuih ge lóuhpòh jáinéui, sóyíh kéuih yāt fonggūng jauh

    _____.
    (yáuh gam ...... dāk gam ......)

6. Q: Néih làihjó Hēunggóng jīhauh ge sāngwuht tùhng yíhchìhn yáuh mātyéh m̀tùhng a?
    A: _____.
    (Búnlòih ...... yìhgā ......)

7. Q: Néih gokdāk Hēunggóng ge gāautūng dím a?

   A: _____.

   (yauh …… yauh ……)

8. Q: Néih deui Hēunggóng ge gēuijyuh wàahngíng (living environment) yáuh mātyéh yanjeuhng a?

   A: Ngóh gokdāk _____.

   (…… dou bātdāklíuh)

9. Q: Kéuih sīk góng mātyéh yúhyìhn a?

   A: Kéuih _____, kèihtā yúhyìhn jauh yātgeui dōu m̀sīk góng la.

   (jihnghaih …… ja)

10. Q: Néih yáuh mātyéh sāangyaht yuhnmohng (wishes) a?

    A: Ngóh hēimohng _____.

    (yuht làih yuht ……)

11. Q: Dímgáai gahnnìhn (recent years) gam dō yàhn yìhmàhn (to migrate) heui ngoihgwok a?

    A: Yáuh dī yàhn yìhmàhn, haih _____; yáuh dī haih

    _____.

    (waihjó ……)

12. Q: Néih jūngyi sihk jīng hóisīn, juhng jūngyi sihk dī mātyéh a?

    A: _____.

    (Chèuihjó …… jīngoih, juhng ……)

4.2. Speech Topics

1. Néih làihjó Hēunggóng gam noih, gokdāk Hēunggóng jeui yáuh doihbíusing ge gíngdím, sihkmaht tùhng sáuseun fānbiht (respectively) haih mātyéh a? Dímgáai néih gám góng nē?

2. Deuiyū ngoihgwok yàuhhaak làih góng, Hēunggóng yáuh dī mātyéh gam kāpyáhn kéuihdeih ge deihfōng a? Kéuihdeih jeui yānséung Hēunggóng ge mātyéh nē?

3. Yáuh dī yàhn hóu jūngyi tái yàuh jyumìhng síusyut góipīnsìhng ge dihnyíng, yáuh dī yàhn jauh béigaau jūngyi tái yùhnbáan (original edition) síusyut. Néih gokdāk tái dihnyíng tùhng tái síusyut yáuh mātyéh yātyeuhng waahkjé m̀tùhng ge deihfōng a? Néih jihgéi béigaau jūngyi bīnyātyeuhng nē?

4. Deuiyū chāantēng tùhng sātnoih chèuhngsó chyùhnmihn gamyīn, néih jihgéi yáuh mātyéh yigin a? Néih ge lahpchèuhng haih dím ge nē?

5. Hóudō yàhn yihngwàih, yùhgwó yātgo hohksāang ge háausíh sìhngjīk hóu hóu, kéuih ge chìhntòuh jauh yātdihng gwōngmìhng. Néih jaan m̀jaansìhng nīgo góngfaat a? Dímgáai nē?

Lesson 6 Proposing casinos
開設賭場

1. Pragmatic factors, Yuti features and linguistic functions
語用因素、語體特徵與語言功能

Yúhyuhng yānsou, yúhtái dahkjīng yúh yúhyìhn gūngnàhng

Pragmatic factors/ Yuti features 語用因素 / 語體特徵	Linguistic function 語言功能
Pragmatic factors: Pragmatic factors: This is a typical scenario for a formal situation, both in terms of content and context, calling for formal features of language. 語用因素： 場合正式，內容嚴肅，所以語體正式。 **Yuti features:** Formality index: 2+ 語體特徵：2+	**Linguistic function:** Defensing In a formal context, advance a defense of your position and provide examples to prove your point. 語言功能：辯護 在正式場合為自己的主張進行辯護，並舉例證明自己的觀點。

Notes on pragmatic knowledge 語用知識	Notes on structure 語言及篇章結構知識
I. Yuti and being vague 語體與虛指 1. Discourse structure in light of pragmatic framework 2. specialists concerned 「有關專家」 II. Related knowledge 相關知識 1. Presentation style in public speech 2. Portugese egg-tart 「葡式蛋撻」 3. Everybody in our society 「廣大市民」	I. Grammar and sentence patterns 語法和句型 1. "làih" in order to; to 2. "géui…laihjí" take for example 3. "yáuh/héi…jokyuhng" play a part; play the role; have effect on 4. "chùhng…làih tái" from the perspective of... 5. "Dōu haih…" 6. Double negative : "m̀wúih m̀ V(O)…" and "m̀wúih…m̀dóu…" 7. "sihfáu" if; whether or not 8. "deui…móuh/yáuh hóuchyu" be (not) good for... 9. "hái…fōngmihn" in relation to; on the topic of 10. "Hóuchíh…jīléui/dī gámge…" 11. "Jēung" pattern 12. "júngkut làih góng" all in all; in a word II. Paragraph and discourse 語段和篇章 1. "sáusīn…kèihchi…lihngngoih…jeuihauh…" Firstly...and then...in addition... finally…

2. Text 🔊

課文 Fomàhn

大家好，首先感謝各位喺百忙之中抽出寶貴時間參加今日嘅專題辯論會，為我哋社會未來嘅發展俾啲意見。頭先幾位代表嘅發言都有一定嘅道理。對於興建賭場呢個建議，政府係持反對意見嘅。以下請容許我解釋吓政府反對開設賭場嘅理由。

Daaihgā hóu, sáusīn gámjeh gokwái hái baak mòhng jījūng chāuchēut bóugwai sìhgaan chāamgā gāmyahtge jyūntàih bihnleuhn wúi, waih ngóhdeih séhwúi meihlòihge faatjín béi dī yigin. Tàuhsīn géiwái doihbíuge faatyìhn dōu yáuh yātdihngge douhléih. Deuiyū hīnggin dóuchèuhng nīgo ginyíh, jingfú haih chìh fáandeui yigin ge. Yíhhah chíng yùhnghéui ngóh gáaisīkháh jingfú fáandeui hōichit dóuchèuhngge léihyàuh.

首先，對於有意見認為開設賭場可以有助於增加政府稅收，政府認為可以有其他方法嚟增加稅收，舉啲例子，好似增加煙酒稅啦、汽車登記稅啦、增加賣地次數等等。社會上有好多反對興建賭場嘅聲音，認為香港已經有賽馬、六合彩同賭波，唔應該進一步鼓勵賭博。政府唔可以因為增加稅收就忽視反對聲音。雖然有意見認為，開設賭場可以起刺激旅遊業呢個作用，吸引更多遊客嚟香港消費，但係近年遊客人數增長太快，由十年前每年一千萬旅客增加到現時嘅七千萬。社會無論喺交通、酒店、定係旅遊業從業員嘅訓練方面都需要有更多嘅配套，先至可以應付更多旅客來港。

Sáusīn, deuiyū yáuh yigin yihngwàih hōichit dóuchèuhng hóyíh yáuhjohyū jānggā jingfú seuisāu, jingfú yihngwàih hóyíh yáuh kèihtā fōngfaat làih jānggā seuisāu, géui dī laihjí, hóuchíh jānggā yīnjáu seui lā, heichē dānggei seui lā, jānggā maaihdeih chisou dángdáng. Séhwúi seuhng yáuh hóudō fáandeui hīnggin dóuchèuhngge sīngyām, yihngwàih Hēunggóng yíhgīng yáuh choimáh, Luhkhahpchói tùhng dóubō, m̀yīnggōi jeun yātbouh gúlaih dóubok. Jingfú m̀hóyíh yānwaih jānggā seuisāu jauh fātsih fáandeui sīngyām. Sēuiyìhn yáuh yigin yìhngwàih, hōichit dóuchèuhng hóyíh héi chigīk léuihyàuh yihp nīgo jokyuhng, kāpyáhn gangdō yàuhhaak làih Hēunggóng sīufai, daahnhaih gahnnìhn yàuhhaak yàhnsou jānggjéung taai faai, yàuh sahp nìhn chìhn múih nìhn yāt chīnmaahn léuihhaak jānggā dou yihnsìhge chāt chīnmaahn. Séhwúi mòuhleuhn hái gāautūng, jáudim, dihnghaih léuihyàuh yihp chùhngyihp yùhn ge fanlihn fōngmihn dōu sēuiyiu yáuh gangdōge puitou, sīnji hóyíh yingfuh gangdō léuihhaak lòih Góng.

其次係香港嘅土地供應不足，目前政府最急切嘅工作係增加房屋嘅土地供應，其實香港係一個缺乏土地嘅地方。大家都知道公屋輪候嘅時間係非常之長。無論係私樓嘅價格，定係一啲公屋轉入去二手市場作為買賣嘅價格，亦都係高到令人難以負擔嘅。我哋起一個賭場嗰度係要犧牲十分之大嘅土地面積。喺一個土地咁缺乏嘅情況底下，我哋係有充分嘅理據去興建賭場。如果興建賭場，就需要更多土地用嚟興建娛樂設施，需要更多土地興建新嘅酒店，嗽香港就會少咗好多地方嚟興建房屋，樓價就好難控制。而家香港普遍認為樓價太高，從呢一點嚟睇，政府都係以興建房屋為優先，而唔係興建賭場。

Kèihchi haih Hēunggóngge tóudeih gūngying bāt jūk, muhkchìhn jingfú jeui gāpchitge gūngjok haih jānggā fòhngngūkge tóudeih gūngying, kèihsaht Hēunggóng haih yātgo kyutfaht tóudeihge deihfōng. Daaihgā dōu jīdou gūngngūkge lèuhnhauh sìhgaan haih fēisèuhngjī chèuhng. Mòuhleuhn haih sīláuge gagaak, dihnghaih yātdī gūngngūk jyun yahpheui yihsáu síhchèuhng jokwàih máaihmaaih ge gagaak, yihkdōu haih gōu dou lihng yàhn nàahnyíh fuhdāam ge. Ngóhdeih héi yātgo dóuchèuhng gódouh haih yiu hēisāng sahpfānjī daaihge tóudeih mihnjīk. Hái yātgo tóudeih gam kyutfahtge chìhngfong dáihah, ngóhdeih haih móuh chūngfahnge léihgeui heui hīnggin dóuchèuhng. Yùhgwó hīnggin dóuchèuhng, jauh sēuiyiu gangdō tóudeih yuhnglàih hīnggin yùhlohk chitsī, sēuiyiu gangdō tóudeih hīnggin sānge jáudim, gám Hēunggóng jauh wúih síujó hóudō deihfōng làih hīnggin fòhngngūk, làuhga jauh hóu nàahn hungjai. Yìhgā Hēunggóng póupin yihngwàih làuhga taai gōu, chùhng nī yātdím làih tái, jingfú dōuhaih yíh hīnggin fòhngngūk wàih yāusīn, yìh m̀haih hīnggin dóuchèuhng.

第三，鄰近地區已經有好多大型賭場，好似澳門、新加坡同馬來西亞，都已經足夠滿足遊客對賭場嘅需求，想去賭場娛樂嘅遊客唔會搵唔到地方。香港冇需要跟隨呢啲地區繼續興建賭場，繼續興建更多賭場只會帶嚟惡性競爭。而且港珠澳大橋已經落成，喺香港澳門同珠海三地，其實大家都有聽過呢個「一小時生活圈」嘅概念。意思即係話我哋喺呢三個地方搭車，其實我哋所需嘅交通時間只需要一個鐘之內。三個地方都有各自嘅特色，大家都知道澳門亦都係一個十分之受歡迎嘅地方。而佢其中一個最大嘅特色就係賭場多。既然喺一個咁近嘅地方就有咁多賭場。點解香港仲需要興建一個賭場呢？大自然嘅風光、各國嘅美食、多元嘅文化，相信呢啲係我哋香港嘅特色。我哋是否需要去同一啲我哋鄰近嘅城市去有一個嘅競爭呢？

Daih sāam, lèuhngahn deihkēui yíhgīng yáuh hóudō daaihyìhng dóuchèuhng, hóuchíh Oumún, Sāngabō tùhng Máhlòihsāinga, dōu yíhgīng jūkgau múhnjūk yàuhhaak deui dóuchèuhngge sēuikàuh, séung heui dóuchèuhng yùhlohkge yàuhhaak m̀wúih wánm̀dóu deihfōng. Hēunggóng móuh sēuiyiu gānchèuih nīdī deihkēui gaijuhk hīnggin dóuchèuhng, gaijuhk hīnggin gangdō dóuchèuhng jíwúih daailàih ngoksing gingjāng. Yìhché Góngjyūou Daaihkiuh yíhgīng lohksìhng, hái Hēunggóng Oumún tùhng Jyūhói sāamdeih, kèihsaht daaihgā dōu yáuh tēnggwo nīgo "yāt síusìh sāngwuht hyūn" ge koinihm. Yisī jīkhaih wah ngóhdeih hái nī sāamgo deihfōng daapchē, kèihsaht ngóhdeih só sēui ge gāautūng sìhgaan jí sēuiyiu yātgo jūng jīnoih. Sāamgo deihfōng dōu yáuh gokjih ge dahksīk, daaihgā dōu jīdou Oumún yihkdōu haih yātgo sahpfānjī sauh fūnyìhng ge deihfōng. Yìh kéuih kèihjūng yātgo jeui daaihge dahksīk jauhhaih dóuchèuhng dō. Geiyìhn hái yātgo gam káhnge deihfōng jauh yáuh gamdō dóuchèuhng. Dímgáai Hēunggóng juhng sēuiyiu hīnggin yātgo dóuchèuhng nē? Daaih jihyìhnge fūnggwōng, gokgwokge méihsihk, dōyùhnge màhnfa, sēungseun nīdī haih ngóhdeih Hēunggóngge dahksīk. Ngóhdeih sihfáu sēuiyiu heui tùhng yātdī ngóhdeih lèuhngahnge sìhngsíh heui yáuh yātgo ge gingjāng nē?

另外，香港近年其他基建工程已經令建築成本增加咗好多，有關專家分析，如果政府決定興建賭場，將會令呢個情況更加嚴重，成本越嚟越高，人手唔夠，最後反而會刺激通脹，影響經濟發展。

Lihngngoih, Hēunggóng gahnnìhn kèihtā gēigin gūngchìhng yíhgīng lihng ginjūk sìhngbún jānggājó hóudō, yáuh gwāan jyūngā fānsīk, yùhgwó jingfú kyutdihng hīnggin dóuchèuhng, jēung wúih lihng nīgo chìhngfong ganggā yìhmjuhng, sìhngbún yuht làih yuht gōu, yàhnsáu m̀gau, jeuihauh fáanyìh wúih chigīk tūngjeung, yínghéung gīngjai faatjín.

最後，興建賭場對社會風氣同治安都有好處。喺社會風氣同治安呢方面，其實係十分之有可能助長非法嘅活動，譬如係好似高利貸啲嘅嘅活動，我哋明白當人沉迷賭博之後要將賭癮戒甩係非常之困難。一個人沉迷賭博唔只係一個人嘅代價，而且都係一家人付出嘅代價。相信呢幾點，可以令大家更加明白，香港特區係唔應該開設賭場嘅。

Jeuihauh, hīnggin dóuchèuhng deui séhwúi fūnghei tùhng jih'ōn dōu móuh hóuchyu. Hái séhwúi fūnghei tùhng jih'ōn nī fōngmihn, kèihsaht haih sahpfānjī yáuh hónàhng johjéung fēifaatge wuhtduhng, peiyùh haih hóuchíh gōuleihtaai dī gámge wuhtduhng, ngóhdeih mìhngbaahk dōng yàhn chàhmmàih dóubok jīhauh yiu jēung dóuyáhn gaailāt haih fēisèuhngjī kwannàahn. Yātgo yàhn chàhmmàih dóubok m̀jí haih yātgo yàhnge doihga, yìhché dōu haih yātgā yàhn fuhchēutge doihga. Sēungseun nī géi dím, hóyíh lihng daaihgā ganggā mìhngbaahk, Hēunggóng dahkkēui haih m̀yīnggōi hōichit dóuchèuhng ge.

總括嚟講，政府認為現時唔係興建賭場嘅時候，但係歡迎社會同廣大市民就呢個問題繼續討論。

Júngkut làihgóng, jingfú yihngwàih yihnsìh m̀haih hīnggin dóuchèuhngge sìhhauh, daahnhaih fūnyìhng séhwúi tùhng gwóngdaaih síhmàhn jauh nīgo mahntàih gaijuhk tóuleuhn.

3. Vocabulary in use 🔊
活用詞彙 Wuhtyuhng chìhwuih

3.1 Common vocabulary

Number	Word	Yale Romanization	POS	English
1	興建	hīnggin	V	to build
2	建議	ginyíh	N/V	suggestion; to suggest
3	容許	yùhnghéui	V	to permit, to allow
4	解釋	gáaisīk	N/V	explanation; to explain
5	開設	hōichit	V	to set up, to establish
6	理由	léihyàuh	N	reason

7	有助於	yáuh joh yū	PH	to be conducive to
8	增加	jānggā	V	to increase
9	次數	chisou	N	number of times
10	鼓勵	gúlaih	N/V	encouragement; to encourage
11	賭博	dóubok	N/V	gambling; to gamble
12	忽視	fātsih	V	to ignore, to neglect
13	刺激	chigīk	V	to stimulate
14	增長	jāngjéung	N/V	growth; to increase
15	訓練	fanlihn	N/V	training, to train
16	應付	yingfuh	V	to deal with, to cope with
17	缺乏	kyutfaht	V	to lack
18	犧牲	hēisāng	V	to sacrifice
19	充分	chūngfahn	Adj	full, ample
20	需要	sēuiyiu	N/V	need; to need
21	更多	gang dō	PH	more
22	樓價	làuhga	N	property price
23	控制	hungjai	V	to control
24	足夠	jūkgau	Adj	enough, sufficient
25	滿足	múhnjūk	V	to satisfy
26	需求	sēuikàuh	N	demand
27	落成	lohksìhng	V	(of buildings) to be completed
28	受歡迎	sauh fūnyìhng	Adj	popular, well-received
29	競爭	gingjāng	N/V	competition; to compete
30	分析	fānsīk	N/V	analysis; to analyze
31	助長	johjéung	V	to encourage (e.g. crimes, evil trends)
32	非法	fēifaat	Adj	illegal
33	高利貸	gōuleihtaai	N	high-interest loan
34	沉迷	chàhmmàih	V	to be addicted to

| 35 | 代價 | doihga | N | price, cost |

3.2 Place words

1	港珠澳大橋	Góng-Jyū-Ou Daaihkìuh	PW	HongKong-Zhuhai-Macao Bridge
2	澳門	Oumún	PW	Macau
3	珠海	Jyūhói	PW	Zhuhai
4	三地	sāam deih	PH	the three places

3.3 About gambling

1	賭場	dóuchèuhng	N	casino
2	賽馬	choimáh	N	horse racing
3	六合彩	Luhkhahpchói	N	Mark Six
4	賭波	dóubō	N/VO	soccer betting; to bet on soccer
5	賭癮	dóuyáhn	N	gambling addiction

3.4 About the government and social issues

1	稅收	seuisāu	N	tax revenue
2	煙酒稅	yīnjáu seui	N	tobacco and alcohol tax
3	汽車登記稅	heichē dānggei seui	N	vehicle registration tax
4	賣地	maaih deih	N/VO	land sale; to sell the land
5	配套	puitou	N	supporting infrastructure
6	土地	tóudeih	N	land
7	供應不足	gūngying bātjūk	PH	the supply is inadequate
8	通脹	tūngjeung	N	inflation
9	社會風氣	séhwúi fūnghei	N	social trend
10	治安	jih'ōn	N	public order

3.5 Other vocabularies

1	旅遊業從業員	léuihyàuhyihp chùhngyihpyùhn	N	tourism practitioner
2	來港	lòih Góng	PH	coming to Hong Kong
3	急切	gāpchit	Adj	eager, urgent
4	房屋	fòhngngūk	N	housing
5	娛樂設施	yùhlohk chitsī	N	recreational facility
6	一小時生活圈	yāt síusìh sāngwuhthyūn	PH	one-hour living circle
7	概念	koinihm	N	concept
8	惡性競爭	ngoksing gingjāng	N	vicious competition
9	風光	fūnggwōng	N	landscape
10	鄰近	lèuhngahn	Adv/N	nearby; vicinity
11	建築成本	ginjūk sìhngbún	N	construction cost

3.6 Useful expressions

1	百忙之中	baak mòhng jījūng	PH	out of one's busy schedule
2	抽出	chāuchēut	RV	to take out
3	寶貴時間	bóugwai sìhgaan	N	precious time
4	專題辯論會	jyūntàih bihnleuhnwúi	N	thematic debate
5	持反對意見	chìh fáandeui yigin	PH	to hold opposing view
6	反對聲音	fáandeui sīngyām	N	opposition voice
7	有關專家	yáuhgwāan jyūngā	N	relevant specialists
8	總括嚟講	júngkut làih góng	PH	in summary
9	廣大市民	gwóngdaaih síhmàhn	PH	the public

4. Notes on language and discourse structure

語言及篇章結構知識 Yúhyìhn kahp pīnjēung gitkau jīsīk

4.1. Grammar and sentence patterns 語法和句型

4.1.1. "làih" in order to; to

1. Ngóh hóyíh géui yātdī laihjí làih gónggóng dóuchèuhng tùhng séhwúi jih'ōn yáuh mātyéh gwāanhaih.

2. Hēunggóng m̀jí yáuh hóu lengge jihyìhn wàahngíng, juhng yáuh yātdī jyútàih gūngyún (theme park) làih kāpyáhn yàuhhaak.

3. Yātdī daaihhohk yuhng jéunghohkgām (scholarship) làih gúlaih nóuhlihkge hohksāang.

4.1.2. "géui......laihjí" take for example

1. Ngóh hóyíh géui yātdī laihjí, gónggóng hohkchìhn gaauyuhkge juhngyiusing (importance).

2. Néih hōi dóuchèuhng sēuiyiu yātdī puitou chitsī, hó m̀hóyíh géui dī laihjí a ?

3. Hēunggóngge daaihhohk fēisèuhng gwokjai fa, géui go laihjí, ngóhge tùhnghohk yáuh Yahtbún yàhn, Hòhngwok yàhn, Yandouh yàhn...

4.1.3. "yáuh /héi......jokyuhng" play a part; play the role; have effect on

1. Nīgo gaiwaahk deui ngóhdeihge séhwúi héi yātgo mātyéh jokyuhng nē?

2. Ngóh gokdāk Gwóngdūng yàhnge tōng fēisèuhng hóuyám, jiyū deui gihnhōng yáuhmóuh jokyuhng, ngóh jānhaih m̀jīdou.

3. Hohkhaauh tùhng gājéung dōu deui síu pàhngyáuhge gaauyuhk héi juhngyiu jokyuhng.

4.1.4. "chùhng......làihtái" from the perspective of...

1. Chùhng gīngjai fōngmihn làihtái, dóuchèuhng deui yātgo sìhngsíh wúih héi yātdī jokyuhng.

2. Nīgo deihfōng chùhng wàahngíng làihtái jānhaih m̀cho, bātgwo gāautūng jauh m̀haih géi fōngbihn.

3. Chùhng sauhhoihjé (victim) gokdouh (angle) làihtái, dōngyìhn hēimohng jeuihfáan (criminal) hóyíh sauhdou jeui chúhngge chìhngfaht (punishment).

4.1.5. "Dōu haih…" means "It would be better to……."

1. Yìhgā hóudō yàhn heui léuihhàhng, gēipiu hóu faai wúih maaihsaai. Néih dōu haih faaidī dehng gēipiu lā.
2. Jihkhòhng bāangēi (direct flight) pèhnggwo jyungēi gamdō, néih dōu haih chóh jihkhòhng bāangēi lā.
3. Sānchíng yìhmàhn hóu màhfàahn ga! Néihdeih dōu haih m̀hóu yìhmàhn lā.
4. Néih yauh yiu fāangūng yauh yiu jiugu gāyàhn, ngóh nám néih dōu haih chéng gūngyàhn hóudī la.
5. Yìhgā lohk gam daaih yúh, ngóhdeih dōu haih làuhhái ngūkkéi hóu la.

4.1.6. Double negative

Two negatives make a strong positive. There are some variations of the pattern:

-   m̀wúih m̀V(O)
-   m̀wúih Vm̀RVE

1. M̀wúih máaih m̀dóu gēipiu ge, néih siháh tīm lā.
2. Néih geibéi kéuih ge dihnjí yàuhgín (email), kéuih m̀wúih sāum̀dóu ge.
3. Yúhgwó ngóh gitfān, ngóh m̀wúih m̀wah béi néih jī ge.
4. Ngóh m̀wúih m̀heui ge, néih fongsām lā.

4.1.7. "sihfáu" if; whether or not

1. Faatjín léuihyàuh haih hóu, daahnhaih taai dō yàuhhaak sihfáu deui nīgo deihfōng yáuh hóuchyu nē ?
2. Néihdeih sihfáu wúih háauleuih hái Hēunggóng máaihláu nē ?
3. Jokwàih yātgo gaauyuhk jyūngā, néih sihfáu líuhgáai Hēunggóngge gīngjai chìhngfong nē ?

4.1.8. "deui…móuh/yáuh hóuchyu" be (not) good for…

1. Nīdī gaiwaahk deui Hēunggóng ge gīngjai yáuh hóuchyu.
2. Jāumuht heui Lèihdóu wáanháh, deui gáamhēng ngaatlihk yáuh hóuchyu.
3. Yám lèuhngchàh deui sāntái yáuh móuh hóuchyu nē?

4.1.9. "hái…fōngmihn" in relation to; on the topic of

1. Hái séhwúi jih'ōn fōngmihn làih tái, ngóh gokdāk Hēunggóng m̀yīnggōi hōichit dóuchèuhng.

2. Kéuih hái gūngjok fōngmihn hóu sìhnggūng, bātgwo hái sāngwuht fōngmihn jauh…

3. Jūnggwok gam daaih, jauhsyun haih Jūnggwokyàhn, hái deihkēui (regional) màhnfa fōngmihn yáuhsìh dōu m̀líuhgáai.

4.1.10. "Hóuchíh ...... jīléui / dī gám ge ......" means "such things as ...... and the like"

1. Hóuchíh sīu yúhjyū a, gāi a jīléui ge yéh taai fèih la, néih dōu haih m̀hóu sihk gam dō la.

2. Kéuih yáuh behng, hóuchíh dī syūn ge, laaht ge jīléui ge yéh, dōu m̀hóyíh sihk.

3. Gitfān yiu jouh hóudō yéh ga, hóuchíh jyuchaak, yíngséung, báaijáu jīléui ge hohngmuhk (item), yiu yuhng hóudō chín ga.

4. Yìhgā heui léuihhàhng hóu fōngbihn, hóuchíh ló chīmjing, máaih gēipiu dī gám ge sáujuhk(procedure), dōu m̀sái jihgéi heui baahn ge la.

4.1.11. "Jēung" pattern

The pattern, "jēung Object V…", can bring the object of a sentence to the position before the main verb. It can be used to express the movement of an object. In addition, it can be used with resultative verbs.

1. Kéuihdeih jēung dī sáutàih hàhngléih fong séuhng hàhngléihgá.

2. Kéuih jēung bouh sáutēuichē béifāan gógo gēichèuhng jīkyùhn.

3. Néih yiu jēung dī gēipiu fonghóu, m̀hóu m̀gin jó a!

4. M̀gōi néih jēung wuhjiu ló chēutlàih.

5. Ngóh móuh jēung nīgihn sih góngbéi kéuih tēng.

6. Deui yīnmàhn làihgóng, yiu kéuihdeih jēung yīnyáhn gaailāt, haih hóu nàahn ge sih.

7. Néih yiu jēung dī gūngfo jouh hóu sīnji hóyíh chēutheui wáan.

8. Yùhgwó néih m̀jēung ōnchyùhn dáai kauhóu, fēigēi héifēi gójahn wúih hóu ngàihhím.

9. Jauhsyun bàhbā màhmā dōu yiu fāangūng, dōu m̀yīnggōi jēung síupàhngyáuh làuh hái ngūkkéi.

* The negative in a 'jēung' sentence is attached to the 'jēung' or to the AV preceding it if there is one.

4.1.12. "júngkut làihgóng" all in all; in a word

1. Júngkut làih góng, jokwàih jingfú, m̀léih Hēunggóng yáuhmóuh dóuchèuhng, ngóhdeih dōu wúih chyùhnlihk wàihwuh (protect) séhwúi jih'ōn.

2. Júngkut làih góng, ngóh fáandeui nīgo gaiwaahk.

3. Chèuihjó máaihyéh, sihkyéh, Hēunggóng juhngyáuh hóu leng ge jihyìhn wàahngíng. Síu pàhngyáuh yáuh jyútàih gūngyún hóyíh wáan, lóuhyàhn hóyíh hàahngháh sāan. Júngkut làih góng, Hēunggóng haih yātgo léuihyàuh tīntòhng.

4.2. Paragraph and discourse 語段和篇章

4.2.1. "Sáusīn…kèihchi…lihngngoih…jeuihauh…" Firstly… and then… in additional… finally….

1. Sáusīn ngóh gokdāk daaihgā dōu tùhngyi Hēunggóng yáuh hóu dō daaihyìhng sēungchèuhng, kèihchi Hēunggóng yáuh saigaai gokdeihge méihsihk, lihngngoih juhng yáuh jihyìhn gínggūn, ngóh sēungseun yàuhhaak jeuihauh yātdihng jūngyi nīgo deihfōng.

2. Ngóh m̀jūngyi nībún syū, sáusīn haih yānwaih ngóh m̀jūngyi dádá saatsaat ge chìhngjit, kèihchi ngóh dōu m̀jūngyi gódī nàahmnéuih ngoichìhng gusih, yìh m̀haih wah nībún syū sédāk m̀hóu.

5. Notes on pragmatic knowledge
語用因素與相關知識 Yúhyuhng yānsou yúh sēunggwāan jīsīk

5.1. Yuti and being vague 語體與虛指

5.1.1. Discourse structure in light of pragmatic framework

5.1.1.1. "各位新聞界嘅朋友 gokwái sānmàhn gaai ge pàhngyáuh"

5.1.1.2. "歡迎 fūnyìhng"

5.1.1.3. "多謝你哋 dōjeh néihdeih"

Appropriateness is the key for speech as a public event but there is usually more than one way of doing the right thing. The official status of the speaker contributes to the tone and the discourse structure of this speech. The linguistic task here is to explain the position of the government regarding the debate over the establishment of casinos in the special economic zone. Among the various possibilities, the speaker chooses to follow the official procedure in terms of format but to adopt a friendly tone, thus we see the use of " 朋友 pàhngyáuh" instead of "reporters" in the greeting, the official welcome at the beginning and the"thank you" at the end.

5.1.2. " 有關專家 yáuhgwāan jyūngā" specialists concerned

The use of vague terms such as "specialists concerned", or "relevant specialists" is often deliberately chosen by the speaker in public speech because the focus is the "specialists", and the term " 有關 yáuhgwāan" provides the speaker with the flexibility to explain it in any way as needed later depending on the circumstances. This is actually a cultural characteristic in Chinese, especially among politicians because they always want to "leave room" in what they say.

Gám jauh yiu chíng yáuhgwāan jyūngā yìhngauháh la.

5.2. Related knowledge 相關知識

5.2.1. Presentation style in public speech

5.2.1.1. " 我本人 ngóh bún yàhn"

5.2.1.2. " 我諗大家都同意 ngóh nám daaihgā dōu tùhngyi"

5.2.1.3. " 我哋都知道 ngóhdeih dōu jīdou"

Similar to what is explained in 5.1.1. above, there are different ways of doing things even though the pragmatic framework is the same. 5.2.1.1. to 5.2.1.3. here is typical of a presentation style in which the speaker adopts a friendly approach by using " 我 " to make it sound more personal, and to make the audience feel that the speaker and the audience actually have the same starting point or share the same perspective by using phrases like " 我 諗大家都同意 ngóh nám daaihgā dōu tùhngyi" (I think we all agree that ……), and " 我 哋都知道 ngóhdeih dōu jīdou" (we all know that ……).

5.2.2. " 葡式蛋撻 pòuhsīk daahntāat" Portugese egg-tart

It is a bakery snack believed to be originated from Portugal and is very popular in Macau. It is well known not only as a snack in itself, but also because of the association with a former governor of Hong Kong before 1997, who reportedly loved to have it either out of personal preference or for political show on various occasions. The use of " 式 sīk", meaning "in the style of" is also getting popular in Chinese, with many combinations such as " 中式 / 西式 / 粵式 / 港式 Jūngsīk/saisīk/yuhtsīk/góngsīk" (Chinese/Western/

Cantonese/Hong Kong style).

Heui Oumún hóyíh sihk Pòuhsīk daahntāat.

Néih yáuhmóuh yám gwo "Góngsīk náaihchàh" a?

5.2.3. "廣大市民 gwóngdaaih síhmàhn" everybody in our society

It is often difficult to distinguish words like "市民 síhmàhn", "公民 gūngmàhn" and "人民 yàhnmàhn". They all refer to people, like the more popular term "大家 daaihgā". Each of them, however, is used in different ways depending on the style and context. While "市民 síhmàhn" and "公民 gūngmàhn" can both be used to refer to the whole class or individuals if together with numbers (e.g. 六位市民 luhkwái síhmàhn), "人民 yàhnmàhn" can only be used to refer to the whole people and is often found in formal situations (中國人民 Jūnggwok yàhnmàhn).

Chíng gwóngdaaih síhmàhn fongsām…

Múihgo síhmàhn dōu yáuh kyùhnleih (rights) tùhng yihmouh (obligations).

6. Contextualized speaking practice

情境說話練習 Chìhnggíng syutwah lihnjaahp

【課前預習】Class preparation

6.1. Please answer the following True/False questions according to the lesson text.

1. Jingfú deuiyū hīnggin dóuchèuhng haih chìh fáandeui yigin ge. (T/F)
2. Jingfú yihngwàih hóyíh yáuh kèihtā fōngfaat làih jānggā seuisāu. (T/F)
3. Séhwúi seuhng yáuh hóudō jīchìh hīnggin dóuchèuhng ge sīngyām, yihngwàih Hēunggóng yíhgīng yáuh choimáh, luhkhahp chói tùhng dóubō, daahnhaih juhng meih gau.(T/F)
4. Séhwúi mòuhleuhn haih gāautūng, jáudim, dihnghaih léuihyàuh chùhngyihp yùhnge fanlihn dōu yáuh jūkgau puitou hóyíh hōichit dóuchèuhng. (T/F)
5. Hēunggóngge tóudeih gūngying bātjūk, jingfú móuh chūngfahn léihgeui heui hīnggin dóuchèuhng. (T/F)

6. Hēunggóng lèuhngahn deihkēui himkyut (in lack of) daaihyìhng dóuchèuhng. (T/F)

7. Yāt síusìh sāngwuht hyūn ge koinihm bāaukut Hēunggóng, Oumún tùhng Gwóngjāu. (T/F)

8. Hēunggóng gahnnìhn kèihtā gēigin gūngchìhng yíhgīng lihng ginjūk sìhngbún jānggājó hóudō. (T/F)

9. Hīnggin dóuchèuhng tùhng séhwúi fūnghei tùhng jih'ōn móuh gwāanhaih. (T/F)

10. Yíngóngge yàhn yihngwàih chàhmmàih dóubok jīhauh yiu gaaidóu haih fēisèuhng kwannàahn ge. (T/F)

6.2 Please explain the following phrases in Cantonese

1 煙酒稅 yīnjáu seui

2 賭波 dóubō

3 一小時生活圈 yāt síusìh sāngwuht hyūn

4 高利貸 gōuleih taai

【課後練習】Post-class exercises

6.3 Fill in the blanks with the given vocabularies. Each vocabulary can be chosen once only.

gáaisīk	gúlaih	fātsih	doihga
kyutfaht	hungjai	hēisāng	múhnjūk
sauh fūnyìhng		gingjāng	chàhmmàih	yingfuh

1. Yìhgā bātyihpsāng wángūng _____ hóu daaih, yātgo jīkwaih (job post) yáuh sèhng baak géi yàhn jāang.

2. Kéuih pìhngyaht fāangūng hóu mòhng, yauh _____ wahnduhng tùhng yāusīk, sóyíh gihnhōng yuht làih yuht chā.

3. Jingfú chīnmaahn m̀hóyíh _____ dāi sāuyahp yàhnsih (low-income persons) deui fòhngngūk ge sēuikàuh.

4. Nītou dihnyíng fēisèuhngjī _____, hóudō yàhn dōu máaih fēi yahp heiyún tái.

5. Kéuih yìhgā heung lóuhsī _____ gán gāmjīu kéuih fāanhohk chìhdou ge yùhnyān.

6. Bàhbā màhmā sèhngyaht dōu _____ dī jáinéui yiu nóuhlihk duhksyū.

7. Jokwàih haakwuh fuhkmouh yàhnyùhn (customer service staff), ngóhdeih wúih jeuhnlihk _____ haakyàhn ge kèihmohng (expectations) tùhng sēuiyiu.

8. Waihjó jiugu gāyàhn, kéuih _____ jó jihgéi daaihbouhfahn ge sīyàhn sìhgaan.

9. Hái Hēunggóng, hohksāang sèhngyaht dōu yiu _____ chāakyihm háausi, sóyíh ngaatlihk hóu daaih.

10. Hóudō dóutòuh (gamblers) yānwaih _____ m̀dóu jihgéi yìh _____ dóubok, yānchí (therefore) fuhchēutjó chàhmchúhng ge_____ .

6.4 Complete the following sentences or answer the following questions using the given patterns.

1. ...... làih ......
   Ngóh yihngwàih jingfú yīnggōi _____ .

2. géui ...... laihjí
   Ngóh séung _____ làih gáaisīk chàhmmàih dóubō wúih yáuh mē mahntàih.

3. deui... héi... jokyuhng
   Hīnggin titlouh_____ .

4. chùhng ...... làih tái
   A: Néih yihngwàih hīnggin dóuchèuhng deui séhwúi yáuh móuh hóuchyu a?
   B: _____ .

5. dōuhaih ......
   Yìhgā tīnhei m̀hóu, ngóhdeih _____ .

6. m̀wúih V m̀ dóu
   Nīgo mahntàih m̀haih hóu nàahn jē, ngóhdeih haih _____ ge.

7. deui ...... yáuh/móuh hóuchyu
   Ngóh yihngwàih sātnoih chèuhngsó chyùhnmihn gamyīn _____ .

8. hái ...... fōngmihn
   A: Néih deui Hēunggóng ge yanjeuhng dím a?
   B: _____ .

9. hóuchíh ...... jīléui ge ......
   Hái Hēunggóng ge jáulàuh, néih hóyíh sihkdóu _____ .

10. jēung ...... fong hái ......
    Chéng néih _____ .

7. Listening and speaking 🔊

聽説練習 Tingsyut lihnjaahp

7.1 Listening comprehension exercise

Please listen to the recording and fill in the blanks with the following words:

Lāaisī Wàihgāsī (Las Vegas)	gīngjai	fūnggaak	síhmàhn
gīngjai dahkkēui	jih'ōn	yìhngjeuhng	séhkēui
gīngjai faatjín	jihyìhn wàahngíng		

1. Syutmìhngwúi ge noihyùhng jyúyiu gwāanyū yīng m̀yīnggōi hái _____ hōichit dóuchèuhng.

2. Jyúyiu fáandeuige léihyàuh haih: dóubok wúih jouhsìhng douhdāk baaihwaaih, yáhnhéi _____ mahntàih.

3. Yíngóngge yàhn góng gīngjai tùhng sìhngsíh yìhngjeuhng gójahnsìh, yuhng Oumún tùhng _____ jouh jingmihn (positive) laihjí.

4. Yíngóngge yàhn yihngwàih yiu háauleuihge juhngdím haih dóuchèuhng deui dōngdeih _____ ge jokyuhng.

5. Tùhngmàaih deui dōngdeih _____ daailàihge yínghéung.

6. Kèihtā háauleuihge yānsou bāaukut: sìhngsíhge chyùhntúng, màhnfa, _____, tùhng dihngwái dángdáng.

7. Yíngóngge yàhn góng yùhgwó hōichit dóuchèuhng, hīnggin puitou tùhng gāautūng chitsī, ngóhdeih yīnggōi gwāanjyu nīdī chitsī wúih m̀wúih yínghéung _____.

8. Jingfú jouh kyutdihng gójahnsìh háauleuihge juhngdím haih _____ tùhng sìhngsíh dihngwái.

9. Hái tàihsīng sìhngsíh _____ nī fōngmihn, sēuiyiu yáuhgwāan jyūgā yìhngau.

10. Syutmìhngwúi ge muhkdīk haih séung lihng gwóngdaaih _____ fongsām, jingfú wúih chyùhnlihk wàihwuh jih'ōn.

7.2 Speech topics

1. Néih yihngwàih dímgáai yáuhdī yàhn wúih chàhmmàih dóubok ge nē? Yùhgwó kéuihdeih gaijuhk chàhmmàih dóubok, wúih yáuh mātyéh hauhgwó nē?

2. Hēunggóng ge fòhngngūk tùhng tóudeih mahntàih yìhm m̀yìhmjuhng a? Dímgáai néih gám góng nē? Fòhngngūk tùhng tóudeih mahntàih deui síhmàhn ge sāngwuht yáuh mē yínghéung a?

3. Yáuh yàhn wah, jingfú yīnggōi hīnggin dōdī dóuchèuhng tùhng yùhlohk chitsī làih chigīk gīngjai jāngjéung. Néih jaan m̀jaansìhng jingfú gámyéung jouh nē? Dímgáai a?

7.3 Speaking exercise: Please use at least 10 of the following vocabularies/patterns to say on the following topic in one to two minutes.

"Yùhgwó jingfú gaiwaahk hīnggin dóuchèuhng, néih jaan m̀jaansìhng a? Dímgáai nē?"

léihyàuh	jānggā	gúlaih	fātsih
yingfuh	kyutfaht	sēuiyiu	jūkgau
fānsīk	fēifaat	chàhmmàih	júngkut làih góng
géui ...... laihjí		yáuh ...... jokyuhng	
chùhng ...... làih tái		deui ...... yáuh/móuh hóuchyu	

8. Additional texts

附加課文 Fuhgā fomàhn

8.1. Additional text 附加課文

今日，我哋嚟講下香港嘅鄰居——澳門。澳門同香港一樣，都曾經係歐洲嘅殖民地。1553 年，葡萄牙 (Pòutòuhnga, Portugal) 人就開始住喺澳門喇，1887 年，澳門成為葡萄牙嘅殖民地。所以澳門雖然唔大，但係經過四百幾年歐洲文化嘅影響，都係一個中西文化融合，同時又有自己特色嘅城市。呢度有香港節奏咁快、壓力咁大，而且比香港多咗一啲浪漫嘅氣氛。

Gāmyaht, ngóhdeih làih góngháh Hēunggóngge lèuhngēui – Oumún. Oumún tùhng Hēunggóng yātyeuhng, dōu chàhnggīng haih Āujāuge jihkmàhndeih. Yāt ńgh ńgh sāam nìhn, Pòuhtòuhngàh yàhn jauh hōichí jyuhhái Oumún la, Yāt baat baat chāt nìhn, Oumún sìhngwàih Pòuhtòuhngàhge jihkmàhndeih. Sóyíh Oumún sēuiyìhn m̀daaih, daahnhaih gīnggwo sei baak géi nìhn Āujāu màhnfage yínghéung, dōu haih yātgo jūngsāi màhnfa yùhnghahp, tùhngsìh yauh yáuh jihgéi dahksīkge sìhngsíh. Nīdouh móuh Hēunggóng jitjau gam faai, ngaatlihk gam daaih, yìhché béi Hēunggóng dōjó yātdī lohngmaahnge heifān.

澳門有國際機場，可以坐飛機去澳門，內地遊客時時喺廣東坐飛機去澳門。如果你喺香港，就要坐船去喇，都係一種唔錯嘅體驗。好多人喺澳門玩嘅時間好短，而且都係匆匆忙忙嘅。有人直接去賭場，有人喺大三巴牌坊 (Daaihsāambā Pàaihfòng, Ruins of St. Paul's) 前面影張相，買啲禮物就走。其實，澳門值得我哋深入了解、慢慢享受。

Oumún yáuh gwokjai gēichèuhng, hóyíh chóh fēigēi heui Oumún, noihdeih yàuhhaak sìhsìh hái Gwóngdūng chóh fēigēi heui Oumún. Yùhgwó néih hái Hēunggóng, jauh yiu chóh syùhn heui la, dōuhaih yātjúng m̀choge táiyihm. Hóudō yàhn hái Oumún wáange sìhgaan hóu dyún, yìhché dōu haih chūngchūngmòhngmòhngge. Yáuh yàhn jihkjip heui dóuchèuhng, yáuh yàhn hái Daaihsāambā Pàaihfòng chìhnmihn yíng jēung séung, máaih dī láihmaht jauh jáu. Kèihsaht, Oumún jihkdāk ngóhdeih sāmyahp líuhgáai, maahnmáan héungsauh.

同香港一樣，美食都係澳門嘅特色。譬如話，一講起澳門，大家第一個就會諗到葡式蛋撻。「葡」就係葡萄牙嘅意思，呢種蛋撻係葡萄牙人帶去澳門嘅，再根據當地人嘅口味做咗一啲改變，譬如話放少啲糖，結果非常受歡迎，成為澳門最有名嘅小食。	Tùhng Hēunggóng yātyeuhng, méihsihk dōu haih Oumúnge dahksīk. Peiyùhwah, yāt gónghéi Oumún, daaihgā daihyātgo jauh wúih námdóu Pòuhsīk Daahntāat. "Pòuh" jauh haih Pòuhtòuhngàh ge yisī, nījúng daahntāat haih Pòuhtòuhngàh yàhn daai heui Oumúnge, joi gāngeui dōngdeih yàhn ge háumeih jouhjó yātdī góibin, peiyùhwah fong síudī tòhng, gitgwó fēisèuhng sauh fūnyìhng, sìhngwàih Oumún jeui yáuhméngge síusihk.
除咗葡式蛋撻，澳門仲有唔少精緻嘅葡國菜餐廳，當然，呢啲葡國菜都係有澳門特色嘅葡國菜。澳門傳統嘅中國菜都唔錯，好似點心、魚蛋、粥之類嘅嘢，同香港嘅一樣咁好食，但係價錢比香港平好多。	Chèuihjó Pòuhsīk Daahntāat, Oumún juhngyáuh m̀síu jīngjige Pòuhgwok choi chāantēng, dōngyìhn, nīdī Pòuhgwok choi dōu haih yáuh Oumún dahksīkge Pòuhgwok choi. Oumún chyùhntúngge Jūnggwok choi dōu m̀cho, hóuchíh dímsām, yùhdáan, jūk jīléuige yéh, tùhng Hēunggóngge yātyeuhng gam hóusihk, daahnhaih gachìhn béi Hēunggóng pèhng hóudō.
澳門唔大，但係有山有海，有古老嘅街道同建築，特別適合慢慢行下、坐下。食啲嘢，飲杯咖啡，睇下當地人嘅生活，過一段輕鬆嘅時間。	Oumún m̀daaih, daahnhaih yáuh sāan yáuh hói, yáuh gúlóuhge gāaidouh tùhng ginjūk, dahkbiht sīkhahp maahnmáan hàahngháh, chóhháh. Sihk dī yéh, yám būi gafē, táiháh dōngdeih yàhnge sāngwuht, gwo yātdyuhn hīngsūngge sìhgaan.

8.2 Additional vocabulary 附加詞彙

Number	Word	Yale Romanization	POS	English
1	歐洲	Āujāu	PW/N	Europe
2	殖民地	jihkmàhndeih	N	colony
3	成為	sìhngwàih	V	to become, to turn into
4	匆忙	chūngmòhng	Adj	in a hurry; in haste
5	精緻	jīngji	Adj	fine, exquisite
6	魚蛋	yùhdáan	N	fish balls
7	粥	jūk	N	porridge; congee

8.3 Please answer the following T/F questions after reading the additional text:

1 Oumún tùhng Hēunggóng dōu chàhnggīng haih Āujāu gwokgāge jihkmàhndeih. (T/F)

2 Oumún sei baak géi nìhn chìhn jauh haih Pòuhtòuhngàhge jihkmàhndeih la. (T/F)

3 Oumún dōu haih yātgo Jūngsāi màhnfa yùhnghahpge deihfōng. (T/F)

4 Noihdeih yàuhhaak sìhsìh chóhsyùhn heui Oumún, nīgo táiyihm hóu yáuh yisī. (T/F)

5 Oumún yáuhméngge gíngdím yáuh dóuchèuhng tùhng Daaihsāambā Pàaihfōng. (T/F)

6 Daahntāat haih Pòuhtòuhngàh yàhn hái Oumún chongjouh (create) ge. (T/F)

7 Oumún yáuh yātdī tùhng Hēunggóng yātyeuhng yáuh dahksīkge síusihk, daahnhaih gwaigwo Hēunggóng. (T/F)

8 Hái Oumún, hóyíh heui daaih sēungchèuhng, yauh hóyíh heui táiháh gúlóuhge gāaidouh tùhng ginjūk. (T/F)

9 Hái Oumún jitjau móuh gam faai, ngaatlihk móuh gam daaih, sīkhahp fongsūng. (T/F)

8.4 Topics for discussions

1 Hóudō ngoihlòih màhnfa heui dou yātgo deihfōng jīhauh dōu wúih faatsāng mātyéh binfa? Néih nám m̀námdóu yātdī laihjí a ?

2 Néih yáuh móuh heuigwo Oumún a? Nèih jūng m̀jūngyi gódouh a ? Dímgáai a ?

3 Néih gokdāk néih wúih jūngyi jyuhhái Oumún dihnghaih Hēunggóng a? Dímgáai a?

8.5 Authentic oral data 1 🔊
真實語料 1

8.6 Authentic oral data 2 🔊
真實語料 2

Lesson 7　Hong Kong for Sports Events

申辦賽事

1. Pragmatic factors, Yuti features and linguistic functions

語用因素、語體特徵與語言功能 Yúhyuhng yānsou, yúhtái dahkjīng yúh yúhyìhn gūngnàhng

Pragmatic factors/ Yuti features 語用因素 / 語體特徵	Linguistic function 語言功能
Pragmatic factors: This is a typical scenario for a formal situation, both in terms of content and context, calling for formal features of language and permitting a confrontational style.	**Linguistic function:** Criticizing List facts to refute someone else's argument while further emphasizing the advantages of your own argument.
語用因素： 場合正式，內容嚴肅，所以語體正式，詞句針鋒相對。	語言功能：反駁 列舉事實來反駁他人觀點，並進一步指出支持自己觀點的有利方面。
Yuti features: Formality index: 2+	
語體特徵：2+	

Notes on pragmatic knowledge 語用知識	Notes on structure 語言及篇章結構知識
I. Yuti，tone and other 語體、口氣與褒貶	I. Grammar and sentence patterns 語法和句型

Notes on pragmatic knowledge 語用知識

I. Yuti，tone and other 語體、口氣與褒貶

1. Describing a task that is hard and thankless in nature「吃力不討好」
2. Absolutely groundless; to refute「…… 絕對唔成立 …… 反駁」
3. The so-called …「所謂嘅勞民傷財」
4. Therefore my conclusion is:「所以我嘅結論係」

II.   Related knowledge 相關知識

1. Olympic equestrian events「奧運馬術比賽」
2. Necessary conditions needed (for a task or event)「天時地利人和」

Notes on structure 語言及篇章結構知識

I. Grammar and sentence patterns 語法和句型

1. "m̀sái góng…,ganggā m̀sái góng…" let alone, not to mention
2. "sówaih" so-called
3. "chàhnggīng" once; used to
4. "Chan nīgo gēiwuih", take this chance to
5. "Yānwaih…ge gwāanhaih", because of…
6. "…jīyāt" and " kèihjūng jīyāt" meaning "one of…"
7. "…jījūng, (kèihjūng)…" and "hóu dō/hóu fūngfu, kèihjūng…" meaning "among…"
8. "sauh (dou)" as a passive marker
9. "chèuihchí yíh/jī ngoih" besides; in addition
10. QW jauh QW
11. "geiyìhn haih gám" , under the circumstances; in that case
12. Use of "béi" to form passive sentences

II. Paragraph and discourse 語段和篇章

1. "yātlàih…, yihlàih…, jeuihauh…" firstly…, secondly…, finally…

2. Text 🔊

課文 Fomàhn

主持人、各位參加辯論會嘅朋友，大家好。頭先嗰位發言人講嘅嘢，我並唔係好認同。首先乜嘢叫做勞民傷財先？如果俾咗好多錢、用咗好多時間、影響普通市民嘅生活，但係香港得唔到好處，嗰樣先至係勞民傷財，吃力不討好。但係舉辦大型國際體育賽事係宣傳香港嘅好機會，係一個投資，而唔係嘥錢。因為如果香港舉辦大型國際體育賽事，唔使講會吸引嚟自唔同地區唔同國家嘅人嚟香港消費，更加唔使講大型賽事會令香港成為世界嘅焦點，對提升香港嘅國際形象有好大嘅幫助。所以所謂嘅勞民傷財呢個論點係絕對唔成立嘅，我喺呢度反駁呢個論點。

Jyúchìh yàhn, gokwái chāamgā bihnleuhn wúi ge pàhngyáuh, daaihgā hóu. Tàuhsīn gówái faatyìhnyàhn góng ge yéh, ngóh bihng m̀haih hóu yihngtùhng. Sáusīn mātyéh giujouh lòuhmàhn sēungchòih sīn? Yùhgwó béijó hóudō chín, yuhngjó hóudō sìhgaan, yínghéung póutūng síhmàhnge sāngwuht, daahnhaih Hēunggóng dāk m̀dóu hóuchyu, gámyéung sīnji haih lòuhmàhn sēungchòih, heklihk bāt tóuhóu. Daahnhaih géuibaahn daaihyìhng gwokjai táiyuhk choisih haih syūnchyùhn Hēunggóng ge hóu gēiwuih, haih yātgo tàuhjī, yìh m̀haih sāaichín. Yānwaih yùhgwó Hēunggóng géuibaahn daaihyìhng gwokjai táiyuhk choisih, m̀sái góng wúih kāpyáhn làihjih m̀tùhng deihkēui m̀tùhng gwokgāge yàhn làih Hēunggóng sīufai, ganggā m̀sái góng daaihyìhng choisih wúih lihng Hēunggóng sìhngwàih saigaaige jīudím, deui tàihsīng Hēunggóngge gwokjai yìhngjeuhng yáuh hóu daaihge bōngjoh. Sóyíh sówaih ge lòuhmàhn sēungchòih nīgo leuhndím haih jyuhtdeui m̀sìhnglahp ge, ngóh hái nīdouh fáanbok nīgo leuhndím.

其實香港對於舉辦大型國際體育賽事有唔少經驗。以前香港曾經舉辦過好多次國際網球賽，最近十幾年香港每年都舉辦國際欖球賽同馬拉松，而且參加人數越嚟越多，好多運動員每年都特登飛嚟香港參加比賽。另外 2008 年北京奧運會，香港負責過馬術比賽，第二年又舉辦過東亞運動會。最近幾年，香港舉辦大型嘅渡海泳比賽，參加比賽嘅人由香港島游水游到去九龍，參加嘅運動員之中，有唔少係外國人嚟嘅。嗰樣就可以知道大型國際體育賽事真係吸引到好多外國人嚟香港。

Kèihsaht Hēunggóng deuiyū géuibaahn daaihyìhng gwokjai táiyuhk choisih yáuh m̀síu gīngyihm. Yíhchìhn Hēunggóng chàhnggīng géuibaahngwo hóudō chi gwokjai móhngkàuh choi, jeuigahn sahp géi nìhn Hēunggóng múihnìhn dōu géuibaahn gwokjai láamkàuh choi tùhng máhlāaichùhng, yìhché chāamgā yàhnsou yuhtlàih yuht dō, hóudō wahnduhng yùhn múihnìhn dōu dahkdāng fēilàih Hēunggóng chāamgā béichoi. Lihngngoih yih-lìhng-lìhng-baat nìhn Bākgīng Ouwahn Wúi, Hēunggóng fuhjaakgwo máhseuht béichoi, daihyih nìhn yauh géuibaahn gwo Dūngnga Wahnduhng Wúi. Jeuigahn géi nìhn, Hēunggóng géuibaahn daaihyìhngge douhhói wihng béichoi, chāamgā béichoige yàhn yàuh Hēunggóng Dóu yàuhséui yàuhdou heui Gáulùhng, chāamgāge wahnduhng yùhn jījūng, yáuh m̀síu haih ngoihgwok yàhn làihge. Gámyéung jauh hóyíh jīdou daaihyìhng gwokjai táiyuhk choisih jānhaih kāpyáhndóu hóudō ngoihgwok yàhn làih Hēunggóng.

我想趁呢個機會講下一啲歷史事實，喺北京舉辦奧運期間，一啲前置功夫，前置功夫包括提高英文水平，一系列嘅英文菜單啦，同埋服務人員嘅應對啦。其實噉樣對於服務業嚟講，其實唔係單一指一個短短嘅奧運效應，而係長期嚟講係對北京有益而無害。因為奧運嘅關係，北京城市整體嘅形象同埋裏面嘅人嘅素質係會大大嘅提高。香港更加唔使講，香港其實喺酒店服務業，我哋嘅英文水平，其實已經達到一定嘅水準。

Ngóh séung chan nīgo gēiwuih gónghâh yātdī lihksí sihsaht, hái Bākgīng géuibaahn Ouwahn kèihgāan, yātdī chìhnji gūngfū, chìhnji gūngfū bāaukut tàihgōu Yīngmàhn séuipìhng, yāt haihlihtge Yīngmàhn choidāan lā, tùhngmàaih fuhkmouh yàhnyùhnge yingdeui lā. Kèihsaht gámyéung deuiyū fuhkmouh yihp làihgóng, kèihsaht m̀haih dāanyāt jí yātgo dyúndyún ge Ouwahn haauhying, yìhhaih chèuhngkèih làihgóng haih deui Bākgīng yáuhyīk yìh mòuh hoih. Yānwaih Ouwahnge gwāanhaih, Bākgīng sìhngsíh jíngtáige yìhngjeuhng tùhngmàaih léuihmihnge yàhn ge soujāt haih wúih daaihdaaih gám tàihgōu. Hēunggóng ganggā m̀sái góng, Hēunggóng kèihsaht hái jáudim fuhkmouh yihp, ngóhdeihge Yīngmàhn séuipìhng, kèihsaht yíhgīng daahtdou yātdihngge séuijéun.

呀，我想講嘅係一啲嘅基建。一啲奧運嘅場所之中，其中北京鳥巢同埋水立方，除咗成為奧運會嘅體育場館，其實亦都可以成為日後嘅一個健身場所。噉樣我相信喺香港如果我哋有類似嘅建築，呢啲建築將會成為香港一個新嘅特色同埋外來遊客一啲嘅參觀景點。

A, ngóh séung góngge haih yātdīge gēigin. Yātdī Ouwahnge chèuhngsó jījūng, kèihjūng Bākgīng Níuhchàauh tùhngmàaih Séuilahpfōng, chèuihjó sìhngwàih Ouwahnwúi ge táiyuhk chèuhnggún, kèihsaht yihkdōu hóyíh sìhngwàih yahthauhge yātgo gihnsān chèuhngsó. Gámyéung ngóh sēungseun hái Hēunggóng yùhgwó ngóhdeih yáuh leuihchíhge ginjūk, nīdī ginjūk jēungwúih sìhngwàih Hēunggóng yātgo sānge dahksīk tùhngmàaih ngoihlòih yàuhhaak yātdī ge chāamgūn gíngdím.

仲有一啲係，潛在嘅影響。我哋知道喺一啲嘅城市如果佢哋舉辦一啲嘅比賽，呀，譬如話係賽車比賽，其實喺比賽期間唔單只係市內嘅人可以觀賞，其實唔少境外嘅電視觀眾都會聚焦喺我哋香港呢一個城市，香港會受到全世界嘅關注。噉樣係會提高香港嘅知名度同埋國際嘅影響力，係有一個正面嘅影響嘅。除此之外，我哋十分之著重一啲本地體育發展，其實對於運動員嚟講亦都係一個好大嘅鼓舞。

Juhngyáuh yātdī haih, chìhmjoihge yínghéung. Ngóhdeih jīdou hái yātdī ge sìhngsíh yùhgwó kéuihdeih géuibaahn yātdī ge béichoi, a, peiyùh wah haih choichē béichoi, Kèihsaht hái béichoi kèihgāan m̀dāanjí haih síhnoih ge yàhn hóyíh gūnséung, kèihsaht m̀síu gíngngoihge dihnsih gūnjung dōu wúih jeuihjīu hái ngóhdeih Hēunggóng nī yātgo sìhngsíh, Hēunggóng wúih sauhdou chyùhn saigaaige gwāanjyu. Gámyéung haih wúih tàihgōu Hēunggóngge jīmìhngdouh tùhngmàaih gwokjaige yínghéung lihk, haih yáuh yātgo jingmihnge yínghéung ge. Chèuihchí jīngoih, ngóhdeih sahpfānjī jeuhkjuhngge yātdī búndeih táiyuhk faatjín, kèihsaht deuiyū wahnduhngyùhn làihgóng yihkdōu haih yātgo hóudaaihge gúmóuh.

我認為香港作為一個國際城市，其實已經具備足夠嘅條件舉辦更多嘅大型國際體育賽事。一嚟香港嘅交通方便，鐵路、公路網絡四通八達，香港嘅塞車問題同其他亞洲城市比較唔算嚴重，二嚟香港嘅機場係全世界最好嘅機場之一，運動員可以喺短時間去到比賽場地。其次係香港有先進嘅通訊網絡，想將喺香港比賽嘅消息發送去邊就可以發送去邊。第三，香港係亞洲以至全世界最安全嘅國際城市，運動員可以放心留喺香港比賽，唔使擔心會有乜嘢危險。呢三方面都表示香港舉辦大型國際體育賽事有晒" 天時地利人和"。所以我嘅結論係香港應該要把握機會，而且比賽場地喺比賽結束之後都可以開放俾市民使用，既然係噉，普通市民都可以得到好處，噉樣點可以話舉辦大型賽事係得不償失呢？我希望大家能夠繼續支持香港申辦大型國際賽事。

Ngóh yihngwàih Hēunggóng jokwàih yātgo gwokjai sìhngsíh, kèihsaht yíhgīng geuihbeih jūkgauge tiuhgín géuibaahn gangdō ge daaihyìhng gwokjai táiyuhk choisih. Yātlàih Hēunggóngge gāautūng fōngbihn, titlouh, gūnglouh móhnglohk sei tūng baat daaht, Hēunggóng ge sākchē mahntàih tùhng kèihtā Ngajāu sìhngsíh béigaau m̀syun yìhmjuhng, yihlàih Hēunggóngge gēichèuhng haih chyùhn saigaai jeuihóuge gēichèuhng jīyāt, wahnduhngyùhn hóyíh hái dyún sìhgaan heuidou béichoi chèuhngdeih. Kèihchi haih Hēunggóng yáuh sīnjeunge tūngseun móhnglohk, séung jēung hái Hēunggóng béichoige sīusīk faatsung heui bīn jauh hóyíh faatsung heui bīn. Daihsāam, Hēunggóng haih Ngajāu yíhji chyùhn saigaai jeui ōnchyùhnge gwokjai sìhngsíh, wahnduhngyùhn hóyíh fongsām làuhhái Hēunggóng béichoi, m̀sái dāamsām wúih yáuh mātyéh ngàihhím. Nī sāam fōngmihn dōu bíusih Hēunggóng géuibaahn daaihyìhng gwokjai táiyuhk choisih yáuh saai "tīnsìh deihleih yàhnwòh". Sóyíh ngóhge gitleuhn haih Hēunggóng yīnggōi yiu bá'ngāak gēiwuih, yìhché béichoi chèuhngdeih hái béichoi gitchūk jīhauh dōu hóyíh hōifong béi síhmàhn síyuhng, geiyìhn haih gám, póutūng síhmàhn dōu hóyíh dākdóu hóuchyu, gámyéung dím hóyíh wah géuibaahn daaihyìhng choisih haih dāk bāt sèuhng sāt nē? Ngóh hēimohng daaihgā nàhnggau gaijuhk jīchìh Hēunggóng sānbaahn daaihyìhng gwokjai choisih.

3. Vocabulary in use 🔊

活用詞彙 Wuhtyuhng chìhwuih

3.1 Common vocabulary

Number	Word	Yale Romanization	POS	English
1	發言人	faatyìhnyàhn	N	spokesperson
2	體育賽事	táiyuhk choisih	N	sports event
3	宣傳	syūnchyùhn	N/V	promotion; to promote
4	投資	tàuhjī	N/V	investment; to invest
5	嘥錢	sāaichín	Adj/VO	wasteful of money; to waste money
6	消費	sīufai	N/V	consumption; to consume
7	焦點	jīudím	N	focus
8	所謂	sówaih	Adj	so-called
9	唔成立	m̀sìhnglahp	PH	invalid
10	反駁	fáanbok	V	to refute
11	論點	leuhndím	N	argument, point of view taken in discussion
12	經驗	gīngyihm	N	experience
13	曾經	chàhnggīng	Adv	to have had the experience of; indicating that an action once happened or a state once existed
14	特登	dahkdāng	Adv	intentionally, deliberately
15	負責	fuhjaak	V	to be responsible for, to be in charge of
16	應對	yingdeui	N/V	response; to respond
17	長期	chèuhngkèih	PH	long-term; over a long period of time
18	體育場館	táiyuhk chèuhnggún	N	sports complex

19	健身場所	gihnsān chèuhngsó	N	fitness centre
20	潛在	chìhmjoih	Adj	potential
21	觀賞	gūnséung	V	to watch, to view and admire
22	電視觀眾	dihnsih gūnjung	N	television audience
23	聚焦	jeuihjīu	V	to focus
24	知名度	jīmìhngdouh	N	popularity
25	正面	jingmihn	Adj	positive
26	著重	jeuhkjuhng	V	to stress, to emphasize
27	鼓舞	gú móuh	N/V	inspiration; to inspire
28	消息	sīusīk	N	news
29	發送	faatsung	V	to send
30	結論	gitleuhn	N	conclusion
31	把握	bá'ngāak	N/V	certainty, assurance; to seize (chances, opportunities)
32	開放	hōifong	V	to open to the public
33	支持	jīchìh	V	to support

3.2 Place names

1	北京鳥巢	Bākgīng Níuhchàauh	PW	Beijing Bird's Nest
2	水立方	Séuilahpfōng	PW	Water Cube

3.3 Sports events

1	網球賽	móhngkàuh choi	N	tennis competition
2	欖球賽	láamkàuh choi	N	rugby competition
3	馬拉松	máhlāaichùhng	N	marathon
4	奧運會	Ouwahnwúi	PN	Olympic Games
5	馬術比賽	máhseuht béichoi	N	equestrian competition

6	東亞運動會	Dūngnga Wahnduhngwúi	PN	East Asian Games
7	渡海泳	douhhóiwihng	N	cross-harbour swimming
8	賽車	choichē	N	car racing

3.4 About transport (gāautūng 交通) and network (móhnglohk 網絡)

1	鐵路	titlouh	N	railway
2	公路網絡	gūnglouh móhnglohk	N	network of highways
3	四通八達	sei tūng baat daaht	PH	extending in all directions
4	塞車	sākchē	Adj/V	congested with traffic; to get stuck in traffic jam
5	通訊網絡	tūngseun móhnglohk	N	communication network

3.5 Other vocabularies

1	頭先	tàuhsīn	Adv	a moment before, amoment ago, just now
2	服務人員	fuhkmouh yàhnyùhn	N	service staff
3	酒店服務業	jáudim fuhkmouh yihp	N	hotel services industry
4	基建	gēigin	N	infrastructure

3.6 Useful expressions

1	勞民傷財	lòuhmàhn sēungchòih	PH	wasting manpower and money; exhausting the people and draining the treasury
2	吃力不討好	heklihk bāttóuhóu	PH	strenuous and unrewarding; arduous and thankless task
3	前置功夫	chìhnji gūngfū	N	preparation efforts
4	奧運效應	Ouwahn haauhying	N	the Olympic effect
5	有益而無害	yáuhyīk yìh mòuhhoih	PH	beneficial and harmless

| 6 | 天時地利人和 | tīn sìh deih leih yàhn wòh | PH | the timing is right, and the geographical and social conditions are favourable |
| 7 | 得不償失 | dāk bāt sèuhng sāt | PH | the loss outweighs the gain |

4. Notes on language and discourse structure
語言及篇章結構知識 Yúhyìhn kahp pīnjēung gitkau jīsīk

4.1. Grammar and sentence patterns 語法和句型

4.1.1. "m̀sái góng…,ganggā m̀sái góng…" let alone, not to mention

1. Kéuih lìhn Bākgīng dōu meih heuigwo, m̀sáigóng chēutgwok, jiyū yìhmàhn jauh ganggā m̀sái góng.

2. Ngóh gokdāk dóuchèuhng m̀haih ngóhdeih sìhngsíhge fūnggaak (style), hōichit dóuchèuhng yauh lòuhmàhn sēungchòih, m̀sái góng wúih yínghéung gīngjai, jiyū séhwúi jihōn jauh ganggā m̀sái góng la.

3. Yùhgwó Hēunggóng géuibaahn daaihyìhng gwokjai táiyuhk choisih, m̀sái góng wúih kāpyáhn làihjih m̀tùhng deihkēui m̀tùhng gwokgāge yàhn làih Hēunggóng sīufai, ganggā m̀sái góng wúih tàihsīng Hēunggóngge gwokjai yìhngjeuhng.

4.1.2. "sówaih" so-called

1. Geiyìhn haih gám, sówaihge "waih síhmàhn jeuhkséung" jauh jānhaih góng daaihwah la.

2. Yihbaak / léuhngbaak mān, nīdī jauh haih néihdeih sówaihge "pùihsèuhng (compensation)" làh?

3. Kéuih jauhhaih néih sówaihge "hóuyàhn" la.

4.1.3. "chàhnggīng" once; used to

1. Hēunggóng chàhnggīng géuibaahngwo hóudō chi gwokjai móhngkàuh béichoi.

2. Kéuih chàhnggīng hái ngàhnhòhng jouhgwo yéh, yìhgā hái ngūkkéi jiugu síu pàhngyáuh.

3. Ngóh chàhnggīng hái Yahtbún jyuhgwo léuhngnìhn, hohkgwo Yahtmán, bātgwo yìhgā dōu m̀geidāksaai la.

4.1.4. "chan…", "chan nīgo gēiwuih", "je nīgo gēiwuih", "leihyuhng nīgo gēiwuih", take this chance to

1. Sēuiyìhn jeuigahn hóu mòhng, daahnhaih ngóh dōu wúih chāamgā néihdeihge wuhtduhng, yānwaih hóyíh chan nīgo gēiwuih tùhng daaihgā ginháh mihn.
2. Chan kéuih juhng meih jáu, néih faaidī mahn kéuih lā.
3. Ngóhdeih yīnggōi chan dūngtīn meih dou heui gódouh léuihhàhng.
4. Chan yìhgā meih hōiwúi, ngóh heui máaih būi gafē sīn.
5. Bātyùh néih chan nīgo sānnìhn gakèih chēutheui wáanháh lā.
6. Néih séung m̀séung chan meih hōijihk túhng sānlòhng sānnèuhng kīngháh gái a?
7. Ngóh séung je nīgo gēiwuih gámjeh …
8. Ngóh gāmyaht góng yāt góng Hēunggóng ge gaauyuhk, dōu je nīgo gēiwuih gaaisiuh yātháh ngóhge hohkhaauh.
9. Hái Hēunggóng, chèuihjó hohk Jūngmàhn, ngóh dōu séung leihyuhng nīgo gēiwuih líuhgáai Hēunggóng màhnfa.

4.1.5. "yānwaih… ge gwāanhaih", because of…

1. Yānwaih yáuh hóudō yàhn ge gwāanhaih, jauh móuh báai johwái.
2. Ngóh m̀máaih haih yānwaih móuh chín ge gwāanhaih.
3. Néih m̀sái gēng béi lóuhsai cháau yàuhyú wo. Lóuhsai m̀hōisām, m̀haih yānwaih néihge gwāanhaih, haih yānwaih kéuih taaitáai ge gwāanhaih..
4. Kéuih m̀chāamgā haih yānwaih néih chāamgā ge gwāanhaih.
5. Yānwaih taai chiùhsāp ge gwāanhaih, ngóhdeih chāutīn ji heui gódouh wáan la.

4.1.6. "…jīyāt" and "kèihjūng jīyāt", meaning "one of…"

1. Bíuyínge jitmuhk hóu fūngfu, kèihjūng jīyāt haih góng siuwá.
2. Ngóh jyuhgwo hóudō deihfōng, Hēunggóng haih kèihjūng jīyāt.
3. Wòhng sīnsāang haih ngóhge Jūnggwok pàhngyáuh jīyāt.
4. Nībún haih ngóh séung máaih ge syū jīyāt.
5. Kéuih haih wúih gaausyū ge sīnsāang jīyāt.
6. Hēunggóng yáuh hóudō yáuhchín ge yàhn, néih haih m̀haih kèihjūng jīyāt a?

4.1.7. "…jījūng, (kèihjūng)…" and "…hóu dō/hóu fūngfu, kèihjūng…", meaning "among…"

1. Tùhnghohk jījūng, yáuhdī jihyuhn daai dī yéh sihk làih tùhng daaihgā fānhéung.
2. Dímsām jījūng, néih jeui jūngyi sihk mātyéh a?
3. Hóigwāan jīkyùhn jījūng, (kèihjūng) yáuh yātgo haih ngóhge tùhnghohk.
4. Kéuihge hàhngléih jījūng, (kèihjūng) yáuh yātgihn m̀ginjó.

Sometimes, only "kèihjūng" is used.

5. Ngóh yáuh hóudō tùhnghohk, kèihjūng yáuh dī háng jihyuhn daai dī yéh sihk làih tùhng daaihgā fānhéung.
6. Máahnwúi ge jitmuhk hóu fūngfu, kèihjūng yātgo haih sīnsāang hohksāang daaih hahpcheung.

4.1.8. "sauh (dou)" as a passive marker

1. Kéuih haih yātgo hóu lóuhsī, hóu sauh hohksāang fūnyìhng.
2. Yātgo yàhnge singgaak (personality) hónàhng sauhdou gātìhngge yínghéung, dōu wúih sauhdou pàhngyáuhge yínghéung.
3. Nīgo gaiwaahk sauhdou gok fōngmihnge pāipìhng (criticism).

4.1.9. "Chèuihchí yíh/jī ngoih" besides; in addition

1. Chèuihchí yíhngoih, ngóh juhng séung gónggháh hōichit dóuchèuhng juhng yáuh mātyéh waaihchyu.
2. Yiu wángūng, gáanlihk (resume), gīngyihm dōu hóu juhngyiu, chèuihchí jīngoih, tēuijinseun (recommendation letter) dōu héi hóu daaihge jokyuhng.
3. Hēunggóng yáuh gūnglahp hohkhaauh, sīlahp hohkhaauh, chèuihchí jīngoih, gwokjai hohkhaauh dōu haih yātjúng syúnjaahk.

4.1.10. QW jauh QW, whatever, whoever, whenever, wherever, …

1. Néih jūngyi sihk géidō jauh géidō.
2. Néih yiu géi daaihge jauh máaih géi daaihge.
3. Néih séung heui géi noih jauh géi noih.
4. Néih géisìh làihdāk jauh géisìh làih.
5. Néih yiu máaih bīngo jauh máaih bīngo.
6. Néih jūngyi heui bīndouh jauh bīndouh.
7. Néih wah yiu māt, màhmā jauh máaih māt.
8. Néih séung dím jouh jauh dím jouh.

9.   Néih yiu tùhng bīngo heui jauh tùhng bīngo heui.

4.1.11. "geiyìhn haih gám" under the circumstances; in that case

1.   Ngóh góng hóudō chi néih dōu m̀tēng. Geiyìhn haih gám, néih m̀sái joi mahn ngóh la.

2.   Sihkyīn deui sihkyīnge yàhn tùhng jāuwàihge yàhn dōu móuh hóuchyu. Geiyìhn haih gám, jauh yīnggōi gamyīn.

3.   Hahgo yuht yáuh sei yaht chèuhng gakèih, geiyìhn haih gám, ngóhdeih jauh ōnpàaih yātchi dyúnsin léuihhàhng (short trip).

4.1.12. Use of "béi" to form passive sentence

"Béi" as co-verb carries the same function as the preposition "by" in English passive sentence. When forming passive sentences in Cantonese, "béi" is used and placed before the person who carries the action (actor) and after the object.

e.g.

Active sentence	Actor	Verb	Object
	kéuih	dálaahnjó	ngóh jek būi
Passive sentence	Object	Actor	Verb
	ngóh jek būi	béi kéuih	dálaahnjó

1.   Nīgo gittā béi Gām sāang máaihjó la!
2.   Nīchi dábō béi gógāan hohkhaauh (ge hohksāang) lódóu daihyāt.
3.   Gāan fóng dī dāng béi kéuih hōijeuhkjó.
4.   Nīdihp sung tùhng dī dímsām béi gógo jīkyùhn sihksaai bo!
5.   Nīgo daahngōu béi dī saimānjái sihksaai.
6.   Góga jeui sān ge dāanchē béi kéuih máaihdóu la!
7.   Gógo chīmjing béi kéuih lódóu la!
8.   Kéuih béi bàhbā sungjó heui Méihgwok duhksyū.

4.2. Paragraph and discourse 語段和篇章

4.2.1. "yātlàih..., yihlàih.., jeuihauh...", firstly..., secondly..., finally...

1.   Ngóhdeih géuihàhng gāmchi ge wuhtduhng, yātlàih béi daaihgā yātgo gēiwuih lihnjaahp, yihlàih hingjūk sānnìhn.

2. Gámyéung sé, yātlàih lengdī, yihlàih chīngchódī.

3. Néih dōu heui lā, yātlàih hóyíh tūhng kéuihdeih kīnggái, yihlàih hóyíh sīk dōdī pàhngyáuh.

4. Yātlàih dī saimānjái dōu daaih la, yihlàih hóusíu gāmouh yiu jouh, sóyíh móuh chéng gūngyàhn.

5. Nīgihn sāam yātlàih taai chèuhng, yihlàih taai gwai, sóyíh ngóh m̀máaih.

6. Yātlàih ngóh m̀sīk dá gōyíhfūkàuh, yihlàih ngóh m̀séung chéngga, sóyíh ngóh m̀heui la.

7. Ngóh yihngwàih Hēunggóng yíhgīng geuihbeih jūkgau ge tìuhgín géuibaahn gangdō ge daaihyìhng gwokjai táiyuhk choisih. Yātlàih, Hēunggóng ge gāautūng fōngbihn, wahnduhngyùhn hóyíh hái dyún sìhgaan heuidou m̀tùhngge béichoi chèuhngdeih; yihlàih, Hēunggóng yáuh sīnjeun ge tūngseun móhnglohk, séung jēung hái Hēunggóng béichoi ge sīusīk faatsung heui bīn jauh hóyíh faatsung heui bīn. Jeuihauh, Hēunggóng haih Ngajāu yíhji chyùhn saigaai jeui ōnchyùhn ge gwokjai sìhngsíh, wahnduhngyùhn hóyíh fongsām làuh hái Hēunggóng béichoi, m̀sái dāamsām wúih yáuh mātyéh ngàihhím.

8. Hóudō yàuhhaak dōu hóu jūngyi làih Hēunggóng léuihhàhng. Yātlàih, Hēunggóng yáuh géi go daaihyìhng jyútàih lohkyùhn, yàuhhaak hóyíh hái gódī deihfōng wáan jeui síu yātléuhng yaht; yihlàih, Hēunggóng yáuh hóu dō m̀tùhng júngleuih ge deihdouh méihsihk. Jeuihauh, Hēunggóng ge gāautūng fōngbihn, jih'ōn yauh hóu, yàuhhaak làih Hēunggóng léuihyàuh, dōu hóyíh hóu ōnchyùhn gám seiwàih heui, m̀sái dāamsām wúih yáuh mātyéh màhfàahn tùhng ngàihhím.

5. Notes on pragmatic knowledge

語用因素與相關知識 Yúhyuhng yānsou yúh sēunggwāan jīsīk

5.1. Yuti, tone and other 語體、口氣與褒貶

5.1.1. "吃力不討好 heklihk bāt tóuhóu" (describing a task that) is hard and thankless in nature

By choosing words and expressions that are derogatory in nature, such as this one, the speaker shows his/her attitude towards what is being talked about. If understanding of the "meaning" from the structure shows knowledge of the speaker, then awareness of the connotation is an indication of the pragmatic proficiency.

- Nīgo gaiwaahk jānhaih heklihk bāt tóuhóu.
- Heklihk bāt tóuhóu ge sih ngóhdeih chùhnglòih dōu m̀jouh.

5.1.2. "…… 絕對唔成立 jyuhtdeui m̀sìhnglahp …… 反駁 fáanbok" absolutely groundless; to refute

Opposite to euphemism, which is highly valued in the Chinese culture when it comes to criticism, direct opposition is not common in most contexts. By describing opinions from others as "absolutely groundless" and clearly expressing the intention of the speaker is to "refute", the speaker here is adopting the argumentation style of direct confrontation. When used properly, such an approach is very powerful but anybody doing this should be fully aware of the possible hostile reaction from the audience.

- Ngóh yihngwàih nīgo gūndím jyuhtdeui m̀sìhnglahp, hahmihn géigo fōngmihn hóyíh fáanbok.
- Néihge gūndím ngóh jyuhtdeui m̀tùhngyi.

5.1.3. " 所謂嘅勞民傷財 sówaih ge lòuhmàhn sēungchòih" the so-called

Again, the use of the word " 所謂嘅 sówaih ge" (so-called) is an indication the speaker's attitude towards what is being described. Obviously, the speaker does not agree to the criticism that applying to host the sports event is " 勞民傷財 lòuhmàhn sēungchòih" (a waste of manpower and money) and therefore put " 所謂嘅 sówaih ge" (so-called) in front of this phrase by the opponents to show his/her position.

- Sówaihge lòuhmàhn sēungchòih…
- Sówaih "yáuhbehng làih m̀dóu", kèihsaht haih kéuih m̀séung làih.

5.1.4. " 所以我嘅結論係 sóyíh ngóhge gitleuhn haih" Therefore my conclusion is:

Referring to the above, the tone of this speech is confrontational at the beginning. There are of course many ways to present one's conclusion and the way here is also very decisive in terms of style. It may sound a little bit pompous in a casual style or with a relatively casual setting, but pragmatically, it is consistent with the overall tone of this argumentation, especially when in combination with all the rhetorical means following this phrase.

- Sóyíh ngóhge gitleuhn haih jīchìh Hēunggóng géuibaahn daaihyìhng choisih.
- Gāngeui sóyáuhge jīlíu (data), ngóhdeihge gitleuhn haih…

5.2. Related knowledge 相關知識

5.2.1. " 奧運馬術比賽 Ouwahn máhseuht béichoi" Olympic equestrian events

This refers to the events during the 2008 Olympic Games, which was hosted by Beijing in China. Hong Kong co-hosted some of the events including the Olympic equestrian events with the facilities available at that time.

- Tīngyahtge máhseuht béichoi hái bīngo máhchèuhng géuihàhng nē?

5.2.2. " 天 時 地 利 人 和 tīnsìh deihleih yàhnwòh" necessary conditions needed (for a task or event)

Literally, "tīn" means the sky, "deih" means the earth, while "yàhn" means the people and collectively, the 3 words together as used here just mean that all the conditions needed for the success of something are available, including the right timing, the convenience (of location or setting) that happens to be around, and the human recourses (or the right kind of connections).

- Jūnggwok yàhn sēungseun yātgihn sih yiu sìhnggūng, yiu yáuh tīnsìh deihleih tùhng yàhnwòh.
- Nīgo gaiwaahk deihleih tùhng yàhnwòh dōu yáuh, hósīk sìhgaan m̀ngāam.

6. Contextualized speaking practice

情境説話練習 Chìhnggíng syutwah lihnjaahp

【課前預習】Class preparation

6.1. Please answer the following True/False questions according to the lesson text.

1　Yíngóngge yàhn yihngwàih géuibaahn daaihyìhng gwokjai choisih haih syūnchyùhn Hēunggóngge hóu gēiwuih. (T/F)

2 Hēunggóng géuibaahngwo hóudō chi gwokjai làahmkàuh choi, gwokjai láamkàuh choi tùhng máhlāaichùhng. (T/F)

3 Yih-lìhng-lìhng-baat nìhn Bākgīng Ouwahnwúi, Hēunggóng fuhjaakjó choichē, yauh géuibaahnjó dūngnga wahnduhngwúi. (T/F)

4 Yíngóngge yàhn jíchēut daaihyìhng gwokjai táiyuhk choisih kāpyáhnjó hóudō ngoihgwok yàhn làih Hēunggóng. (T/F)

5 Yíngóngge yàhn yuhng Bākgīng géuibaahn Ouwahn ge laihjí jīchìh Hēunggóng géuibaahn daaihyìhng béichoi. (T/F)

6 Hēunggóng yùhgwó yáuh hóuchíh Séuilahpfōng ge ginjūk m̀wúih daailàih hóuchyu.(T/F)

7 Daaihyìhng gwokjai táiyuhk choisih mòuhjoh (cannot help) búndeih táiyuhk faatjín. (T/F)

8 Hēunggóng ge sākchē mahntàih tùhng kèihtā Ngajāu sìhngsíh chā m̀dō. (T/F)

9 Hēunggóngge gēichèuhng haih chyùhn saigaai jeuihóuge gēichèuhng jīyāt. (T/F)

10 Hēunggóng haih Ngajāu yíhji chyùhn saigaai jeui ōnchyùhnge gwokjai sìhngsíh. (T/F)

6.2. Please explain the following phrases in Cantonese

1 四通八達 seitūng baatdaaht
2 吃力不討好 heklihk bāt tóuhóu
3 基建 gēigin
4 天時地利人和 tīnsìh deihleih yàhnwòh

【課後練習】 Post-class exercises

6.3 Fill in the blanks with the given vocabularies. Each vocabulary can be chosen once only.

syūnchyùhn	tàuhjī	sāaichín	sīufai
jīudím	gīngyihm	fuhjaak	yingdeui
chìhmjoih	gūnséung	jingmihn	jeuhkjuhng
bá'ngāak	hōifong		

1. Yih-lìhng-lìhng-baat nìhn Ouwahnwúi yàuh Jūnggwok Bākgīng _____ géuibaahn.

2. Hái daaihhohk duhksyū sìhkèih nàhnggau chēutgwok làuhhohk, haih yātgo hóu hóu ge hohkjaahp táiyihm, néih yiu hóu hóu _____ gāmchi ge gēiwuih a.

3. Yùhgwó néih séung faaidī chóuhdóu chín máaihláu, jauh m̀hóu sèhngyaht _____ máaih gam dō yéh.

4. Chèuihjó hái ūkkéi jīngoih, Hēunggóng síhmàhn juhng hóyíh hái sēungchèuhng a, jáubā a, sihksi (restaurants) a dángdáng ge deihfōng _____ daaihyìhng ge táiyuhk choisih.

5. Síu-mìhng sèhngyaht m̀síusām jouh cho yéh, jīhauh béi lóuhsai naauh gójahnsìh móuh baahnfaat _____.

6. Gāmyaht Saigaaibūi (World Cup) ge choisih _____ haih Bāsāi deui Faatgwok.

7. Titlouh Bokmahtgún yàuh gāmyaht héi míhnfai _____ béi síhmàhn tùhng yàuhhaak chāamgūn.

8. Ngóh yihngwàih Hēunggóng yīnggōi faatjín dōdī m̀tùhng ge léuihyàuh gíngdím làih chigīk _____, gámyéung deui Hēunggóng ge gīngjai yáuh _____ jokyuhng.

9. Nīgāan chāantēng jeui _____ sihkmaht ge jātsou, kéuihdeih ge fuhjaakyàhn yihngwàih jíyiu sihkmaht jātsou hóu jauh nàhnggau kāpyáhn dōdī yàhn làih bōngchan (come to shop/eat), yùhgwó móuh bītyiu dōu m̀wúih fā (spend) taai dō chín jouh _____.

10. Hóudō Hēunggóng yàhn dōu jūngyi máaih gúpiu (shares) tùhng máaih láu, daahnhaih ngóh yihngwàih _____ ge yéh yáuh hóudō _____ fūnghím, yùhgwó hái nī fōngmihn móuh māt _____ jauh jeui hóu síusāmdī.

6.4 Complete the following sentences or answer the following questions using the given patterns.

1. m̀sái góng ......, ganggā m̀sái góng ......
   Yùhgwó fuhmóuh m̀fā sìhgaan tùhng sāmgēi (efforts) jēung jáinéui gaauhóu,
   _____.

2. chàhnggīng ......
   A: Dímgáai kéuih góng Póutūngwá góngdāk gam hóu gé?
   B: Yānwaih kéuih_____.

3. chan nīgo gēiwuih ......
   Nàahndāk gāmyaht chyùhnbouh yàhn dōu hái douh, ngóh séung _____.

4. Yānwaih ...... ge gwāanhaih
   _____,wuhtduhng dou chí gitchūk, dōjeh gokwái!

5. ...... jījūng, kèihjūng ......
   A: Néih jeui jūngyi sihk mātyéh a?
   B: _____.

6. sauhdou ...... yínghéung
   Gāmchi ge wuhtduhng _____ chéuisīu.

7. chèuihchí jī ngoih, ……

    A: Múihnìhn yáuh dī mātyéh táiyuhk choisih a?

    B: Yáuh máhlāaichùhng lā, móhngkàuh choi lā; _____.

8. Néih …… mātyéh ……, ngóh jauh …… mātyéh ……

    Gāmyaht haih néih ge sāangyaht, _____.

9 geiyìhn haih gám,……

    A: Búnlòih ngóhdeih gāmyaht yeukjó heui hàahngsāan, daahnhaih tīnmàhntòih (Hong Kong Observatory) wah yātjahngāan hónàhng wúih lohk daaihyúh wóh…

    B: _____.

10 N₁ béi N₂ V ……

    A: Dímgáai kéuih gāmyaht gam m̀hōisām gé?

    B: Yānwaih _____.

11 Sówaih…… kèihsaht haih……

    A: Néih jī m̀jīdou "Léuhng màhn sāam yúh" haih mātyéh a?

    B: _____.

7. Listening and speaking 🔊

聽説練習 Tingsyut lihnjaahp

7.1 Listening comprehension exercise

Please listen to the recording and answer the following T/F questions:

1. Hēunggóng yíhgīng yáuh sìhnggūng géuibaahn daaihyìhng gwokjai táiyuhk choisihge gīngyihm. (T/F)

2. Hēunggóng chàhnggīng géuibaahn Ouwahn máhseuht béichoi tùhng dūnggwai wahnduhng wúi. (T/F)

3. Daaihyìhng wahnduhngwúi wúih waih búngóng wahnduhng yùhn tàihgūng bíuyìhn gēiwuih tùhng lìhng ganggā dō síhmàhn gwāanjyu kéuihdeih. (T/F)

4. Hēunggóng yáuh jūkgauge gūngguhng táiyuhk chitsī tùhng béichoi chèuhngdeih. (T/F)

5. Yùhgwó jēung gauh gēichèuhng góigin sìhngwàih táiyuhkgún, Hēunggóng wúih yáuh yātjoh hóyíh yùhngnaahp sāam maahn yàhnge chèuhnggún. (T/F)

6. Jingfú hóyíh jēung béichoi ōnpàaih dou lèuhngahnge Oumún, Sāmjan, Seuhnghói tùhng Bākgīng nīdī sìhngsíh. (T/F)

7. Hēunggóng géuibaahn daaihyìhng choisih ge léuhng daaih yáuhleih tìuhgín: gāautūng fōngbihn tùhng wàahngíng yāulèuhng. (T/F)

8. Hēunggóng sìhngsíh yīsāan làhmhói, hūnghei jātsou hóu, daahnhaih himkyut (lacking) meih hōifaatge gāauyéh deihkēui. (T/F)

9. Hēunggóng yìhnleuhn jihyàuh, gokjúng boudouh dōu m̀sauh haahnjai. (T/F)

10. Yíngóngge yàhn yihngwàih géuibaahn choisih hóyíh waih Hēunggóng daailàih wuhtlihk, tàihgōu Hēunggóngge jīmìhngdouh tùhng chūkjeun (boost up) gīngjai. (T/F)

7.2 Speech topics

1. Yātgo gwokgā, deihkēui waahkjé sìhngsíh géuibaahn daaihyìhng táiyuhk choisih, deui gódouh ge gāautūng, gēigin, gīngjai faatjín tùhng síhmàhn ge sāngwuht yáuh mātyéh yínghéung a?

2. Néih jaan m̀jaansìhng Hēunggóng jingfú (waahkjé néih ge gwokgā ge jingfú) sānbaahn daaihyìhng táiyuhk choisih a? Dímgáai nē?

3. Yáuh dī yàhn wah Hēunggóng taaigwo jeuhkjuhng gīngjai tùhng gāmyùhng faatjín, fātsihjó (ignored) táiyuhk tùhng màhnfa wuhtduhng. Dímgáai nē? Néih ge gwokgā yáuh móuh gám ge chìhngfong a?

7.3 Speaking exercise: Please use at least 10 of the following vocabularies/patterns to say on the following topic in one to two minutes.

"Yātgo gwokgā, deihkēui waahkjé sìhngsíh kyutdihng géuibaahn daaihyìhng táiyuhk wuhtduhng, sēuiyiu háauleuih (consider) dī mātyéh nē?"

syūnchyùhn	sāaichín	gīngyihm	dahkdāng
fuhjaak	chèuhngkèih	jingmihn	bá'ngāak
jīchìh	chàhnggīng	jīmìhngdouh	chèuihchí jī ngoih
táiyuhk choisih	táiyuhk chèuhnggún		
geiyìhn haih gám	m̀sái góng ......, ganggā m̀sái góng		

8. Additional texts
附加課文 Fuhgā fomàhn

8.1 Additional text 附加課文

最近，布達佩斯(Boudaaht puisī, Budapest)宣佈唔再申請舉辦 2024 年奧運會。以前已經有加拿大多倫多（Dōlèuhndō, Toronto）、美國波士頓（Bōsihdéun, Boston）、德國漢堡（Honbóu, Hamburg）、意大利羅馬（Lòhmáh, Rome）退出申辦，呢個時候申辦城市就只有法國巴黎（Bālàih, Paris）同美國洛杉磯（Lohk chaamgēi, Los Angeles）。2028 年嘅奧運會，連一個申辦嘅國家都冇。結果，奧組委（Ou jóu wái, Olympic Organizing Committee）一次決定咗兩屆奧運會嘅舉辦城市，2024 年喺巴黎，2028 年喺洛杉磯舉辦。

Jeuigahn, Boudaahtpuisī syūnbou m̀joi sānchíng géuibaahn yih-lìhng-yih-sei nìhn Ouwahnwúi. Yíhchìhn yíhgīng yáuh Gānàhdaaih Dōlèuihdō, Méihgwok Bōsihdéun, Dākgwok Honbóu, Yidaaihleih Lòhmáh teuichēut sānbaahn, nīgo sìhhauh sānbaahn sìhngsíh jauh jíyáuh Faatgwok Bālàih tùhng Méihgwok Lohk Chaamgēi. Yih-lìhng-yih-baat nìhn ge Ouwahnwúi, lìhn yātgo sānbaahnge gwokgā dōu móuh. Gitgwó, Ou jóuwái yātchi kyutdihngjó léuhnggaai Ouwahnwúige géuibaahn sìhngsíh, yih-lìhng-yih-sei nìhn hái Bālàih, yih-lìhng-yih-baat nìhn hái Lohk Chaamgēi géuibaahn.

呢個情況有啲尷尬。

Nīgo chìhngfong yáuhdī gaamgaai.

仲記唔記得上個世紀最後幾次奧運會？無論係洛杉磯、首爾（Sáuyíh, Seoul），定係巴賽隆拿（Bāchoilùhngnàh, Barcelona），奧運會都對當地經濟、城市形象甚至國家形象帶嚟好處。北京申辦咗兩次，最後成功舉辦咗 2008 年嘅奧運會，令全世界認識一個新嘅北京、新嘅中國。噉，喺乜嘢時候開始，舉辦奧運會冇咗以前嘅吸引力呢？

Juhng gei m̀geidāk seuhnggo saigéi jeuihauh géichi Ouwahnwúi? Mòuhleuhn haih Lohk Chaamgēi, Sáuyíh, dihnghaih Bāchoilùhngnàh, Ouwahnwúi dōu deui dōngdeih gīngjai, sìhngsíh yìhngjeuhng sahmji gwokgā yìhngjeuhng daailàih hóuchyu. Bākgīng sānbaahnjó léuhng chi, jeuihauh sìhnggūng géuibaahnjó yih lìhng lìhng baat nìhn ge Ouwahnwúi, lihng chyùhn saigaai yihngsīk yātgo sānge Bākgīng, sānge Jūnggwok. Gám, hái mātyéh sìhhauh hōichí, géuibaahn Ouwahnwúi móuhjó yíhchìhnge kāpyáhn lihk nē?

首先，當然係越嚟越多國家認為舉辦奧運會咁大型嘅賽事係勞民傷財。21 世紀嘅幾次奧運會都冇為舉辦國家帶嚟經濟方面嘅好處，用咗大量資金修建嘅運動場館喺大賽之後唔再有用，變成廢墟，城市經濟都冇因此而發展起嚟。因此，喺一啲言論比較自由嘅國家，市民對舉辦奧運會嘅了解越深入，佢哋就越反對申辦。

Sáusīn, dōngyìhn haih yuht làih yuht dō gwokgā yihngwàih géuibaahn Ouwahnwúi gam daaihyìhngge choisih haih lòuhmàhn sēungchòih. Yihsahpyāt saigéige géi chi Ouwahnwúi dōu móuh waih géuibaahn gwokgā daailàih gīngjai fōngmihnge hóuchyu, yuhngjó daaihleuhng jīgām sāuginge wahnduhng chèuhnggún hái daaihchoi jīhauh m̀joi yáuhyuhng, binsìhng faihēui, sìhngsíh gīngjai dōu móuh yānchí yìh faatjín héilàih. Yānchí, hái yātdī yìhnleuhn béigaau jihyàuhge gwokgā, síhmàhn deui géuibaahn Ouwahnwúige líuhgáai yuht sāmyahp, kéuihdeih jauh yuht fáandeui sānbaahn.

波士頓反對申辦嘅人認為，如果政府將大量人力、財力放喺奧運會上面，噉，用喺提高教育品質、改善城市基礎設施方面嘅預算就一定會減少。而令更多學生得到高水平嘅教育、解決交通問題先至係波士頓人民更加需要嘅。佢哋話：「我哋唔會用納稅人嘅錢去辦一場三個星期嘅聚會。」漢堡人都有類似嘅想法，佢哋認為，如果有市民連住嘅地方都冇，點可能用錢去修建運動場呢？

Bōsihdéun fáandeui sānbaahnge yàhn yihngwàih, yùhgwó jingfú jēung daaihleuhng yàhnlihk, chòihlihk fonghái Ouwahnwúi seuhngmihn, gám, yuhnghái tàihgōu gaauyuhk bánjāt, góisihn sìhngsíh gēichó chitsī fōngmihnge yuhsyun jauh yātdihng wúih gáamsíu. Yìh lihng gangdō hohksāang dākdóu gōu séuipìhngge gaauyuhk, gáaikyut gāautūng mahntàih sīnji haih Bōsihdéun yàhnmàhn ganggā sēuiyiu ge. Kéuihdeih wah: "Ngóhdeih m̀wúih yuhng naahpseui yàhnge chín heui baahn yātchèuhng sāamgo sīngkèihge jeuihwuih." Honbóu yàhn dōu yáuh leuihchíhge séungfaat, kéuihdeih yihngwàih, yùhgwó yáuh síhmàhn lìhn jyuhge deihfōng dōu móuh, dím hónàhng yuhng chín heui sāugin wahnduhngchèuhng nē?

8.2 Additional vocabulary 附加詞彙

Number	Word	Yale Romanization	POS	English
1	宣佈	syūnbou	V	to announce, to declare
2	尷尬	gaamgaai	Adj	awkward; embarrassed
3	資金	jīgām	N	capital; fund
4	修建	sāugin	V	to build, to construct
5	廢墟	faihēui	N	ruins; debris

6	人力	yàhnlihk	N	manpower; labour power
7	財力	chòihlihk	N	financial resources
8	預算	yuhsyun	N	budget
9	納稅人	naahpseui yàhn	N	taxpayer

8.2 Please answer the following T/F questions after reading the additional text:

1 Yáuh chātgo sìhngsíh dásyun sānbaahn yih-lìhng-yih-sei nìhn ge Ouwahnwúi. (T/F)

2 Sānbaahn yih-lìhng-yih-baat nìhnge Ouwahnwúi, jíyáuh Méihgwok Lohkchaamgēi. (T/F)

3 Géuibaahn Ouwahnwúi deui Sáuyíh yáuh hóuchyu, daahnhaih deui Bāchoilùhngnàh móuh hóuchyu. (T/F)

4 Bākgīng sānchínggwo léuhngchi, daahnhaih dōu móuh sìhnggūng. (T/F)

5 Sāugin wahnduhngchèuhng sēuiyìhn yuhng hóudō chín, daahnhaih wahnduhngwúi gitchūk jīhauh juhng hóyíh leihyuhng. (T/F)

6 Daaihyìhng táiyuhk choisih m̀yātdihng hóyíh faatjín sìhngsíh gīngjai. (T/F)

7 Yātdī síhmàhn m̀haih taai líuhgáai sānbaahn Ouwahnwúi ge chìhngfong, sóyíh fēisèuhng fáandeui. (T/F)

8 Bōsihdéunge síhmàhn yihngwàih, fonghái Ouwahnwúi seuhngmihnge yàhnlihk, chòihlihk dōu taaisíu. (T/F)

9 Yātdī Bōsihdéun yàhn gokdāk jingfú yīnggōi sáusīn gáaikyut gaauyuhk tùhng sìhngsíh gāautūng mahntàih. (T/F)

10 Honbóu yàhn yihngwàih, síhmàhn yáuh deihfōng jyuh sīnji haih jeui juhngyiu ge sih. (T/F)

8.4 Topics for discussions

1 Néih gokdāk géuibaahn Ouwahnwúi deui yātgo sìhngsíh hóuchyu dō dihnghaih waaihchyu dō?

2 Dímgáai yìhgā géuibaahn Ouwahnwúi móuh yíhchìhn gam daaih kāpyáhnlihk nē?

3 Néih tùhng m̀tùhngyi nīpīn màhnjēungge táifaat nē? Dímgáai nē?

8.5 Authentic oral data 1 🔊
真實語料 1

8.6 Authentic oral data 2 🔊
真實語料 2

Lesson 8 Holidays and cultures
節日文化

1. Pragmatic factors, Yuti features and linguistic functions
語用因素、語體特徵與語言功能
Yúhyuhng yānsou, yúhtái dahkjīng yúh yúhyìhn gūngnàhng

Pragmatic factors/ Yuti features 語用因素 / 語體特徵	Linguistic function 語言功能
Pragmatic factors: This is a typical scenario for a formal situation, both in terms of content and context, calling for formal features of language.	**Linguistic function:** Drawing Conclusion Focusing on a certain topic, use historical and cultural perspectives to gradually elaborate your viewpoint.
語用因素： 場合正式，內容嚴肅，所以語體正式。	語言功能：歸納 針對某個問題，從歷史、文化講起，循循善誘，提出自己的看法。
Yuti features: Formality index: 2	
語體特徵：2	

Notes on pragmatic knowledge 語用知識	Notes on structure 語言及篇章結構知識

I. Yuti and being modest 語體與自謙
  1. Being modest
 	
II. Related knowledge 相關知識
  1. Five important holidays according to the lunar calendar「五大農曆節日」
  2. To give red packet money「派利是」
  3. Holidays with a religious flavor「帶宗教色彩嘅節日」
  4. Red-letter days「『紅字』，『紅假』，『紅日』and『公眾假期』」
  5. Buddha's Birthday「佛誕」
  6. Religious factions「宗教派別」
	I. Grammar and sentence patterns 語法和句型
	  1. "jihkdāk……ge haih" something that is worthy of...
	  2. "yíh……wàihlaih" take...as an example
	  3. "chùhng……hōichí/héi", "yàuh…V héi" start with; begin with
	  4. "gēibún seuhng" on the whole; mainly; basically
	  5. "Adj. dou…" and "(VO)V dou…"
	  6. "Gwāanhaih dou……" be related to
	  7. "Séung m̀V(O) dōu m̀dāk"
	
	II. Paragraph and discourse 語段和篇章
	  1. "jeui adj./V ge haih…juhngyáuh jauhhaih…jiyū…" the most…then…in addition to that…
	  2. "bātgwo chùhng lihng yāt fōngmihn heui tái", however if looking from another perspective

2. Text 🔊

課文 Fomàhn

各位，關於是否增設伊斯蘭教節同道教節為公眾假期呢個問題呢，我個人嘅睇法係噉嘅：

Gokwái, gwāanyū sihfáu jāngchit Yīsīlàahngaau jit tùhng Douhgaau jit wàih gūngjung gākèih nīgo mahntàih nē, ngóh goyàhnge táifaat haih gámge:

首先對於增設呢兩個節日為公眾假期我並唔反對。大家都知道香港係一個多元化嘅國際大城市，增加節日代表社會對於不同宗教信仰同文化一視同仁，同時又可以俾市民放多兩日紅假。另外如果政府、宗教團體趁呢個機會舉辦一啲同節日有關嘅活動，有可能為香港嘅旅遊業同埋經濟帶嚟一啲好處，噉就好值得。

Sáusīn deuiyū jāngchit nī léuhnggo jityaht wàih gūngjung gakèih ngóh bihng m̀fáandeui. Daaihgā dōu jīdou Hēunggóng haih yātgo dōyùhnfage gwokjai daaih sìhngsíh, jānggā jityaht doihbíu séhwúi deuiyū bāttùhng jūnggaau seunyéuhng tùhng màhnfa yāt sih tùhng yàhn, tùhngsìh yauh hóyíh béi síhmàhn fong dō léuhngyaht hùhngga. Lihngngoih yùhgwó jingfú, jūnggaau tyùhntái chan nīgo gēiwuih géuibaahn yātdī tùhng jityaht yáuhgwāange wuhtduhng, yáuh hónàhng waih Hēunggóngge léuihyàuh yihp tùhngmàaih gīngjai daailàih yātdī hóuchyu, gám jauh hóu jihkdāk.

不過從另一方面去睇，同樣係因為香港係一個國際大城市，除咗伊斯蘭教、道教之外，仲有好多其他宗教派別，好似係印度教、猶太教等等，佢哋喺香港都係好緊要嘅。我覺得唔需要為伊斯蘭教同道教嘅節日設立公眾假期，最大嘅一個理由係，我覺得政府唔可以選擇支持某一啲宗教，而唔支持另一啲宗教。目前香港嘅公眾假期，大多數係傳統節日，好似農曆新年、清明節、端午節、中秋節、重陽節等等，我哋喺呢幾日放假係因為要進行一啲傳統嘅活動，新年要拜年、派利是，端午節要扒龍船，重陽節要拜山，等等，放假係咗方便市民做呢啲事。仲有就係歷史上一啲重要嘅日子，譬如香港回歸、國慶、會有官方嘅紀念活動。至於聖誕節、復活節、喺香港，已經成為一種傳統，以聖誕節為例，香港人習慣咗喺聖誕假期一家大細放假去長線旅行，從聖誕開始去到新曆新年放假休息下。聖誕節除咗喺教會內部，喺香港呢啲節日嘅宗教味道已經唔係特別明顯喇。但係伊斯蘭教同道教嘅節日就唔一樣喇，香港人喺呢啲日子放假會做啲乜嘢呢？政府都冇理由公開慶祝呢啲節日。至於佛誕，香港本來有佛誕，設佛誕呢個假期有歷史原因。雖然佛誕係一個帶宗教色彩嘅節日，但係算係一個例外。

Bātgwo chùhng lihng yāt fōngmihn heui tái, tùhngyeuhng haih yānwaih Hēunggóng haih yātgo gwokjai daaih sìhngsíh, chèuihjó Yīsīlàahngaau, Douhgaau jīngoih, juhng yáuh hóudō kèihtā jūnggaau paaibiht, hóuchíh haih Yandouhgaau, Yàuhtaaigaau dángdáng, kéuihdeih hái Hēunggóng dōu haih hóu gányiu ge. Ngóh gokdāk m̀sēuiyiu waih Yīsīlàahngaau tùhng Douhgaauge jityaht chitlahp gūngjung gakèih, jeuidaaihge yātgo léihyàuh haih, ngóh gokdāk jingfú m̀hóyíh syúnjaahk jīchìh máuh yātdī jūnggaau, yìh m̀jīchìh lihng yātdī jūnggaau. Muhkchìhn Hēunggóngge gūngjung gakèih, daaihdōsou haih chyùhntúng jityaht, hóuchíh Nùhnglihk Sānnìhn, Chīngmìhng jit, Dyūnńgh jit, Jūngchāu jit, Chùhngyèuhng jit dángdáng, ngóhdeih hái nī géi yaht fongga haih yānwaih yiu jeunhàhng yātdī chyùhntúngge wuhtduhng, Sānnìhn yiu baainìhn, paai laihsih, Dyūnńgh jit yiu pàh lùhngsyùhn, Chùhngyèuhng jit yiu baaisāan, dángdáng, fongga haih waihjó fōngbihn síhmàhn jouh nīdī sih. Juhngyáuh jauhhaih lihksí seuhng yātdī juhngyiu ge yahtjí, peiyùh Hēunggóng wùihgwāi, gwokhing, wúih yáuh gūnfōngge geinihm wuhtduhng. Jiyū Singdaan jit, Fuhkwuht jit, hái Hēunggóng yíhgīng sìhngwàih yātjúng chyùhntúng, yíh Singdaan jit wàih laih, Hēunggóng yàhn jaahpgwaanjó hái Singdaan gakèih yātgā daaihsai fongga heui chèuhngsin léuihhàhng, chùhng Singdaan hōichí heuidou Sānlihk Sānnìhn fongga yāusīkháh. Singdaan jit chèuihjó hái gaauwúi noihbouh, hái Hēunggóng nīdī jityaht ge jūnggaau meihdouh yíhgīng m̀haih dahkbiht mìhnghín la. Daahnhaih Yīsīlàahngaau tùhng Douhgaauge jityaht jauh m̀yātyeuhng la, Hēunggóng yàhn hái nīdī yahtjí fongga wúih jouh dī mātyéh nē? Jingfú dōu móuh léihyàuh gūnghōi hingjūk nīdī jityaht. Jiyū Fahtdaan, Hēunggóng búnlòih móuh Fahtdaan, chit Fahtdaan nīgo gakèih yáuh lihksí yùhnyān. Sēuiyìhn Fahtdaan haih yātgo daaih jūnggaau sīkchói ge jityaht, daahnhaih syunhaih yātgo laihngoih.

如果真係要一視同仁，好多喺香港每年都會慶祝嘅節日，好似萬聖節、感恩節、又或者瑞典嘅「聖露西亞日」、菲律賓嘅「朋友節」、泰國嘅「潑水節」、尼泊爾嘅新年，係咪都應該要增加一啲公眾假期俾佢哋呢？如果講對宗教信仰公平嘅話，我覺得而家嘅安排就好公平。至於唔同國家嘅文化，中國人社會基本上當然遵從中國文化，香港嘅外國人咁多，唔通韓國嘅節日、法國嘅節日、愛爾蘭嘅節日，我哋全部都要設立公眾假期咩？

Yùhgwó jānhaih yiu yātsih tùhng yàhn, hóudō hái Hēunggóng múih nìhn dōu wúih hingjūkge jityaht, hóuchíh Maahnsing jit, Gámyān jit, yauh waahkjé Seuihdín ge "Sing Louhsāi'nga yaht", Fēileuhtbānge "Pàhngyáuh jit", Taaigwokge "Putséui jit", Nèihpokyíhge Sānnìhn, haih maih dōu yīnggōi yiu jānggā yātdī gūngjung gakèih béi kéuihdeih nē? Yùhgwó góng deui jūnggaau seunyéuhng gūngpìhngge wah, ngóh gokdāk yìhgāge ōnpàaih jauh hóu gūngpìhng. Jiyū m̀tùhng gwokgā ge màhnfa, Jūnggwok yàhn séhwúi gēibúnseuhng dōngyìhn jēunchùhng Jūnggwok màhnfa, Hēunggóngge ngoihgwok yàhn gam dō, m̀tūng Hòhngwokge jityaht, Faatgwokge jityaht, Ngoiyíhlàahnge jityaht, ngóhdeih chyùhnbouh dōu yiu chitlahp gūngjung gakèih mē?

最後一點想補充嘅係，增加一個公眾假期，係咪要喺另外一啲假期嗰度減少返啲呢？如果淨係增加一兩個節日，而唔減少其他假期，嗰公眾假期會唔會太多呢？公眾假期太多，第一個出嚟反對嘅一定係啲大老闆。佢哋會話，平時已經忙到要加班，休息一日，公司就會唔見幾多幾多錢，關係到錢嘅問題，佢哋想唔反對都唔得。如果增設伊斯蘭教節同道教節，嗰新年假期同埋聖誕節係咪應該放少啲呢？但係新年假期同聖誕節本來就放得唔多，再減嘅話，香港人會唔會唔高興呢？所以討論呢個問題嘅時候，需要考慮好多方面嘅問題，而且要照顧社會上唔同人嘅聲音，我認為唔可以隨便改變公眾假期嘅安排。呢個係我個人嘅睇法，多謝大家。

Jeuihauh yāt dím séung bóuchūng ge haih, jānggā yātgo gūngjung gakèih, haih maih yiu hái lihngngoih yātdī gakèih gódouh gáamsíu fāan dī nē? Yùhgwó jihnghaih jānggā yāt léuhnggo jityaht, yìh m̀gáamsíu kèihtā gakèih, gám gūngjung gakèih wúih m̀wúih taai dō nē? Gūngjung gakèih taai dō, daihyātgo chēutlàih fáandeuige yātdihng haih dī daaih lóuhbáan. Kéuihdeih wúih wah, pìhngsìh yíhgīng mòhngdou yiu gābāan, yāusīk yātyaht, gūngsī jauh wúih m̀gin géidō géidō chín, gwāanhaih dou chín ge mahntàih, kéuihdeih séung m̀fáandeui dōu m̀dāk. Yùhgwó jāngchit Yīsīlàahngaau jit tùhng Douhgaau jit, gám Sānnìhn gakèih tùhngmàaih Singdaan jit haih maih yīnggōi fong síudī nē? Daahnhaih Sānnìhn gakèih tùhng Singdaan jit búnlòih jauh fongdāk m̀dō, joi gáam ge wah, Hēunggóng yàhn wúih m̀wúih m̀gōuhing nē? Sóyíh tóuleuhn nīgo mahntàihge sìhhauh, sēuiyiu háauleuih hóudō fōngmihnge mahntàih, yìhché yiu jiugu séhwúiseuhng m̀tùhng yàhn ge sīngyām, ngóh yihngwàih m̀hóyíh chèuihbín góibin gūngjung gakèihge ōnpàaih. Nīgo haih ngóh goyàhnge táifaat, dōjeh daaihgā.

3. Vocabulary in use 🔊

活用詞彙 Wuhtyuhng chìhwuih

3.1 Common vocabulary

Number	Word	Yale Romanization	POS	English
1	關於	gwāanyū	Adv	regarding, concerning, about
2	是否	sihfáu	PH	whether
3	增設	jāngchit	V	to establish an additional or a new … (e.g. organization, course, facility, service)
4	公眾假期	gūngjung gakèih	N	public holiday
5	多元化	dōyùhnfa	PH	diversified; diversification
6	節日	jityaht	N	festival
7	宗教信仰	jūnggaau seunyéuhng	N	religious belief
8	一視同仁	yāt sih tùhng yàhn	PH	to treat all alike without discrimination
9	紅假	hùhngga	N	public holiday (lit. "red holiday")
10	大多數	daaihdōsou	Adv/N	mostly; the majority
11	傳統節日	chyùhntúng jityaht	N	traditional festival
12	國慶	gwokhing	N	national day
13	官方	gūnfōng	Adj	official
14	紀念活動	geinihm wuhtduhng	N	commemorative activity
15	一家大細	yātgā daaihsai	PH	the whole family
16	長線旅行	chèuhngsin léuihhàhng	PH	long-haul trip
17	教會	gaauwúi	N	church
18	內部	noihbouh	Att/N	internal; internal part
19	宗教味道	jūnggaau meihdouh	N	religious flavour

20	明顯	mìhnghín	Adj	obvious
21	公開	gūnghōi	Adj/Adv/V	open (not secret); openly; to make known to the public
22	至於	jiyū	CV	as for
23	歷史原因	lihksí yùhnyān	N	historical reason
24	例外	laihngoih	N	exception
25	基本上	gēibúnseuhng	Adv	basically
26	遵從	jēunchùhng	V	to comply with
27	設立	chitlahp	V	to establish, to set up, to found
28	補充	bóuchūng	V	to supplement, to add
29	減少	gáamsíu	V	to reduce
30	大老闆	daaih lóuhbáan	N	big boss
31	加班	gābāan	V	to work overtime
32	高興	gōuhing	Adj	happy
33	改變	góibin	N/V	change; to change
34	個人	goyàhn	Adj	personal, individual

3.2 Place names

1	瑞典	Seuihdín	PW	Sweden
2	菲律賓	Fēileuhtbān	PW	the Philippines
3	泰國	Taaigwok	PW	Thailand
4	尼泊爾	Nèihpokyíh	PW	Nepal
5	愛爾蘭	Ngoiyíhlàahn	PW	Ireland

3.3 About religions and festivals

| 1 | 宗教團體 | jūnggaau tyùhntái | N | religious organization |
| 2 | 宗教派別 | jūnggaau paaibiht | N | religious faction |

3	印度教	Yandouhgaau	PN	Hinduism
4	猶太教	Yàuhtaaigaau	PN	Judaism
5	伊斯蘭教節	Yīsīlàahngaaujit	PN	Islamic Festival
6	道教節	Douhgaaujit	PN	Taoist Festival
7	農曆新年	Nùhnglihk Sānnìhn	PN	Lunar New Year
8	清明節	Chīngmìhngjit	PN	Ching Ming Festival
9	端午節	Dyūnńghjit	PN	Dragon Boat Festival
10	中秋節	Jūngchāujit	PN	Mid-Autumn Festival
11	重陽節	Chùhngyèuhngjit	PN	Chung Yeung Festival
12	拜年	baainìhn	VO	to pay a New Year call
13	派利是	paai laihsih	VO	to give out red packets
14	扒龍船	pàh lùhngsyùhn	VO	to row the dragon boat
15	拜山	baaisāan	VO	to sweep the grave
16	回歸	wùihgwāi	PH	handover (of Hong Kong to China)
17	聖誕節	Singdaanjit	PN	Christmas
18	復活節	Fuhkwuhtjit	PN	Easter
19	新曆新年	Sānlihk Sānnìhn	PN	New Year (according to Gregorian calendar)
20	佛誕	Fahtdaan	PN	Birthday of Buddha
21	萬聖節	Maahnsingjit	PN	Halloween
22	感恩節	Gámyānjit	PN	Thanksgiving Day
23	瑞典嘅「聖露西亞日」	Seuihdín ge "Sing Louhsāi'nga Yaht"	PN	Saint Lucia's Day in Sweden
24	菲律賓嘅「朋友節」	Fēileuhtbān ge "Pàhngyáuhjit"	PN	Kapangyawan Festival in the Philippines
25	泰國嘅「潑水節」	Taaigwok ge "Putséuijit"	PN	Songkran Festival in Thailand

4. Notes on language and discourse structure

語言及篇章結構知識 Yúhyìhn kahp pīnjēung gitkau jīsīk

4.1. Grammar and sentence patterns 語法和句型

4.1.1. "jihkdāk…ge haih" something that is worthy of...

1. Jihkdāk jyuyige haih, yùhgwó nīdī yáuh Jūnggaau sīkchóige jityaht dihngwaih gakèih, hóyíh jiugudou bāttùhng júngjuhkge sēuiyiu.

2. Jihkdāk gōuhing (happy)ge haih, yuht làih yuht dō yàhn hōichí líuhgáai wàahngíng bóuwuhge juhngyiusing (importance).

3. Yìhnleuhn jihyàuh (freedom of speech) fēisèuhng juhngyiu, daahnhaih jihkdāk jyuyige haih m̀hóyíh yínghéung kèihtā yàhn.

4.1.2. "yíh……wàihlaih" take...as an example

1. Yíh Hēunggóng wàihlaih, Jūnggwokyàhn jim (consist of) daaih dōsou, nùhnglihk (lunar calendar) tùhng sānlihk (solar calendar) dōu yuhng.

2. Hēunggóngge daaihhohk gwokjaifa ge chìhngdouh dōu hóu gōu, yíh ngóhdeihge daaihhohk wàihlaih, ngoihjihk lóuhsī jim baakfahnjī sāamsahp.

3. Hóudō sìhngsíh dōu géuibaahngwo daaihyìhng choisih, tàihgōujó gwokjai jīmìhng douh. Yíh Sáuyíh wàihlaih, yātgáu baatbaat nìhn Ouwahn jīhauh, Sáuyíh binsìhng jó yātgo léuihyàuh yihtdím.

4.1.3. "chùhng……hōichí/héi", "yàuh …… V héi" start with; begin with; start an action from……

1. Chùhng yātgáu gáugáu nìhn hōichí, Hēunggóng jēung sei yuht baat houh Fahtdaan lihtwàih gūngjung gakèih.

2. Oumún yàuh seibaak nìhn chìhn hōichí jauh yáuh Pòuhtòuhngàh yàhn gēuijyuh, sóyíh Oumún sauh Pòuhtòuhngàh màhnfa yínghéung.

3. Chùhng tīngyaht héi, ngóh yiu jouh dōdī wahnduhng, sihk síudī m̀gihnhōngge yéh.

4. Kéuih meih hohkgwo Gwóngdūngwá, sóyíh yiu yàuh daihyāt bāan duhkhéi.

5. Yàuh gáandāan ge sih jouhhéi, jauh m̀gokdāk nàahn ge la.

6. Yīngmàhn jih haih yàuh jóbīn séhéi ge.

7. Jēung sīnsāang sahpnìhn chìhn hái nīgāan gūngsī yàuh dāi jouhhéi, yìhgā yíhgīng haih gīngléih la.

8. Néih séung jīdou ngóh dímyéung hohk Gwóngdūngwá, ngóh jauh yiu yàuh daihyāt chi tēng Gwóngdūng gō gónìhn gónghéi.

4.1.4. "gēibún seuhng" on the whole; mainly; basically

1. Nīdī jityaht gēibún seuhng fáanyíng (reflect)jó Hēunggóngge dōyùhn màhnfa.
2. Kéuih dahkbiht jūngyi Yahtbún maahnwá, gēibúnseuhng daaih bouhfahn kéuih dōu táigwo.
3. Jeuigahn taai mòhng, jāumuhtge sìhgaan gēibún seuhng dōu hái ngūkkéi yāusīk, bīndouh dōu m̀séung heui.

4.1.5. "Adj. dou……" and "(VO)V dou……"

- "Adj.dou ……", this pattern means "so Adj. that…"

1. Nīgihn hàhngléih chúhngdou ló m̀dóu.
2. Ngóh deui geuk guihdou kéih m̀dóu.
3. Nījēung dang saidou chóh m̀lohk.
4. Kéuih guihdou hàahng m̀dóu.
5. Kéuih hōisāmdou (lìhn) góng dōu góng m̀chēut.
6. Ngóh mòhngdou (lìhn) faahn dōu móuh sihk.
7. Kéuih gēngdou (lìhn) hàaih dōu móuh jeuk jauh jáujó chēutheui.
8. Kéuih guihdou (lìhn) boují dōu m̀séung tái.
9. Ngóh gēngdou (lìhn) sēng dōu chēut m̀dóu.
10. Kéuih ngohdou (lìhn) syutwah dōu góng m̀chēut.

- "(VO) V dou ……."

This pattern means 'do something so much that……'

1. Séjih sédou sáu tung.
2. Jouhyéh jouhdou (lìhn) faahn dōu m̀geidāk sihk.
3. Kéuih tùhng pàhngyáuh kīnggái kīngdou m̀séung séuhngtòhng.
4. Ngóh hàahngjó léuhng go géi jūngtàuh, hàahngdou geuk tung.
5. Gógo síupàhngyáuh sìhsìh dōu wáandou (lìhn) gūngfo dōu móuh jouh.

4.1.6. "gwāanhaih dou……" be related to

1. Nīgo haih yātgo hóu fūkjaahpge mahntàih, gwāanhaih dou yātgo séhwúi ge gajihkgūn (values) tùhng màhnjuhk jīngsàhn (ethnic spirit).

2. Yātgo sìhngsíh yīng m̀yīnggōi hōichit dóuchèuhng, m̀jíhaih gīngjai mahntàih, juhng gwāanhaih dou sìhngsíh yìhngjeuhng (image).

3. Nīgihn sih gwāanhaih dou goyàhn leihyīk (benefit), sóyíh daaihgā yīnggōi gónggóng jihgéige séungfaat.

4.1.7. séung m̀ V(O) dōu m̀dāk

This pattern means 'cannot but......'. A combination of two negative forms is used to give a strong positive meaning.

1. Tīngyaht yiu chāakyihm, séung m̀duhksyū dōu m̀dāk.

2. Yìhgā hóu yeh la, séung m̀fāan ngūkkéi dōu m̀dāk.

3. Yiu hái Hēunggóng jouhsih, séung m̀hohk Gwóngdūngwá dōu m̀dāk.

4. Yānwaih hauhbihn móuhsaai wái, sóyíh séung m̀chóh chìhnbihn ge wái dōu m̀dāk.

5. Ngūkkéi móuh yéh sihk, séung m̀chēutgāai sihkfaahn dōu m̀dāk.

4.2. Paragraph and discourse 語段和篇章

4.2.1. "Jeui Adj/V ge haih…juhngyáuh jauhhaih…jiyū…" the most…then…in addition …

1. Jeui juhngyiu ge dōngyìhn haih Sānnìhn, yìhnhauh jauhhauh Chīngmìhng jit, nīgo sìhhauh yiu heui soumouh (sweep the grave), juhngyáuh jauh haih Dyūnngh jit, Jūngchāujit, Chùhngyèuhng jit.

2. Nīchi làih Hēunggóng, jeui juhngyiu ge haih gin pàhngyáuh, juhngyáuh jauhhaih tái yātgo yíncheung wúi (music concert), jiyū máaihyéh jauh m̀haih jeui juhngyiu la.

3. Sānnìhnge sìhhauh, ngóh jeui jūngyige jauhhaih yáuh leihsih sāu, juhngyáuh jauh haih sihkyéh, jiyū kèihtāge yéh jauh m̀haih gam juhngyiu la.

4.2.2. "bātgwo chùhng lihng yāt fōngmihn heui tái", however if looking from another perspective.

1. Hīnggin dóuchèuhng haih deui gīngjai yáuh hóuchyu, bātgwo chùhng lihng yāt fōngmihn heui tái, deui sìhngsíh yìhngjeuhng yáuh hóu daaihge fuhmín yínghéung (negative influence).

2. Jouh sāangyi haih yātgo hóuge wánchín baahnfaat, bātgwo chùhng lihng yāt fōngmihn heui tái, jouh sāangyige ngaatlihk dōu géi daaih.

5. Notes on pragmatic knowledge

語用因素與相關知識 Yúhyuhng yānsou yúh sēunggwāan jīsīk

5.1. Yuti and being modest 語體與自謙

5.1.1. Being modest

5.1.1.1. "我個人嘅睇法係 …Ngóh goyàhnge táifaat haih…"

5.1.1.2. "呢個係我個人嘅睇法 Nīgo haih ngóh goyàhnge táifaat"

5.1.1.3. "我都簡單講講我嘅睇法 Ngóh dōu gáandāan gónggóng ngóhge táifaat"

5.1.1.4. "拋磚引玉 pāaujyūn yáhnyuhk"

5.1.1.5. "我對 … 其實所知甚少" ngóh deui… kèihsaht sójī sahmsíu

While being modest is a very important part of the Chinese culture, how it is manifested by language is part of the pragmatic knowledge that needs to be acquired. In a formal situation like this, it is common to minimize any contribution by the speaker and to maximize what is said or done by others (5.1.1.1& 5.1.1.2), while what the speaker is going to say is something "simple" (5.1.1.3), and is figuratively referred to as a "brick" that will facilitate the appearance of "jade"(5.1.1.4). Expression (5.1.1.5) shows that the speaker being humble and said that he/she has very limited knowledge in certain topic.

- Néihge faatyìhn fēisèuhng yáuh yisī. Hahmihn, ngóh dōu gáandāan gónggóng ngóhge táifaat, m̀syun haih māatyéh yíngóng, jíhaih séung tùhng daaihgā gāaulàuh yātháh, hēimohng yáuh yātgo pāaujyūn yáhnyuhk ge jokyuhng lā.

- Ngóh deui m̀tùhng màhnfa ge jityaht kèihsaht só jī sahmsíu, gāmyaht làihdou nīdouh jyúyiu haih heung daaihgā hohkjaahp. Ngóh goyàhn ge táifaat haih……

5.2. Related knowledge 相關知識

5.2.1. "五大農曆節日 ńgh daaih nùhnglihk jityaht" five important holidays according to the lunar calendar

According to the lunar calendar, there are five important holidays including the Lunar New Year, the Chingming Festival, Dragan Boat Festival, the Mid-autumn Festival and the Chungyeung (Double Nine) Festival. The folk stories behind these festivals are important cultural knowledge that may affect the appropriate use of Chinese.

- Yíh Hēunggóng wàih laih, yáuh ńgh daaih nùhnglihk jityaht: nùhnglihk sānnìhn hái saigaaiseuhng hóudō yáuh Wàhyàhn ge deihkēui dōu yáuh hingjūk wuhtduhng.

5.2.2. "派利是 paai laihsih" to give red packet money

The word "laihsih" (red packet) is one of the many varieties referring to the same activity: giving money in the red envelope (or '紅包 hùhngbāau' in Mandarin Chinese) during the Chinese New Year. Different places have different "rules of thumb" regarding the same activity and the violation of which may result in awkwardness or may be considered offensive. A typical saying is "恭喜發財，利是逗來 Gūnghéi faatchòih, laihsih dauhlòih"，but usually only children will say that to grown-ups and it is almost a life long lesson for all CSL speakers to learn the "利是文化" and the appropriate ways of referring to it in Chinese.

- Nùhnglihk sānnìhn, ngóhdeih máaih nìhnfo, tip fāichēun, tái móuhsī, sihk nìhngōu, paai laihsih,… hái Jūnggwok gwo nùhnglihk sānnìhn m̀sīk laihsih màhnfa jānhaih m̀dāk.

5.2.3. "帶宗教色彩嘅節日 daai jūnggaau sīkchóige jityaht" holidays with a religious flavor

Many holidays were first originated from a certain religion but the religious meaning of the holiday was gradually fading because the holiday is now highly commercialized. A typical example would be the Christmas holidays, especially in places where Christianity is not practiced. Similarly, quite a few holidays in the Chinese culture have drifted away from the original story, such as the original meaning of "年 nìhn" was a monster (as told in one version of the story behind the Chinese New Year). Understanding of the religious and cultural meanings behind holidays, however, is often important in the appropriate use of Chinese related to these holidays.

- Hēunggóng juhng yáuh yātdī daai jūnggaau sīkchóige jityaht, peiyùh Gēidūkgaau ge Fuhkwuhtjit tùhng Singdaanjit, Fahtgaau ge Fahtdaan.
- Hóu dō jityaht kèihsaht tùhng dōngdeih ge jūnggaau màhnfa yúuh mahtchit ge lyùhnhaih.

5.2.4. "'紅字'、'紅假'、'紅日'、'公衆假期' 'hùhngjih', 'hùhngga', 'hùhngyaht', 'gūngjung gakèih'" red-letter days, public holidays

Most calendars would mark holidays and the most common of which in Hong Kong is to mark them red. Thus all holidays are often referred to as "red-letter days" or simply (and literally) "red days". It should be noted that, although weekends are often marked red as well, they are seldom referred to as red-letter days.

- Gūngjung gakèih jauhhaih Hēunggóng síhmàhn pìhngsìh góng ge "hùhng jih", "hùhng ga" waahkjé giu "hùhng yaht".
- Hēunggóng ge yahtlihk seuhngmihn Sīngkèihyaht dōu haih hùhngsīk ge.

5.2.5. " 佛誕 Fahtdaan" Buddha's Birthday

Referring to the 8th day of the 4th month according to the Lunar Calendar in China, which usually falls in May. It is also celebrated in Thailand and many other Asian countries, but the specific day for the celebration may be different from place to place. In Hong Kong, it became a public holiday in 1998 and, among the many celebrations, the ones held in Po Lin Monastery with the Big Buddha are well known to most.

- Jeuigahn yáuh yàhn tàihchēut, chèuihjó Fahtdaan tùhng Singdaanjit jīngoih,…
- Tēngginwah gāmnìhn Fahtdaan Daaihyùhsāan (Lantau Island) Bóulìhnjí (Po lin monestary) yáuh daaihyìhng hingjūk wuhtduhng, néih wúih m̀wúih heui a?

5.2.6. " 宗教派別 jūnggaau paaibiht" Religious factions

In the Hong Kong contact, this refers to many different groups within each religion, be it Christian, Buddhism, Daoism or Muslim. Each faction may have its own way of referring to certain things, activities or ceremonies and the proper understanding of these terms are important for the appropriate use of Chinese by CSL learners. Teachers are usually very friendly and are not easily offended by mistakes in words or a religious nature, but believers may not be as "friendly" and may treat certain mistakes as blasphemous.

- Waihjó bíusih deui gokgo jūnggaau paaibiht ge juhngsih,….
- Hēunggóng lihklòih jyūnjuhng m̀tùhng ge jūnggaau seunyéuhng, sóyíh yìhgā Hēunggóng ge jūnggaau paaibiht dahkbiht dō.

6. Contextualized speaking practice

情境説話練習 Chìhnggíng syutwah lihnjaahp

【課前預習】Class preparation

6.1. Please answer the following True/False questions according to the lesson text.

1 Yíngóngge yàhn yihngwàih jingfú yīnggōi jāngchit léuhnggo jityaht jouh gūngjung gakèih. (T/F)

2 Jānggā jityaht doihbíu séhwúi m̀wúih deui m̀tùhng jūnggaau tùhng màhnfa yātsih tùhng yàhn. (T/F)

3 Yíngóngge yàhn yihngwàih jingfú hóyíh jí syúnjaahk jīchìh máuh yātdī jūnggaau. (T/F)

4 Nùhnglihk Sānnìhn, Chīngmìhng jit dángdáng, hái nī géi yaht fongga haih yānwaih síhmàhn yātdihng yiu chēutngoih léuihyàuh. (T/F)

5 Lihksíseuhng yātdī juhngyiuge yahtjí, peiyùh Hēunggóng wùihgwāi, gwokhing, wúih yáuh màhngāange chyùhntúng wuhtduhng. (T/F)

6 Maahnsing jit, Gámyān jit, Nèihpokyíhge Sānnìhn haih Hēunggóng móuhyàhn wúih hingjūkge jityaht. (T/F)

7 Yíngóngge yàhn yihngwàih yùhwó jíhaih jānggā yāt léuhnggo jityaht, yìh m̀gáamsíu kèihtā gakèih, gūngjung gakèih wúih taai dō.(T/F)

8 Yíngóngge yàhn yihngwàih fáandeui jānggā gūngjung gakèih ge yàhn yātdihng bāaukut daaih lóuhbáan. (T/F)

9 Yíngóng ge yàhn yihngwàih dōjó gakèih Hēunggóng yàhn wúih m̀hōisām. (T/F)

10 Yíngóngge yàhn yihngwàih tóuleuhn ge sìhhauh sēuiyiu háauleuih dō fōngmihn, yìhché yiu jiugu séhwúi seuhng m̀tùhngge sīngyām. (T/F)

6.2. Please explain the following phrases in Cantonese

1 紅假 hùhngga

2 清明 Chīngmìhng

3 端午 Dyūnńgh

4 中秋 Jūngchāu

5 重陽 Chùhngyèuhng

【課後練習】Post-class exercises

6.3 Fill in the blanks with the given vocabularies. Each vocabulary can be chosen once only.

gūnfōng   mìhnghín   gūnghōi   dōyùhnfa

jēunchùhng   bóuchūng   gābāan   yātgā daaihsai

gōuhing   laihngoih   daaihdōsou   yātsih tùhngyàhn

1. Gūngsī deui sóyáuh yùhngūng (employees) _____, mòuhleuhn bīngo jouhdāk hóu dōu hóyíh gā yàhngūng.

2. Yīsāng hái góngjoh seuhng gaau yahnfúh (pregnant women) hái wàaihyahn kèihgāan yīnggōi sihk mātyéh làih _____ yìhngyéuhng (nutritions).

3. Múihgo yàhn dōu yīnggōi jēunsáu faatleuht (obey the law), bīngo dōu móuh _____.

4. Néih yiu _____ lóuhbáan ge jísih (instructions), jēung gūngjok jouhhóu.

5. Waih hingjūk Hēunggóng wùihgwāi Jūnggwok yihsahp jāunìhn, jingfú jēung wúih géuihàhng yātlìhnchyun (a series of) _____ wuhtduhng.

6. Hēunggóng haih yātgo _____ ge séhwúi, nàhnggau yùhngnaahp (accept) m̀tùhng ge màhnfa tùhng sīngyām.

7. Waihjó jīdou sihgín ge jānseung (truth), yáuh síhmàhn yīukàuh jingfú bouhmùhn _____ noihbouh màhngín.

8. Nīpáai gūngsī sāangyi hóu hóu, sóyíh ngóhdeih gogo sīngkèih dōu yiu _____.

9. Néihdeih hóu! Ngóh giu Síu-kèuhng, haih gūngsī sānlàih ge tùhngsih, hóu _____ nàhnggau yihngsīk daaihgā.

10. Múihfùhng chèuhng gakèih, hóudō _____ dōu wúih chēutgwok léuihyàuh.

11. Gīngjai m̀hóu, làih Hēunggóng ge yàuhhaak béi gauhnín _____ gáamsíu.

12. Hóudō gāautūng gūnggeuih nìhnnìhn dōu gāga (increase the price), _____ síhmàhn dōu gámdou sahpfānjī bātmúhn (discontent).

6.4 Complete the following sentences or answer the following questions using the given patterns.

1. jihkdāk ...... ge haih ……

   Hēunggóng màhnfa jījūng, jeui _____.

2. yíh ...... wàih laih,……

   Hēunggóng ge fòhng'ūk tùhng tóudeih mahntàih jānhaih hóu yìhmjuhng,

   _____.

3. chùhng ...... héi

   Síubā gūngsī _____ jāngchit hohksāang yāuwaih (discount).

4. gēibún seuhng, ...

   A: Néih deui Hēunggóng ge gaauyuhk yáuh mātyéh táifaat a?

   B: _____.

5. V dou ......

   Kéuih jeuigahn chàhmmàih dágēi, yáuhsìh juhng _____.

6. gwāanhaih dou ......

   A: Deui hohksāang làih góng, dímgáai háausi sìhngjīk gam juhngyiu?

   B: Yānwaih háausi sìhngjīk _____.

7. séung m̀ V (O) dōu m̀dāk

   Gāmyaht haih ngóh taaitáai ge sāangyaht, _____.

7. Listening and speaking 🔊

聽說練習 Tingsyut lihnjaahp

7.1 Listening comprehension exercise

Please listen to the recording and fill in the blanks with the following words:

nùhnglihk	yihngtùhnggám	Fuhkwuhtjit	daihyih	Chīngmìhngjit
jityaht	sei yuht chō baat	lòuhgūng	Húnggaau	gūngjung

1. Chùhng màhnfa séhwúihohk gokdouh, _____ haih hóu fūkjaahpge mahntàih.

2. Hēunggóng chèuihjó yuhng yèuhnglihk wàih gēichó ge jityaht jīngoih, juhngyáuh

   ńghdaaih_____ jityaht.

3. _____ gójahnsìh, ngóhdeih wúih soumouh, geinihm séijóge chānyàhn.

4. Nīdī jityaht deuiyū jāngkèuhng màhnfa_____, màhnjuhk yìhngjeuihlihk dōu

   yáuh jīkgihk jokyuhng.

5. Hēunggóng dōu yáuh yātdī daai jūnggaau sīkchói ge jityaht, hóuchíh Gēidūkgaau ge

   _____ tùhng Singdaanjit, Fahtgaauge Fahtdaan.

6. Nīdī daai jūnggaau sīkchóige jityaht haih_____ gakèih.

7. Faatdihng gakèih dángyū (equal) _____ gakèih, múih nìhn jíyáuh sahpyìh yaht,

8. Hēunggóng séhwúi yáuh m̀tùhngge jūnggaau, chèuihjó Yīsīlàahngaau tùhng Douhgaau, juhng yáuh_____Yandouh gaau dángdáng.

9. Gāngeui sēunggwāan diuhchàh, chyùhngóng yáuh 12.5% ge yàhn haih Fahtgaau tòuh, yàhnsou gánchiyū (preceded only by) Gēidūkgaau, haih Hēunggóng_____ daaihge jūnggaau.

10. Yāt gáu gáu gáu nìhn hōichí, Hēunggóng jēung _____ge Fahtdaan lihtwàih gūngjung gakèih.

7.2 Speech topics

1. Chéng néih heung tùhnghohk gaaisiuh néih ge gwokgā ge chyùhntúng jityaht tùhngmàaih yáuhgwāan nīgo/nīdī chyùhntúng jityaht ge gūnfōng hingjūk/geinihm wuhtduhng.

2. Gahnlòih Hēunggóng yáuh jūnggaau tyùhntái tàihchēut yiu jāngchit gūngjung gakèih, yáuh mātyéh léihgeui nē? Chùhng jingfú, lóuhbáan, yùhngūng (employees) waahkjé gātìhng ge gokdouh, jāngchit gūngjung gakèih yáuh mātyéh hóu tùhngmàaih m̀hóu ge deihfōng a?

3. Néih yihngwàih Hēunggóng (waahkjé néih ge gwokgā) syun m̀syunhaih yātgo dōyùhnfa séhwúi a? Chéng néih fānhéungháh néih ge táifaat.

7.3 Speaking exercise: Please use at least 10 of the following vocabularies/patterns to say on the following topic in one to two minutes.

"Hái Hēunggóng (waahkjé néih ge gwokgā), géisìh yáuh gūngjung gakèih a? Gūngjung gakèih gójahnsìh, daaihdōsou yàhn wúih jouh mātyéh nē?"

jityaht	hùhngga	gābāan	gōuhing
laihngoih	gūnfōng	goyàhn	jiyū
mìhnghín	gūnghōi	jūnggaau seunyéuhng	
yātgā daaihsai		gēibúnseuhng	yíh ...... wàih laih
chùhng ...... hōichí		séung m̀ V (O) dōu m̀dāk	

8. Additional texts

附加課文 Fuhgā fomàhn

8.1 附加課文 Additional text

最近二十年嚟，中國人嘅渡假方式發生咗一啲變化，節日文化都向住多元化嘅方向發展。

Jeuigahn yihsahp nìhn làih, Jūnggwok yàhnge douhga fōngsīk faatsāngjó yātdī binfa, jityaht màhnfa dōu heungjyuh dōyùhnfage fōngheung faatjín.

1999 年，中國政府決定農曆新年、五一勞動節同十一國慶日呢三個節日都放三日假，再將呢三日同前後兩個週末放埋一齊，噉樣就有七日長假，呢個長假叫做「黃金周」。七日嘅長假，越嚟越有錢嘅中國人會做乜嘢呢？當然係旅行。

Yāt-gáu-gáu-gau nìhn, Jūnggwok jingfú kyutdihng Nùhnglihk Sānnìhn, Ngh yāt lòuhduhng jit tùhng Sahp yāt gwokhing yaht nī sāamgo jityaht dōu fong sāamyaht ga, joi jēung nī sāamyaht tùhng chìhnhauh léuhnggo jāumuht fongmàaih yātchàih, gámyéung jauh yáuh chātyaht chèuhngga, nīgo chèuhngga giujouh "wòhnggām jāu (golden week)". Chātyahtge chèuhngga, yuhtlàih yuht yáuhchínge Jūnggwok yàhn wúih jouh mātyéh nē? Dōngyìhn haih léuihhàhng.

從 1999 年嘅第一個黃金周開始，中國利用長假出國旅行嘅人就越嚟越多。以國慶黃金周為例，第一個黃金周嘅旅遊人次達到 2800 萬，2017 年更加增加到 7.1 億！可以想像，長假期間旅遊業、零售業、餐飲業、娛樂業嘅收入都一年比一年多，對經濟發展有好多好處。

Chùhng yāt-gáu-gáu-gáu nìhnge daih yātgo Wòhnggām Jāu hōichí, Jūnggwok leihyuhng chèuhngga chēutgwok léuihhàhngge yàhn jauh yuhtlàih yuht dō. Yíh Gwokhing Wòhnggām Jāu wàihlaih, daihyātgo Wòhnggām Jāuge léuihyàuh yàhnchi daahtdou yih chīn baat baakmaahn, yih-lìhng-yāt-chāt nìhn ganggā jānggā dou chāt dím yāt yīk! Hóyíh séungjeuhng, chèuhngga kèihgāan léuihyàuh yihp, lìhngsauh yihp, chāanyám yihp, yùhlohk yihpge sāuyahp dōu yātnìhn béi yātnìhn dō, deui gīngjai faatjín yáuh hóudō hóuchyu.

甚至好似農曆新年呢種傳統節日，中國人嘅習慣都改變緊。以前農曆新年嘅時候，就算我哋離開得再遠，都要諗辦法返到家鄉，同屋企人一齊食下飯、睇下電視、探下親戚、傾下一年嘅生活。依家，中國人開始離開家鄉，全家人一齊去另外一個環境優美、氣候溫暖嘅地方，渡過一個愉快嘅新年。海南 (Hóinàahm, Hainan Province) 同泰國 (Taaigwok, Thailand) 都成為旅遊首選。

Sahmji hóuchíh Nùhnglihk Sānnìhn nījúng chyùhntúng jityaht, Jūnggwok yàhnge jaahpgwaan dōu góibingán. Yíhchìhn Nùhnglihk Sānnìhnge sìhhauh, jauhsyun ngóhdeih lèihhōidāk joi yúhn, dōu yiu nám baahnfaat fāandou gāhēung, tùhng ngükkéi yàhn yātchàih sihkháhfaahn, táiháh dihnsih, taamháh chānchīk, kīngháh yātnìhnge sāngwuht. Yīgā, Jūnggwok yàhn hōichí lèihhōi gāhēung, chyùhngā yàhn yātchàih heui lihngngoih yātgo wàahngíng yāuméih, heihauh wānnyúhnge deihfōng, douhgwo yātgo yuhfaaige Sānnìhn. Hóinàahm tùhng Taaigwok dōu sìhngwàih léuihyàuh sáusyún.

聖誕節、情人節 (Chìhngyàhn jit, Valentine's Day) 呢啲外來嘅節日，並唔係中國嘅法定假期，都受到唔少年輕人嘅歡迎。聖誕節嘅時候，大型商場門口擺好聖誕樹、掛起燈飾，無論你係唔係基督徒，都可以享受到節日嘅氣氛。情人節嗰陣時，年青人送禮物俾男女朋友，浪漫一下。依家過母親節、父親節嘅中國人都越嚟越多。

Singdaanjit, Chìhngyàhn jit nīdī ngoihlòihge jityaht, bihng m̀haih Jūnggwokge faatdihng gakèih, dōu sauhdou m̀síu nìhnhīngyàhnge fūnyìhng. Singdaanjitge sìhhauh, daaihyìhng sēungchèuhng mùhnháu báaihóu Singdaansyuh, gwahéi dāngsīk, mòuhleuhn néih haih m̀haih Gēidūktòuh, dōu hóyíh héungsauhdóu jityahtge heifān. Chìhngyàhn jit gójahnsìh, nìhnchīngyàhn sung láihmaht béi nàahmnéuih pàhngyáuh, lohngmaahn yātháh. Yīgā gwo Móuhchān jit, Fuhchān jit ge Jūnggwok yàhn dōu yuht làih yuht dō.

2008 年，清明、端午、中秋都開始成為中國嘅法定假期，對於繼承傳統文化、增強民族認同感都起咗積極嘅作用。

Yih-lìhng-lìhng-baat nìhn, Chīngmìhng, Dyúnnǵh, Jūngchāu dōu hōichí sìhngwàih Jūnggwokge faatdihng gakèih, deuiyū gaisìhng chyùhntúng màhnfa, jāngkèuhng màhnjuhk yihngtùhnggám dōu héijó jīkjihkge jokyuhng.

8.2 Additional vocabulary 附加詞彙

Number	Word	Yale Romanization	POS	English
1	五一勞動節	Ńgh yāt lòuhduhng jit	N	May 1, Labor Day
2	十一國慶	Sahp yāt gwokhing	N	October 1, National Day
3	黃金周	wòhnggām jāu	N	golden week
4	人次	yàhnchi	N	person-time
5	溫暖	wānnyúhn	Adj	warm
6	首選	sáusyún	N / Att.	first choice; preferences; preferred
7	掛	gwa	V	to hang, to put up
8	彩燈	chóidāng	N	illumination; colorful lights
9	相愛	sēungngoi	V/Adj	to fall in love; in love with
10	繼承	gaisìhng	V	to inherit, to succeed, to carry on

8.3 Please answer the following T/F questions after reading the additional text:

1 Jūnggwok ge jityaht màhnfa yuhtlàih yuht dōyùhnfa. (T/F)
2 Gwokhing jit ge chātyaht chèuhngga giujouh "wòhnggām jāu". (T/F)
3 Wòhnggām jāuge sìhhauh, hóudō Jūnggwok yàhn dōu wúih heui léuihhàhng. (T/F)
4 Wòhnggām jāuge léuihyàuh yàhnchi tùhng léuihyàuh sāuyahp dōu jānggājó. (T/F)
5 Tùhng gāyàhn yātchàih sihkfaahn, tái dihnsih, taam chānchīk dōu haih Nùhnglihk Sānnìhn ge chyùhntúng wuhtduhng. (T/F)
6 Yìhgā, Nùhnglihk Sānnìhn ge sìhhauh yātdihng yiu fāan gāhēung. (T/F)
7 Yùhgwó Nùhnglihk Sānnìhn chēutheui léuihhàhng, móuhyàhn heui Taaigwok. (T/F)
8 Nìhnhīngyàhn béigaau jūngyi Singdaanjit, Chìhngyàhnjit nīdī ngoihlòih jityaht. (T/F)
9 Móuhchān jit, Fuhchān jit haih Jūnggwokge chyùhntúng jityaht. (T/F)
10 Chīngmìhng, Dyūnnǵh, Jūngchāu yātjihk dōu haih Jūnggwokge faatdihng gayaht. (T/F)

8.4 Topics for discussions

1 Jūnggwok yáuh bīndī faatdihng gakèih nē? Néihge gwokgā nē?

2 Dímgáai wah Jūnggwokge jityaht yuht làih yuht dōyùhnfa?

3 Chéng néih góngháh néih jeui jūngyi ge jityaht.

8.5 Authentic oral data 1 🔊
真實語料 1

8.6 Authentic oral data 2 🔊
真實語料 2

Lesson 9　Law and society
法律與社會

1. Pragmatic factors, Yuti features and linguistic functions
語用因素、語體特徵與語言功能

Yúhyuhng yānsou, yúhtái dahkjīng yúh yúhyìhn gūngnàhng

Pragmatic factors/ Yuti features 語用因素 / 語體特徵	Linguistic function 語言功能
Pragmatic factors: Pragmatic factors: A forum with experts is typically a formal situation, especially when the focus of discussion is related to legal issues. Thus the appropriate style of language would be characterized by formal features. **語用因素：** 專業研討會，特別是內容與法律有關的場合，一般都比較正式，所以在這種場合得體的語言應該也比較正式。 **Yuti features:** Formality index: 2+ **語體特徵：**2+	**Linguistic function:** Discussion Comprehensively evaluating a multifaceted subject from different, even opposite, perspectives to discuss an issue. **語言功能：**闡述 綜合考慮多方面因素，從不同的、甚至是相反的角度來討論某一問題。

Notes on pragmatic knowledge 語用知識	Notes on structure 語言及篇章結構知識
I. Politeness and ways to refer to family members 禮貌與稱謂 1. I'm not an expert in the legal field. 「我唔係法律專家」 2. Different levels of formality with kinship terms :Mother「母親」 3. Family members「家人」 II. Related knowledge 相關知識 1. Not yet perfect, not yet complete 「唔太完善、唔太健全」 2. Focused news「熱點新聞」 3. A male person whose last name is "Mok" 「姓莫嘅男人」 4. Suspect (crime)「疑犯」 5. Public opinion of the society「社會輿論」	I. Grammar and sentence patterns 語法和句型 1. "…héi séuhnglàih" 2. "jiu nīgo chìhngyìhng làih tái/góng" 3. "jíyiu…jauh…" as long as, …then… 4. "yáuhdī Adj Adj déi " 5. "yātdaan…jauh…" once...then... 6. "mòuhleuhn…dōu…" no matter 7. "yàuhkèihsih" especially; particularly 8. "chùhng……ge gokdouh" from the perspective of… 9. "gīnggwo……" after… II. Paragraph and discourse 語段和篇章 1. "Sáusīn…gānjyuh…yàuhyū yíhseuhngge yùhnyān…"first...then...for above reasons... 2. "yùhgwó…yìhché…gám…" if...and...then/ so...

2. Text 🔊

課文 Fomàhn

各位專家、各位朋友，大家好。好高興今日能夠參加呢一個研討會。作為香港教育界嘅代表，我係持反對意見嘅。我並唔係從事法律相關工作嘅人，所以只可以從普通市民嘅角度去睇同性婚姻應否合法化呢個問題。	Gokwái jyūngā, gokwái pàhngyáuh, daaihgā hóu. Hóu gōuhing gāmyaht nàhnggau chāamgā nī yātgo yìhntóu wúi. Jokwàih Hēunggóng gaauyuhkgaaige doihbíu, ngóh haih chìh fáandeui yigin ge. Ngóh bihng m̀haih chùhngsih faatleuht sēunggwāan gūngjokge yàhn, sóyíh jí hóyíh chùhng póutūng síhmàhnge gokdouh heui tái tùhngsing fānyān yīngfáu hahpfaatfa nīgo mahntàih.

我今日帶咗啲新聞同數據嚟同大家分享。到底點解同性婚姻一時之間好似成為咗世界熱點新聞，大家都爭相討論起上嚟，變成討論熱點。首先喺2015年美國最高法院判同性婚姻係合法，受到憲法保障。自此之後我哋見到其實喺世界各國嘅 facebook 嘅用家都用一個彩虹嘅標記嚟到支持同性戀者。冇錯我哋知道人係的確係有唔同嘅自由。無論係言論自由、出版自由、定係戀愛自由，其實我哋知道同性戀，法律並有禁止。只不過係喺同性婚姻呢一個議題上面，我哋需要小心。

Ngóh gāmyaht daaijó dī sānmàhn tùhng sougeui làih tùhng daaihgā fānhéung. Doudái dímgáai tùhngsing fānyān yātsìh jīgāan hóuchíh sìhngwàihjó saigaai yihtdím sānmàhn, daaihgā dōu jāngsēung tóuleuhnhéi séuhnglàih, binsìhng tóuleuhn yihtdím. Sáusīn hái yih-lìhng-yāt-ńgh nìhn Méihgwok jeuigōu faatyún pun tùhngsīng fānyān haih hahpfaat, sauhdou hinfaat bóujeung. Jihchí jīhauh ngóhdeih gindóu kèihsaht hái saigaai gokgwokge *facebook* ge yuhnggā dōu yuhng yātgo chóihùhng ge bīugei làihdou jīchìh tùhngsinglyúnjé. Móuhcho ngóhdeih jīdou yàhn haih dīkkok haih yáuh m̀tùhngge jihyàuh. Mòuhleuhn haih yìhnleuhn jihyàuh, chēutbáan jihyàuh, dihnghaih lyúnngoi jihyàuh, kèihsaht ngóhdeih jīdou tùhngsinglyún, faatleuht bihng móuh gamjí. Jíbātgwo haih hái tùhngsing fānyān nī yātgo yíhtàih seuhngmihn, ngóhdeih sēuiyiu síusām.

喺香港，同性戀一早已經唔係非法嘅嘑。90年代開始，政府唔再話同性戀係非法嘅嘑，但係兩個同性戀者想喺香港結婚仲係唔可以。雖然越嚟越多人贊成香港應該好似歐洲一啲國家噉，俾同性戀者結婚，不過其實好多香港人都仲未可以接受嗰樣嘅關係。因為多數人覺得結婚係一男一女嘅事，如果結咗婚之後想要 BB，嗰 BB 最好要有父親同母親。呢方面，同性戀者做唔到。佢哋如果領養一個 BB，BB 就會永遠生活喺一個同性戀嘅家庭裏面。我哋可以睇下同性婚姻對小朋友嘅影響。有數據指出同性婚姻嘅小朋友，我哋知道係嚟自領養啦，佢哋比較起傳統婚姻，異性婚姻嘅小孩子，佢哋學業上嘅表現同埋人際關係都係有一個極大嘅差距。照呢個情形嚟睇，我哋唔係單單要考慮，係唔係容許成年人有嗰樣嘅自由嚟到結合，我哋都需要諗下一啲相關嘅影響。

Hái Hēunggóng, tùhngsing lyún yātjóu yíhgīng m̀haih fēifaat ge la. Gáusahp nìhndoih hōichí, jingfú m̀joi wah tùhngsinglyún haih fēifaat ge la, daahnhaih léuhnggo tùhngsinglyúnjé séung hái Hēunggóng gitfān juhnghaih m̀hóyíh. Sēuiyìhn yuht làih yuht dō yàhn jaansìhng Hēunggóng yīnggōi hóuchíh Ngāujāu yātdī gwokgā gám, béi tùhngsinglyúnjé gitfān, bātgwo kèihsaht hóudō Hēunggóng yàhn dōu juhng meih hóyíh jipsauh gámyéungge gwāanhaih. Yānwaih dōsou yàhn gokdāk gitfān haih yāt nàahm yāt néuih ge sih, yùhgwó gitjófān jīhauh séung yiu bìhbī, gám bìhbī jeui hóu yiu yáuh fuhchān tùhng móuhchān. Nī fōngmihn, tùhngsinglyúnjé jouh m̀dóu. Kéuihdeih yùhgwó líhngyéuhng yātgo bìhbī, bìhbī jauh wúih wíhngyúhn sāngwuht hái yātgo tùhngsinglyúnge gātìhng léuihmihn. Ngóhdeih hóyíh táiháh tùhngsing fānyān deui síu pàhngyáuhge yínghéung. Yáuh sougeui jíchēut tùhngsing fānyānge síu pàhngyáuh, ngóhdeih jīdou haih làihjih líhngyéuhng lā, kéuihdeih béigaauhéi chyùhntúng fānyān, yihsing fānyānge síuhàaihjí, kéuihdeih hohkyihp seuhng ge bíuyihn tùhngmàaih yàhnjai gwāanhaih dōu haih yáuh yātgo gihk daaih ge chākéuih. Jiu nīgo chìhngyìhng làih tái, ngóhdeih m̀haih dāandāan yiu háauleuih, haih m̀haih yùhnghéui sìhngnìhn yàhn yáuh gámyéungge jihyàuh làihdou githahp, ngóhdeih dōu sēuiyiu námháh yātdī sēunggwāange yínghéung.

就算兩個人唔打算要 BB，都唔代表我哋就可以俾佢哋結婚。當然，佢哋可以話，同邊個結婚，係個人自由，應該係自己揀嘅。同性戀者話，喺香港結婚，需要雙方嘅證婚人，而且要有人反對。所以如果佢哋嘅父母或者家人唔反對，外面嘅人唔反對，噉樣佢哋兩個人結婚，就冇問題㗎。呢點我唔反對，因為呢個係佢哋私人嘅問題。但係我想講，呢個社會，有好多嘢，係冇可能只要佢哋兩個人想點就點嘅。譬如話，兩個男人喺街上面拖住手行路，或者有啲人睇到只係覺得有啲怪怪哋都唔定。但係如果參加一個晚會，主持人介紹佢哋兩個嘅時候，應該點樣介紹呢？如果一個姓張嘅男人同一個姓陳嘅男人手拖手行出嚟，噉應該介紹張先生同張太太定係陳先生同陳太太呢？呢個已經去到文化方面嘅問題嘑。我哋幾千年，都未試過噉樣結婚嘅，而家忽然有人話想改變，噉就一定有好多嘢需要跟住改先至得。

最近有啲同性戀者出嚟話政府要俾佢哋「已婚人士免稅額」，噉兩個人一齊可以交少啲稅。有啲人話一旦佢哋結咗婚，就係「二人家庭」，可以兩個人一齊申請公屋。噉呢個就係社會民生問題嘑，大多數人要為咗嗰啲少數人改變成個社會咁耐以嚟嘅制度，噉樣大家係咪已經準備好呢？而家呢個社會已經同以前嘅社會有好大嘅唔同，而家嘅社會無論結唔結婚都可以一齊生活，但係如果同性婚姻合法化，萬一兩個人嘅關係出現問題，而且佢哋有小朋友，噉法律上應該點樣處理呢？呢啲問題尤其是法律問題就更加複雜。同埋如果同性婚姻係合乎人權，噉我哋將來亦都要喺呢個邏輯底下，從人權嘅角度考慮，多人婚姻係唔係都應該獲得法律嘅保障呢？

Jauhsyun léuhnggo yàhn m̀dásyun yiu bìhbī, dōu m̀doihbíu ngóhdeih jauh hóyíh béi kéuihdeih gitfān. Dōngyìhn, kéuihdeih hóyíh wah, tùhng bīngo gitfān haih goyàhn jihyàuh, yīnggōi haih jihgéi gáan ge. Tùhngsinglyúnjé wah, hái Hēunggóng gitfān, sēuiyiu sēungfōng ge jingfānyàhn, yìhché yiu móuh yàhn fáandeui. Sóyíh yùhgwó kéuihdeihge fuhmóuh waahkjé gāyàhn m̀fáandeui, ngoihmihnge yàhn m̀fáandeui, gámyéung kéuihdeih léuhnggo yàhn gitfān jauh móuh mahntàih la. Nī dím ngóh m̀fáandeui, yānwaih nīgo haih kéuihdeih sīyàhnge mahntàih. Daahnhaih ngóh séung góng, nīgo séhwúi, yáuh hóudō yéh, haih móuh hónàhng jíyiu kéuihdeih léuhnggo yàhn séung dím jauh dím ge. Peiyùhwah, léuhnggo nàahmyán hái gāai seuhngmihn tōjyuh sáu hàahnglouh, waahkjé yáuhdī yàhn táidóu jíhaih gokdāk yáuhdī gwaaigwáaidéi dōu m̀dihng. Daahnhaih yùhgwó chāamgā yātgo máahnwúi, jyúchìhyàhn gaaisiuh kéuihdeih léuhnggo ge sìhhauh, yīnggōi dímyéung gaaisiuh nē? Yùhgwó yātgo sing Jēung ge nàahmyán tùhng yātgo sing Chàhnge nàahmyán sáu tō sáu hàahng chēutlàih, gám yīnggōi gaaisiuh Jēung sīnsāang tùhng Jēung taaitáai dihnghaih Chàhn sīnsāang tùhng Chàhn taaitáai nē? Nīgo yíhgīng heuidou màhnfa fōngmihn ge mahntàih la. Ngóhdeih géi chīn nìhn, dōu meih sigwo gámyéung gitfān ge, yìhgā fātyìhn yáuh yàhn wah séung góibin, gám jauh yātdihng yáuh hóudō yéh sēuiyiu gānjyuh gói sīnji dāk.

Jeuigahn yáuhdī tùhngsinglyúnjé chēutlàih wah jingfú yiu béi kéuihdeih "yíhfān yàhnsih míhnseui ngáak", gám léuhnggo yàhn yātchàih hóyíh gāau síudī seui. Yáuhdī yàhn wah yātdaan kéuihdeih gitjófān, jauhhaih "yihyàhn gātìhng", hóyíh léuhnggo yàhn yātchàih sānchíng gūngngūk. Gám nīgo jauh haih séhwúi màhnsāng mahntàih la, daaih dōsou yàhn yiu waihjó gódī síusou yàhn góibin sèhnggo séhwúi gam noih yíhlàihge jaidouh, gámyéung daaihgā haih maih yíhgīng jéunbeih hóu nē? Yìhgā nīgo séhwúi yíhgīng tùhng yíhchìhn ge séhwúi yáuh hóu daaih ge m̀tùhng, yìhgā ge séhwúi mòuhleuhn git m̀gitfān dōu hóyíh yātchàih sāngwuht, daahnhaih yùhgwó tùhngsing fānyān hahpfaatfa, maahnyāt léuhnggo yàhnge gwāanhaih chēutyìhn mahntàih, yìhché kéuihdeih yáuh síu pàhngyáuh, gám faatleuht seuhng yīnggōi dímyéung chyúhléih nē? Nīdī mahntàih yàuhkèihsih faatleuht mahntàih jauh ganggā fūkjaahp. Tùhngmàaih yùhgwó tùhngsing fānyān haih hahpfùh yàhnkyùhn, gám ngóhdeih jēunglòih yihkdōu yiu hái nīgo lòhchāp dáihah, chùhng yàhnkyùhnge gokdouh háauleuih, dōyàhn fānyān haih m̀haih dōu yīnggōi wohkdāk faatleuhtge bóujeung nē?

經過以上嘅分析之後，我認為我哋嘅社會仲未準備好。因此我認為同性戀者唔可以喺香港結婚。喺呢一個議題上我嘅立場係十分之清晰，我係持反對嘅意見。多謝各位。	Gīnggwo yíhseuhngge fānsīk jīhauh, ngóh yihngwàih ngóhdeih ge séhwúi juhngmeih jéunbeih hóu. Yānchí ngóh yihngwàih tùhngsinglyúnjé m̀hóyíh hái Hēunggóng gitfān. Hái nī yāt go yíhtàih seuhng ngóhge lahpchèuhng haih sahpfānjī chīngsīk, ngóh haih chìh fáandeuige yigin. Dōjeh gokwái.

3. Vocabulary in use 🔊

活用詞彙 Wuhtyuhng chìhwuih

3.1 Common vocabulary

Number	Word	Yale Romanization	POS	English
1	從事	chùhngsih	V	to engage in (work)
2	法律	faatleuht	N	law
3	分享	fānhéung	V	to share
4	到底	doudái	Adv	after all
5	爭相	jāngsēung	V	to fall over each other in rush to
6	憲法	hinfaat	N	constitution
7	保障	bóujeung	N/V	protection; to ensure and protect
8	言論自由	yìhnleuhn jihyàuh	N	freedom of speech
9	出版自由	chēutbáan jihyàuh	N	freedom of publication
10	戀愛自由	lyún'ngoi jihyàuh	N	freedom of love
11	禁止	gamjí	V	to prohibit, to ban
12	接受	jipsauh	V	to accept
13	指出	jíchēut	V	to point out
14	學業	hohkyihp	N	(one's) academic studies
15	表現	bíuyihn	N	performance

16	人際關係	yàhnjai gwāanhaih	N	interpersonal relationship
17	極大	gihk daaih	PH	huge, enormous
18	差距	chākéuih	N	gap, disparity
19	成年人	sìhngnìhnyàhn	N	adult
20	雙方	sēungfōng	PH	both parties
21	一旦	yātdaan	Adv	in case, once
22	公屋	gūng'ūk	N	public housing estate
23	社會民生	séhwúi màhnsāng	N	social livelihood
24	透過	taugwo	CV	through
25	尤其是	yàuhkèihsih	Adv	especially
26	複雜	fūkjaahp	Adj	complicated
27	合乎	hahpfùh	V	to conform to
28	人權	yàhnkyùhn	N	human rights
29	邏輯	lòhchāp	N	logic
30	考慮	háauleuih	V	to consider

3.2 Proper nouns

1	最高法院	jeui gōu faatyún	PN	Supreme Court
2	已婚人士免稅額	yíhfān yàhnsih míhnseuingáak	PN	Married Person's Allowance
3	婚姻法	fānyān faat	PN	Marriage Law

3.3 About family and marriage

1	同性戀合法化	tùhngsinglyún hahpfaatfa	PH	legalization of homosexuality
2	同性婚姻	tùhngsing fānyān	N	same-sex marriage
3	父親	fuhchān	N	father
4	母親	móuhchān	N	mother
5	領養	líhngyéuhng	V	to adopt (child)

6	小孩子	síuhàaihjí	N	child
7	傳統婚姻	chyùhntúng fānyān	N	traditional marriage
8	異性	yihsing	N	the opposite sex
9	結合	githahp	V	to marry, to be united in wedlock
10	證婚人	jingfānyàhn	N	wedding witness
11	二人家庭	yihyàhn gātìhng	PH	two-person household
12	合法夫妻	hahpfaat fūchāi	N	legitimate couple
13	多人婚姻	dōyàhn fānyān	N	multi-person marriage

3.4 Other vocabularies

1	數據	sougeui	N	data
2	用家	yuhnggā	N	user
3	跟住	gānjyuh	Adv/V	then; to follow
4	彩虹	chóihùhng	N	rainbow
5	標記	bīugei	N	symbol, sign, mark
6	晚會	máahnwúi	N	evening party
7	主持人	jyúchìhyàhn	N	host, MC

3.5 Useful expressions

1	相關工作	sēunggwāan gūngjok	PH	related work
2	一時之間	yātsìh jīgāan	PH	all of a sudden
3	討論熱點	tóuleuhn yihtdím	N	hot-debate issue
4	自此之後	jih chí jīhauh	PH	since then, henceforth
5	唔係單單要考慮	m̀haih dāandāan yiu háauleuih	PH	not only need to consider

4. Notes on language and discourse structure

語言及篇章結構知識 Yúhyìhn kahp pīnjēung gitkau jīsīk

4.1. Grammar and sentence patterns 語法和句型

4.1.1. " -héiséuhnglàih" is a verb ending which shows or describes an action of a verb beginning or occurring. It can be translated as "when…" or "once…".

- "héi séuhng làih" can be used to evaluate an action.

1. Sēuiyìhn kéuih sìhsìh dōu jūngyi góngsíu, daahnhaih yāt jouhhéi yéh séuhnglàih jauh hóu yihngjān.

   (Although he loves to joke, but once he starts working, he works seriously.)

2. Kéuih yāt gónghéi nī gihn sih séuhnglàih jauh hóu nāu.

   (Whenever this issue is mentioned, he gets very angry.)

3. M̀hóu daai gam dō yéh, wáanhéiséuhnglàih wúih hīngsūng dī.

   (Don't bring too much with you, so that when you play, you will be more at ease.)

4. Deui sān hàaih yáuh dī jaak, hàahnghéiséuhnglàih wúih hóu sānfú.

5. Néih góng jauh yùhngyih, daahnhaih jouhhéiséuhnglàih jauh hóu nàahn la.

   (It's easy for you to say, but it's hard when you actually do it.)

- "héi séuhng làih" can be translated as "Suddenly (fātyìhngāan)......", and it is usually used to refer to weather conditions or human emotions.

1. Ngóh m̀jī dímgáai kéuih haamhéiséuhnglàih.

   (I didn't know why she suddenly began to cry.)

2. Gāmjīu juhng hóu hóutīn, gú m̀dou lohkhéi yúh séuhnglàih.

   (It was fine this morning suddenly it began raining.)

3. Yùhgwó dáhéi fūng séuhnglàih jauh móuh syùhn hàahng ge la.

   (No boat will be sailing if there is a typhoon.)

4.1.2. "Jiu nīgo chìhngyìhng làih tái/góng"

This pattern means that "according to this situation" and is often used in a rather formal situation.

1. Gāmnìhn ngóhdeih hohkhaauh ge hohksāang yàhnsou gáamsíu. Jiu nīgo chìhngyìhng

làih góng, ngóhdeih m̀wúih joi pingchíng (to hire) sānge jīkyùhn (staff).

2.   Yìhgā tīnhei ngoklyuht (bad), hóudō hòhngbāan (flights) dōu yiu chéuisīu. Jiu nīgo chìhngyìhng làih tái, léuihhaak hónàhng yiu dáng dou daihyih yaht sīnji hóyíh séuhnggēi.

3.   Nībāan hohksāang ge hohkyihp bíuyihn yātheung dōu hóu hóu, pìhngsìh ge háausíh sìhngjīk dōu sēungdōng m̀cho. Jiu nīgo chìhngyìhng làih góng, kéuihdeih yīnggōi hóyíh yahpdóu sāmyìh (favourite, adoring) ge daaihhohk duhksyū.

4.   Gahnnìhn lèuhngahn deihkēui ge dóuchèuhng yuht hōi yuht dō, yìhché chàhmmàih dóubok ge yàhn yihkdōu yuht làih yuht dō, mahntàih yuht làih yuht yìhmjuhng. Jiu nīgo chìhngyìhng làih tái, ngóh yihngwàih Hēunggóng jingfú m̀yīnggōi hīnggin dóuchèuhng làih chigīk gīngjai.

4.1.3.   "jíyiu…, jauh…" as long as, …then…

1.   Waahkjé haih gobiht laihjí, daahnhaih jíyiu yáuh nījúng sih ge chyùhnjoih (existence), deui séhwúi jauhwúih yáuh hóudaaihge yínghéung.

2.   Jíyiu néih nóuhlihk, jauh yātdihng wúih sìhnggūng.

3.   Jíyiu síu pàhngyáuh gihnhōng, bàhbā màhmā jauh fongsām.

4.1.4.   "yáuhdī Adj. Adj. déi", a little bit Adj.

1.   Dī chēung dáhōisaai, ngóh yáuhdī dungdúngdéi.

2.   Yìhgā sahpyih dím la, ngóh yáuhdī ngohngódéi.

3.   Kéuih m̀chēutsēng, hóuchíh yáuhdī nāunāudéi.

4.   Ngóh jeuk taai dō sāam, yìhgā yáuhdī yihtyítdéi.

5.   Ngóh yìhgā juhng yáuhdī báaubáaudéi, sóyíh m̀séung sihkfaahn jyuh.

The adjective used in this pattern should be monosyllabic and also reduplicated, and the reduplicated one is changed into High Rising tone except when its original tone is High Level or High Rising.

4.1.5.   "yātdaan…, jauh…" once...then...

1.   Yātdaan yātgo yàhn beih pun séiyìhng (death penalty), maahnyāt (in case) yáuh puncho, nīgo chongh (mistake) jauh hóunàahn bóugau (to remedy).

2.   Yātdaan yáuh yīnyáhn, jauh hóunàahn m̀sihkyīn.

3.   Yātdaan faatsāng deihjan (earthquake), jauh yiu wán ōnchyùhnge deihfōng jaahmbeih (temporary shelter).

4.1.6. "mòuhleuhn…, dōu…" no matter

1. Mòuhleuhn yātgo yàhn jouhjó mātyéh waaihsih, dōu m̀hóyíh pun kéuih séiyìhng (death penalty).

2. Jūnggwok yàhn hóu juhngsih gaauyuhk, mòuhleuhn haih síuhohk, jūnghohk, daaihhohk gingjāng (competition) dōu hóu gīkliht (severe).

3. Yùhgwó pòhngbīn yáuh yàhn sihkyīn, mòuhleuhn néih jihgéi sihk m̀sihk, gihnhōng dōu wúih sauh yínghéung.

4.1.7. "yàuhkèihsih" especially; particularly

1. Hái yātgo gwokgā, hóu dō faatleuht mahntàih dōu sēuiyiu síusām chyuléih, yàuhkèihsih séiyìhng nīgo mahntàih.

2. Hēunggóngge wàahngíng géihóu, yàuhkèihsih hái daaihhohk fuhgahn, yáuh sāan yáuh séui, yauh leng yauh gōnjehng.

3. Ngóh gokdāk Jūngmàhn géi nàahn, yàuhkèihsih Jūngmàhnjih.

4.1.8. "chùhng…ge gokdouh" from the perspective of…

1. Ngóh gokdāk yātgo gwokgā yīng m̀yīnggōi yáuh séiyìhng haih yātgihn daaihsih, ngóh hóyíh chùhng yātbūn yàhnge gokdouh gónggóng ngóhge táifaat.

2. Tùhngsing fānyān hahpfaatfa, nīgo mahntàih hóu fūkjaahp, ngóh yihngwàih daaihgā yīnggōi chùhng m̀tùhng ge gokdouh tóuleuhn.

3. Gwāanyū yihnsìh (now) hohksāang gūngfo sihfáu taai dō ge mahntàih, ngóhdeih yiu chùhng hohksāang ge gokdouh námháh.

4.1.9. "gīnggwo…" after…

1. Gīnggwo diuhchàh, faatyihn gógo yàhn haih mòuhgū (innocent) ge.

2. Gīnggwo bunnìhnge jéunbeih, kéuih sānchíngdóu kéuih séung heuige daaihhohk la.

3. Gīnggwo géinìhnge faatjín, nīgo sìhngsíh yáuh hóudaaihge binfa.

4.2. Paragraph and discourse 語段和篇章

4.2.1. "Sáusīn…gānjyuh…yàuhyū yíhseuhngge yùhnyān…" first…and then…for above reasons…

1. Sáusīn, séiyìhng lihng síhmàhn gokdāk m̀syūfuhk, gānjyuh pun yātgo yàhn séiyìhng haih yātgo juhngdaaihge kyutdihng, kèihchi (and then)…yàuhyū yíhseuhng ge yùhnyān, ǹgóh deui séiyìhng yáuhsó bóulàuh (reservation).

2. Sáusīn, ngóh deui nīfahn gūng yáuh hingcheui. Gānjyuh, ngóh séung hái Hēunggóng sāngwuht… yàuhyū yíhseuhngge yùhnyān ngóh séung hái nīgāan gūngsī gūngjok.

3. Sáusīn, nīgāan jūnghohk deihdím hóu káhn. Gānjyuh kéuihdeihge hohkfai pèhngdī… Yàuhyū yíhseuhngge yùhnyān, ngóh hēimohng sung ngóhge jáinéui làih nīgāan hohkhaauh duhksyū.

4.2.2. "Yùhgwó…yìhché…gám…" if...and...then/so...

1. Yùhgwó sauhhoihjé (victim) gāyàhn yáuh gámge yuhnmohng, yìhché kéuihdeihge yīukàuh haih hahpléihge (reasonable), gám ngóh gokdāk kéuihdeihge yuhnmohng yīnggōi dākdou jyūnjuhng.

2. Yùhgwó nīgāan hohkhaauhge hohkfai gam gwai, yìhché yauh gaaudāk m̀haihgéi hóu, gám ngóh gokdāk néih yīnggōi háauleuih kèihtā hohkhaauh.

3. Yùhgwó chēutnín ge jōugām (rent) tùhng gāmnín chām̀dō, yìhché ngóh yauh wándóu sānge tùhngfóng, gám ngóh juhng séung jōu néihge dāanwái.

5. Notes on pragmatic knowledge

語用因素與相關知識 Yúhyuhng yānsou yúh sēunggwāan jīsīk

5.1. Politeness and ways to refer to family members 禮貌與稱謂

5.1.1. "我唔係法律專家 ngóh m̀haih faatleuht jyūngā" I'm not an expert in the legal field.

Being modest is a very important part of the Chinese culture, which is behind many common expressions found in public speech. When the speaker says "I'm not an expert in this field", it may or may not be true but the use of expressions similar to this is often expected among Chinese audiences. Thus the lack of it may sometimes contribute to the impression that the pragmatic competence of the speaker (if he/she is a CSL learner) can be further improved.

Ngóh m̀haih faatleuht jyūngā, daahnhaih…
Ngóh deui Hēunggóng m̀haihgéi líuhgáai, bātgwo…

5.1.2. Different levels of formality with kinship terms: "母親 móuhchān" mother

Although both "媽媽màhmā" and "母親móuhchān" can be used to refer to one's mother, the former is often used in face-to-face situations or, if not, with some emotional attachment, while the latter is a more factual and objective term when referring to one's mother. When used figuratively or used in names of organizations, books, etc, however "母親 móuhchān" is acceptable in combinations such as "母親的抉擇 móuhchān dīk kyutjaahk", literally "mothers' choice" (a charity organization helping children without family and pregnant teenagers).

Kéuihge màhmā deui kéuih fēisèuhng hóu.
Gāmyaht haih Móuhchān jit (Mothers' day), hóudō yàhn chēutheui yámchàh.

5.1.3. "家人 gāyàhn" family members

Similar to "母親 móuhchān" as explained above, "家人 gāyàhn" is used as an objective term to refer to family members. The scope of "家人 gāyàhn", however, is much larger in Chinese than what is usually thought of in English, because it may include members of the extended family, such as grandparents, or even uncles and aunties.

Sauhhoihjé ge gāyàhn yáuh gámyéungge yuhnmohng…
Chíng néih bōng ngóh mahnhauh néihge gāyàhn.

5.2. Related knowledge 相關知識

5.2.1. "唔太完善m̀taai yùhnsihn、唔太健全 m̀taai gihnchyùhn" not yet perfect, not yet complete

The use of "太 taai" does not always mean "too (as in too much)" in English. Rather, it is a hedge to soften the tone, especially when the speaker believes that the comments made may be somewhat offensive, or politically not correct. Here, instead of saying the rule of law is "唔完善 m̀yùhnsihn" and "唔健全 m̀gihnchyùhn", putting 太 after the negation makes the comment much less harsh. The awareness of the effect from blunt negative statements and the ability to use words and expressions to soften the negative effect is considered part of the pragmatic competence.

Hái yātgo faatjih juhng m̀taai yùhnsihn, m̀taai gihnchyùhnge gwokgā…
Sēuiyìhn kéuihge taaidouh m̀haih taai hóu…

5.2.2. "熱點新聞 yihtdím sānmàhn" focused news

Language is certainly "alive" from a sociolinguistic perspective and the most active part of language use is often found in social media and other virtual platforms provided by the Internet, which creates "hot spots" in the news from time to time. To be able to pay attention to such hot spots with relevant language features is an indication of both language proficiency level and pragmatic ability.

Ngóh námhéi géi nìhnchìhnge yātgo yihtdím sānmàhn…

5.2.3. "姓莫嘅男人 sing Mohk ge nàahmyán" a male person whose last name is "Mok"

Each culture has different ways of referring to a person depending on the relationship, the context and the purpose in which such a person is named. In the legal context, there are certain terms which are regarded as "factual and neutral", such as the one used here. Usually you will not refer to your friends and colleagues in such a way as it may appear impolite, or it may give people the impression that you have something to hide.

Yātgo sing Jēung ge nàahmyán beih pun séiyìhng (death penalty),…
Ngóh yáuh yātgo sing Sītòuhge pàhngyáuh.

5.2.4. "疑犯 yìhfáan" suspect(crime)

In a legal discourse, certain terms are expected to be used in order to convey the impression of a formal, solemn style, such as "疑犯 yìhfáan" here. It is combination of the use of such terms, the relatively unique way of referring to a person (as explained above), and the adoption of certain grammatical features that contributes to the appropriateness in terms of style.

Nīgihn ongín (case) ge yìhfáan sìhngyihng (admit)…
Néih yihngwàih yìhfáan góngge yéh hó m̀hóseun a?

5.2.5. "社會輿論 séhwúi yùhleuhn" public opinion of the society

Given the formal setting and the content area covered here, the use of formal and abstract terms, as opposed to concrete and specific words, is more appropriate and can be treated as an indication of proficiency level and pragmatic competence.

Séhwúi yùhleuhn dōu tùhngyi nījúng jeuihfáan (criminal) yīnggōi sauhdou chìhngfaht (punishment).

Faatleuht chìhngjeuih (procedure) yáuhsìh wúih sauhdou séhwúi yùhleuhn gōnyuh (interfere).

6. Contextualized speaking practice

情境説話練習 Chìhnggíng syutwah lihnjaahp

【課前預習】 Class preparation

6.1 Please answer the following True/False questions according to the lesson text.

1　Yíngóngge yàhn fáandeui tùhngsing fānyān hahpfaatfa. (T/F)

2　Yih-lìhng-yāt-nǵh nìhn Méihgwok jeui gōu faatyún pun tùhngsing fānyān haih m̀sauhdou faatleuht bóujeung ge. (T/F)

3　Hái Hēunggóng, tùhngsing lyún haih fēifaat ge. (T/F)

4　Yuht làih yuht dō yàhn jaansìhng Hēunggóng yīnggōi hóuchíh Ngāujāu yātdī gwokgā gám, béi tùhngsinglyúnjé gitfān. (T/F)

5　Yíngóngge yàhn yihngwàih hóudō Hēunggóng yàhn juhng meih hóyíh jipsauh tùhngsinglyúnjé gitfān. (T/F)

6　Yíngóngge yàhn tàihchēut yáuh sougeui jíchēut tùhngsing fānyānge síu pàhngyáuh, tùhng chyùhntúng fānyānge síu pàhngyáuh béigaau, léuhngjé hohkyihp seuhng ge bíuyihn tùhng yàhnjai gwāanhaih chā m̀dō. (T/F)

7　Yíngóngge yàhn yihngwàih tùhngsing fānyān gwāanhaihdou màhnfa fōngmihnge mahntàih. (T/F)

8　Yíngóngge yàhn tàihchēut sānchíng gūngngūkge laihjí heui gáaisīk tùhngsing fānyān gwāanhaihdou séhwúi jīyùhn mahntàih. (T/F)

9　Yíngóngge yàhn yihngwàih chùhng yàhnkyùhn gokdouh háauleuih, gokdāk dōyàhn fānyān dōu yīnggōi wohkdāk faatleuhtge bóujeung. (T/F)

10　Yíngóngge yàhn yihngwàih ngóhdeihge séhwúi juhngmeih jéunbeih hóu tùhngsing fānyān hahpfaat fa. (T/F)

【課後練習】 Post-class exercises

6.2 Fill in the blanks with the given vocabularies. Each vocabulary can be chosen once only.

chùhngsih	taugwo	jāngsēung	bóujeung
gamjí	jipsauh	jíchēut	bíuyihn
chākéuih	fūkjaahp	hahpfùh	háauleuih

1. Nīgo mahntàih hóu _____, néih béi dī sìhgaan ngóh námháh, jīhauh joi fūkfāan néih.

2. Síu-mìhng múihgo yuht ge sāuyahp (income) fēisèuhngjī m̀wándihng, kéuih gokdāk sāngwuht hóu móuh _____.

3. Jingfú ginyíh lahpfaat _____ heung sahpbaatseui yíhhah ge chīngsiunìhn maaih jáu.

4. Wahnduhngyùhn hái nīchèuhng béichoi ge _____ fēisèuhngjī hóu.

5. Síu-mìhng jouh yéh hóu síusām, múihgihn sih dōu yātdihng wúih _____ dāk hóu chīngchó sīnji jouh kyutdihng.

6. Hái yātgo jyūntàih bihnleuhnwúi seuhng, m̀síu chāamgājé dōu _____ bíudaaht jihgéi ge yigin.

7. Kéuih fahn yàhn hóu gujāp (stubborn), m̀yùhngyih _____ kèihtā yàhn ge yigin tùhng pāipìhng (criticism).

8. Lóuhsai wah, m̀ _____ bīujéun (standard) ge cháanbán (product) m̀hóyíh hái síhchèuhng chēutsauh (offer for sale).

9. Chàhn lóuhsī _____ gaauhohk gūngjok yíhgīng yahgéi nìhn la.

10. Yáuh jyūngā _____, yùhgwó wūyíhm (pollution) mahntàih yātlouh gám gaijuhk lohkheui, hauhgwó (consequence) jēung wúih hóu yìhmjuhng.

11. Kùhngyàhn tùhng yáuhchínyàhn jīgāan ge _____ hóu daaih, yàuhkèihsih séhwúi deihwaih tùhng sāngwuht jātsou fōngmihn.

12. Néih hóyíh _____ dihnyàuh heung gūngsī bíudaaht jihgéi ge yigin.

6.3 Complete the following sentences or answer the following questions using the given patterns.

1. V héi (O) séuhnglàih
   Kéuih yāt _____ jauh hóu hōisām.

2. Jiu nīgo chìhngyìhng làih tái, ……
   Yìhgā haih fàahnmòhng sìhgaan, mòuhleuhn bīndouh dōu hóu sākchē.
   _____.

3. jíyiu ...... jauh ......

   A: Dímyéung hóyíh hōisāmdī nē?

   B: _____.

4. yáuhdī Adj Adj déi

   Nīdouh _____, dáng ngóh jeukfāan gihn sāam sīn.

5. yātdaan ...... jauh ......

   Heui ngoihdeih léuihhàhng, chīnkèih yiu síusām. _____.

6. mòuhleuhn ...... dōu ......

   Nīgāan jáulàuh _____.

7. yàuhkèihsih ......

   Kéuih deui Hēunggóng ge lihksí tùhng màhnfa hóu yáuh yihngsīk,

   _____.

8. chùhng ...... ge gokdou, ...

   A: Néih yihngwàih jingfú jāngchit gūngjung gakèih deui séhwúi yáuh mātyéh jokyuhng a?

   B: _____.

9. gīnggwo ......

   _____, ngóhdeih jūngyū doujó muhkdīkdeih (destination) la.

7. Listening and speaking 🔊

聽説練習 Tingsyut lihnjaahp

7.1 Listening comprehension exercise

Please listen to the recording and answer the following T/F questions:

1. Yíngóngge noihyùhng jyúyiu haih gwāanyū yīng m̀yīnggōi faichèuih (abolish) séiyìhng (captial punishment) (T/F)

2. Yíngóngge yàhn yihngwàih mòuhleuhn yātgo yàhn jouhjó mātyéh, kèihtā yàhn dōu haih móuhkyùhn kyutdihng kéuihge sāngséi. (T/F)

3. Yíngóngge yàhn gokdāk faatleuht tùhng jaidouh hóyíh yáuhkyùhn mōkdyuht kèihtā yàhn ge sāngmihng. (T/F)

4. Yíngóngge yàhn yihngwàih sēuiyìhn séiyìhng haih yātgo hóu juhngdaaihge kyutdihng,

daahnhaih jouhsìhng ge cho (mistake) haih hóyíh nèihbóu (remedy)ge. (T/F)

5. Yíngóngge yàhn yihngwàih faatleuht yíhgīng yùhnsihn, gihnchyùhnge gwokgā, hái séiyìhng nīgo mahntàih seuhng ganggā yiu síusām chyúhléih. (T/F)

6. Yíngóngge yàhn tàihchēut kèuhnggāan (rape) saatyàhn(murder) on (cases) ge laihjí heui jīchìh kéuihge leuhndím (discussion points). (T/F)

7. Yíngóngge yàhn deui séiyìhngge taaidouh haih wàaihyìh (suspicious) tùhng yáuh bóulàuh (reserve) ge. (T/F)

8. Yíngóngge yàhn tàihchēut hái sauhhoihjé (victim) ge gokdouh, deuiyū séiyìhngge táifaat haih yātyeuhngge. (T/F)

9. Hái faatleuhtge gokdouh, jaidihng faatleuht ge yātgo muhkdīk haih lihng yàhn m̀gám (dare not) faahnjeuih. (T/F)

10. Yíngóngge yàhn haih chùhng yātgo póutūng yàhn ge gokdouh yihngwàih yīnggōi faichèuih séiyìhng. (T/F)

7.2 Speech topics

1. Néih yihngwàih mātyéh haih "yìhnleuhn jihyàuh" a? "Yìhnleuhn jihyàuh" yáuh géi juhngyiu nē? Jingfú yīnggōi dímyéung bóujeung m̀tùhng yàhn ge yìhnleuhn jihyàuh nē?

2. "Tùhngsing fānyān" tùhng "chyùhntúng fānyān" yáuh mātyéh fānbiht a? Néih yihngwàih yùhgwó "tùhngsing fānyān" hahpfaatfa, wúih deui séhwúi daailàih mātyéh yínghéung nē?

3. Yáuh yàhn wah faatleuht hóyíh gáaikyut sóyáuh ge mahntàih, daahnhaih yihk yáuh yàhn wah faatleuht jí wúih waih yàhn daailàih gang dō ge mahntàih. Néih jihgéi yáuh mātyéh táifaat a?

7.3 Speaking exercise: Please use at least 10 of the following vocabularies/patterns to say on the following topic in one to two minutes.

"Hēunggóng séhwúi yìhgā mihndeui mātyéh mahntàih a? Yáuh mātyéh baahnfaat hóyíh gáaikyut waahkjé gáamsíu nīgo/nīdī mahntàih nē?"

bóujeung	bíuyihn	chākéuih	gūng'ūk
taugwo	fūkjaahp	hahpfùh	yàhnkyùhn
háauleuih	yàuhkèihsih	yìhnleuhn jihyàuh	
yàhnjai gwāanhaih		séhwúi màhnsāng	yātdaan ...... jauh ......
mòuhleuhn ...... dōu		jiu nīgo chìhngyìhng làih tái, ...	

8. Additional texts

附加課文 Fuhgā fomàhn

8.1. 附加課文 Additional text

最近，一個中國留學生喺日本俾人殺死，佢嘅媽媽非常痛苦，要求判兇手死刑。我哋當然好理解呢位媽媽嘅心情，都尊重佢嘅願望，但係其實喺日本，一般嘅殺人兇手係好難被判死刑嘅。除咗日本，一啲歐美國家完全冇死刑，如果係非常嚴重嘅犯罪，法院可能判一百年兩百年，等罪犯一生都要喺監獄裏面生活，都唔會主動結束罪犯嘅生命。

Jeuigahn, yātgo Jūnggwok làuhhohksāang hái Yahtbún béi yàhn saatséi, kéuihge màhmā fēisèuhng tungfú, yīukàuh pun hūngsáu séiyìhng. Ngóhdeih dōngyìhn hóu léihgáai nīwái màhmāge sāmchìhng, dōu jyūnjuhng kéuihge yuhnmohng, daahnhaih kèihsaht hái Yahtbún, yātbūnge saatyàhn hūngsáu haih hóunàahn beih pun séiyìhng ge. Chèuihjó Yahtbún, yātdī Āuméih gwokgā yùhnchyùhn móuh séiyìhng, yùhgwó haih fēisèuhng yìhmjuhngge faahnjeuih, faatyún hónàhng pun yātbaak nìhn léuhng baak nìhn, dáng jeuihfáan yātsāng dōu yiu hái gāamyuhk léuihmihn sāngwuht, dōu m̀wúih jyúduhng gitchūk jeuihfáange sāngmihng.

喺中國，我哋有「殺人填命」噉樣嘅講法，但係你或者唔知道，其實中國喺唐朝（Tòhngchìuh, Tang Dynasty）就已經廢除過死刑，喺歷史書裏面就可以睇到。至於點解要廢除死刑，孔子（Húngjí, Confucius）講過「上天有好生之德」或者係最好嘅理由。另外一個原因係同宗教有關嘅，唐朝嘅時候流行佛教（Fahtgaau, Buddhism），而佛教係唔支持死刑嘅。不過，唐朝廢除死刑嘅時間只有十幾年。或者唐朝嘅皇帝（Wòhngdai, Emperor）嘅睇法對日本呢個鄰居有一啲影響。

Hái Jūnggwok, ngóhdeih yáuh "saatyàhn tìhnmehng" gámyéungge góngfaat, daahnhaih néih waahkjé m̀jīdou, kèihsaht Jūnggwok hái Tòhngchìuh jauh yíhgīng faichèuihgwo séiyìhng, hái lihksí syū léuihmihn jauh hóyíh táidóu. Jiyū dímgáai yiu faichèuih séiyìhng, Húngjí gónggwo, "seuhngtīn yáuh housāng jīdāk" waahkjé haih jeuihhóuge léihyàuh. Lihngngoih yātgo yùhnyān haih tùhng jūnggaau yáuhgwāange, Tòhngchìuhge sìhhauh làuhhàhng Fahtgaau, yìh Fahtgaau haih m̀jīchìh séiyìhngge. Bātgwo, Tòhngchìuh faichèuih séiyìhngge sìhgaan jíyáuh sahp géi nìhn. Waahkjé Tòhngchìuhge Wòhngdaige táifaat deui Yahtbún nīgo lèuhngēui yáuh yātdī yínghéung.

到咗十八世紀，意大利（Yidaaihleih, Italy）嘅一啲法律學家都開始反對死刑，佢哋認為死刑唔能夠令壞人變成好人，而且，國家唔應該有剝奪普通人生命嘅權力。十九世紀尾，歐洲唔少國家都開始考慮廢除死刑。當時日本啱啱就向西方學習，因此喺日本有人提出要廢除死刑。所以日本對死刑嘅態度非常謹慎，即使係一啲非常嚴重、惡劣嘅殺人事件，殺人犯最後都只係被判無期徒刑（mòuhkèih tòuhyìhng, Life Sentence）。

所以我哋可以睇到，有啲人雖然"罪該萬死"，但係世界各國其實都一直討論緊死刑係唔係應該存在，各國都努力平衡法律同人權嘅關係。就係，按照現代人嘅睇法，一定會有越嚟越多嘅國家廢除死刑，不過，需要一個接受嘅過程。

Doujó sahpbaat saigéi, Yidaaihleihge yātdī faatleuht hohkgā dōu hōichí fáandeui séiyìhng, kéuihdeih yihngwàih séiyìhng m̀nàhnggau lihng waaihyàhn binsìhng hóuyàhn, yìhché, gwokgā m̀yīnggōi yáuh mōkdyuht póutūng yàhn sāngmihngge kyùhnlihk. Sahpgáu saigéi méih, Āujāu m̀síu gwokgā dōu hōichí háauleuih faichèuih séiyìhng. Dōngsìh Yahtbún ngāamngāam jauh heung sāifōng hohkjaahp, yānchí hái Yahtbún yáuh yàhn tàihchēut yiu faichèuih séiyìhng. Sóyíh Yahtbún deui séiyìhngge taaidouh fēisèuhng gánsahn, jīksí haih yātdī fēisèuhng yìhmjuhng, ngoklyuhtge saatyàhn sihgín, saatyàhnfáan jeuihauh dōu jíhaih beih pun mòuhkèih tòuhyìhng.

Sóyíh ngóhdeih hóyíh táidóu, yáuhdī yàhn sēuiyìhn "jeuih gōi maahn séi", daahnhaih saigaai gokgwok kèihsaht dōu yātjihk tóuleuhngán séiyìhng haih m̀haih yīnggōi chyùhnjoih, gokgwok dōu nóuhlihk pìhnghàhng faatleuht tùhng yàhnkyùhnge gwāanhaih, jauhhaih, onjiu yihn doih yàhn ge táifaat, yātdihng wúih yáuh yuhtlàih yuht dōge gwokgā faichèuih séiyìhng, bātgwo, sēuiyiu yātgo jipsauhge gwochìhng.

8.2 附加詞彙 Additional vocabulary

Number	Word	Yale Romanization	POS	English
1	一般	yātbūn	Adj	general, common, ordinary
2	監獄	gāamyuhk	N	prison, jail
3	理由	léihyàuh	N	reason, argument, justification
4	宗教	jūnggaau	N	religion
5	世紀	saigéi	N	century
6	法學家	faathohk gā	N	jurist, jurisconsult, legist
7	反對	fáandeui	V	to oppose
8	變成	binsìhng	V	to become, to turn into
9	人權	yàhnkyùhn	N	human rights
10	過程	gwochìhng	N	process

1 殺人填命 saatyàhn tìhnmehng: A life for a life.

2 上天有好生之德 seuhngtīn yáuh housāng jīdāk: Heaven's care for every living thing.

3 罪該萬死 jeuih gōi maahn séi: be guilty of a crime for which one deserves to die ten thousand deaths.

8.3 Please answer the following T/F questions after reading the additional text:

1 Yātgo Jūnggwok làuhhohksāang gokdāk Yahtbún yīnggōi yiu yáuh séiyìhng. (T/F)

2 Hái Yahtbún, saatyàhn hūngsáu yātbūn wúih beih pun séiyìhng. (T/F)

3 Yahtbún tùhng yātdī Āuméih gwokgā dōu yáuh séiyìhng. (T/F)

4 Yáuhdī jeuihfáan wúih hái gāamyuhk léuihmihn séijó, yānwaih yáuh séiyìhng. (T/F)

5 Jūnggwok yàuh Tòhngchìuh hōichí jauh móuh séiyìhng. (T/F)

6 Húngjí tùhng Fahtgaauge táifaat dōu haih Tòhngchìuh faichèuih séiyìhngge léihyàuh. (T/F)

7 Yātdī Yidaaihleih faathohkgā fáandeui séiyìhng, yānwaih séiyìhng m̀wúih jēung jeuihfáan binsìhng hóuyàhn. (T/F)

8 Nīpīn màhnjēung yihngwàih, Yahtbún sauhdou Jūnggwok tùhng Āujāuge yínghéung sóyíh faichèuihjó séiyìhng. (T/F)

9 Jeuigahn yātléuhng baak nìhn, saigaai gokgwokge yàhn hōichí háauleuih séiyìhng yīng ṁyīnggōi chyùhnjoih. (T/F)

10 Yuht làih yuht síu gwokgā yáuh séiyìhng. (T/F)

8.4 Topics for discussions

1 Néih tùhng ṁtùhngyi "saatyàhn tìhnmehng" nīgo góngfaat nē?

2 Chéng néih góngháh néihge gwokgā deui séiyìhngge taaidouh.

3 Néih gokdāk juhngyáuh mātyéh faatleuht yīnggōi góibin nē? Dímgáai nē?

8.5 Authentic oral data 1 [related in content, beyond Text] 🔊
真實語料 1

8.6 Authentic oral data 2 [related in content, beyond Text] 🔊
真實語料 2

Lesson 10 Environmental Protection
環境保護

1. Pragmatic factors, Yuti features and linguistic functions
語用因素、語體特徵與語言功能

Yúhyuhng yānsou, yúhtái dahkjīng yúh yúhyìhn gūngnàhng

語用因素 / 語體特徵 Pragmatic factors/ Yuti features	語言功能 Linguistic function
Pragmatic factors: Expressing thanks in public is often associated with a formal, and sometimes ceremonial situation. It calls for formal features of language as well as formulaic chunks. 語用因素： 公開致謝一般為正式場合，語體正式，因為儀式的需要會出現某些約定俗成的套話。 **Yuti features:** Formality index: 2+ 語體特徵：2+	**Linguistic function:** Expressing Gratitude and Review Expressing gratitude in a formal context, and focusing on a specific undertaking, point out shortcomings and inefficiencies while affirming the undertaking's success, simultaneously providing affirmation and motivation to further improve. 語言功能：致謝與回顧 在正式場合致謝，並針對某項工作，在肯定成績的同時指出不足的方面和未盡的事宜，既有肯定又有督促。

Notes on pragmatic knowledge 語用知識	Notes on structure 語言及篇章結構知識
I. Yuti, formulaic expressions and exaggerating 語體、套話與誇張 　1. Order in greeting people「尊稱的順序」 　2. Person in charge「負責人」 　3. Millions thanks「萬分感謝」 II. Related knowledge 相關知識 　1. Have got certain achievement 「取得一定嘅成績」 　2. "Green" banquet「環保宴」 　3. Coastal park「海岸公園」 　4. Discourage (lit. pour cold water)「潑冷水」	I. Grammar and sentence patterns 語法和句型 　1. "jihchùhng……(yíhlàih)" since… 　2. "bīndouh wúih/hónàhng…" 　3. Use "chān" to express personal experience：chānngáahn、chānyíh、chānháu、chānsáu、chānjih 　4. "haih yiu V" / "haih m̀ …" 　5. "hái……hah" under… 　6. "bihngché" and; as well as 　7. "kèihjūng" within 　8. "m̀joi…" no longer; not any more 　9. "yāt M yauh yāt M" II. Paragraph and discourse 語段和篇章 　1. "Chèuihjó…juhng…yauh…"apart from...furthermore...also... 　2. "m̀jí…juhng…" not only..., but also...

2. Text 🔊

課文 Fomàhn

大家好，我係「綠色香港」嘅負責人陳國強。今日獲邀請嚟參加呢個活動，我覺得十分榮幸。首先我要多謝環境局俾我一個機會可以喺呢度向各位善長仁翁表達「綠色香港」對你哋嘅萬分感謝。環保工作大家都知道係一項長時間嘅投資，係一個唔可以睇到即時效果嘅工作。自從十年前，我哋提議政府推行「清潔維港計劃」嘅時候，我哋開始環保工作，嗰陣時好多人都潑我冷水，話海水已經污染咗幾十年，邊度可能改善到呀？嗰陣時聽到最多人話，搞環保，會影響經濟發展，會搞到佢哋搵唔到食，賺唔到錢，仲親耳聽到有人話你係要做都冇辦法。好彩當時有各位嘅支持，喺呢十年嘅努力下，香港嘅環保工作已經取得一定嘅成績，今日維多利亞港比十年前乾淨咗好多。香港變得更加吸引，遊客更加鍾意香港，對我哋嘅旅遊業同埋經濟都有好處，呢啲都係大家有目共睹嘅。

Daaihgā hóu, ngóh haih "Luhksīk Hēunggóng" ge fuhjaak yàhn Chàhn Gwok Kèuhng. Gāmyaht wohk yīuchíng làih chāamgā nīgo wuhtduhng, ngóh gokdāk sahpfān wìhnghahng. Sáusīn ngóh yiu dōjeh Wàahngíngguhk béi ngóh yātgo gēiwuih hóyíh làih nīdouh heung gokwái sihnjéung yàhnyūng bíudaaht "Luhksīk Hēunggóng" deui néihdeihge maahnfān gámjeh. Wàahnbóu gūngjok daaihgā dōu jīdou haih yāthohng chèuhng sìhgaange tàuhjī, haih yātgo m̀hóyíh táidóu jīksìh haauhgwóge gūngjok. Jihchùhng sahp nìhn chìhn, ngóhdeih tàihyíh jingfú tēuihàhng "Chīnggit Wàih Góng gaiwaahk"ge sìhhauh, ngóhdeih hōichí wàahnbóu gūngjok, gójahnsìh hóudō yàhn dōu put ngóh láahng séui, wah hóiséui yíhgīng wūyíhmjó géi sahp nìhn, bīndouh hónàhng góisihndóu a? Gójahnsìh tēngdóu jeui dō yàhn wah, gáau wàahnbóu, wúih yínghéung gīngjai faatjín, wúih gáaudou kéuihdeih wán m̀dóu sihk, jaahn m̀dóu chín, juhng chānyíh tēngdóu yáuh yàhn wah néih haih yiu jouh dōu móuh baahnfaat. Hóuchói dōngsìh yáuh gokwái ge jīchìh, hái nī sahp nìhn ge nóuhlihk hah, Hēunggóngge wàahnbóu gūngjok yíhgīng chéuidāk yātdihngge sìhngjīk, gāmyaht Wàihdōleihnga Góng béi sahp nìhn chìhn gōnjehngjó hóudō. Hēunggóng bindāk ganggā kāpyáhn, yàuhhaak ganggā jūngyi Hēunggóng, deui ngóhdeihge léuihyàuh yihp tùhngmàaih gīngjai dōu yáuh hóuchyu. Nīdī dōu haih daaihgā yáuh muhk guhng dóu ge.

呢十年，我哋每年都收到唔少嘅捐款，令我哋可以做大量環保工作，其中我哋舊年做咗一個保護郊野公園雀鳥嘅項目，並且組織咗清潔沙灘運動，培訓少年環保大使，清潔海岸公園等等。在此我向所有幫助我哋嘅人士表示衷心嘅感謝。

Nī sahp nìhn, ngóhdeih múih nìhn dōu sāudóu m̀síuge gyūnfún, lihng ngóhdeih hóyíh jouh daaihleuhng wàahnbóu gūngjok, kèihjūng ngóhdeih gauhnín jouhjó yātgo bóuwuh gāauyéh gūngyún jeukníuhge hohngmuhk, bihngché jóujīkjó chīnggit sātāan wahnduhng, pùihfan siunìhn wàahnbóu daaihsi, chīnggit hóingohn gūngyún dángdáng. Joihchí ngóh heung sóyáuh bōngjoh ngóhdeihge yàhnsih bíusih chūngsām ge gámjeh.

最近兩年，我哋喺每個屋邨舉辦垃圾分類計劃。香港講環保講咗三十幾年，而家亞洲好多地區好似日本同台灣已經實行垃圾分類好多年，但係香港仲係啱啱開始冇幾耐，而且參加嘅都係自願嘅。呢個計劃最大嘅困難，係處理垃圾分類嘅成本越嚟越高，好多公司都因為覺得太麻煩唔再同我哋合作。喺呢個時候，我哋得到在座各位嘅幫助，解決咗一個又一個嘅困難。除咗捐錢之外，仲幫我哋請義工，聯絡香港各區嘅屋邨參加垃圾分類計劃，又搵咗一啲支持環保嘅公司同我哋合作。舊年我哋一共收到港幣三百七十萬嘅捐款，請到超過二百個義工幫手，我哋嘅義工有啲係中學生、大學生，有啲係家庭主婦，有啲係退休人士，有啲係唔同行業嘅專業人士。今日在座有好多都係義工，你哋唔怕辛苦，唔介意喺環境好差嘅地方幫手，唔介意長時間工作，連周末都要去唔同嘅屋邨回收垃圾，冇咗你哋，呢個計劃唔會成功。

Jeuigahn léuhng nìhn, ngóhdeih hái múihgo ngūkchyūn géuibaahn laahpsaap fānleuih gaiwaahk. Hēunggóng góng wàahnbóu góngjó sāamsahp géi nìhn, yìhgā Ngajāu hóudō deihkēui hóuchíh Yahtbún tùhng Tòihwāan yíhgīng sahthàhng laahpsaap fānleuih hóudō nìhn, daahnhaih Hēunggóng juhng haih ngāamngāam hōichí móuh géi noih, yìhché chāamgāge dōu haih jihyuhnge. Nīgo gaiwaahk jeui daaih ge kwannàahn, haih chyúhléih laahpsaap fānleuihge sìhngbún yuht làih yuht gōu, hóudō gūngsī dōu yānwaih gokdāk taai màhfàahn m̀joi tùhng ngóhdeih hahpjok. Hái nīgo sìhhauh, ngóhdeih dākdóu joihjoh gokwái ge bōngjoh, gáaikyutjó yātgo yauh yātgo ge kwannàahn. Chèuihjó gyūnchín jīngoih, juhng bōng ngóhdeih chéng yihgūng, lyùhnlok Hēunggóng gokkēuige ngūkchyūn chāamgā laahpsaap fānleuih gaiwaahk, yauh wánjó yātdī jīchìh wàahnbóuge gūngsī tùhng ngóhdeih hahpjok. Gauhnín ngóhdeih yātguhng sāudóu góngbaih sāam baak chātsahp maahn ge gyūnfún, chéngdóu chīugwo yih baakgo yihgūng bōngsáu, ngóhdeihge yihgūng yáuhdī haih jūnghohksāang, daaihhohksāang, yáuhdī haih gātìhngjyúfúh, yáuhdī haih teuiyāu yàhnsih, yáuhdī haih m̀tùhng hòhngyihpge jyūnyihp yàhnsih. Gāmyaht joihjoh yáuh hóudō dōu haih yihgūng, néihdeih m̀pa sānfú, m̀gaaiyi hái wàahngíng hóu chā ge deihfōng bōngsáu, m̀gaaiyi chèuhng sìhgaan gūngjok, lìhn jāumuht dōu yiu heui m̀tùhngge ngūkchyūn wùihsāu laahpsaap, móuhjó néihdeih, nīgo gaiwaahk m̀wúih sìhnggūng.

最後我想趁呢個機會感謝各位咁耐以嚟對本會嘅支持，你哋咁多年嚟有錢出錢，有力出力，唔只令我哋嘅環保工作做得更好，仲令到多咗香港人重視環保，認識到環保係生活嘅一部分，明白到環保同經濟發展係分唔開嘅。呢個係在座各位努力嘅成果。記住我哋「綠色香港」嘅宗旨，希望「每人做多啲，將來好過啲」。期待大家繼續支持我哋嘅工作，令呢個城市越嚟越靚，越嚟越清潔，環境越嚟越好。多謝大家！

Jeuihauh ngóh séung chan nīgo gēiwuih gámjeh gokwái gam noih yíhlàih deui búnwúige jīchìh, néihdeih gam dō nìhn làih yáuh chín chēutchín, yáuhlihk chēutlihk, m̀jí lihng ngóhdeihge wàahnbóu gūngjok jouhdāk gang hóu, juhng lihngdou dōjó Hēunggóng yàhn juhngsih wàahnbóu, yihngsīkdou wàahnbóu haih sāngwuhtge yāt bouhfahn, mìhngbaahkdou wàahnbóu tùhng gīngjai faatjín haih fānm̀hōi ge. Nīgo haih joihjoh gokwái nóuhlihk ge sìhnggwó. Geijyuh ngóhdeih "Luhksīk Hēunggóng"ge jūngjí, hēimohng "múih yàhn jouh dōdī, jēunglòih hóu gwo dī". Kèihdoih daaihgā gaijuhk jīchìh ngóhdeihge gūngjok, lihng nīgo sìhngsíh yuht làih yuht leng, yuht làih yuht chīnggit, wàahngíng yuht làih yuht hóu. Dōjeh daaihgā!

3. Vocabulary in use 🔊

活用詞彙 Wuhtyuhng chìhwuih

3.1 Common vocabulary

Number	Word	Yale Romanization	POS	English
1	負責人	fuhjaakyàhn	N	person in charge
2	獲邀請	wohk yīuchíng	PH	to be invited
3	表達	bíudaaht	V	to express
4	環保工作	wàahnbóu gūngjok	N	environmental protection work
5	即時	jīksìh	Adj / Adv	immediate; immediately
6	自從	jihchùhng	CV	(of time) from, since

7	潑我冷水	put ngóh láahngséui	PH	to discourage me, to throw cold water on me
8	海水	hóiséui	N	seawater
9	改善	góisihn	V	to improve
10	搵唔到食	wán m̀dóu sihk	PH	cannot make a living
11	賺唔到錢	jaahn m̀dóu chín	PH	cannot earn money
12	親耳聽到	chānyíh tēngdóu	PH	to hear something with one's own ears
13	好彩	hóuchói	Adj/ Adv	lucky; luckily
14	當時	dōngsìh	Adv	at that time
15	有目共睹	yáuh muhk guhng dóu	PH	obvious to everyone
16	捐款	gyūnfún	N	donation
17	雀鳥	jeukníuh	N	bird
18	項目	hohngmuhk	N	project, item
19	組織	jóujīk	N/V	organization; to organize
20	培訓	pùihfan	N/V	training; to train (personnel)
21	海岸公園	hóingohn gūngyún	N	marine park
22	屋邨	ngūkchyūn	N	housing estate
23	自願	jih'yuhn	Adv	voluntarily
24	困難	kwannàahn	Adj/N	difficult; difficulty
25	義工	yihgūng	N	volunteers
26	聯絡	lyùhnlok	V	to contact
27	各區	gokkēui	PH	each district
28	行業	hòhngyihp	N	industry
29	在座	joihjoh	PH	to be present (at a meeting, banquet, etc.)
30	宗旨	jūngjí	N	(of associations, clubs, etc.) aim, purpose

3.2 Proper nouns

1	綠色香港	Luhksīk Hēunggóng	PN	Green Hong Kong
2	陳國強	Chàhn Gwok-kèuhng	PN	Chan Kwok-keung
3	清潔維港計劃	Chīnggit Wàih Góng Gaiwaahk	PN	"Clean Up Victoria Harbour" scheme
4	清潔沙灘運動	Chīnggit Sātāan Wahnduhng	PN	"Beach Clean-up" campaign
5	環保大使	wàahnbóu daaihsi	PH	Green Ambassador
6	垃圾分類計劃	Laahpsaap Fānleuih Gaiwaahk	PN	Waste Sorting Campaign

3.3 People

1	少年	siunìhn	N	early youth; youngster
2	家庭主婦	gātihng jyúfúh	N	housewife
3	退休人士	teuiyāu yàhnsih	N	retired people
4	專業人士	jyūnyihp yàhnsih	N	professionals

3.4 Useful expressions

1	善長仁翁	sihnjéung yàhnyūng	PH	philanthropists
2	萬分感謝	maahnfān gámjeh	PH	million of thanks
3	表示衷心嘅感謝	bíusih chūngsām ge gámjeh	PH	to express my/our heartfelt thanks
4	有錢出錢，有力出力	yáuh chín chēut chín, yáuh lihk chēut lihk	PH	if you have money, donate some to the poor; if you have strength, help others with your hands

4. Notes on language and discourse structure

語言及篇章結構知識 Yúhyìhn kahp pīnjēung gitkau jīsīk

4.1. Grammar and sentence patterns 語法和句型

4.1.1. "jihchùhng......(yíhlàih)" , since...

1. Jihchùhng jouhjó nīgo gūngjok yíhlàih, ngóh hohkjó hóudō yáuhyuhng ge jīsīk, dōjeh gokwáige bōngjoh.
2. Jihchùhng sìhnggūng sānbaahn Ouwahn yíhlàih, nīgo sìhngsíhge gīngjai faatjíndāk hóu faai.
3. Jihchùhng sīkjó néih, ngóh hōisāmjó hóudō.

4.1.2. "bīndouh wúih/hónàhng...... ?"

There is a rhetorical question which means something "cannot happen".

1. Kéuih syūjó chín, bīndouh wúih hōisām ā ?
2. Kéuih yìhgā yauh yiu fāangūng yauh yiu jiugu síupàhngyáuh, bīndouh hónàhng yáuh sìhgaan léih néih a?
3. Gódouh gam chòuh, bīndouh hónàhng duhkdóu syū ā ?
4. Kéuih hóu guih, bīndouh wúih yáuh jīngsàhn tùhng néih wáan a?
5. Kéuih gam ngaan héisān, bīndouh hónàhng jéunsìh (punctual) dou a?
6. Kéuih chàhmmàih sihkyīn, yámjáu, sāntái bīndouh wúih hóu a?

4.1.3. Use "chān" to express personal experience: chānngáahn、chānyíh、chānháu、chānsáu、chānjih

1. Jihchùhng jouhjó nīfahn gūngjok, ngóh chānngáahn táidóu hóudō sēuiyiu bōngjohge yàhn.
2. Yahmhòh (any) sih, yùhgwó m̀haih néih chānngáahn táidóu, chānyíh tēngdóuge, jauh m̀hóu chèuihbín sēungseun.
3. Ngóhge hóu pàhngyáuh sāangyaht, ngóh chānsáu jouhjó go daahngōu béi kéuih, juhng chānjih sungdou kéuih ngūkkéi tīm.

4.1.4. haih......

Sometimes 'haih' is used to show emphasis or insistence to do something.

1. Ngóh hyun kéuihdeih m̀hóu ngaaigāau, daahnhaih kéuihdeih haih yiu ngaai.
2. Sēuiyìhn gāmyaht tīnhei m̀hóu, daahnhaih kéuih haih yiu heui hàahngsāan.
3. Sēuiyìhn gódouh yauh chòuh, hūnghei yauh m̀hóu, daahnhaih kéuih haih yiu heui gódouh jyuh.
4. Sihkyīn yáuh hoih mòuh yīk, daahnhaih kéuih haih yiu sihk.
5. Sēuiyìhn nīfahn gūngjok mātyéh dōu hóu, daahnhaih kéuih haih m̀jouh.
6. Gódī sēuiyìhn haih bātlèuhng sihou, daahnhaih kéuih haih m̀háng gaai.

4.1.5. "hái...hah", under...

1. Hái gokwái tùhng séhwúi gokgaaige bōngjoh hah, hái nī sahpnìhn léuihbihn, ngóhdeih yáuh hóu mìhnghín (obvious) ge jeunbouh.
2. Hái lóuhsī tùhng tùhnghohkge bōngjoh hah, ngóhge Jūngmàhn jeunbouhjó hóudō.
3. Hái nījúng gingjāng gīkliht ge chìhngfong hah, yiu wándóu hóugūng jānhaih m̀yùhngyih.
4. Yùhgwó fuhmóuh (parents) sìhsìh ngaaigāau, síu pàhngyáuh hái nījúng wàahngíng hah jéungdaaih, yātdihng m̀hōisām.

4.1.6. "bihngché" and; as well as

1. Waihjó bóuwuh hóiyèuhng (Ocean) sāngmaht, tàihgōu síhmàhnge wàahnbóu yisīk, bihngché tàihgūng yùhlohk sīuhàahn (entertainment) chèuhngsó (venue) béi síhmàhn, jingfú chitlahp hóingohn (shore) gūngyún.
2. Nīchi làih Hēunggóng, ngóhdeih chāamgūnjó géigāan daaihhohk, bihngché tùhng lóuhsī tùhnghohk kīngjó hóudō yéh.
3. Jingfú tūnggwojó géi tìuh tùhng wàahnbóu yáuhgwāan ge faatleuht, bihngché jēung wàahnbóu gaauyuhk gāyahpdou hohkhaauhge fochìhng léuihbihn, hēimohng tàihgōu Hēunggóng síhmàhn ge wàahnbóu yisīk.

4.1.7. "kèihjūng" within

1. Ngóh gūngsī kèihjūng yātgo tùhngsih yānwaih yiu sāang bìhbī fongga.
2. Hēunggóng yáuh géigo gūngyún, kèihjūng yātgo jauh hái ngóh ngūkkéi fuhgahn.
3. Gam dō go jityaht, kèihjūng ngóh jeui jūngyige jauh haih nùhnglihk sānnìhn.

4.1.8. "m̀joi Adj/V." no longer; not any more

1. Yáuhdī hohksāang wah, hái hohkhaauh hohkdóuge yéh, jouhyéhge sìhhauh m̀joi yáuh yuhng.

2. Jihchùhng seuhngchi faatyihn kéuih góng daaihwah, ngóh jauh m̀joi sēungseun kéuih la.

3. Nīdī daaihyìhng béichoi yùhnjó jīhauh, dī wahnduhng chèuhng jauh m̀joi yáuh yuhng, jānhaih lohngfai (waste).

4.1.9. "yāt M yauh yāt M" again and again

1. Hái nī sahp nìhn léuihbihn, ngóhdeih yātchi yauh yātchi bōngjoh kéuihdeih.

2. Kéuih sijó yātgihn yauh yātgihn, géisìh sīnji gáandóu a?

3. Kéuih geijó yātfūng yauh yātfūngge kàuhjīk seun (job application letter), daahnnhaih móuh yātgāan gūngsī chéng kéuih mihnsíh.

4.2. Paragraph and discourse 語段和篇章

4.2.1. "Chèuihjó… juhng… yauh…", apart from… furthermore… also

1. Nīchi ge yìhntóuwúi, chèuihjó hóyíh faatbíu jihgéi ge táifaat, juhng hóyíh tēngdóu jyūngā (specialists) ge yigin, yauh yáuh gēiwuih tóuleuhn gāaulàuh (exchange), jānhaih yātchi hóu hóu ge hohkjaahp gēiwuih.

2. Ngóhdeih chèuihjó yiu háauleuih yàhnsáu (labour force) ge mahntàih, juhng yiu háauleuih dehng chèuhngdeih (venue) ge mahntàih, jeuihauh yauh yiu táiháh tīnhei pui m̀puihahp, baahn yātgo yíncheungwúi jānhaih m̀yùhngyih.

4.2.2. "m̀jí… juhng… ", not only…, but also…

1. Ngóhdeih nīgo gaiwaahk m̀jí yáuh hóudō yàhn gyūnchín, juhng yáuh hóudō yihgūng bōngsáu.

2. Kéuih m̀jí deui nīfahn gūng yáuh hingcheui, kéuih juhng séung hái Hēunggóng sāngwuht… yàuhhyū yíhseuhngge yùhnyān kéuih séung hái nīgāan gūngsī gūngjok.

3. Nīgāan jūnghohk deihdím m̀jí hóu káhn, juhng yáuh kéuihdeihge hohkfai pèhngdī… Yàuhhyū yíhseuhngge yùhnyān, ngóh hēimohng sung ngóhge jáinéui làih nīgāan hohkhaauh duhksyū.

5. Notes on pragmatic knowledge

語用因素與相關知識 Yúhyuhng yānsou yúh sēunggwāan jīsīk

5.1. Yuti, formulaic expressions and exaggerating 語體、套話與誇張

5.1.1. 尊稱的順序 order in greeting people

尊敬嘅各位領導，各位慈善家，各位志願者朋友：jyūngingge gokwái líhngdouh, gokwái chìhsihngā, gokwái jiyuhnjé pàhngyáuh:

The use of "尊敬嘅 jyūngingge" is relatively new in Chinese but is becoming one of the formulaic expressions in public speech, especially in formal and ceremonial settings like this one. Please also note the order of the greeting in the Chinese culture, starting from government officials. If there is more than one, it will follow their official ranks, with the highest in rank coming first. In many cases, the name and official title of the officials are also used. The use of "各位" is also standard in such a context.

- Jyūngingge gokwái líhngdouh, gokwái chìhsihngā, gokwái tùhnghòhng,…

5.1.2. "負責人 fuhjaak yàhn" person in charge

The speaker can actually say the official title (… 主席 jyújihk，… 總裁 júngchòih，… 首席執行官 sáujihk jāphàhnggūn，etc.) of someone when he has to tell people that he is the number one person in the institution. Using "負責人 fuhjaak yàhn", however, sound; less pompous to most people. In this context this is an example to show modest as expected by many in the Chinese culture. There is of course another possibility that the speaker is not really holding the number one post but just acting as one. In such a case the use of "負責人 fuhjaakyàhn" is a representation of reality and will surely avoid the somewhat awkward term "acting". In either event, it is pragmatically appropriate to use it in this context.

- Jihchùhng jouhjó nīgāan gūngsīge fuhjaak yàhn jīhauh…
- Chíng néih giu nīdouhge fuhjaak yàhn chēutlàih…

5.1.3. "萬分感謝 maahnfān gámjeh" millions thanks

There are many ways to express thanks in Chinese and, similar to the use of "millions" in English, the use of "萬 maahn" (literally "ten thousand") is an overstatement. It is interesting, but perhaps mathematically does not make sense, to see the use of number in front of thanks by the Chinese people. No matter whether you hear "十分 sahpfān", "十二分 sahpyih fān", "萬分 maahnfān" or, "萬二分 maahnyih fān", it just means "many" when used together with "感謝 gámjeh". As a CSL learner, you may explore the reasons behind and find many explanations, then trying to determine which is more convincing than others, or you can simply leave that aside and just remember them as a chunk when you want to express thanks. It is not wise, however, to try to invent your own number and create new combinations by using other numbers (you can make up one and ask your teacher whether it makes sense!).

- Hái nīdouh doihbíu ngóhge gūngsī heung gokwái ji maahnyihfān gámjeh!
- Sahpfān gámjeh daaihgā gwoheui bunnìhn deui ngóhdeihge bōngjoh tùhng gúlaih.

5.2. Related knowledge 相關知識

5.2.1. "取得一定嘅成績 chéuidāk yātdihng ge sìhngjīk" have got certain achievement

Don't confuse the use of "一定 yātdihng" here with the other meaning that you have learned, as in "佢一定會嚟 kéuih yātdihng wúih làih" (Surely he will come). In this context, the speaker is telling the audience that they have done a lot and achieved many goals but he uses "一定 yātdihng" in front of "成績 sìhngjīk" (achievement) to downplay his own success. As explained many times by now, this is just another example of trying to be modest, which fits in the expectation of the Chinese culture and is therefore appropriate.

- Ngóhdeihge gūngsī hái gokfōngmihn chéuidāk yātdihngge sìhngjīk.
- Gīnggwo fanlihn jīhauh, ngóhge Yīngmàhn séuijéun (standard) yáuh yātdihngge tàihgōu.

5.2.2. "環保宴 wàahnbóu yin" "Green" banquet

The concept of environmental protection is getting popular and, because of that, we are encountering words and phrases that we didn't have today. "環保宴 wàahnbóu yin" is one of them. The use of "環保 wàahnbóu" in this way is relatively new and the meaning is not yet fixed, thus we have the parenthesis to help explain exactly what we mean by that.

- Wàahnbóu yin jauh haih móuh yùhchige yinwuih (banquet).
- Wàahnbóu heichēge dahkdím jauhhaih yuhng dihn m̀yuhng heiyàuh.

5.2.3. "海岸公園 hóingohn gūngyún" coastal park

Hong Kong is an island with a long coast line. The reservation of natural habitats along the coast is a big issue in environmental protection. Any contributions made in this area is important to the sustainable development of Hong Kong, which explains why the speaker chose to have this item mentioned while he expressed thanks.

- Hóingohn gūngyún m̀jí wàahnbóu, juhng hóyíh béi síhmàhn yáuh yātgo sīuhàahnge deihfōng.

5.2.4. "潑冷水 put láahng séui" discourage (lit. pour cold water)

Similar to the word order above, combination of phrases are learned and cannot always be created at will. We can say "潑冷水 put láahng séui", often used to indicating any acts or words to discourage somebody from doing something. We cannot, however, say "潑熱水 put yiht séui" if we want to encourage somebody to do something.

- Hohksāang hóu yáuh yihtchìhng, jouh lóuhsīge jauh m̀yīnggōi put láahngséui.
- Ngóh séung jouh sāangyi, daahnhaih néih sìhsìh put ngóh láahng séui.

6. Contextualized speaking practice

情境説話練習 Chìhnggíng syutwah lihnjaahp

【課前預習】Class preparation

6.1. Please answer the following True/False questions according to the lesson text.

1. Chàhn Gwok Kèuhng haih "Luhksīk Hēunggóng" ge fuhjaak yàhn. (T/F)
2. Jihchùhng ńgh nìhn chìhn, yíngóng ge yàhn tàihyíh jingfú tēuihàhng "Chīnggit wàihgóng gaiwaahk". (T/F)
3. Hóudō yàhn yihngwàih hóiséui yíhgīng wūyíhmjó géi sahp nìhn, kéuihdeih gokdāk yíngóngge yàhn ge gaiwaahk móuh baahnfaat góisihn wàahngíng. (T/F)
4. Jeuigahn léuhng nìhn, yíngóngge yàhn hái sóyáuh hohkhaauh géuibaahn laahpsaap fānleuih gaiwaahk. (T/F)

5. Yíngóngge yàhn tàihdou (mentioned) Yahtbún tùhng Nàahmhòhn (South Korea) yíhgīng sahthàhng laahpsaap fānleuih hóudō nìhn.(T/F)

6. Yíngóngge yàhn jíchēut jeui daaih ge kwannàahn, haih chyúhléih laahpsaap fānleuihge sìhngbún yuhtlàih yuht gōu. (T/F)

7. Chìhnnín "Luhksīk Hēunggóng" sāudóu góngbaih sāam baak chātsahp maahnge gyūnfún, tùhng chéngdóu chīugwo nghbaak wái yihgūng bōngsáu. (T/F)

8. Yihgūng bāaukut síuhohksāang, jūnghohksāang, gātìhng jyúfúh tùhng teuiyāu yàhnsih. (T/F)

9. Yíngóngge yàhn hēimohng Hēunggóng yàhn juhngsih wàahnbóu, yihngsīk wàahnbóu haih sāngwuhtge yāt bouhfahn, mìhngbaahk wàahnbóu tùhng gīngjai faatjín haih fān m̀hōi ge. (T/F)

10. "Luhksīk Hēunggóng" ge jūngjí haih "jingfú jouh dōdī, jēunglòih hóu gwo dī". (T/F)

6.2. Please explain the following phrases in Cantonese

1　綠色香港 Luhksīk Hēunggóng
2　負責人 fuhjaak yàhn
3　環保大使 wàahnbóu daaihsí
4　義工 yihgūng
5　專業人士 jyūnyihp yàhnsih

【課後練習】 Post-class exercises

6.3 Fill in the blanks with the given vocabularies. Each vocabulary can be chosen once only.

góisihn	jaahnchín	hóuchói	put láahngséui
gyūnfún	pùihfan	jihyuhn	wándóu sihk
kwannàahn	lyùhnlok	hòhngyihp	yáuh muhk guhng dóu

1. Ngóh námjyuh hóu sām bōng yàhn jē, dímjī béi yàhn _____.

2. Lóuhbáan wah ngóh jouh yéh jouhdāk m̀haih géi hóu, giu ngóh nám baahnfaat _____ gūngjok bíuyihn wóh.

3. Kéuih ge gūngjok bíuyihn _____, haih jihkdāk daaihgā yānséung ge.

4. Jihchùhng bàhbā móuhjó fahn gūng jīhauh, kéuihdeih yātgā hōichí yáuh gīngjai _____.

5. Kéuih daaihhohk bātyihp jīhauh chùhngsih faatleuht sēunggwāan ge _____.

6. _____ yáuh hóudō baahnfaat, laihyùh bōng yàhn dágūng, jihgéi hōi gūngsī jouh sāangyi, tàuhjī máaih gúpiu dángdáng.

7. Waihjó tàihsīng (raise) fuhkmouh jātsou, ngóhdeih ge gūngsī kwāidihng sóyáuh yùhngūng (staff) múihnìhn dōu yiu jipsauh jeui síu yātchi _____.

8. Chùhngsih ngaihseuht tùhng yāmngohk (music) ge gūngjok, sāuyahp (income) yauh dāi yauh m̀wándihng, bīndouh _____ a?

9. Ngóhdeih gēikau ngāamngāam sāudóu yātbāt _____, hēimohng hóyíh yuhng làih bōngjoh yáuh sēuiyiu ge yàhn.

10. Nīgo séhkēui jūngsām hóu noih dōu chéng m̀dóu yàhn làih gūngjok, _____ pìhngsìh juhng yáuh géi go yihgūng _____ làih bōngháh sáu ja. Yùhgwó néih dākhàahn séung gwolàih bōngháh sáu ge, chéng _____ ngóhdeih.

6.4 Fill in the blanks with the given words with "chān-". Each word can be chosen once only.

chānngáahn   chānyíh   chānháu   chānsáu   chānjih

1. Ngóh _____ tēngdóu kéuih wah kéuih jihgéi haih tùhngsinglyúnjé.

2. Fūnyìhng daaihgā séuhnglàih ngóh ūkkéi, gāmyaht ngóh wúih _____ hahchyùh (to cook a meal), hēimohng gokwái séungmín lā!

3. Ngóh pàhngyáuh _____ jíngjó jēung sāangyahtkāat sung béi ngóh.

4. Ngóh _____ táigin néih lóuhgūng tùhng lihng yāt go néuihyán yātchàih hàahnggāai sihkfaahn.

5. Seuhngchi ge sih gáaudou néih gam màhfàahn, sóyíh ngóh gāmyaht séung _____ tùhng néih góng sēng "deuim̀jyuh".

6.5 Complete the following sentences or answer the following questions using the given patterns.

1. jihchùhng ...... yíhlàih

_____, Hēunggóng ge wàahngíng wūyíhm mahntàih yuht làih yuht yìhmjuhng.

2. bīndouh hónàhng ......

Néih yauh yiu fāangūng yauh yiu jiugu gāyàhn, _____ a?

3. haih yiu V

Sēuiyìhn hóudō yàhn dōu hyun kéuih m̀hóu dóuchín, daahnhaih kéuih

_____.

4. hái ...... hah

   Ngóh _____ wándóu gūngjok.

5. ......, bihngché ......

   A: Chàhmmàih dóuchín yáuh mātyéh hoihchyu a?

   B: _____.

6. kèihjūng ......

   Hēunggóng yáuh hóudō wàahngíng mahntàih, _____.

7. m̀joi ......

   Nīgāan chāantēng ge sihkmaht tùhng fuhkmouh jātsou dōu chādou bātdāklíuh, ngóhdeih

   yíhhauh _____.

8. yāt M yauh yāt M ......

   Yìhgā gīngjai m̀hóu, gūngsī ge yùhngūng _____.

7. Listening and speaking

聽說練習 Tingsyut lihnjaahp

7.1 Listening comprehension exercise 🔊))

Please listen to the recording and fill in the blanks with the following words:

yisīk	hiptìuh	fochìhng	gāhaauh hahpjok
faiséui	síu pàhngyáuh	hah yātdoih	hóingohn gūngyún
hóiyèuhng sāngmaht		Wàahnbóu Daihyātsin	

1. Yíngóngge yàhn haih yātgo wàahnbóu tyùhntái _____ge fuhjaak yàhn.

2. Wàahnbóu Daihyātsin tùhng kèihtā wàahnbóu tyùhntái hōijín (start) ge wàahnbóu wuhtduhng, hái tàihgōu séhwúige wàahnbóu _____fōngmihn chéuidāk yātdihng sìhngjīk.

3. Yíngóngge yàhn hóu hōisām Lahpfaatwúi tūnggwo gākèuhng _____tùhng faihei pàaihfong gúnjaige faatlaih.

4. Daaih bouhfahnge hohkhaauh yíhgīng jēung wàahnbóu gāyahp dou _____ léuihmihn, lihng hah yātdoih yáuh wàahnbóu yisīk.

5. Yíngóngge yàhn hēimohng daaihgā gaijuhk gwāansām tùhng jīchìh léuhnghohng juhngdím gūngjok, daihyāt bāaukut _____ge ginchit.

6. Hóingohn gūngyún nīgo gaiwaahk haih waihjó bóuwuh _____, tàihgōu
   síhmàhnge wàahnbóu yisīk, tùhng tàihgūng wàahnbóu hói seuhng wuhtduhng.

7. Daih yihhohng juhngdím gūngjok haih, tūnggwo _____, jēung laahpsaap
   fānleuih tùhng wùihsāu nīdī chousī chùhng hohkhaauh tēuigwóng dou gātìhng sāngwuht
   yahpmihn.

8. Hái hohkhaauh tēuihàhng wàahnbóu gaauyuhk ge jeui daaih jeungngoih haih gātìhng
   sāngwuht tùhng hohkhaauh gaauyuhk meih nàhnggau _____.

9. _____ hái hohkhaauh yihngsīkdou wàahnbóuge juhngyiusing, bihng hohkyíh
   jiyuhng, wuht hohk wuht yuhng.

10. Yíngóngge yàhn hēimohng jēung wàahnbóu chousī lohksahtdou ngóhdeih sāngwuhtge
    gokfōngmihn, yàuhkèihsih lohksaht dou _____ge sāngwuht.

7.2 Speech topics

1. Néih yihngwàih Hēunggóng (waahkjé néih ge gwokgā) ge wàahngíng wūyíhm mahntàih yìhm
   m̀yìhmjuhng a? Dímgáai nē? Chéng néih géui yātdī laihjí, tùhng tùhnghohk fānhéungháh.

2. Néih yihngwàih yìhgā síhmàhn ge wàahnbóu yisīk (awareness of environmental protection)
   gōu m̀gōu a? Jingfú tùhng wàahnbóu jóujīk hóyíh jouh dī mātyéh làih tàihgōu (to raise)
   síhmàhn ge wàahnbóu yisīk nē?

3. Néih haih yātgo wàahnbóu jóujīk ge fuhjaakyàhn, néih yìhgā hái yātgo gūnghōi wuhtduhng
   seuhng daapjeh (to express thanks) síhmàhn yātlouh yíhlàih deui néihdeih ge jīchìh, bihngché
   fūyuh (to appeal) joihjoh yàhnsih gyūnchín jīchìh néihdeih.

7.3 Speaking exercise: Please use at least 10 of the following vocabularies/patterns to say on the following topic in one to two minutes.

"Jūnghohk bātyihpsāng tùhng daaihhohk bātyihpsāng jauhyihp (to obtain employment), mihndeui
mātyéh kwannàahn a?"

jīksìh	góisihn	hóuchói	dōngsìh
jihyuhn	kwannàahn	hòhngyihp	bíudaaht
m̀joi	jaahn chín	wán sihk	put láahngséui
jihchùhng ...... yíhlàih		bīndouh hónàhng ...... a?	
yāt M yauh yāt M		......, bihngché	

8. Additional texts

附加課文 Fuhgā fomàhn

8.1 Additional text 附加課文

如果有朋友住喺北京，你會發現一個奇怪嘅現象，如果天氣唔錯，佢哋就特別鍾意喺微信（Mèihseun, Wechat）發放各種藍天白雲嘅相。係唔係北京人特別鍾意自然呢？可能係。但係更加有可能嘅係，北京嘅空氣太差喇，藍天白雲太少喇。

Yùhgwó yáuh pàhngyáuh jyuhhái Bākgīng, néih wúih faatyihn yātgo kèihgwaaige yihnjeuhng, yùhgwó tīnhei m̀cho, kéuihdeih jauh dahkbiht jūngyi hái Mèihseun faatfong gokjúng làahmtīn baahkwàhnge séung. Haih m̀haih Bākgīng yàhn dahkbiht jūngyi jihyìhn nē? Hónàhng haih. Daahnhaih ganggā yáuh hónàhngge haih, Bākgīngge hūnghei taaichā la, làahmtīn baahkwàhn taai síu la.

北京人嘅手機上面，除咗有微信呢種APP，一般嚟講，仲有空氣品質指數嘅APP。出門之前，除咗睇睇有冇落雨，使唔使帶遮，都要睇下空氣品質點樣，使唔使戴口罩——呢個已經係北京人嘅生活必需品喇。

Bākgīng yàhn ge sáugēi seuhngmihn, chèuihjó yáuh Mèihseun nījúng APP, yātbūn làihgóng, juhng yáuh hūnghei bánjāt jísouge APP. Chēutmùhn jīchìhn, chèuihjó tái tái yáuhmóuh lohkyúh, sáim̀sái daai jē, dōu yiu táiháh hūnghei bánjāt dímyéung, sái m̀sái daai háujaau – nīgo yíhgīng haih Bākgīng yàhn ge sāngwuht bītsēui bán la.

唔只係北京，中國北部、東部嘅大部分地方都存在空氣污染嘅問題，喺北京附近嘅河北省（Hòhbāk sáang, Heibei Province），河北省嘅幾個城市更加係年年都喺空氣污染排行榜上面「名列前茅 (top of the list)」。嚴重嘅空氣污染對人嘅身體健康帶嚟極大嘅傷害，尤其是小朋友，而如果媽媽喺懷孕期間呼吸有毒空氣，仲會影響下一代嘅健康。

M̀jí haih Bākgīng, Jūnggwok bākbouh, dūngbouh ge daaih bouhfahn deihfōng dōu chyùhnjoih hūnghei wūyíhmge mahntàih, hái Bākgīng fuhgahnge Hòhbāk sáang, Hòhbāk sáang ge géigo sìhngsíh ganggā haih nìhnnìhn dōu hái hūnghei wūyíhm pàaihhàhng bóng seuhngmihn "mìhngliht chìhn màauh (top of the list)". Yìhmjuhng ge hūnghei wūyíhm deui yàhnge sāntái gihnhōng daailàih gihk daaihge sēunghoih, yàuhkèihsíh síu pàhngyáuh, yìh yùhgwó màhmā hái wàaihyahn kèihgāan fūkāp yáuhduhk hūnghei, juhng wúih yínghéung hah yātdoihge gihnhōng.

記者柴靜（Chàaih Jihng）就係一個媽媽，佢喺 2015 年拍攝嘅紀錄片《蒼穹之下》（Chōngkùhng jīhah, Under the Dome）對空氣污染問題進行咗深入嘅調查，紀錄片播出之後，迅速喺全國引起極大嘅關注同熱烈嘅討論。

Geijé Chàaih Jihng jauh haih yātgo màhmā, kéuih hái yih lìhng yāt ńgh nìhn paaksipge geiluhk pín "Chōngkùhng jīhah" deui hūnghei wūyíhm mahntàih jeunhàhngjó sāmyahpge diuhchàh, geiluhkpín bochēut jīhauh, seunchūk hái chyùhngwok yáhnhéi gihk daaihge gwāanjyu tùhng yihtlihtge tóuleuhn.

《蒼穹之下》提到造成中國北方空氣污染嘅一個重要原因：就係唔合理嘅能源使用。或者仲有其他嘅原因，譬如話城市發展得太快，建築工地太多，國家監管唔夠……空氣問題其實係喺各種因素嘅共同作用之下造成嘅，因此，要改善空氣品質，唔係一項簡單嘅任務，需要時間，都需要大量嘅人力財力。

"Chōngkùhng jīhah" tàihdou jouhsìhng Jūnggwok bākfōng hūnghei wūyíhm ge yātgo juhngyiu yùhnyān: jauhhaih m̀hahpléihge nàhngyùhn síyuhng. Waahkjé juhngyáuh kèihtāge yùhnyān, peiyùhwah sìhngsíh faatjíndāk taai faai, ginjūk gūngdeih taai dō, gwokgā gāamgún m̀gau… Hūnghei mahntàih kèihsaht haih hái gokjúng yānsouge guhngtùhng jokyuhng jīhah jouhsìhngge, yānchí, yiu góisihn hūnghei bánjāt, m̀haih yāthohng gáandāange yahmmouh, sēuiyiu sìhgaan, dōu sēuiyiu daaihleuhngge yàhnlihk chòihlihk.

生活喺霧霾之下嘅北京人，有啲人考慮移民，或者將小朋友送去國外，更加多嘅人只係可以出門嘅時候戴口罩，喺屋企裏面放幾部空氣清新機。不過，我哋都睇到，市民嘅環保意識不停提高，佢哋用自己嘅實際行動保護環境，同時都要求政府努力解決環境惡化嘅問題。

Sāngwuht hái mouhmàaih jīhah ge Bākgīng yàhn, yáuhdī yàhn háauleuih yìhmàhn, waahkjé jēung síupàhngyáuh sung heui gwokngoih, ganggā dō ge yàhn jíhaih hóyíh chēutmùhn ge sìhhauh daai háujaau, hái ngūkkéi léuihmihn fong géibouh hūnghei chīngsān gēi. Bātgwo, ngóhdeih dōu táidóu, síhmàhnge wàahnbóu yisīk bāttìhng tàihgōu, kéuihdeih yuhng jihgéige sahtjai hàhngduhng bóuwuh wàahngíng, tùhngsìh dōu yīukàuh jingfú nóuhlihk gáaikyut wàahngíng ngokfage mahntàih.

8.2 附加詞彙 Additional vocabulary

Number	Word	Yale Romanization	POS	English
1	指數	jísou	N	index; exponent
2	戴	daai	V	to wear, to put on
3	口罩	háujaau	N	mask
4	必需品	bītsēui bán	N	necessities
5	排行榜	pàaihhàhng bóng	N	ranking list
6	播出	bochēut	V	to broadcast
7	熱烈	yihtliht	Adj	enthusiastic; fervent; ardent
8	能源	nàhngyùhn	N	energy; energy resources
9	工地	gūngdeih	N	construction site; building site
10	監管	gāamgún	V	to watch and control, to supervise
11	霧霾	mouhmàaih	N	haze
12	空氣清新機	hūnghei chīngsān gēi	N	air cleaner; air purifier

8.3 Please answer the following T/F questions after reading the additional text:

1 Bākgīng dahkbiht leng, sóyíh Bākgīng yàhn jūngyi làahmtīn baahkwàhn ge séung. (T/F)

2 Hóudō Bākgīng yàhnge sáugēi seuhngmihn dōu yáuh hūnghei bánjāt yáuhgwāange APP. (T/F)

3 Bākgīng sìhsìh lohkyúh, hūnghei dōu m̀hóu, chēutmùhn yiu daai jē tùhng háujaau. (T/F)

4 Chèuihjó Bākgīng, Jūnggwok kèihtā deihfōng dōu móuh hūnghei wūyíhm mahntàih. (T/F)

5 Hòhnàahm sáang ge hūnghei wūyíhm mahntàih yìhmjuhng. (T/F)

6 Chàaih Jihngge geiluhkpín sauhdou hóudō yàhnge gwāanjyu, dōu yáhnhéi hóudō tóuhleuhn. (T/F)

7 Jūnggwok wūyíhm mahntàihge yùhnyān haih yānwaih móuhchín. (T/F)

8 Hūnghei mahntàih sēuiyìhn yìhmjuhng, daahnhaih yùhgwó nóuhlihk, yīnggōi hóufaai hóyíh gáaikyut. (T/F)

9 Yáuhdī yàhn yānwaih hūnghei mahntàih, dásyun lèihhōi Jūnggwok. (T/F)

10 Gáaikyut wàahngíng mahntàih, sēuiyiu síhmàhn tùhng jingfúge guhngtùhng nóuhlihk. (T/F)

8.4 Topics for discussions

1 Néih gokdāk Jūnggwokge wàahngíng mahntàih, haih mātyéh yùhnyān jouhsìhngge nē?

2 Yùhgwó néih jyuhhái hūnghei wūyíhm yìhmjuhngge deihfōng, yáuh mātyéh baahnfaat sāngwuht nē?

3 Néih gokdāk yiu gáaikyut wàahngíng mahntàih, jingfú tùhng síhmàhn yīnggōi jouh dī mātyéh nē?

8.5 Authentic oral data 1 🔊
真實語料 1

8.6 Authentic oral data 2 🔊
真實語料 2

General Review L1-L10

1. Speaking topics

1. Yùhgwó yātgo yàhn chàhmmàih dóubok, deuiyū kéuih jihgéi goyàhn, gātìhng, tùhng sèhnggo séhwúi wúih yáuh mātyéh yínghéung a?

2. Deuiyū jingfú hīnggin dóuchèuhng tùhng yùhlohk chitsī ge ginyíh, m̀tùhng ge yàhn fānbiht (respectively) pàhng mātyéh léihgeui jaansìhng waahkjé fáandeui nē?

3. Yùhgwó yātgo gwokgā/sìhngsíh géuibaahn daaihyìhng gwokjai táiyuhk choisih, sihchìhn (before the event) yiu jouhhóu dī mātyéh chìhnji gūngfū sīn a? (Peiyùhwah, táiyuhk chèuhnggún fōngmihn, gāautūng chitsī fōngmihn, fuhkmouh yàhnyùhn ge pùihfan fōngmihn, dángdáng)

4. Néih yihngwàih jingfú yīnggōi dímyéung gúlaih gang dō síhmàhn jīkgihk (actively) chāamgā táiyuhk wuhtduhng a?

5. Néih yihngwàih yātgo dōyùhnfa ge séhwúi yīnggōi haih dímyéung ge nē? Chéng néih géui yātdī laihjí.

6. Néih gokdāk Hēunggóng (waahkjé néih ge gwokgā) múihnìhn ge gūngjung gakèih jūk m̀jūkgau a? Sēui m̀sēuiyiu lihngngoih joi jāngchit gūngjung gakèih nē? Dímgáai néih gám góng a?

7. Yìhgā Hēunggóng (waahkjé néih ge gwokgā) yáuh mātyéh séhwúi màhnsāng mahntàih a? Néih yihngwàih nīdī séhwúi màhnsāng mahntàih ge yùhnyān haih mātyéh a?

8. Néih yáuh móuh hingcheui chùhngsih tùhng faatleuht yáuh gwāan ge gūngjok a? Dímgáai a?

9. Yìhgā Hēunggóng (waahkjé néih ge gwokgā) ge hūnghei (air) jātsou tùhng hóiséui jātsou dím a? Dímyéung hóyíh góisihn hūnghei jātsou tùhng hóiséui jātsou nē?

10. Yìhgā séhwúi mihndeui hóudō m̀tùhng ge mahntàih, hóuchíh gīngjai mahntàih a, fòhngngūk tùhng tóudeih mahntàih a, wàahnbóu mahntàih a, gaauyuhk mahntàih a dángdáng. Néih yihngwàih jingfú yīnggōi yāusīn (to take priority) chyúhléih mātyéh mahntàih sīn nē?

2. Make a sentence with each of the following vocabulary.

1. gáaisīk

2. fuhjaak

3. góibin

4. góisihn

5. mìhnghín

6. yáuh muhk guhng dóu

7. gingjāng

8. jingmihn

9. chùhngsih

10. yāt sih tùhng yàhn

11. bóujeung

12. kyutfaht

13. put láahngséui

14. hōifong

15. gūnghōi

16. fūkjaahp

3. Make a sentence with each of the following pattern.

1. jēung Obj. V ......

2. jihchùhng ...... yíhlàih ......

3. yātdaan ...... jauh ......

4. yàuh ...... V héi

5. m̀sái góng ......, ganggā m̀sái góng ......

4. Oral Skills Practice

4.1. Complete the following sentences or answer the following questions using the given patterns.

1. Yìhgā go tīn hóu haak, yātjahn hónàhng wúih lohk daaihyúh, néih _____.
    (dōuhaih ...... lā)

2. Gahnlòih kéuih máahnmáahn dōu yiu gābāan, sóyíh _____.
    (Adj. dou ......)

3. _____, kéuih jūngyū (eventually) háaudóu léihséung ge sìhngjīk, yahpdóu
    só héingoi ge daaihhohk la.
    (gīnggwo ......)

4. _____, gāmnín gūngsī ge sāangyi béi gauhnín síujó baak fahn jī sahp.
    (sauhdou ...... yínghéung)

5. Yìhgā hóudō Hēunggóng yàhn gūngjok hóu mòhng, yauh kyutfaht wahnduhng tùhng yāusīk,
    _____.
    (bīndouh wúih ...... a?)

6. Q: Sihk mātyéh deui sāntái gihnhōng, sihk mātyéh deui sāntái móuhyīk a?

A: _____.

(hóuchíh …… jīléui ge ……)

7. Q: Néih jeui jūngyi tái mātyéh táiyuhk choisih a?

A: _____.

(…… jījūng, kèihjūng ……)

8. Q: Yātgo gwokgā/sìhngsíh géuibaahn daaihyìhng táiyuhk choisih, yáuh mātyéh hóuchyu a?

A: _____.

(……, bihngché ……)

9. Q: Dímyéung hóyíh faaidī hohksīk yātjúng yúhyìhn a?

A: _____.

(jíyiu …… jauh ……)

10. Q: Dímgáai yáuh dī Hēunggóng yàhn gam jeuhkjuhng tàuhjī a?

A: _____.

(gwāanhaih dou ……)

11. Q: Néih yihngwàih chāantēng chyùhnmihn gamyīn yáuh mātyéh hóuchyu tùhng waaihchyu a?

A: _____.

(chùhng …… làih tái)

12. Q: Néih gokdāk waahtchèuhngsaan haih yātjúng dímyéung ge wahnduhng a?

A: Ngóh gokdāk _____.

(V héi séuhng làih ……)

4.2. Speech Topics

1. Néih jī m̀jīchìh jingfú hōichit dóuchèuhng tùhng yùhlohk chitsī làih góisihn gīngjai a? Dímgáai nē?

2. Chéng néih fānsīkháh, yātgo gwokgā/sìhngsíh géuibaahn daaihyìhng gwokjai táiyuhk choisih, deui nīgo gwokgā/sìhngsíh yáuh mātyéh hóuchyu (laihyùh jīmìhngdouh, gwokjai yìhngjeuhng, gīngjai, síhmàhn ge sāngwuht dángdáng).

3. Hēunggóng (waahkjé néih ge gwokgā) yātnìhn yáuh géidō yaht gūngjung gakèih a? Yùhgwó lihngngoih joi jāngchit gūngjung gakèih, gám wúih deui séhwúi jouhsìhng mātyéh yínghéung nē? Chéng néih chùhng lóuhbáan, yùhngūng (employees), gīngjai, gātìhng dángdáng ge gokdouh fānsīkháh.

4. Yáuh dī yàhn wah, tùhngsing fānyān wúih yínghéung sèhnggo séhwúi ge douhdāk lèuhnléih (morals and ethics), sahmji wúih deui hahyātdoih jouhsìhng fuhmín (negative) yínghéung. Néih tùhng m̀tùhngyi nīgo góngfaat a?

5. Néih haih yātgo wàahnbóu jóujīk ge fuhjaakyàhn, yìhgā néih hái yātgo yìhntóuwúi seuhng, heung daaihgā gáaisīk Hēunggóng ge wàahngíng mahntàih, bihngché fūyuh joihjoh gokwái jīkgihk (actively) jīchìh wàahnbóu gūngjok.

Appendices 附錄

Appendix I: Index of pragmatic points 語用點索引

Appendix II: Index of grammatical points 語法點索引

226

Appendix III: Index of vocabulary in use 活用詞彙總表

Yale Romanization	Word	POS	English	Lesson number	Page number
gokwái	各位	PH	every; everybody	Lesson 1	6
lòihjih	來自	V	to come from	Lesson 1	6
tóu sāng tóu jéung	土生土長	PH	locally born and bred	Lesson 1	6
wìhnghahng	榮幸	Adj	to be honored	Lesson 1	6
gámjeh	感謝	N/V	thanks; to thank; to be grateful	Lesson 1	6
daaihyìhng	大型	Adj	large-scale	Lesson 1	6
jínsīu wuhtduhng	展銷活動	N	trade fair	Lesson 1	6
jínsih	展示	V	to show	Lesson 1	6
pìhngtòih	平台	N	platform	Lesson 1	6
kāpyáhn	吸引	Adj/V	attractive; to attract	Lesson 1	6
jyumìhng	著名	Adj	famous, well-known	Lesson 1	6
sìhngsíh gínggūn	城市景觀	N	urban landscape	Lesson 1	6
kaumaht	購物	N/V	shopping; to do shopping	Lesson 1	6
sáusīk	首飾	N	jewelry	Lesson 1	6
jāp pèhngfo	執平貨	VO	to buy cheap products	Lesson 1	6
pàaihjí	牌子	N	brand	Lesson 1	6
jyútàih lohkyùhn	主題樂園	PW	theme park	Lesson 1	6
jihyìhn fūnggíng	自然風景	N	natural scenery	Lesson 1	6
sīngíng	仙境	N	fairyland	Lesson 1	6

Yale Romanization	Word	POS	English	Lesson number	Page number
wàihjyuh	圍住	V	to surround	Lesson 1	6
séyi	寫意	Adj	enjoyable, relaxed	Lesson 1	6
gūngwōng	觀光	V	to go sightseeing	Lesson 1	7
fūngtóu yàhnchìhng	風土人情	N	local conditions and customs	Lesson 1	7
lihksí màhnfa	歷史文化	N	history and culture	Lesson 1	7
bánsèuhng	品嚐	V	to taste (food and drinks)	Lesson 1	7
chigīk	刺激	Adj	exciting	Lesson 1	7
chèuih chí jī ngoih	除此之外	PH	besides, in addition	Lesson 1	7
heihauh wānwòh	氣候溫和	PH	the climate is moderate	Lesson 1	7
yáuhsihn houhaak	友善好客	PH	friendly and hospitable	Lesson 1	7
gíngdím	景點	N	tourist spot, tourist attraction	Lesson 1	7
fuhkmouh jātsou	服務質素	N	quality of service	Lesson 1	7
guhkjéung	局長	N	Director of Bureau	Lesson 1	7
yihpgaai ge pàhngyáuh	業界嘅朋友	PH	friends from the industry	Lesson 1	7
lòihbān	來賓	N	guest	Lesson 1	7
tùhnghòhng	同行	N	people of the same industry	Lesson 1	7
Làuh Gā-bóu	劉家寶	PN	Lau Ka-po	Lesson 1	7
Hēunggóng Léuihyàuh Faatjín Guhk	香港旅遊發展局	PN	Hong Kong Tourism Board	Lesson 1	7
Dūngfōng Jī Jyū	東方之珠	PN	Pearl of the Orient	Lesson 1	7
síhkēui	市區	PW	urban area	Lesson 1	7
Lèihdóu	離島	PW	Outlying island(s)	Lesson 1	7
Dūngpìhngjāu	東平洲	PW	Tung Ping Chau	Lesson 1	7
gāauyéh gūngyún	郊野公園	PW	country park	Lesson 1	7

Yale Romanization	Word	POS	English	Lesson number	Page number
deihjāt gūngyún	地質公園	PW	geopark	Lesson 1	7
léuihyàuh yihpgaai	旅遊業界	N	tourism industry	Lesson 1	8
gok hòhng gok yihp	各行各業	PH	all walks of life	Lesson 1	8
gīngjai jīchyúh	經濟支柱	N	economic pillar	Lesson 1	8
tàuhsān daaihjihyìhn	投身大自然	PH	to throw oneself into the nature	Lesson 1	8
fongsūng sānsām	放鬆身心	PH	to relax the body and mind	Lesson 1	8
gwokgā kāp	國家級	PH	national level	Lesson 1	8
léuihyàuh hohngmuhk	旅遊項目	N	tourism project	Lesson 1	8
chìhjuhk faatjín	持續發展	PH	to sustain the development	Lesson 1	8
faatsīuyáu	發燒友	N	enthusiast	Lesson 1	8
waahtchèuhngsaan	滑翔傘	N	paragliding	Lesson 1	8
waahtlohng fūngfàahn	滑浪風帆	N	windsurfing	Lesson 1	8
tái páaumáh	睇跑馬	VO	to watch horse racing	Lesson 1	8
yáuh doihbíu sing	有代表性	Adj	typical	Lesson 2	25
choihaih	菜系	N	cuisine	Lesson 2	25
jīng	蒸	V	to steam	Lesson 2	25
yùhchyūn	漁村	N	fishing village	Lesson 2	25
gāaisíh	街市	N	wet market	Lesson 2	25
hóiséui wūyíhm	海水污染	PH	marine pollution	Lesson 2	25
bóuchìh	保持	V	to keep, to maintain	Lesson 2	25
gūngying	供應	N/V	supply; to supply	Lesson 2	25
máhtàuh	碼頭	N	pier	Lesson 2	25
yéuhng	養	V	to keep (animals)	Lesson 2	25
waihsāng	衛生	Adj/N	hygienic; hygiene	Lesson 2	25
yìhmgaak	嚴格	Adj	strict	Lesson 2	25

Yale Romanization	Word	POS	English	Lesson number	Page number
bīujéun	標準	Adj/N	standard	Lesson 2	25
táiyihm	體驗	N/V	experience, to learn through practice, to learn through one's personal experience	Lesson 2	25
yānséung	欣賞	V	to admire, to appreciate	Lesson 2	25
tēuigaai	推介	N/V	recommendation; to recommend	Lesson 2	25
yàuhhaak	遊客	N	tourist	Lesson 2	25
saaigōn	曬乾	RV	to dry in the sun	Lesson 2	25
binsìhng	變成	RV	to become, to change into	Lesson 2	25
bóulàuh	保留	V	to reserve, to retain	Lesson 2	26
mauhyihk jūngsām	貿易中心	N	trade centre	Lesson 2	26
yàhn lòih yàhn wóhng	人來人往	PH	many people hurrying back and forth	Lesson 2	26
tàihyíh	提議	N/V	suggestion; to suggest, to propose	Lesson 2	26
sáuseun	手信	N	souvenir	Lesson 2	26
gauh ginjūk	舊建築	N	old building and structure	Lesson 2	26
lihngyātmihn	另一面	PH	the other side	Lesson 2	26
Hēunggóng Hóisīn Hipwúi	香港海鮮協會	PN	Hong Kong Seafood Association	Lesson 2	26
Hóinàahm Dóu	海南島	PW	Hainan Island	Lesson 2	26
Oujāu	澳洲	PW	Australia	Lesson 2	26
Yùhnlóhng	元朗	PW	Yuen Long	Lesson 2	26
Sāigung	西貢	PW	Sai Kung	Lesson 2	26
Nàahm'ngādóu	南丫島	PW	Lamma Island	Lesson 2	26
Tyùhnmùhn	屯門	PW	Tuen Mun	Lesson 2	26

Yale Romanization	Word	POS	English	Lesson number	Page number
Léihyùhmùhn	鯉魚門	PW	Lei Yue Mun	Lesson 2	26
Wàihdōleihnga Góng	維多利亞港	PW	Victoria Harbour	Lesson 2	26
Daaih'ou	大澳	PW	Tai O	Lesson 2	26
Seuhngwàahn	上環	PW	Sheung Wan	Lesson 2	26
Sāiyìhngpùhn	西營盤	PW	Sai Ying Pun	Lesson 2	26
Hàahmyùh Lāan	鹹魚欄	PW	Salted Fish Market	Lesson 2	26
Hóiméi Gāai	海味街	PW	Dried Seafood Street	Lesson 2	26
Sāi Góng Sìhng	西港城	PW	Western Market	Lesson 2	26
Yīhohk Bokmahtgún	醫學博物館	PW	Museum of Medical Sciences	Lesson 2	27
Syūn Jūng-sāan Geinihm Gún	孫中山紀念館	PW	Dr Sun Yat-sen Museum	Lesson 2	27
lùhnghā	龍蝦	N	lobster	Lesson 2	27
hāmáih	蝦米	N	dried shrimp	Lesson 2	27
hājeung	蝦醬	N	shrimp paste	Lesson 2	27
yùhfán	魚粉	N	fish meal	Lesson 2	27
yùhlouh	魚露	N	fish sauce	Lesson 2	27
hàahmyú	鹹魚	N	salted fish	Lesson 2	27
hóiméi	海味	N	dried seafood	Lesson 2	27
yùhchyūn fūngmeih	漁村風味	N	taste of fishing village	Lesson 2	27
beihfūngtòhng	避風塘	N	typhoon shelter	Lesson 2	27
yāuyùh kèih	休漁期	PH	fishing moratorium	Lesson 2	27
leuihyìhng	類型	N	type	Lesson 3	47
gúdoih	古代	N	ancient times	Lesson 3	47
lòihwóhng	來往	N/V	contact, dealings; to come and go	Lesson 3	47

Yale Romanization	Word	POS	English	Lesson number	Page number
jūnggaau	宗教	N	religion	Lesson 3	47
dihnsihkehk	電視劇	N	TV drama	Lesson 3	47
yìhngjeuhng	形象	N	image	Lesson 3	47
wūjōu	污糟	Adj	dirty	Lesson 3	47
faatjín	發展	N/V	development; to develop	Lesson 3	47
góipīn	改編	V	to adapt, to rearrange, to reorganize	Lesson 3	47
síusyut	小説	N	novel	Lesson 3	47
sésaht	寫實	Adj	appearing to be existing or happening in fact	Lesson 3	47
geiluhk	記錄	N/V	record; to record	Lesson 3	47
yùhnbún	原本	Adj/ Adv	original; originally	Lesson 3	47
chìhngjit	情節	N	plot	Lesson 3	47
saijit	細節	N	details	Lesson 3	47
chūkdouh	速度	N	speed	Lesson 3	47
chitgai	設計	N/V	design; to design	Lesson 3	47
dá dá saat saat	打打殺殺	PH	blood and guts, fighting and killing	Lesson 3	47
fūchín	膚淺	Adj	shallow, superficial, skin-deep	Lesson 3	47
chìhngdouh	程度	N	degree, level	Lesson 3	48
sīuhín	消遣	N	pastime	Lesson 3	48
Dūngnàahm'nga	東南亞	PW	Southeast Asia	Lesson 3	48
Daahtmàhnsāi Mahtmáh	達文西密碼	PN	Da Vinci Code (movie & novel)	Lesson 3	48
yàhnmaht jyuhngei	人物傳記	N	biography	Lesson 3	48

Yale Romanization	Word	POS	English	Lesson number	Page number
fāanyihk màhnhohk	翻譯文學	N	translated literature	Lesson 3	48
léuihyàuh syū	旅遊書	N	travel guide	Lesson 3	48
jinjāng gusih	戰爭故事	N	war story	Lesson 3	48
gīngdín mìhngjyu	經典名著	N	the classics	Lesson 3	48
jīngtaam síusyut	偵探小説	N	detective novel	Lesson 3	48
ngoichìhng síusyut	愛情小説	N	romantic novel	Lesson 3	48
fēisèuhngjī	非常之	Adv	very, extremely	Lesson 4	66
geuih jāngyíhsing	具爭議性	Adj	controversial	Lesson 4	66
tàihmuhk	題目	N	topic	Lesson 4	66
màauhtéuhn	矛盾	Adj/N	contradictory; contradiction	Lesson 4	66
dīkkok	的確	Adv	indeed	Lesson 4	66
yíhtàih	議題	N	issue	Lesson 4	66
lahpchèuhng	立場	N	standpoint	Lesson 4	67
chīngsīk	清晰	Adj	clear	Lesson 4	67
baak fahn jī baak	百分之百	PH	a hundred percent; absolutely	Lesson 4	67
jaansìhng	贊成	V	to approve of, to be in favour of	Lesson 4	67
gēichó	基礎	N	foundation	Lesson 4	67
ngàihhoih	危害	V	to endanger, to harm	Lesson 4	67
tóuleuhn	討論	N/V	discussion; to discuss	Lesson 4	67
hūnggāan	空間	N	space	Lesson 4	67
sahpfānjī	十分之	Adv	very, fully	Lesson 4	67
sèuhng gin	常見	Adj	common	Lesson 4	67
hah yāt doih	下一代	N	the next generation	Lesson 4	67

Yale Romanization	Word	POS	English	Lesson number	Page number
gaaiyīn	戒煙	VO	to quit smoking	Lesson 4	67
móuhyīk	冇益	Adj	unhelpful, not beneficial	Lesson 4	67
gaailāt	戒甩	RV	to successfully quit (a habit)	Lesson 4	67
jihyàuh	自由	Adj/N	free; freedom	Lesson 4	67
sihou	嗜好	N	hobby	Lesson 4	67
fáandeui	反對	V	to oppose	Lesson 4	67
búnsān	本身	N	self, itself	Lesson 4	67
leihyīk	利益	N	benefit	Lesson 4	67
séhwúi	社會	N	society	Lesson 4	67
hahgong	下降	V	to decrease	Lesson 4	67
gātìhng	家庭	N	family	Lesson 4	67
méihmúhn	美滿	Adj	happy, good and perfect (for marriage or family)	Lesson 4	67
sēungjeuih	相聚	V	to gather together	Lesson 4	67
léihgeui	理據	N	justification	Lesson 4	67
jihsī	自私	Adj	selfish	Lesson 4	67
gūngpìhng	公平	Adj	fair	Lesson 4	67
haahnjai	限制	N/V	restriction; to restrict	Lesson 4	68
júnggit	總結	N/V	conclusion; to conclude	Lesson 4	68
mōkdyuht	剝奪	V	to deprive	Lesson 4	68
chyùhnmihn gamyīn	全面禁煙	PH	total ban on smoking	Lesson 4	68
gáamsíu kāpyīn	減少吸煙	PH	to reduce smoking	Lesson 4	68
yīn meih	煙味	N	smoke smell	Lesson 4	68
yīnyáhn héi	煙癮起	PH	to have an urge to smoke	Lesson 4	68
yīnmàhn	煙民	N	smoker	Lesson 4	68

Yale Romanization	Word	POS	English	Lesson number	Page number
kāpyīn kēui	吸煙區	N	smoking area	Lesson 4	68
waahn ngàahm	患癌	VO	to suffer from cancer	Lesson 4	68
yīnhàuh ngàahm	咽喉癌	N	cancer of the pharynx and larynx	Lesson 4	68
háuhōng ngàahm	口腔癌	N	oral cavity cancer	Lesson 4	68
fai ngàahm	肺癌	N	lung cancer	Lesson 4	68
wàaihyahn	懷孕	V	to be pregnant	Lesson 4	68
tāiyìh	胎兒	N	fetus	Lesson 4	68
yahnfúh	孕婦	N	pregnant woman	Lesson 4	68
beih máhngám	鼻敏感	N	nasal allergy	Lesson 4	68
yīlìuh faiyuhng	醫療費用	N	medical expenses	Lesson 4	68
sātnoih chèuhngsó	室內場所	N	indoor place	Lesson 4	69
kyùhnwāi jaahpji	權威雜誌	N	reputed journal	Lesson 4	69
yuhngbán	用品	N	articles for use	Lesson 4	69
fuhjoh yihtsin	輔助熱線	N	assistance hotline	Lesson 4	69
sāmléih fuhdouh	心理輔導	N	psychological counselling	Lesson 4	69
chóifóng	採訪	N/V	news gathering; to interview and gather news	Lesson 4	69
jídihng	指定	V	to appoint, to assign	Lesson 4	69
pàhng mātyéh fáandeui	憑乜嘢反對	PH	what to base on to oppose	Lesson 4	69
yáuh hoih mòuh yīk	有害無益	PH	harmful and unhelpful	Lesson 4	69
hūnghei m̀làuhtùng	空氣唔流通	PH	poorly ventilated	Lesson 4	69
hó chìhjuhk faatjín	可持續發展	PH	sustainable development	Lesson 4	69
gúnléih	管理	N/V	management; to manage	Lesson 5	86
bouhfahn	部分	N	part	Lesson 5	86
tūngsèuhng	通常	Adv	usually, ordinarily	Lesson 5	86

Yale Romanization	Word	POS	English	Lesson number	Page number
hōibaahn	開辦	V	to set up	Lesson 5	86
fochìhng	課程	N	course, curriculum	Lesson 5	86
gāaidyuhn	階段	N	stage	Lesson 5	86
jeuhngjīng	象徵	N/V	symbol; to symbolize	Lesson 5	86
nóuhlihk	努力	V	to strive, to make an effort	Lesson 5	86
héingoi	喜愛	V	to be fond of	Lesson 5	86
léihséung	理想	Adj/N	ideal	Lesson 5	86
tàihgūng	提供	V	to provide	Lesson 5	86
sìhngjīk	成績	N	achievement, academic result	Lesson 5	86
sāmchou	深造	V	to pursue advanced studies	Lesson 5	86
yāujāt	優質	Att	high-quality; of high quality	Lesson 5	86
jeunsāu	進修	V	to pursue further studies	Lesson 5	86
jījoh	資助	N/V	subsidy; to subsidize	Lesson 5	86
séuipìhng	水平	N	level, standard	Lesson 5	86
wándihng	穩定	Adj	stable	Lesson 5	86
bātyihpsāng	畢業生	N	graduate	Lesson 5	86
gwōngmìhng	光明	Adj	bright	Lesson 5	86
chìhntòuh	前途	N	prospects	Lesson 5	86
chūngchūngmòhngmòhng	匆匆忙忙	PH	in a hurry	Lesson 5	86
làuhhohksāang	留學生	N	overseas student; student studying abroad	Lesson 5	87
chīugwo	超過	V	to exceed, to surpass	Lesson 5	87
sīngyuh	聲譽	N	reputation	Lesson 5	87
sīnjeun	先進	Adj	advanced (for equipment, technology, etc.)	Lesson 5	87

Yale Romanization	Word	POS	English	Lesson number	Page number
pùihyéuhng	培養	V	to cultivate	Lesson 5	87
gwokjaifa	國際化	PH	internationalization；internationalized	Lesson 5	87
sihyéh	視野	N	field of vision	Lesson 5	87
gwāanhaih	關係	N	relations; relationship	Lesson 5	87
juhngsih	重視	V	to attach importance to	Lesson 5	87
yāusau	優秀	Adj	outstanding, excellent	Lesson 5	87
yātfahnjí	一份子	PH	a member of, a part of	Lesson 5	87
yàuhyū	由於	Adv	due to	Lesson 5	87
héungsauh	享受	N/V	enjoyment; to enjoy	Lesson 5	87
gōu jātsou	高質素	PH	high-quality, of high quality	Lesson 5	87
Luhk Síu-waih	陸小慧	PN	Luk Siu-wai	Lesson 5	87
Gaauyuhk Guhk	教育局	PN	Education Bureau	Lesson 5	87
gaauyuhk gaai	教育界	N	education sector	Lesson 5	87
hohk chìhn gaauyuhk	學前教育	N	pre-primary education	Lesson 5	87
míhnfai gaauyuhk	免費教育	N	free education	Lesson 5	87
sīyàhn gēikau	私人機構	N	private organization	Lesson 5	87
fēi màuhleih gēikau	非牟利機構	N	non-profit-making organisation	Lesson 5	88
yauyìhyún	幼兒園	N	nursery	Lesson 5	88
yaujihyún	幼稚園	N	kindergarten	Lesson 5	88
gōujūng	高中	Att/N	senior secondary	Lesson 5	88
jyūnseuhng fochìhng	專上課程	N	post-secondary programme	Lesson 5	88
baat daaih	八大	PH	the eight major universities in Hong Kong	Lesson 5	88
hohksih hohkwái	學士學位	PN	Bachelor's Degree	Lesson 5	88

Yale Romanization	Word	POS	English	Lesson number	Page number
fu hohksih	副學士	PN	Associate Degree	Lesson 5	88
gōukāp màhnpàhng	高級文憑	PN	Higher Diploma	Lesson 5	88
yìhngausāng fochìhng	研究生課程	N	postgraduate programme	Lesson 5	88
syúnduhk	選讀	V	to choose to study (e.g. courses, curriculum)	Lesson 5	88
sīkjihleuhng	識字量	N	repertoire of words (number of words that one knows)	Lesson 5	88
yuhtduhk nàhnglihk	閱讀能力	N	reading literacy	Lesson 5	88
léuhngmàhn sāamyúh	兩文三語	PH	biliteracy and trilingualism	Lesson 5	88
tàuhjī	投資	N/V	invesment; to invest	Lesson 5	88
wàahngíng yāuméih	環境優美	PH	the environment is beautiful	Lesson 5	88
gūngguhng gāautūng	公共交通	N	public transport	Lesson 5	88
fōngbihn	方便	Adj/V	convenient; to make things easy	Lesson 5	88
sáuwaih	首位	PH	to be in the first place	Lesson 5	88
faatjín lohkheui	發展落去	PH	keep on developing	Lesson 5	88
yàuhyū sìhgaan gwāanhaih	由於時間關係	PH	due to time constraints	Lesson 5	89
dou chí gitchūk	到此結束	PH	that's the end (of …)	Lesson 5	89
dōyùhn màhnfa	多元文化	PH	multi-culturalism	Lesson 5	89
gwokjai kāp yàhnchòih	國際級人才	N	talented people at international level	Lesson 5	89
hīnggin	興建	V	to build	Lesson 6	113
ginyíh	建議	N/V	suggestion; to suggest	Lesson 6	113
yùhnghéui	容許	V	to permit, to allow	Lesson 6	113

Yale Romanization	Word	POS	English	Lesson number	Page number
gáaisīk	解釋	N/V	explanation; to explain	Lesson 6	113
hōichit	開設	V	to set up, to establish	Lesson 6	113
léihyàuh	理由	N	reason	Lesson 6	113
yáuh joh yū	有助於	PH	to be conducive to	Lesson 6	114
jānggā	增加	V	to increase	Lesson 6	114
chisou	次數	N	number of times	Lesson 6	114
gúlaih	鼓勵	N/V	encouragement; to encourage	Lesson 6	114
dóubok	賭博	N/V	gambling; to gamble	Lesson 6	114
fātsih	忽視	V	to ignore, to neglect	Lesson 6	114
chigīk	刺激	V	to stimulate	Lesson 6	114
jāngjéung	增長	N/V	growth; to increase	Lesson 6	114
fanlihn	訓練	N/V	training, to train	Lesson 6	114
yingfuh	應付	V	to deal with, to cope with	Lesson 6	114
kyutfaht	缺乏	V	to lack	Lesson 6	114
hēisāng	犧牲	V	to sacrifice	Lesson 6	114
chūngfahn	充分	Adj	full, ample	Lesson 6	114
sēuiyiu	需要	N/V	need; to need	Lesson 6	114
gang dō	更多	PH	more	Lesson 6	114
làuhga	樓價	N	property price	Lesson 6	114
hungjai	控制	V	to control	Lesson 6	114
jūkgau	足夠	Adj	enough, sufficient	Lesson 6	114
múhnjūk	滿足	V	to satisfy	Lesson 6	114
sēuikàuh	需求	N	demand	Lesson 6	114
lohksìhng	落成	V	(of buildings) to be completed	Lesson 6	114

Yale Romanization	Word	POS	English	Lesson number	Page number
sauh fūnyìhng	受歡迎	Adj	popular, well-received	Lesson 6	114
gingjāng	競爭	N/V	competition; to compete	Lesson 6	114
fānsīk	分析	N/V	analysis; to analyze	Lesson 6	114
johjéung	助長	V	to encourage (e.g. crimes, evil trends)	Lesson 6	114
fēifaat	非法	Adj	illegal	Lesson 6	114
gōuleihtaai	高利貸	N	high-interest loan	Lesson 6	114
chàhmmàih	沉迷	V	to be addicted to	Lesson 6	114
doihga	代價	N	price, cost	Lesson 6	115
Góng-Jyū-Ou Daaihkìuh	港珠澳大橋	PW	HongKong-Zhuhai-Macao Bridge	Lesson 6	115
Oumún	澳門	PW	Macau	Lesson 6	115
Jyūhói	珠海	PW	Zhuhai	Lesson 6	115
sāam deih	三地	PH	the three places	Lesson 6	115
dóuchèuhng	賭場	N	casino	Lesson 6	115
choimáh	賽馬	N	horse racing	Lesson 6	115
Luhkhahpchói	六合彩	N	Mark Six	Lesson 6	115
dóubō	賭波	N/VO	soccer betting; to bet on soccer	Lesson 6	115
dóuyáhn	賭癮	N	gambling addiction	Lesson 6	115
seuisāu	稅收	N	tax revenue	Lesson 6	115
yīnjáu seui	煙酒稅	N	tobacco and alcohol tax	Lesson 6	115
heichē dānggei seui	汽車登記稅	N	vehicle registration tax	Lesson 6	115
maaih deih	賣地	N/VO	land sale; to sell the land	Lesson 6	115
puitou	配套	N	supporting infrastructure	Lesson 6	115
tóudeih	土地	N	land	Lesson 6	115

Yale Romanization	Word	POS	English	Lesson number	Page number
gūngying bātjūk	供應不足	PH	the supply is inadequate	Lesson 6	115
tūngjeung	通脹	N	inflation	Lesson 6	115
séhwúi fūnghei	社會風氣	N	social trend	Lesson 6	115
jih'ōn	治安	N	public order	Lesson 6	115
léuihyàuhyihp chùhngyihpyùhn	旅遊業從業員	N	tourism practitioner	Lesson 6	116
lòih Góng	來港	PH	coming to Hong Kong	Lesson 6	116
gāpchit	急切	Adj	eager, urgent	Lesson 6	116
fòhng'ngūk	房屋	N	housing	Lesson 6	116
yùhlohk chitsī	娛樂設施	N	recreational facility	Lesson 6	116
yāt síusìh sāngwuhthyūn	一小時生活圈	PH	one-hour living circle	Lesson 6	116
koinihm	概念	N	concept	Lesson 6	116
ngoksing gingjāng	惡性競爭	N	vicious competition	Lesson 6	116
fūnggwōng	風光	N	landscape	Lesson 6	116
lèuhngahn	鄰近	Adv/N	nearby; vicinity	Lesson 6	116
ginjūk sìhngbún	建築成本	N	construction cost	Lesson 6	116
baak mòhng jījūng	百忙之中	PH	out of one's busy schedule	Lesson 6	116
chāuchēut	抽出	RV	to take out	Lesson 6	116
bóugwai sìhgaan	寶貴時間	N	precious time	Lesson 6	116
jyūntàih bihnleuhnwúi	專題辯論會	N	thematic debate	Lesson 6	116
chìh fáandeui yigin	持反對意見	PH	to hold opposing view	Lesson 6	116
fáandeui sīngyām	反對聲音	N	opposition voice	Lesson 6	116
yáuhgwāan jyūngā	有關專家	N	relevant specialists	Lesson 6	116
júngkut làih góng	總括嚟講	PH	in summary	Lesson 6	116
gwóngdaaih síhmàhn	廣大市民	PH	the public	Lesson 6	116

Yale Romanization	Word	POS	English	Lesson number	Page number
faatyìhnyàhn	發言人	N	spokesperson	Lesson 7	135
táiyuhk choisih	體育賽事	N	sports event	Lesson 7	135
syūnchyùhn	宣傳	N/V	promotion; to promote	Lesson 7	135
tàuhjī	投資	N/V	investment; to invest	Lesson 7	135
sāaichín	嘥錢	Adj/VO	wasteful of money; to waste money	Lesson 7	135
sīufai	消費	N/V	consumption; to consume	Lesson 7	135
jīudím	焦點	N	focus	Lesson 7	135
sówaih	所謂	Adj	so-called	Lesson 7	135
m̀sìhnglahp	唔成立	PH	invalid	Lesson 7	135
fáanbok	反駁	V	to refute	Lesson 7	135
leuhndím	論點	N	argument, point of view taken in discussion	Lesson 7	135
gīngyihm	經驗	N	experience	Lesson 7	135
chàhnggīng	曾經	Adv	to have had the experience of; indicating that an action once happened or a state once existed	Lesson 7	135
dahkdāng	特登	Adv	intentionally, deliberately	Lesson 7	135
fuhjaak	負責	V	to be responsible for, to be in charge of	Lesson 7	135
yingdeui	應對	N/V	response; to respond	Lesson 7	135
chèuhngkèih	長期	PH	long-term; over a long period of time	Lesson 7	135
táiyuhk chèuhnggún	體育場館	N	sports complex	Lesson 7	135
gihnsān chèuhngsó	健身場所	N	fitness centre	Lesson 7	136
chìhmjoih	潛在	Adj	potential	Lesson 7	136

Yale Romanization	Word	POS	English	Lesson number	Page number
gūnséung	觀賞	V	to watch, to view and admire	Lesson 7	136
dihnsih gūnjung	電視觀眾	N	television audience	Lesson 7	136
jeuihjīu	聚焦	V	to focus	Lesson 7	136
jīmìhngdouh	知名度	N	popularity	Lesson 7	136
jingmihn	正面	Adj	positive	Lesson 7	136
jeuhkjuhng	著重	V	to stress, to emphasize	Lesson 7	136
gú móuh	鼓舞	N/V	inspiration; to inspire	Lesson 7	136
sīusīk	消息	N	news	Lesson 7	136
faatsung	發送	V	to send	Lesson 7	136
gitleuhn	結論	N	conclusion	Lesson 7	136
bá'ngāak	把握	N/V	certainty, assurance; to seize (chances, opportunities)	Lesson 7	136
hōifong	開放	V	to open to the public	Lesson 7	136
jīchìh	支持	V	to support	Lesson 7	136
Bākgīng Níuhchàauh	北京鳥巢	PW	Beijing Bird's Nest	Lesson 7	136
Séuilahpfōng	水立方	PW	Water Cube	Lesson 7	136
móhngkàuh choi	網球賽	N	tennis competition	Lesson 7	136
láamkàuh choi	欖球賽	N	rugby competition	Lesson 7	136
máhlāaichùhng	馬拉松	N	marathon	Lesson 7	136
Ouwahnwúi	奧運會	PN	Olympic Games	Lesson 7	136
máhseuht béichoi	馬術比賽	N	equestrian competition	Lesson 7	136
Dūng'nga Wahnduhngwúi	東亞運動會	PN	East Asian Games	Lesson 7	137
douhhóiwihng	渡海泳	N	cross-harbour swimming	Lesson 7	137
choichē	賽車	N	car racing	Lesson 7	137

Yale Romanization	Word	POS	English	Lesson number	Page number
jāngchit	增設	V	to establish an additional or a new ... (e.g. organization, course, facility, service)	Lesson 8	158
gūngjung gakèih	公眾假期	N	public holiday	Lesson 8	158
dōyùhnfa	多元化	PH	diversified; diversification	Lesson 8	158
jityaht	節日	N	festival	Lesson 8	158
jūnggaau seunyéuhng	宗教信仰	N	religious belief	Lesson 8	158
yāt sih tùhng yàhn	一視同仁	PH	to treat all alike without discrimination	Lesson 8	158
hùhngga	紅假	N	public holiday (lit. "red holiday")	Lesson 8	158
daaihdōsou	大多數	Adv/N	mostly; the majority	Lesson 8	158
chyùhntúng jityaht	傳統節日	N	traditional festival	Lesson 8	158
gwokhing	國慶	N	national day	Lesson 8	158
gūnfōng	官方	Adj	official	Lesson 8	158
geinihm wuhtduhng	紀念活動	N	commemorative activity	Lesson 8	158
yātgā daaihsai	一家大細	PH	the whole family	Lesson 8	158
chèuhngsin léuihhàhng	長線旅行	PH	long-haul trip	Lesson 8	158
gaauwúi	教會	N	church	Lesson 8	158
noihbouh	內部	Att/N	internal; internal part	Lesson 8	158
jūnggaau meihdouh	宗教味道	N	religious flavour	Lesson 8	158
mìhnghín	明顯	Adj	obvious	Lesson 8	159
gūnghōi	公開	Adj/ Adv/V	open (not secret); openly; to make known to the public	Lesson 8	159
jiyū	至於	CV	as for	Lesson 8	159
lihksí yùhnyān	歷史原因	N	historical reason	Lesson 8	159

Yale Romanization	Word	POS	English	Lesson number	Page number
laihngoih	例外	N	exception	Lesson 8	159
gēibúnseuhng	基本上	Adv	basically	Lesson 8	159
jēunchùhng	遵從	V	to comply with	Lesson 8	159
chitlahp	設立	V	to establish, to set up, to found	Lesson 8	159
bóuchūng	補充	V	to supplement; to add (opinion)	Lesson 8	159
gáamsíu	減少	V	to reduce	Lesson 8	159
daaih lóuhbáan	大老闆	N	big boss	Lesson 8	159
gābāan	加班	V	to work overtime	Lesson 8	159
gōuhing	高興	Adj	happy	Lesson 8	159
góibin	改變	N/V	change; to change	Lesson 8	159
goyàhn	個人	Adj	personal, individual	Lesson 8	159
Seuihdín	瑞典	PW	Sweden	Lesson 8	159
Fēileuhtbān	菲律賓	PW	the Philippines	Lesson 8	159
Taaigwok	泰國	PW	Thailand	Lesson 8	159
Nèihpokyíh	尼泊爾	PW	Nepal	Lesson 8	159
Ngoiyíhlàahn	愛爾蘭	PW	Ireland	Lesson 8	159
jūnggaau tyùhntái	宗教團體	N	religious organization	Lesson 8	159
jūnggaau paaibiht	宗教派別	N	religious faction	Lesson 8	159
Yandouhgaau	印度教	PN	Hinduism	Lesson 8	160
Yàuhtaaigaau	猶太教	PN	Judaism	Lesson 8	160
Yīsīlàahngaaujit	伊斯蘭教節	PN	Islamic Festival	Lesson 8	160
Douhgaaujit	道教節	PN	Taoist Festival	Lesson 8	160
Nùhnglihk Sānnìhn	農曆新年	PN	Lunar New Year	Lesson 8	160
Chīngmìhngjit	清明節	PN	Ching Ming Festival	Lesson 8	160

Yale Romanization	Word	POS	English	Lesson number	Page number
Dyūnnǵhjit	端午節	PN	Dragon Boat Festival	Lesson 8	160
Jūngchāujit	中秋節	PN	Mid-Autumn Festival	Lesson 8	160
Chùhngyèuhngjit	重陽節	PN	Chung Yeung Festival	Lesson 8	160
baainìhn	拜年	VO	to pay a New Year call	Lesson 8	160
paai laihsih	派利是	VO	to give out red packets	Lesson 8	160
pàh lùhngsyùhn	扒龍船	VO	to row the dragon boat	Lesson 8	160
baaisāan	拜山	VO	to sweep the grave	Lesson 8	160
wùihgwāi	回歸	PH	handover (of Hong Kong to China)	Lesson 8	160
Singdaanjit	聖誕節	PN	Christmas	Lesson 8	160
Fuhkwuhtjit	復活節	PN	Easter	Lesson 8	160
Sānlihk Sānnìhn	新曆新年	PN	New Year (according to Gregorian calendar)	Lesson 8	160
Fahtdaan	佛誕	PN	Birthday of Buddha	Lesson 8	160
Maahnsingjit	萬聖節	PN	Halloween	Lesson 8	160
Gámyānjit	感恩節	PN	Thanksgiving Day	Lesson 8	160
Seuihdín ge "Sing Louhsāi'nga Yaht"	瑞典嘅「聖露西亞日」	PN	Saint Lucia's Day in Sweden	Lesson 8	160
Fēileuhtbān ge "Pàhngyáuhjit"	菲律賓嘅「朋友節」	PN	Kapangyawan Festival in the Philippines	Lesson 8	160
Taaigwok ge "Putséuijit"	泰國嘅「潑水節」	PN	Songkran Festival in Thailand	Lesson 8	160
chùhngsih	從事	V	to engage in (work)	Lesson 9	179
faatleuht	法律	N	law	Lesson 9	179
fānhéung	分享	V	to share	Lesson 9	179
doudái	到底	Adv	after all	Lesson 9	179

Yale Romanization	Word	POS	English	Lesson number	Page number
jāngsēung	爭相	V	to fall over each other in rush to	Lesson 9	179
hinfaat	憲法	N	constitution	Lesson 9	179
bóujeung	保障	N/V	protection; to ensure and protect	Lesson 9	179
yìhnleuhn jihyàuh	言論自由	N	freedom of speech	Lesson 9	179
chēutbáan jihyàuh	出版自由	N	freedom of publication	Lesson 9	179
lyún'ngoi jihyàuh	戀愛自由	N	freedom of love	Lesson 9	179
gamjí	禁止	V	to prohibit, to ban	Lesson 9	179
jipsauh	接受	V	to accept	Lesson 9	179
jíchēut	指出	V	to point out	Lesson 9	179
hohkyihp	學業	N	(one's) academic studies	Lesson 9	179
bíuyihn	表現	N	performance	Lesson 9	180
yàhnjai gwāanhaih	人際關係	N	interpersonal relationship	Lesson 9	180
gihk daaih	極大	PH	huge, enormous	Lesson 9	180
chākéuih	差距	N	gap, disparity	Lesson 9	180
sìhngnìhnyàhn	成年人	N	adult	Lesson 9	180
sēungfōng	雙方	PH	both parties	Lesson 9	180
yātdaan	一旦	Adv	in case, once	Lesson 9	180
gūng'ūk	公屋	N	public housing estate	Lesson 9	180
séhwúi màhnsāng	社會民生	N	social livelihood	Lesson 9	180
taugwo	透過	CV	through	Lesson 9	180
yàuhkèihsih	尤其是	Adv	especially	Lesson 9	180
fūkjaahp	複雜	Adj	complicated	Lesson 9	180
hahpfùh	合乎	V	to conform to	Lesson 9	180
yàhnkyùhn	人權	N	human rights	Lesson 9	180

Yale Romanization	Word	POS	English	Lesson number	Page number
lòhchāp	邏輯	N	logic	Lesson 9	180
háauleuih	考慮	V	to consider	Lesson 9	180
jeui gōu faatyún	最高法院	PN	Supreme Court	Lesson 9	180
yíhfān yàhnsih míhnseuingáak	已婚人士免稅額	PN	Married Person's Allowance	Lesson 9	180
fānyān faat	婚姻法	PN	Marriage Law	Lesson 9	180
tùhngsinglyún hahpfaatfa	同性戀合法化	PH	legalization of homosexuality	Lesson 9	180
tùhngsing fānyān	同性婚姻	N	same-sex marriage	Lesson 9	180
fuhchān	父親	N	father	Lesson 9	180
móuhchān	母親	N	mother	Lesson 9	180
líhngyéuhng	領養	V	to adopt (child)	Lesson 9	180
síuhàaihjí	小孩子	N	child	Lesson 9	181
chyùhntúng fānyān	傳統婚姻	N	traditional marriage	Lesson 9	181
yihsing	異性	N	the opposite sex	Lesson 9	181
githahp	結合	V	to marry, to be united in wedlock	Lesson 9	181
jingfānyàhn	證婚人	N	wedding witness	Lesson 9	181
yihyàhn gātìhng	二人家庭	PH	two-person household	Lesson 9	181
hahpfaat fūchāi	合法夫妻	N	legitimate couple	Lesson 9	181
dōyàhn fānyān	多人婚姻	N	multi-person marriage	Lesson 9	181
sougeui	數據	N	data	Lesson 9	181
yuhnggā	用家	N	user	Lesson 9	181
gānjyuh	跟住	Adv/V	then; to follow	Lesson 9	181
chóihùhng	彩虹	N	rainbow	Lesson 9	181
bīugei	標記	N	symbol, sign, mark	Lesson 9	181

Yale Romanization	Word	POS	English	Lesson number	Page number
máahnwúi	晚會	N	evening party	Lesson 9	181
jyúchìhyàhn	主持人	N	host, MC	Lesson 9	181
sēunggwāan gūngjok	相關工作	PH	related work	Lesson 9	181
yātsìh jīgāan	一時之間	PH	all of a sudden	Lesson 9	181
tóuleuhn yihtdím	討論熱點	N	hot-debate issue	Lesson 9	181
jih chí jīhauh	自此之後	PH	since then, henceforth	Lesson 9	181
m̀haih dāandāan yiu háauleuih	唔係單單要考慮	PH	not only need to consider	Lesson 9	181
fuhjaakyàhn	負責人	N	person in charge	Lesson 10	200
wohk yīuchíng	獲邀請	PH	to be invited	Lesson 10	200
bíudaaht	表達	V	to express	Lesson 10	200
wàahnbóu gūngjok	環保工作	N	environmental protection work	Lesson 10	200
jīksìh	即時	Adj / Adv	immediate; immediately	Lesson 10	200
jihchùhng	自從	CV	(of time) from, since	Lesson 10	200
put ngóh láahngséui	潑我冷水	PH	to discourage me, to throw cold water on me	Lesson 10	201
hóiséui	海水	N	seawater	Lesson 10	201
góisihn	改善	V	to improve	Lesson 10	201
wán m̀dóu sihk	搵唔到食	PH	cannot make a living	Lesson 10	201
jaahn m̀dóu chín	賺唔到錢	PH	cannot earn money	Lesson 10	201
chānyíh tēngdóu	親耳聽到	PH	to hear something with one's own ears	Lesson 10	201
hóuchói	好彩	Adj/ Adv	lucky; luckily	Lesson 10	201
dōngsìh	當時	Adv	at that time	Lesson 10	201

Yale Romanization	Word	POS	English	Lesson number	Page number
yáuh muhk guhng dóu	有目共睹	PH	obvious to everyone	Lesson 10	201
gyūnfún	捐款	N	donation	Lesson 10	201
jeukníuh	雀鳥	N	bird	Lesson 10	201
hohngmuhk	項目	N	project, item	Lesson 10	201
jóujīk	組織	N/V	organization; to organize	Lesson 10	201
pùihfan	培訓	N/V	training; to train (personnel)	Lesson 10	201
hóingohn gūngyún	海岸公園	N	marine park	Lesson 10	201
ngūkchyūn	屋邨	N	housing estate	Lesson 10	201
jih'yuhn	自願	Adv	voluntarily	Lesson 10	201
kwannàahn	困難	Adj/N	difficult; difficulty	Lesson 10	201
yihgūng	義工	N	volunteers	Lesson 10	201
lyùhnlok	聯絡	V	to contact	Lesson 10	201
gokkēui	各區	PH	each district	Lesson 10	201
hòhngyihp	行業	N	industry	Lesson 10	201
joihjoh	在座	PH	to be present (at a meeting, banquet, etc.)	Lesson 10	201
jūngjí	宗旨	N	(of associations, clubs, etc.) aim, purpose	Lesson 10	201
Luhksīk Hēunggóng	綠色香港	PN	Green Hong Kong	Lesson 10	202
Chàhn Gwok-kèuhng	陳國強	PN	Chan Kwok-keung	Lesson 10	202
Chīnggit Wàih Góng Gaiwaahk	清潔維港計劃	PN	"Clean Up Victoria Harbour" scheme	Lesson 10	202
Chīnggit Sātāan Wahnduhng	清潔沙灘運動	PN	"Beach Clean-up" campaign	Lesson 10	202
wàahnbóu daaihsi	環保大使	PH	Green Ambassador	Lesson 10	202

Yale Romanization	Word	POS	English	Lesson number	Page number
Laahpsaap Fānleuih Gaiwaahk	垃圾分類計劃	PN	Waste Sorting Campaign	Lesson 10	202
siunìhn	少年	N	early youth; youngster	Lesson 10	202
gātìhng jyúfúh	家庭主婦	N	housewife	Lesson 10	202
teuiyāu yàhnsih	退休人士	N	retired people	Lesson 10	202
jyūnyihp yàhnsih	專業人士	N	professionals	Lesson 10	202
sihnjéung yàhnyūng	善長仁翁	PH	philanthropists	Lesson 10	202
maahnfān gámjeh	萬分感謝	PH	million of thanks	Lesson 10	202
bíusih chūngsām ge gámjeh	表示衷心嘅感謝	PH	to express my/our heartfelt thanks	Lesson 10	202
yáuh chín chēut chín, yáuh lihk chēut lihk	有錢出錢，有力出力	PH	if you have money, donate some to the poor; if you have strength, help others with your hands	Lesson 10	202

Appendix IV: Lesson texts in standard written Chinese
課文（書面語版）

Lesson 1

東方之珠

局長先生、各位業界的朋友、各位來賓，大家好。

我是來自旅遊業界的劉家寶。先讓我來介紹一下自己，我是土生土長的香港人，我很榮幸能夠在這裏介紹香港。首先我要借這個機會在這裏代表業界向香港旅遊發展局表示感謝，感謝旅發局舉辦這次大型展銷活動，給各行各業一個展示香港的平台。

香港有一個很美麗的名字叫做「東方之珠」，這麼小的香港每年可以吸引這麼多遊客，旅遊業是香港最重要的經濟支柱之一。其中的原因，首先，我們有著名的城市景觀——譬如尖沙咀、中環、山頂。然後是購物方面，如果你想在香港買東西，有很多不同的選擇。例如去撿便宜貨你可以去旺角，幾十元一件的衣服，又便宜又耐穿的鞋子，又有一些女士們非常喜歡的首飾，只是在旺角你也可以找到。如果你不是太喜歡撿便宜貨，你可以去中環一些高級的商場買名牌貨物。世界各國的牌子你也可以找到。我們有大型主題樂園，還有很多其他城市很難找到的自然風景。離市區不遠的地方，就有郊野公園或離島，遊客立刻就可以投身大自然，放鬆身心。香港的東平洲就是國家級的地質公園，那裏的石頭非常的特別，好像仙景一樣。你在香港中文大學附近的碼頭乘小船，大概一個多小時。很多人都會在那裏玩一整天。繞著小島走一圈，就可以在碼頭附近的士多吃一些特色食物。這樣過一天真的很寫意。

說起來，遊客來到香港，就會發現在香港不單可以觀光和娛樂，還可以了解這裏的風土人情和歷史文化，品嚐這裏的美食。喜歡刺激的運動愛好者呢，可以試試滑翔傘、滑浪風帆這樣的活動，又或者進去馬場看賽馬。除此以外，香港氣候溫和，交通方便，香港人友善好客，很多遊客來過還想再來。

在這裏我要特別感謝旅遊業的同行，因為你們多年的努力，香港得以成為國際旅遊城市。我希望政府往後繼續支持旅遊業，讓我們業界可以開發新的景點和旅遊項目，改善服務質量，讓旅遊業持續發展，愈做愈好，讓更多人認識香港。

謝謝。

Lesson 2

香港美食

我代表香港海鮮協會向各位推廣香港旅遊的魅力。廣東菜是中國最有代表性的菜系之一，而廣東菜最特別的就是蒸海鮮。香港以前是一個漁村，二百年前，香港很多人住在船上面，需要經常出海。今天雖然水上人愈來愈少，但是香港的漁村風味還能在離島和避風塘找到。香港的海鮮來自不同的地方，有的離香港比較近，例如廣東、海南島，有的離香港比較遠，例如菲律賓、印尼、甚至澳洲附近來的，所以海鮮的種類很豐富。吃海鮮，不一定要上酒樓，香港每個街市每天都買到海鮮，就算打風下大雨，都一樣買到最新鮮的。

近年海水污染，每年又有「休漁期」，為了保持海鮮的供應，養海鮮變成另外一個選擇。香港的元朗、西貢和南丫島的碼頭，我們還能看見很多人養魚、養蝦、養龍蝦。香港自己養的海鮮，客人可以放心地吃，既新鮮又衛生，因為我們有嚴格的衛生標準。吃海鮮，是所有來香港旅行的人一定要做的。除了西貢和離島，香港仔、元朗、屯門、鯉魚門都是吃海鮮的好地方。如果想試一下新的體驗，銅鑼灣避風塘也是值得去的，客人可以在船上面一邊吃海鮮，一邊欣賞維多利亞港的夜景。不管你是否喜歡吃海鮮，我也推介遊客去走一走逛一逛，認識一下香港的文化。至於喜歡吃海鮮的朋友也就不用多說了。

香港是海邊的城市，幾百年以來，都離不開魚。除了海鮮，香港人還喜歡將一些魚曬乾，變成蝦米呀、蝦醬呀、魚粉呀、魚露呀、鹹魚呀等等。很多遊客都知道，大澳還保留了以前漁村的風味，所以特地去大澳買蝦醬。如果不想去這麼遠，香港島的上環和西營盤有很多售賣海味的店鋪，香港人叫那裏做「鹹魚欄」或者「海味街」，那裏一百年前已經是很熱鬧的貿易中心，附近的碼頭人來人往。我提議來香港旅行的人一定要去上環逛一逛，這樣不但能買一些海味做紀念品，還可以看一下附近的舊建築，比如西港城啦、醫學博物館啦、孫中山紀念館啦，知道多一些香港的歷史。我代表香港海鮮協會，歡迎世界各地的遊客來這裏體驗香港的另一面。

Lesson 3

樂在閱讀

你問我平常看些甚麼樣的書呢？我從小就喜歡看書，小學的時候是，大學的時候也是，現在開始工作還是很喜歡看書。我喜歡很多類型的書。我喜歡看歷史書、人物傳記、翻譯文學和旅遊書。首先說一下歷史書。我平常去書店，一定會留意有沒有一些和中國、日本及東南亞相關的新書。我對古代歷史特別有興趣，我最近不是看中國歷史就是看日本歷史。

古代的中國和日本有很多來往，有些中國人去了日本做生意，而日本無論是宗教、建築、藝術、音樂都受到中國很多方面的影響。最近買了一本書，是關於一千三百年前一般中國人的日常生活，例如他們平常穿些什麼樣的衣服呀、買菜去哪裏買呀、病了去哪裏看醫生呀、去旅行要準備些甚麼呀等等。我發現他們的生活和電影裏面或者電視劇裏面的形象有很大的差別。譬如說街上其實很髒，晚上不能隨便外出，還有普通人很難找到乾淨的水做飯和洗澡，生活也挺苦、挺慘的。

除了歷史書以外，我也喜歡看一些人物傳記。這一類的書比較容易看。因為它的故事發展特別吸引。乘車的時候看也可以。人物傳記通常都分為兩類，一類就是改編成為小說的，一類就是比較寫實的記錄。改編成為小說的人物傳記，為了讓故事比較吸引，通常都會加入一些原本沒有在那個人身上發生的事情，一些寫實性的人物傳記通常就會把一些細節或者那個人的成長，很忠實的記錄下來。所以兩類的人物傳記都有他們各自吸引讀者的地方。兩類我都喜歡看。

我是一個小說迷，各國的小說我都經常看。台灣發行的翻譯小說一向都是非常的多，但是這幾年我也買多了很多大陸出版的翻譯小說，因為他們翻譯的速度很快，而且書的設計愈來愈好，種類愈來愈多。你平常這麼喜歡看書，你一定知道很多外國的文學和小說不單翻譯為中文，還保留了原來的文字，你能一邊看中文，一邊看英文；或者一邊看中文，一邊看日文。無論如何，我覺得看小說能放鬆心情，我不喜歡那些打打殺殺的戰爭故事，我比較膚淺，也不喜歡那些經典名著，我不是看愛情小說，就是看偵探小說，當你進入了小說的世界，就會忘記很多生活中的麻煩事，有些時候我會想如果好像小說裏面的人那樣，我會怎樣做。我中學時代非常喜歡看愛情小說，喜歡到差點連飯也不吃的程度。有些小說還會改編成為電影，我會去看小說改編的電影，也是一個有趣的消遣。電影《達文西密碼》你也看過了，真是好看得不得了，原版小說你看過沒有呀？這本書我可以送給你，我已經看完了。

Lesson 4

無煙香港

室內場所應不應該全面禁煙，我自己也明白是一個特別具爭議性的題目，因為我自己的家裏也是有人吸煙的。所以當我們外出吃飯的時候也面對不少的矛盾。一方面我們也想遷就家人，另一方面我們也明白其實，吸煙的確是對自己和身邊的人的健康都有一個特別大的影響。所以在這個議題上我自己的立場是非常的清晰。我自己是百分之百贊成酒樓餐館和室內公共場所應該全面禁煙的。

首先我們要留意一個很重要的基礎，就是吸煙危害健康，是人命關天的大事。相信在這一個觀點上是絕對沒有討論的空間的。權威雜誌上有數字顯示其實吸煙的人，他們患癌的機會特別高。無論是咽喉癌，口腔癌，肺癌都是非常的常見。進一步來看我們也知道其實吸煙也是會影響下一代。如果懷孕的人她是有吸煙的習慣，胎兒的發展是會嚴重受到影響。另一方面當我們看見，市面上有很多戒煙用品、戒煙中心啦、輔助熱線啦、心理輔導啦等等，其實也都證明了一些人是知道吸煙對健康是沒有益處，但是戒掉是特別的困難。

沒錯，有些人說吸煙是個人的選擇和自由，你喜歡吸煙，跟我沒有關係。不過個人的選擇和自由是必須建立在不影響其他人的基礎上的。意思是如果你在巴士上吸煙，其他乘客聞到了煙味覺得不舒服，難道要他們下車嗎？那你這樣就是影響了他們呢。這個情形就像幾個人在圖書館裏面大聲說話一樣。聊天是他們的自由，但是在圖書館裏面大聲說話就一定影響其他想安靜讀書的人，讓其他人不開心。

或者有些人會說，不是的，吸煙和喝酒一樣，都是一個人的嗜好而已。我喜歡吸煙，你喜歡喝啤酒，我不反對你在室內公共場所喝啤酒了，你憑甚麼反對我吸煙。雖然我覺得啤酒的味道很臭，很奇怪，但是我不會去管你。你們覺得這個講法對不對呢？我想說，其實吸煙和喝酒是不一樣的。所有人都知道吸煙對身體有害無益，而且吸二手煙的害處比吸煙本身還要多。就算我自己不吸煙，但是在室內空氣不流通的場所，吸了他人的煙，我也一樣會病。聽說有些人因為這樣就患肺癌死了。他們不吸煙也有肺癌，為甚麼？就是因為吸二手煙的關係。何況在酒樓和餐廳這些地方有很多小孩子、老人、孕婦、還有香港有很多人鼻敏感。如果其他人吸煙，對他們無論怎樣也有影響。所以為了社會大多數人的利益，其實室內禁煙是好的，因為這一個方法可以幫人去盡量減少吸煙。長遠來說，室內禁煙是對我們社會可持續發展是有一個特別大的益處，譬如說醫療費用，整體社會的醫療費用我相信是會下降，對於家庭的美滿，家人能夠更加多的時間去相聚。所以在各方面的理據下，其實我們明白室內禁煙是對個人和社會整體都有好處的。

我很明白，對於煙民來說，吸煙不單是嗜好，還是生活習慣。他們煙癮來的時候，他們要特地走到很遠，真是挺麻煩挺不方便的。不過，我覺得不可以因為這樣就不理會其他人。在室內公共場所就需要照顧其他人的需要，不能這麼自私的。如果因為你的自由，影響了其他人，這樣社會就會更加不公平。其實有的城市甚至室外都不可以吸煙，這裏只是室內不能吸，還算挺自由了。我知道你們的採訪時間有限制，所以我想總結，我贊成室內公共場所全面禁煙的同時，政府應該指定一些吸煙區，不應該剝奪煙民吸煙的自由。

Lesson 5

香港教育

局長先生、各位業界的朋友、各位來賓，大家好。

我是來自教育界的陸小慧。我很榮幸有這個機會在這裏介紹一下香港的教育。香港的教育主要由教育局來管理。可以分為幾個部分。第一個部分是學前教育。通常就是三歲至六歲期間。學前教育有幼兒園和幼稚園，其中有私人機構，其他也有一些非牟利機構來開辦。在私人機構開辦的也好，非牟利機構開辦的也好，每一個家庭都可以按照自己的需要來選擇幼稚園。接著就是十二年免費教育。小學一年級至六年級，然後就是初中，中一至中三，接著就是中四至中六高中的課程。在高中階段 DSE 這個英文字就象徵著高中學生的生活。這個時期就是為了這個考試每天這樣努力，希望可以進到自己所喜愛的大學。如果 DSE 的成績理想，就可以進入專上課程的階段。專上課程當然有香港八大所提供的學士學位課程。但是如果成績並不是太好，就要選擇一些其他的課程了。比方說副學士或者是高級文憑課程等等。完成專上學位後，如果不想立刻工作，希望繼續深造，香港的大學也提供優質的研究生課程讓希望繼續進修的學生選讀。從學前教育開始，然後到小學教育，接著中學教育，最後到專上教育，政府都提供不少的資助。香港的教育其實在世界來說，水平都是十分的穩定。包括香港大學畢業生的英語水平，和小學生的識字量和閱讀能力，其實都是排在世界的首位。相信香港的教育發展下去還是有一個光明的前途。

每天我們走在街上，除了看到匆匆忙忙的香港人之外，還有來自不同國家的遊客，但是我們可能不是每天都看到在香港讀書的留學生。其實每年來香港留學的學生有超過三萬，香港的學校在世界上有非常好的聲譽。我們有先進的設備，由於香港很多大學都希望培養學生有國際化的視野的關係，加上政府很重視對教育的投資，我們可以從世界不同的地方請到優秀的老師。另外，香港是世界上最安全的城市之一，這裏的生活水平比較高，大學裏面環境優美，城市公共交通方便。有些留學生因為在這裏讀書而愛上香港，畢業以後還留在香港，成為香港社會的一份子。

由於時間關係，我很快的介紹了香港的教育。我的介紹到此結束。我相信香港作為一個擁有多元文化的國際城市，香港的教育環境可以培養出兩文三語的國際級人才。我們歡迎所有人士來香港享受高質量的教育。

謝謝各位。

Lesson 6

開設賭場

大家好，首先感謝各位在百忙之中抽出寶貴時間參加今天的專題辯論會，為我們社會未來的發展給些意見。剛才幾位代表的發言都有一定的道理。對於興建賭場這個建議，政府是持反對意見的。以下請容許我解釋一下政府反對開設賭場的理由。

首先，對於有意見認為開設賭場可以有助於增加政府稅收。政府認為可以有其他方法來增加稅收，舉些例子，好像增加煙酒稅、汽車登記稅啦、增加賣地次數等等。社會上有很多反對興建賭場的聲音，認為香港已經有賽馬、六合彩和足球賭博，不應該進一步鼓勵賭博。政府不可以因為增加稅收就忽視反對聲音。雖然有意見認為，開設賭場可以起刺激旅遊業這個作用，吸引更多遊客來香港消費，但是近年遊客人數增長太快，由十年前每年一千萬旅客增加到現時的七千萬。社會不論是交通、酒店、還是旅遊業從業員的訓練方面都需要有更多的配套，才可以應付更多旅客來港。

其次是香港的土地供應不足，目前政府最急切的工作是增加房屋的土地供應，其實香港是一個缺乏土地的地方。大家都知道公屋輪候時間非常長。無論是私樓的價格，還是一些公屋轉到二手市場作為買賣的價格，都高得讓人難以負擔。我們興建一個賭場便要犧牲非常大的土地面積。在一個這樣缺乏土地的情況底下我們是沒有充分的理據去興建賭場的。如果興建賭場，就需要更多土地用來興建娛樂設施，需要更多土地興建新的酒店，這樣香港就會少了很多地方來興建房屋，樓價就很難控制。現在香港普遍認為樓價太高，在這一點來說，政府還是以興建房屋為優先，而不是興建賭場。

第三，鄰近地區已經有很多大型賭場，好像澳門、新加坡和馬來西亞，都已經足夠滿足遊客對賭場的需求，想去賭場娛樂的遊客不會找不到地方。香港沒需要跟隨這些地區繼續興建賭場，繼續興建更多賭場只會帶來惡性競爭。而且港珠澳大橋已經落成。在香港澳門和珠海三地，其實大家都有聽過這個「一小時生活圈」的概念。意思即是説我們在這三個地方乘車，我們所需的交通時間只需要一個小時之內。三個地方都有各自的特色，大家都知道澳門也是一個非常受歡迎的地方。而它其中一個最大的特色就是賭場多。既然在一個這樣近的地方有這麼多的賭場。為甚麼香港還需要興建一個賭場呢？大自然的風光、各國的美食、多元的文化，相信這些是我們香港的特色。我們是否需要去和一些我們鄰近的城市去有一個競爭呢？

另外，香港近年其他基建工程已經導致建築成本增加了很多，有關專家分析，如果政府決定興建賭場，將會使這個情況更加嚴重，成本愈來愈高，人手不夠，最後反而會刺激通脹，影響經濟發展。

最後，興建賭場對社會風氣和治安也沒有好處。在社會風氣和治安這方面，其實是十分有可能助長非法的活動，譬如是好像高利貸這類的活動，我們明白當人沉迷賭博後要把賭癮戒掉是非常的困難的。一個人沉迷賭博不只是一個人的代價，而且也是一家人付出的代價。相信這數點，可以讓大家更加明白，香港特區是不應該開設賭場的。

總括來說，政府認為現時不是興建賭場的時候，但是歡迎社會和廣大市民就這個問題繼續討論。

Lesson 7

申辦賽事

主持人、各位參加辯論會的朋友，大家好。剛才那位發言人說的意見，我並不是很認同。首先甚麼叫作勞民傷財？如果給了很多錢、用了很多時間、影響普通市民的生活，但是香港得不到好處，這樣才是勞民傷財，吃力不討好。但是舉辦大型國際體育賽事是宣傳香港的好機會，是一個投資，而不是浪費金錢。因為如果香港舉辦大型國際體育賽事，不用說會吸引來自不同地區不同國家的人來香港消費，更不用說大型賽事會讓香港成為世界的焦點，對提升香港的國際形象有很大的幫助。所以所謂的勞民傷財這個論點是絕對不成立的，我想在這裏反駁這個論點。

其實香港對於舉辦大型國際體育賽事有不少經驗。以前香港曾經舉辦過很多次國際網球賽，最近十幾年香港每年都舉辦國際欖球賽和馬拉松，而且參加人數愈來愈多，很多運動員每年都特地飛來香港參加比賽。另外 2008 年北京奧運會，香港負責過馬術比賽，第二年又舉辦東亞運動會。最近幾年，香港舉辦大型的渡海泳比賽，參加比賽的人由香港島游泳到九龍，參加的運動員之中，有不少是外國人。這樣就可以知道大型國際體育賽事真的吸引了很多外國人來香港。

我想藉這個機會說一下一些歷史事實，在北京舉辦奧運期間，一些前置的功夫，包括提高英語水平，一系列的英語的菜單，和服務人員的應對。這樣對於服務業來說，其實不是單指一個短短的奧運效應，而是長期來說對北京有益而無害，因為奧運的關係，北京城市整體的形象和裏面的素質會大大的提高。香港就更不用說，香港其實在酒店服務業，我們的英語水平，其實已經達到一定的水準。

啊，我想說的是一些的基建。一些奧運的場所之中，其中北京鳥巢和水立方，除了成為奧運會的體育場館，其實也都可以成為日後的一個健身場所。這樣我相信在香港，如果我們有類似的建築，這些建築將會成為香港一個新的特色和外來遊客一些的參觀景點。

還有一些是潛在的影響。我們知道在一些的城市，如果他們舉辦一些的比賽，譬如說是賽車，其實在比賽期間不單是市內的人可以觀賞，其實不少境外的電視觀眾都會聚焦在我們香港這一個城市，香港會受到全世界的關注。這樣是可以提高香港的知名度和國際的影響力，是有一個正面的影響。除此以外，我們十分著重的一些本地體育發展，其實對於運動員來說也是一個很大的鼓舞。

我認為香港作為一個國際城市，其實已經具備足夠的條件舉辦更多的大型國際體育賽事。一來香港的交通方便，鐵路、公路網絡四通八達，香港的塞車問題和其他亞洲城市比較不算嚴重，二來香港的機場是全世界最好的機場之一，運動員可以在短時間去到比賽場地。其次是香港有先進的通訊網絡，想把在香港比賽的消息發送去哪裏就可以發送去哪裏。第三，香港是亞洲以至全世界最安全的國際城市，運動員可以放心留在香港比賽，不用擔心會有甚麼危險。這三方面都表示香港舉辦大型國際體育賽事有了「天時地利人和」。所以我的結論是香港應該要把握機會，而且比賽場地在比賽結束後也能開放給市民使用。既然如此，普通市民可以得到好處，這樣怎麼可以說舉辦大型賽事是得不償失呢？我希望大家能夠繼續支持香港申辦大型國際賽事。

Lesson 8

節日文化

各位，關於是否增設伊斯蘭教節和道教節為公眾假期這個問題呢，我個人的看法是這樣的：

首先對於增設這兩個節日為公眾假期我並不反對。大家都知道香港是一個多元化的國際大城市，增加節日代表社會對於不同宗教信仰和文化一視同仁，同時又可以讓市民多放兩天紅假。另外如果政府、宗教團體趁這個機會舉辦一些和節日有關的活動，有可能為香港的旅遊業和經濟帶來一些好處，這樣就很值得。

不過從另一方面去看，同樣是因為香港是一個國際大城市，除了伊斯蘭教、道教外，還有很多其他宗教派別，好像是印度教、猶太教等，他們在香港都是很重要的。我覺得不需要為伊斯蘭教和道教的節日設立公眾假期，最大的一個理由是我覺得政府不能選擇支持某一些宗教，而不支持另一些宗教。目前香港的公眾假期，大多數是傳統節日，好像農曆新年、清明節、端午節、中秋節、重陽節等等，我們在這幾天放假是因為要進行一些傳統的活動，新年要拜年派利是，端午節要扒龍船，重陽節要拜山，等等，放假是為了方便市民做這些事。還有就是歷史上一些重要的日子，譬如香港回歸、國慶，都有官方的紀念活動。至於聖誕節、復活節，在香港，已經成為一種傳統，以聖誕節為例，香港人習慣了在聖誕假期一家大小放假去長線旅行，從聖誕開始到新曆新年放假休息一下。聖誕節除了在教會內部，在香港這些節日的宗教味道已經不是特別明顯了。但是伊斯蘭教和道教的節日就不一樣了，香港人在這些日子放假會做甚麼呢？政府也沒有理由公開慶祝這些節日。至於佛誕，香港本來沒有佛誕，設佛誕這個假期有歷史原因。雖然佛誕是一個帶宗教色彩的節日，但是算是一個例外。

如果真的要一視同仁，很多在香港每年都會慶祝的節日，好像萬聖節、感恩節、或者是瑞典的「聖露西亞日」、菲律賓的「朋友節」、泰國的「潑水節」、尼泊爾的新年，是否也應該要增加一些公眾假期給他們呢？如果説對宗教信仰公平的話，我覺得現在的安排就很公平。至於不同國家的文化，中國人社會基本上當然遵從中國文化，香港的外國人這麼多，難道韓國的節日、法國的節日、愛爾蘭的節日，我們全部都要設立公眾假期嗎？

最後一點想補充的是，增加一個公眾假期，是否要在另外一些假期那裏減少呢？如果只是增加一兩個節日，而不減少其他假期，那公眾假期會不會太多呢？公眾假期太多，第一個出來反對的一定是一些大老闆。他們會説，平常已經忙得要加班，休息一天，公司就會損失多少多少的錢，關係到錢的問題，想不反對也不能。如果增設伊斯蘭教節和道教節，那新年假期和聖誕節是不是應該少放一些呢？但是新年假期和聖誕節本來就放得不多，再減少的話，香港人會不會不高興呢？所以討論這個問題的時候，需要考慮很多方面的問題，而且要照顧社會上不同人的聲音，我認為不可以隨便改變公眾假期的安排。這個是我個人的看法，謝謝大家。

Lesson 9

法律與社會

各位專家、各位朋友，大家好。好高興今天能夠參加這一個研討會。作為香港教育界的代表，我是持反對意見的。我並不是從事法律相關工作的人，所以只可以從普通市民的角度去看同性婚姻應否合法化這個問題。

我今天帶來了一些新聞和數據來和大家分享。到底為甚麼同性婚姻一時之間好像成為了世界熱點新聞，大家也在爭相討論起來，變成討論熱點。首先是 2015 年美國最高法院判同性婚姻合法，受到憲法保障。自此以後我們見到其實在世界各國的 facebook 的用家都用一個彩虹的標記來到支持同性戀者。沒錯我們知道人是的確是有不同的自由。無論是言論自由、出版自由、還是戀愛自由，其實我們知道同性戀，法律並沒有禁止。只不過是在同性婚姻這一個議題上面，我們需要小心。

在香港，同性戀早已經不是非法的了。90 年代開始，政府不再説同性戀是非法的了，但是兩個同性戀者想在香港結婚還是不可以。雖然愈來愈多人贊成香港應該好像歐洲一些國家那樣，讓同性戀者結婚，不過其實很多香港人都還未能接受這樣的關係。因為多數人覺得結婚是一男一女的事，如果結了婚以後想要小孩子，那小孩子最好要有父親和母親。這方面，同性戀者不能做到。他們如果領養一個小孩子，小孩子就會生活在一個同性戀的家庭裏面。我們可以看一下同性婚姻對小朋友的影響。有數據指出同性婚姻的小朋友，我們知道是來自領養的，他們比較起一般傳統婚姻、異性婚姻的小孩子，他們學業上的表現和人際關係都有一個極大的差距。按照這個情形來看，我們不是單單要考慮，是不是容許成年人有這樣的自由來到結合，我們也需要想一下一些相關的影響。

就算兩個人不打算要小孩子，也不代表我們就可以讓他們結婚。當然，他們可以說，和哪個人結婚，是個人自由，應該是自己選擇的。同性戀者說，在香港結婚，需要雙方的證婚人，而且要沒有人反對。所以如果他們的父母或者家人不反對，外面的人不反對，這樣他們兩個人結婚，就沒有問題了。這點我不反對，因為這個是他們私人的問題。但是我想說，這個社會，有很多東西，是沒可能只要他們兩個人想怎樣就怎樣的。譬如說，兩個男人在街上拖著手走路，或許有些人看了也只是覺得有點怪怪的也說不定。但是如果參加一個晚會，主持人介紹他們兩個的時候，應該怎樣介紹？如果一個姓張的男人和一個姓陳的男人手拖著手走出來，那應該介紹張先生和張太太還是陳先生和陳太太呢？這個已經去到文化方面的問題了。我們幾千年，都沒有試過這樣結婚的，現在忽然有人說想改變，那就一定有很多東西需要跟著改正才行。

最近有些同性戀者出來說要政府給他們「已婚人士免稅額」，這樣兩個人一齊可以少交一點稅。有些人說一旦他們結了婚，就是「二人家庭」，可以兩個人一齊申請公屋。那這個就是社會民生問題了，大多數人要為了那些少數人改變整個社會這麼長久以來的制度，這樣大家是否已經準備好呢？現在這個社會已經跟以前的社會有很大的差別，現在的社會無論結不結婚都可以一起生活，但是如果同性婚姻合法化，萬一兩個人的關係出現問題，而且他們有小朋友，那法律上應該怎樣處理呢？那些問題尤其是法律問題就更加複雜。而且如果同性婚姻是合乎人權，那我們將來也都要在這一種邏輯底下，從人權的角度考慮，多人婚姻是不是也應該獲得法律的保障呢。

經過以上的分析後，我認為我們的社會還未準備好。因此我認為同性戀者不可以在香港結婚。在這一個議題上我的立場是十分明確的，我是持反對的意見。謝謝各位。

Lesson 10

保護環境

大家好，我是「綠色香港」的負責人陳國強。今天獲邀請來參加這個活動，我覺得十分榮幸。首先我要感謝環境局給我一個機會能在這裏向各位善長仁翁表達「綠色香港」對你們的萬分感謝。環保工作大家都知道是一項長時間的投資，是一個不能看到即時效果的工作。從十年前開始，我們提議政府推行「清潔維港計劃」的時候，我們開始環保工作，那時很多人都潑我冷水，說海水已經污染了幾十年，怎麼可能改善？那時聽到最多人說，做環保工作，會影響經濟發展，會讓他們沒了工作，賺不到錢，還親耳聽到有人說你是要做也沒辦法。幸好當時有各位的支持，在這十年的努力下，香港的環保工作已經取得一定的成績，今天維多利亞港比十年前乾淨了很多。香港變得更加吸引，遊客更加喜歡香港，對我們的旅遊業和經濟都有好處，這些都是大家有目共睹的。

這十年，我們每年都收到不少的捐款，讓我們可以做大量環保工作，其中我們去年做了一個保護郊野公園雀鳥的項目，並且組織了清潔沙灘運動，培訓少年環保大使，清潔海岸公園等等。在此我向所有幫助我們的人士表示衷心的感謝。

最近兩年，我們在每個屋邨舉辦垃圾分類計劃。香港說環保說了三十幾年，現在亞洲很多地區好像日本和台灣已經實行垃圾分類很多年，但是香港還是剛剛開始不太久，而且參加的都是自願的。這個計劃最大的困難，是處理垃圾分類的成本愈來愈高，很多公司都因為覺得太麻煩不再和我們合作。這個時候，我們得到在座各位的幫助解決了一個又一個的困難。除了捐款外，還幫我們聘請義工，聯絡香港各區的屋邨參加垃圾分類計劃，又找了一些支持環保的公司和我們合作。去年我們一共收到港幣三百七十萬的捐款，請到超過二百位義工幫忙，我們的義工有些是中學生、大學生，有些是家庭主婦，有些是退休人士，有些是不同行業的專業人士。今天在座有很多都是義工，你們不怕辛苦，不介意在環境很差的地方幫忙，不介意長時間工作，甚至周末都要去不同的屋邨回收垃圾。沒了你們，這個計劃不會成功。

最後我想藉這個機會感謝各位這麼長時間以來對本會的支持，你們這麼多年來有錢出錢，有力出力，不但讓我們的環保工作做得更好，還讓更多香港人重視環保，認識到環保是生活的一部分，明白到環保和經濟發展是分不開的。這是在座各位努力的成果。記著我們「綠色香港」的宗旨，希望「每人做多啲，將來好過啲」。期待大家繼續支持我們的工作，讓這個城市愈來愈美麗，愈來愈清潔，環境愈來愈好。謝謝大家！

Appendix V: Suggested answers 建議答案

Lesson 1

6.1. 1~5 TFTFF   6~10 TTFFT

7.1. 1~5 TFFTT   6~10 TFFFT

Lesson 2

6.1. 1~5 TFTTF   6~10 FFFTT

7.1.

1.méihsihk 2.yámchàh 3.dímsām

4.daaihpàaihdong 5.chīngdaahm

6.lóuhfó tōng   7.jūngyeuhk

8.pùhnchoi 9.hóisīn 10.Chāutīn

Lesson 3

6.1. 1~5 TFFTT   6~10 TTTFF

7.1. 1~5 TFFTF   6~10 FFTTF

Lesson 4

6.1. 1~5 TFTFT   6~10 FFTTF

7.1. 1. jīchìh 2.chāantēng 3.wūyíhm

     4. fahohk mahtjāt 5.hūnghei làuhtūng

     6. síu pàhngyáuh 7.bātnàhng

     8. fójōi 9.kāpyīnkēui 10.geihseuht

Lesson 5

6.1. 1~5 TFFFT   6~10 TFFTF

7.1. 1~5 TFTTF   6~10 TTTFF

Lesson 6

6.1. 1~5 TTFFT   6~10 FFTFT

7.1. 1. gīngjai dahkkēui 2. jih'ōn

     3. Lāaisī Wàihgāsī 4. gīngjai

5. séhkēui   6. fūnggaak

7. jihyìhn wàahngíng   8.gīngjai faatjín

9. yìhngjeuhng   10. síhmàhn

Lesson 7

6.1. 1~5 TFFTT   6~10 FFFTT

7.1. 1~5 TFFTF   6~10 FTFTT

Lesson 8

6.1. 1~5 FFFFF   6~10 FTTFT

7.1. 1. jityaht   2. Nùhnglihk

     3. Chīngmìhng jit   4. yihngtùhng gám

     5. Fuhkwuhtjit   6. gūngjung

     7. lòuhgūng   8. Húnggaau

     9. daihyih   10. sei yuht chō baat

Lesson 9

6.1. 1~5 TFFTT   6~10 FTFTT

7.1. 1~5 TTFFF   6~10 TTFTF

Lesson 10

6.1. 1~5 TFTFF   6~10 TFFTF

7.1. 1. Wàahnbóu Daihyātsin   2. yisīk

     3. faiséui   4. fochìhng

     5. Hóingohn gūngyún

     6. hóiyèuhng sāngmaht

     7. gāhaauh hahpjok   8. hiptìuh

     9. síu pàhngyáuh   10. hah yātdoih

Appendix VI: Yuti Features of Book 1, 2 and 3
語體特徵索引（全三冊）

語體分類	篇目	説話者 / 聽眾	地點	話題 / 內容
	L1	老師、學生	校園、教室	初次見面
	L2	老師、學生、職員路人	教室、校園	詢問、問路和指路
	L3	同學	校園、宿舍	邀約
	L4	同學 學生 服務員、客人	校園、餐廳、店舖	講價
	L5	同學 學生	校園、宿舍、電話	留言 邀約
1 非正式	L6	同學 朋友	校園、餐廳 教室	推介、介紹事物
I	L7	學生、商店老闆 同學	宿舍、餐廳 教室	描述 介紹事物
	L8	同學、朋友 旅行社職員、客人	宿舍、餐廳 旅行社	計劃、說明情況
	L9	同學 朋友	宿舍、餐廳	請求幫助
	L10	同學	校園、宿舍	籌備活動、致謝（非正式）

1 非正式	II	L1	同學 同事	校園 公司	介紹（半正式） 介紹食物、設施
		L2	仲介、客戶 男女朋友	物業中介公司	諮詢
		L3	朋友	餐廳	建議 討論
		L4	朋友	家	評論電影
		L5	朋友 同事	餐廳	解釋、討論對事物的法
		L6	同學 家人	教室、宿舍、電話	提醒注意事項
1+ 半正式	II	L7	同學、朋友 護士、探病的人	校園、電話 醫院	拒絕及婉拒
		L8	職員、乘客／客人 職員、顧客	機場 理髮店	表達不滿
		L9	同學 同事	校園 公司飯堂	比較及討論事物
	III	L1	普通市民	座談會、電台、電視節目	旅遊、城市介紹
		L2	美食愛好者	展銷會	飲食介紹
		L3	閱讀愛好者	座談會、討論會等	興趣
		L5	教育界代表	介紹會	行業介紹
2/2+ 正式／官方	II	L10	職員、大眾	記者招待會	致歉
	III	L4	與會嘉賓	專業研討會	提出意見
		L8	有關專家	學術研討會	文化問題、歸納
		L6	政府官員	新聞說明會	表達立場、辯護
		L7	相關人士	辯論會	反駁
		L9	普通市民	討論會	法律問題、闡述
		L10	團體負責人	典禮	致謝、總結

Notes:

1. 非正式語體：

一般描述：非正式語體的特點是放鬆、親切、隨意，其目的是取消或淡化距離感。典型的非正式語體在語境（人／地／時）和內容方面往往受以下因素影響：

- 人：熟人和朋友之間，同學之間，說話者的相對地位和文化背景與聽眾沒有明顯區別（或雖有上對下的區別但說話者刻意淡化）。
- 地：非工作、非官方地點，比如朋友同學在飯店小聚、郊遊等。
- 時：非工作、非官方時段，比如雖然在教室，但是並非上課時間。
- 內容：話題一般以日常生活為主，比如寒暄、就餐、出行、購物等。

2. 半正式語體：

一般描述：介於"非正式"和"正式／官方"之間的語體，可以是同輩或熟人在非正式場合討論正式話題，也可以是地位和文化背景有明顯差異的人談論一般的話題，或者雖然場合和話題都比較正式，但交流者希望拉近與對方距離等等，這些均會產生此類"半正式"語體，其目的往往取決於說話者的主觀願望。典型的半正式語體在語境（人／地／時）和內容方面往往受以下因素影響：

- 人：範圍廣，說話者的相對地位和文化背景與聽眾可以有也可以沒有明顯區別。
- 地：可以包括下至非正式，上至正式／官方語體的一切地點。
- 時：可以括囊下至非正式，上至正式／官方語體的一切時段。
- 內容：話題可以包羅萬象，生活或公務各種話題均可，但說話者必須根據語境做出正確判斷甚麼是合適或不合適的話題。

3. 正式／官方語體：

一般描述：正式／官方語體的特點是有規有矩，有約定俗成的做法，其目的是強調權威或表示尊重，有明顯距離感。典型的正式／官方語體在語境（人／地／時）和內容方面往往受以下因素影響：

- 人：有上下、尊卑、長幼之分，說話者的相對地位和文化背景與聽眾有明顯區別，說話的時候必須根據自己的地位採用表示尊敬（比如幼對長，下對上）或展示權威的語言。
- 地：工作或官方儀式所在地，比如學術會議、各類典禮等。
- 時：工作、教學、會議或官方活動期間。
- 內容：話題一般與公務相關，要傳遞的資訊比較嚴肅，比如某些學術會議或某個官方慶典的主題。

Appendix VII: Liguistic fuctions of Book 1, 2 and 3 語言功能索引（全三冊）

I

	Linguistic functions	語言功能
L1	Introducing (informal)	自我介紹（非正式）
L2	Querying	詢問
L3	Inviting (informal)	邀約（非正式）
L4	Bargaining the price	講價
L5	Leaving messages	留言
L6	Giving recommendation	推介
L7	Describing	描述
L8	Explaining	說明
L9	Asking for help	求助
L10	Expressing thanks (informal)	致謝（非正式）

II

	Linguistic functions	語言功能
L1	Introducing (semi-formal)	介紹（半正式）
L2	Consulting	諮詢

L3	Suggesting ideas	建議
L4	Commenting	評論
L5	Explaining	解釋
L6	Reminding	提醒
L7	Refusing	拒絕
L8	Complaining	投訴
L9	Comparing	比較
L10	Apologizing	致歉

III

Linguistic functions		語言功能
L1	Persuading	勸說
L2	Detailed description	詳細描述
L3	Exploring	深入探討
L4	Expressing Opinion	發表意見
L5	Introducing (formal)	介紹 (正式)
L6	Defensing	辯護
L7	Criticizing	反駁
L8	Drawing Conclusion	歸納
L9	Discussing	闡述
L10	Expressing Gratitude and Review	致謝與回顧

Appendix VIII: Pragmatic points of Book 1, 2 and 3
語用點索引（全三冊）

I

Pragmatic points	Remarks
Greeting expressions	I-L1-5.1.1
Chinese names	I-L1-5.1.2
Omission of pronoun in Chinese	I-L1-5.2.1
Starting questions with "chíngmahn"	I-L1-5.2.2
Saying "thank you" in Cantonese: "m̀gōi" verses "dōjeh"	I-L1-5.2.3
Good morning: Greeting people in the morning.	I-L1-5.2.4
Greeting with: heui bīndouh a?	I-L2-5.1.1
Saying goodbye in Cantonese	I-L2-5.1.2
Asking for agreement using: hóu m̀hóu a?	I-L2-5.2.1
The treatment of two-syllable verbs in V-not-V questions	I-L2-5.2.2
Welcome greetings in shops	I-L3-5.1.1
The use of "yiu" vs "séung yiu"	I-L3-5.1.2
The use of "yáuhdī"	I-L3-5.2.1
Greeting with "hóu noih móuh gin"	I-L4-5.1.1
Greeting with "sihkjó faahn meih a?"	I-L4-5.1.2
Auxiliary verb "hóyíh" and verb particle "-dāk"	I-L4-5.2.1
Making a request, "béi ngóh táitái"	I-L4-5.2.2
See you then: "dou sìh gin"	I-L5-5.1.1

Asking for agreement: "dím a?"	I-L5.5.2.1
Metaphorical use of "deihfõng"	I-L6-5.1.1
Accepting and refusing politely	I-L6-5.1.2
Quality assessment with "m̀dāk"	I-L6-5.2.1
Useful expressions to introduce people	I-L6-5.2.2
Confirming with "haih m̀haih a?"	I-L7-5.1.1
Phone calls: calling and receiving	I-L7-5.1.2
Making reservations	I-L7-5.1.3
Polite way to request people to do things for you, "màhfàahn néih…"	I-L7-5.2.1
Asking questions with "dímgáai" and "jouh māt"	I-L7-5.2.2
Offering, accepting and refusing help politely	I-L7-5.2.3
Making decision	I-L8-5.1.1
Introducing a different topics	I-L8-5.1.2
Making a choice with "dihnghaih"	I-L8-5.2.1
Revisit various meanings of "dím"	I-L9-5.1.1
Asking for help "dím syun"	I-L9-5.1.2
The use of "yáuh yàhn"	I-L9-5.2.1
Expressing congratulations	I-L10-5.1.1
Expressing good wishes	I-L10-5.1.2
Saying farewell	I-L10-5.2.1

II

Pragmatic points	Remarks
How to greet people in front of a class	II-L1-5.1
Casual and semi-formal style of expressions	II-L1-5.2
A polite way to refuse other people's request with the use of verb suffix "-háh"	II-L1-5.3
Draw people's attention to a topic with "haih nē"	II-L1-5.4

Consulting people at the first encounter	II-L2-5.1
Renting a flat in Hong Kong	II-L2-5.2
Telling people some information ambiguously	II-L2-5.3
Suggesting ideas in a casual way	II-L3-5.1
Denoting surprise and checking the truth of an unexpected state of affairs	II-L3-5.2
Reduction of words in a conversation	II-L3-5.3
Ending a conversation	II-L3-5.4
Difference between "góng" and "wah"	II-L4-5.1
Confirming one's condition and corresponding in accordance with the other party's reply	II-L4-5.2
Expressing agreement or assent	II-L4-5.3
Denoting familiarity	II-L5-5.1
Playing down a fact by using "jē"	II-L5-5.2
Interjection in a conversation	II-L5-5.3
Pass time in Chinese New Year in Canton (VO: gwonìhn 過年)	II-L6-5.1
Chinese soup	II-L6-5.2
Concept of "ancestral home town"	II-L6-5.3
Deflecting a compliment	II-L6-5.4
Filling a pause in a sentence	II-L7-5.1
Repetition of the same word or phrase	II-L7-5.2
Converting nouns to verbs	II-L7-5.3
Refusing someone's request by saying "hóu nàahnjouh"	II-L7-5.4
Checking someone's identity with a question "néih haih kéuih bīnwái a?"	II-L7-5.5
Interjection to express disapproval or objection	II-L8-5.1
Expressing unfriendly tone even calling someone "daaihlóu"	II-L8-5.2
A casual way to call someone	II-L8-5.3
Sortal classifiers and generic classifiers	II-L9-5.1

Describing thick and thin	II-L9-5.2
Transition from informal to formal style	II-L10.5.1
A mild and roundabout way to refuse other people's request	II-L10.5.2

<h2 style="text-align:center">III</h2>

Pragmatic points	Lesson number
Honorable guests and friends「各位來賓，各位朋友」	III-L1-5.1.1
Let me introduce myself「我介紹一下自己」	III-L1-5.1.2
Born and grow up here「土生土長」	III-L1-5.2.1
Bureau of Tourism and Development「旅發局」	III-L1-5.2.2
Multi-culture「多元文化」	III-L1-5.2.3
People「addicted」to a hobby「發燒友」	III-L1-5.2.4
Race course「馬場」	III-L1-5.2.5
The use of sentence final particles 句末語氣詞：呢，啦，啊等	III-L2-5.1.1
Heaven of delicious food「美食天堂」	III-L2-5.2.1
Hong Kong style「tea restaurant」「茶餐廳」	III-L2-5.2.2
Foregin helpers「外籍傭工 (菲傭)」	III-L2-5.2.3
Cantonese style herbal tea「廣式涼茶」	III-L2-5.2.4
Indigenous inhabitants「原居民」	III-L2-5.2.5
Indigenous food: Pot-dish「盆菜」	III-L2-5.2.6
Eating is the most important thing in life「民以食為天」	III-L2-5.2.7
Pardon my shallowness「可能係我個人比較膚淺」	III-L3-5.1.1
Things like fighting and killing「打打殺殺嘅嘢」	III-L3-5.2.1
The four famous literary works「四大名著」	III-L3-5.2.2
Very interested in....「……迷」	III-L3-5.2.3
Thanks for the opportunity「謝謝……機會」	III-L4-5.1.1
Knowing that you have a time limit「知道你哋嘅採訪有時間限制」	III-L4-5.1.2

Three meals a day「一日三餐」	III-L4-5.2.1
Second-hand smoking「二手煙」	III-L4-5.2.2
Journals with authority「權威雜誌」	III-L4-5.2.3
How can you (lit. "depending on what")「憑乜嘢」	III-L4-5.2.4
A matter of life and death「人命關天嘅大事」	III-L4-5.2.5
Addictive to smoking「煙癮起」	III-L4-5.2.6
Honorable leaders and guests「各位領導，各位嘉賓」	III-L5-5.1.1
I'm hornored「(我)好榮幸」	III-L5-5.2.1
Due to the limitation of time「由於時間關係」	III-L5-5.2.2
My introduction will stop here「我嘅介紹到此結束」	III-L5-5.2.3
Thank you all「謝謝大家」	III-L5-5.2.4
Two written languages and three spoken forms「兩文三語」	III-L5-5.2.5
Discourse structure in light of pragmatic framework	III-L6-5.1.1
specialists concerned「有關專家」	III-L6-5.1.2
Presentation style in public speech	III-L6-5.2.1
Portugal style egg-tart「葡式蛋撻」	III-L6-5.2.2
Everybody in our society「廣大市民」	III-L6-5.2.3
Describing a task that is hard and thankless in nature「吃力不討好」	III-L7-5.1.1
Absolutely groundless; to refute「……絕對唔成立……反駁」	III-L7-5.1.2
The so-called ...「所謂嘅勞民傷財」	III-L7-5.1.3
Therefore my conclusion is:「所以我嘅結論係」	III-L7-5.1.4
Olympic equestrian events「奧運馬術比賽」	III-L7-5.2.1
Necessary conditions needed (for a task or event)「天時地利人和」	III-L7-5.2.2
Being modest	III-L8-5.1.1
Five important holidays according to the luna calendar「五大農曆節日」	III-L8-5.2.1
To give laisee money「派利是」	III-L8-5.2.2

Holidays with a religious flavor「帶宗教色彩的節假日」	III-L8-5.2.3
Red-letter days「『紅字』，『紅假』，『紅日』」	III-L8-5.2.4
Buddha's Birthday「佛誕節」	III-L8-5.2.5
Religious factions「宗教派別」	III-L8-5.2.6
I'm not an expert in the legal field.「我唔係法律專家」	III-L9-5.1.1
Different levels of formality with kinship terms :Mother「母親」	III-L9-5.1.2
Family members「家人」	III-L9-5.1.3
Not yet perfect, not yet complete「唔太完善、唔太健全」	III-L9-5.2.1
Focused news「熱點新聞」	III-L9-5.2.2
A male person whose last name is "Mok"「姓莫嘅男人」	III-L9-5.2.3
Suspect (crime)「疑犯」	III-L9-5.2.4
Public opinion of the society「社會輿論」	III-L9-5.2.5
Order in greeting people「尊稱的順序」	III-L10-5.1.1
Person in charge「負責人」	III-L10-5.1.2
Millions thanks「萬分感謝」	III-L10-5.1.3
Have got certain achievement「取得一定嘅成績」	III-L10-5.2.1
"Green」banquet「環保宴」	III-L10-5.2.2
Costal park「海岸公園」	III-L10-5.2.3
Discourage (lit. pore cold water)「潑冷水」	III-L10-5.2.4

Appendix IX: Grammatical points of Book 1, 2 and 3
語法點索引（全三冊）

I

Preposition "lèih"	I-L7-4.1.2
Asking and giving direction	I-L7-4.1.3
Questions word "dím"/"dímyéung"	I-L7-4.1.4
Sentence-end particles in Cantonese	I-L7-4.1.5
Verb-object (VO) structure	I-L8-4.1.1
Comparative constructions	I-L8-4.1.2
"waahkjé" and "dihnghaih"	I-L8-4.1.3
The usage of "tùhng" and "yātchàih"	I-L8-4.1.4
The usage of "juhng" (also)	I-L8-4.1.5
"daap" and "chóh" as a co-verb telling means of transportation	I-L8-4.1.6
Resultative verb "dóu"	I-L8-4.1.7
Asking and giving direction (Con't)	I-L8-4.1.8
Directional complements	I-L9-4.1.1
Comparative construction (Con't)	I-L9-4.1.2
If… , then…: "Yùhgwó…jauh…"	I-L10-4.1.1
The use of "tùhng" meaning "for"	I-L10-4.1.2
The use of "-yùhn" to indicate finished action	I-L10-4.1.3
More use of "jauh" as an adverb	I-L10-4.1.4
Comparative constructions (con't)	I-L10-4.1.5
Becoming more and more: "yuht làih yuht…" , "yuht V yuht…"	I-L10-4.1.6

II

Grammatical points	Remarks
Experiental action "gwo" and existential questions "yáuh móuh"	II-L1-4.1
Verb-object compounds in a sentence	II-L1-4.2
Verb suffix "-háh"	II-L1-4.3
Particle "ga"	II-L1-4.4
Subordinate clauses "although…nevertheless"	II-L1-4.5

Causative and resultative constructions with "jíng" and "gáau"	II-L6-4.5
Indicating the source and nature of knowledge expressed in the sentence with "ā ma" particle	II-L7-4.1
Double sentence final particles meaning "only" or "that's all"	II-L7-4.2
Describing habits with "bātnāu"	II-L7-4.3
Giving force to a rhetorical question: m̀tūng…?	II-L7-4.4
VOV	II-L7-4.5
Rhetorical "bīndouh…?"	II-L8-4.1
Indicating warning, suggestion, or eagerness: ā làh	II-L8-4.2
"Béi" serving as "let" or "allow"	II-L8-4.3
"Hái…jīhah/dáihah"	II-L8-4.4
Comparision of adjective: VO Vdāk Adj gwo	II-L8-4.5
The use of "mòuhleuhn"	II-L9-4.1
Elaborating ideas or reasons step by step: yātlàih…yihlàih	II-L9-4.2
The use of "m̀gwaaidāk"	II-L9-4.3
More resultative verbs (RV): "-màaih", "-sìhng", "jihngfāan", "gáaudihm"	II-L9-4.4
More patterns on "hóuchíh"	II-L9-4.5
Take advantage of (time, opportunity, etc): chan…	II-L10-4.1
Use of "béi" to form passive sentence	II-L10-4.2
For the sake or benfit of: waihjó	II-L10-4.3
Difference between "deui" and "heung"	II-L10-4.4

III

Grammatical points	Remarks
Sentence particle, "lā", "a", used for listing items or examples	III-L1-4.1.1
"yauh…yauh…"	III-L1-4.1.2
jihnghaih… ja / jē	III-L1-4.1.3
"hóuchíh……yātyeuhng" just like...	III-L1-4.1.4

"Jeun yāt bouh" further; go a step further	III-L4-4.1.2
"Lihng yàhn (gámdou)…" to make one (feels)…	III-L4-4.1.3
Rhetorical questions with"m̀tūng…mē"	III-L4-4.1.4
"pàhng……" rely on; base on	III-L4-4.1.5
"Sēuiyìhn…, daahnhaih… "	III-L4-4.1.6
« Búnlòih…sāumēi…"	III-L4-4.1.7
"Mòuhleuhn dím dōu…"	III-L4-4.1.8
"Sáusīn…jeun yāt bouh…lihng yāt fōngmihn…jeuihauh…"; first…, furthermore…, on the other hand…, in the end…	III-L4-4.2.1
"…. yauh hóu, … yauh hóu "	III-L5-4.1.1
"waihjó……" in order to; for; for the sake of	III-L5-4.1.2
Using "só+V+ge" to form one kind of nominal construction	III-L5-4.1.3
Emphasizing a negation with "bihng"	III-L5-4.1.4
"m̀hóu … jyuh" and "m̀hóu … jyuh"	III-L5-4.1.5
"yàuhyū……ge gwāanhaih" because of; due to	III-L5-4.1.6
Making "-ize" and "-ify" verbs with"-fa"	III-L5-4.1.7
More about manner of action	III-L5-4.1.8
"Adj. jó dī"	III-L5-4.1.9
"yáuh gam … dāk gam…"	III-L5-4.1.10
"…yáuh…, kèihjūng…,kèihtā……" there is…, among (which)…, and the other…	III-L5-4.2.1
"chùhng…héi/hōichí, …, (yìhnhauh)…, gānjyuh…, (jeuihauh)…" to begin with…(then)…, next…, in the end…	III-L5-4.2.2
"làih" in order to; to	III-L6-4.1.1
"géui…laihjí" take for example	III-L6-4.1.2
"yáuh/héi…jokyuhng" play a part; play the role; have effect on	III-L6-4.1.3
"chùhng…làih tái" from the perspective of…	III-L6-4.1.4
"Dōu haih…"	III-L6-4.1.5
Double negative: "m̀wúih m̀ V(O)" and "m̀wúih…m̀dóu…"	III-L6-4.1.6

"sihfáu" if; whether or not	III-L6-4.1.7
"deui…móuh/yáuh hóuchyu" be (not) good for...	III-L6-4.1.8
"hái…fōngmihn" in relation to; on the topic of	III-L6-4.1.9
"Hóuchíh…jīléui / dī gámge…"	III-L6-4.1.10
"Jēung" pattern	III-L6-4.1.11
"júngkut làih góng" all in all; in a word	III-L6-4.2.1
"sáusīn…kèihchi…lihngngoih…jeuihauh…" Firstly...and then...in addition... finally…	III-L6-4.2.2
"m̀sái góng…,ganggā m̀sái góng…" let alone, not to mention	III-L7-4.1.1
"sówaih" so-called	III-L7-4.1.2
"chàhnggīng" once; used to	III-L7-4.1.3
"Chan nīgo gēiwuih", take this chance	III-L7-4.1.4
"Yānwaih…ge gwāanhaih", because of…	III-L7-4.1.5
"…jīyāt" and "kèihjūng jīyāt" "meaning one of …"	III-L7-4.1.6
"…jījūng, (kèihjūng)…" and "…hóu dō/hóu fūngfu, kèihjūng…" meaning "among"	III-L7-4.1.7
"sauh (dou)" as a passive marker	III-L7-4.1.8
"chèuihchí yíh/jī ngoih" besides; in addition	III-L7-4.1.9
QW jauh QW	III-L7-4.1.10
"geiyìhn haih gám" , under the circumstances; in that case	III-L7-4.1.11
Use of "béi" to form passive sentences	III-L7-4.1.12
"yātlàih…, yihlàih…, jeui hauh…" firstly…, secondly…, finally…	III-L7-4.2.1
"jihkdāk……ge haih" something that is worthy of...	III-L8-4.1.1
"yíh……wàihlaih" take...as an example	III-L8-4.1.2
"chùhng……hōichí/héi", "yàuh… V héi", start with; begin with	III-L8-4.1.3
"gēibún seuhng" on the whole; mainly; basically	III-L8-4.1.4
"Adj. dou…" and "(VO) V dou…"	III-L8-4.1.5
"Gwāanhaih dou……." be related to	III-L8-4.1.6
"Séung m̀V (O) dōu m̀dāk"	III-L8-4.1.7

"jeui adj./v ge haih…juhngyáuh jauhhaih…jiyū…" the most…then…in addition to that…	III-L8-4.2.1
"bātgwo chùhng lihng yāt fōngmihn heui tái", however if looking from another perspective	III-L8-4.2.2
"…héi séuhnglàih"	III-L9-4.1.1
"jiu nīgo chìhngyìhng làih tái/góng"	III-L9-4.1.2
"jíyiu…jauh…" as long as, …then…	III-L9-4.1.3
"yáuhdī Adj Adj déi "	III-L9-4.1.4
"yātdaan…jauh…" once...then...	III-L9-4.1.5
"mòuhleuhn…dōu…" no matter	III-L9-4.1.6
"yàuhkèihsih" especially; particularly	III-L9-4.1.7
"chùhng……ge gokdouh" from the perspective of…	III-L9-4.1.8
"gīnggwo……" after…	III-L9-4.1.9
"Sáusīn…gānjyuh…yàuhyū yíhseuhng ge yùhnyān…"first...then...for above reasons...	III-L9-4.2.1
"yùhgwó…yìhché…gám…" if...and...then/so...	III-L9-4.2.2
"jihchùhng……(yíhlàih)" since…	III-L10-4.1.1
"bīndouh wúih/hónàhng…"	III-L10-4.1.2
Use "chān" to express personal experience: chānngáahn、chānyíh、chānháu、chānsáu、chānjih	III-L10-4.1.3
"haih yiu V" / "haih m̀…"	III-L10-4.1.4
"hái……hah" under…	III-L10-4.1.5
"bihngché" and; as well as	III-L10-4.1.6
"kèihjūng" within	III-L10-4.1.7
"m̀joi…" no longer; not any more	III-L10-4.1.8
"yāt M yauh yāt M"	III-L10-4.1.9
"Chèuihjó…juhng…yauh…"apart from...furthermore...also...	III-L10-4.2.1
"m̀jí…juhng…" not only..., but also…	III-L10-4.2.2